PHAL Eden's bride.

Phalen, Daniel

T5-ADA-439

Guernsey Memorial Library
3 Court Street
Norwich, NY 13815
GuernseyMemorialLibrary.org

EDEN'S BRIDE

SUMERIAN CHRONICLES I

DANIEL PHALEN

Creston Hall Press

EDEN'S BRIDE. Copyright © 2017 by Daniel Phalen. All rights reserved.
Cover by Damonza.com
Published: March 2017 by Creston Hall Press

ISBN-10: 0-971-29712-6
ISBN-13: 978-0-971-29712-8

This is a work of fiction. Names, characters, organizations, places, events, and incidents are either products of the author's imagination or are used fictitiously.

No part of this book may be reproduced or stored in a retrieval system, or transmitted in any form or by any means, electronic, mechanical, photocopying, recording, or otherwise, without express written permission of the publisher.

10 9 8 7 6 5 4 3 2 1

For Sue, empowered, loved, lovely

Map of Sumer

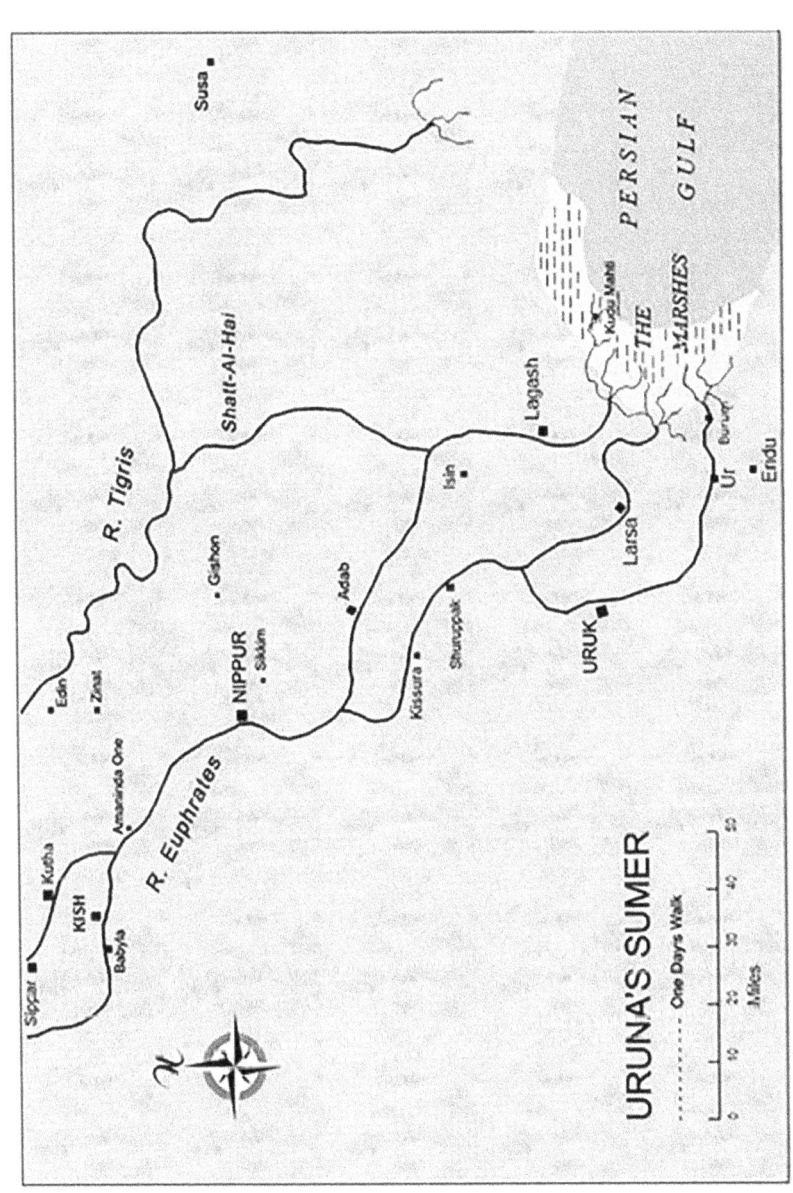

City of Nippur

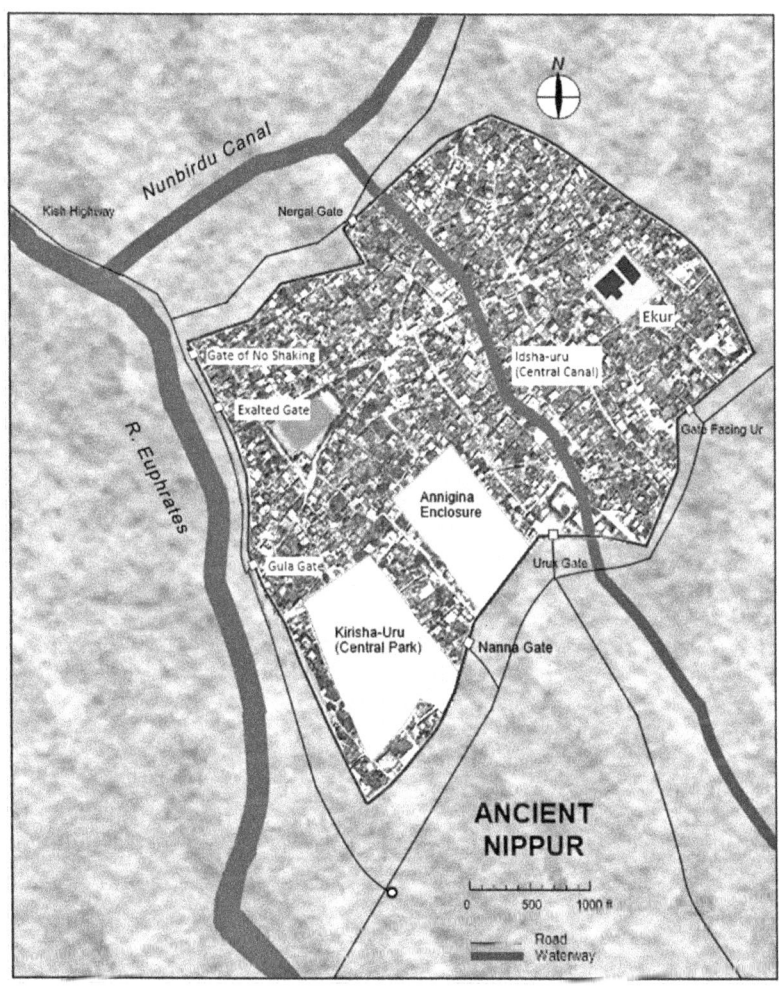

Character Brief

Uruna Kumta	(oo-*ROO*-nuh *KOOM*-tah) queen of Nippur, seeker of The Sight, keeper of Serpenthood; also Entu, or high priestess
Anu	(*AH*-noo) hunter, fighter, Uruna's lover, Hanza scion
Rahnee	(*RAH*-nee) mystic, witch, ancient seer, ghost, Anu's ally
Tezu-Mah	(teh-zoo-*MAH*) short for Teguzzu-Mah, Hani for "Hunts With No Fear"; their name for Anu; legendary lion hunter
Arn-Gar	(a.k.a. Gar) Nord blacksmith and Uruna's devoted bodyguard
Retha	(*RETH*-uh) Uruna's loyal assistant; Gar's daughter; Serpenthood acolyte; Uruna's loyal assistant; scorned as a halfbreed
Enguda	(en-*GOO*-duh) also Bull Priest, or "the Bull"; corruption of Sumerian *en* (king), *gud* (bull or ox); also *guda'abzu*
Kukhmet	(kook-*MET*) Uruna's king cobra, Serpenthood gatekeeper
Shua-Kinar	(*SHOO*-uh kin-*NAR*) Uruna's close friend and mentor, once high priestess; also Kinar or Kikki
Borok	(*BORE*-awk) Enguda's brutal Nafti henchman, captain of Uruk's Gunzek army
Heganna	(hey-*GAHN*-uh) from Sumerian *heĝal* [PLENTY], richest woman in Sumer, Anu's mother
Lilla	Anu's sister, councillor at Eanna temple in Uruk; Heganna's envoy
Milsah	(*MILL*-suh) Gar's Sumerian wife, Retha's mother

Udea Seddua	(oo-*DEE*-uh *SED*-oo-uh) Queen of Eanna at Uruk, aged weakling
Niccaba Seddua	(*NICK*-uh-buh *SED*-oo-uh) Uruna's mentor and mother figure; stalwart keeper of tradition
Lasheen	(lah-*SHEEN*) Anu's savior nurse, Borok's victim; a Bedouin ancestor
Marduk Imhalla	(*MAR*-duke) Enguda's son and suitor choice for Uruna
Nashi	Uruna's early mentor; mystic desert crone
Kalumma-Dalla	Nippur's high priestess of agriculture
Nabi Gahn	(nah-bee-*GAHN*) Anu's former mentor; master of stealth, weapons, combat
Jabali	(jah-*BAH*-lee) marsh dweller headman of Kudu Mahti
Pana	(*PAH*-nuh) Hani orphan boy, Anu's helpmate in the *ghana*
Hanza	(*HAHN*-zuh) northern clan of landowners centered around Nippur
Seddua	(*SED*-oo-uh) southern clan of land-owners based around Uruk
Hani	(*HAH*-nee) aboriginal marsh dwellers
Gunzek	(*GUN*-zek) insurgent race of brutal savages; Enguda's soldiers
Kurg	Invading barbarians from the northern steppes; also savage, fearsome fighters

NOTE: See Glossary at the back of this book for a guide to pronunciation

THE GHANA

CHAPTER ONE
A String of Failures

Sumer, ca 3,200 BC

The first hint of disaster began as a faint warning buzz inside her head. She lay supine on the coupling stone deep inside Nippur's most sacred hall, vaguely aware of mystic runes inscribed on the ceiling, cobras poised at each foot and shoulder, the pungent odor of incense, the sceptre's bobbing shadow-dance in the brazier's flickering glow. Her consort had taken her to the threshold. Now his bleak stare signaled an impasse. Why had he stopped?

She did not want this husband, despite her lifelong imperative to be the instrument of the god's desire and not her own. Nevertheless, she surrendered will and prejudice to the divine and pleaded for the ecstasy to return.

Instead, the strident hum infected her mind with dread and confusion, demanded her undivided attention as it vied with the serpent song still coursing through her veins. The persistent wail would rip her from the thrall and end all hope for the precious gift.

Too soon! Oh, do not end it now!

Beneath eyelids leaden with stupor she saw Apilsha from Azziz lift his gaze to stare straight ahead into a fanged maw poised to deliver swift death. All four serpents remained on station, their slit-eyed stares focused on the petitioner who had brought their queen to the First Door of ascension. Had they too heard the keening intrusion? Did they heed a call from a higher source?

She strained to recover some essence of herself, but the potent blend of wine and venom in her system clouded her thoughts. Whether she or Apilsha had prepared the vital mixture was a detail rendered moot by a more pressing matter.

She had stopped breathing!

Enshiggu-god, do not take me yet!

The humming sound only rose higher in pitch, up and up to a maddening, all-consuming whine that threatened to cleave her head in two, as piercing agony wrenched every fiber of her body.

She arched her back and jerked upright, completely out of trance.

The scream ceased at once, cut off like a snuffed candle, the pain swept away with it. Her breathing was steady, normal, as though the anguish had never happened.

Her betrothed cowered near the woolen carpet's fringe, his eyes wide with terror, his naked body quaking. The four cobras stood erect at the corners of the dais, to all appearances undisturbed by the episode.

Drawing her knees together, she rolled into a crouch. The spirit presence hadn't left her altogether, and she polled the nether regions of her being for evidence she remained intact.

She was still Uruna Kumta, queen and anointed high priestess of temple Ekur. The Mothers had appointed her magistrate and governor of the eight northern provinces. She was the divinely ordained regent of the spirit guardian of Serpenthood prophecy. She had walked the serpent path since first hearing the god's voice as a child. Fourteen of her twenty-six years she had spent perfecting the ritual. Yet each attempt had fallen short. Was she to blame for Apilsha's premature climax? Should she have been more careful with his instruction?

The god answered back: The flaw is with the man, in whom

ambition overrules reason.

There it was, the selfsame trait so condemned by the Mothers as typically male. She had opposed their blind bigotry with her own steadfast conviction that a man, any man, might rightly show wisdom and compassion if given the chance.

She looked down at her thighs and clenched her jaw. Apparently not this man. It was an all-too-familiar story. Once again the ceremony was over, her appeal for prophecy denied.

She lurched to her feet and screamed.

𒌓 𒅆 𒆜 𒎙

Nippur at night shone bright upon the Sumerian plain, a twinkling diadem kissing the river's gentle brow, her lighted windows a mirror of the starry heavens. Beloved of keen minds and industrious spirits, she commanded a vantage like no other for a hundred miles in any direction. Her sanctuary was a godly gift to her people. Her majestic beauty purified and warmed the heart.

Yet on this night, her twenty thousand voices were stilled in an unsettled hush. From Nergal Gate to the Pillar of Nanna, not a foot stirred her dusty streets. The cook pots were put away, the evening banter cut short, as citizens held their collective breath for a sign from the temple in their midst.

Ekur rested its pillars on a raised platform twenty feet above the streets. Host to daily rites of supplication and gratitude, its tabernacle received prayers and offerings from a people enriched by the food of the land and the river's steady flow. Gardens atop the second tier were tended by ranks of Great Mother's most faithful, priestess and acolyte alike. Its halls rang daily with the hurly-burly of holy service to god and man. Ekur was the sacred home of the most high goddess Inanna.

But if Ekur was for the gods, Aniginna was for the godly. Aniginna, or "One-Fifth Enfolding," the product of eleven generations of

Sumerian industry, held all the splendor one could wish for. A haven from the sere world of sunbaked silt, its enclosure ran six hundred paces in length by three hundred across. The city's nine-foot outer wall crossed its southern end to form a perimeter that was less an obstacle to passage than a definition between secular and sacred ground.

Bisecting its length like a bejeweled strap, a slender rectangular pool reflected Sumer's eternal blue by day and twinkling canopy by night. Tamarisk limbs dipped feathery fronds above secluded ponds where yellow carp glided to and fro in watery seclusion. Colonnades of date palms towered above thickets of oleander and drifts of hyacinth and aster. On every stair a flower pot. A tree tub before every postern.

On either side of its broad concourse ran the houses of government. Along the northeast edge stood House of Decrees for the lawmakers and House of Commerce for trade, followed by House of Safekeeping, a warehouse for religious artifacts and relics. Facing them from the other side were Abundant Life, hospital and public commissary, Judgment, for the courts, and Ancient Spirits, the abode of Inanna's servants past. Across the far end lay Serpenthood, seat of wisdom and knowledge, and host for Sumer's eternal quest of prophecy.

The signal that arrested so much attention tonight would herald the result of an auspicious rite being carried out not inside Ekur herself, but within Serpenthood's Hall of Sacred Union.

Lay folk were not supposed to know what went on within that chamber, but everyone did. The Sumerian soul thrived on gossip. Even the deaf old cobbler on Road of Laboring Mothers knew the queen's business tonight.

She was up there sitting cross-legged with her snakes, each with enough venom to kill forty men.

She slept with four cobras and sacrificed a husband every year. Heard so from the tent maker.

Left her mother's womb bearing an asp in either hand.

Her eyes were the color of smoke, and her beauty turned men to stone.

In a single night she had taken sixty lovers.

She could cast a spell over the river and travel on the wings of gods.

The man from Azziz was with her. Not a prince, mind you, but a tailor.

Six times would he mix the magic potion. Six times would his manhood bring her to ecstasy. Before dawn's first light she would have The Sight.

Or not.

None had succeeded before, not in fourteen years of trying, so if the tailor failed, the cobras would give him a quick death and he'd dwell thereafter in a garden with Inanna. Or something like that.

And then the queen would scour the world for the next suitor—well, maybe not the queen herself, but temple emissaries. And in another year or so, same thing all over again.

Would tonight be any different? One could only hope. Would the queen emerge a prophet for the people and guide Sumer to lasting peace and prosperity? None could say, but it was high time she did.

All this speculation had been exhausted before the supping hour ended. Now Ekur's ruling caste waited like everyone else, seated at their game tables, lying in their beds, perched on window sills or rooftops. Such fervent anticipation, while a yellow-eyed cobra tested queen and suitor thrice and thrice more, seeking the worthy. Perhaps tonight...

R-R-AUGH!

A woman's guttural roar of disgust leaped from the chamber of Sacred Union, rang through the hallway past effigies of Inanna, Nin, Damuzi, and Enshiggu, echoed down the Stairway of Purest Love, and burst into the sleeping quarters of Lukur priestess Shua Kinar like the unwelcome howl of a fiend from hell.

Kinar rolled from her pallet and slipped her feet into the embroidered sandals set out each night by her handmaid. In her forty-two years she had seldom heard such distress at any hour, much less past midnight. But tonight was far too extraordinary an occasion to cause surprise.

Great Mother in heaven, not another failure, Kinar moaned to herself as she swept a shawl about her shoulders and shuffled into action. Shaking sleep from her head, she gathered her wits with a weary sigh and lit a taper before heading upstairs.

She reached Serpenthood's hallway ahead of a gaggle of ladies rousted from their sleep as well, and was halfway down the corridor when her second in rank, Ku-Aya, caught up.

"I surely hope this is the last of her nonsense," the elder woman muttered, struggling to match Kinar's pace. "She'll have to listen to reason now."

"Uruna listens to no one but that cobra."

"We granted her wish to continue the rite, and we can take it away. Council always has the final word."

"Don't be too sure, my dear. She still has the will of the people firmly in her grasp."

Several more women fell in behind to form a reluctant march through the darkened central corridor, their stubby tapers providing scarcely enough light to avoid stumbling into the grooved pavement tiles. Serpenthood creaked like a decrepit old woman. Her clay bones were in desperate need of repair, a dereliction zealously withheld from the public by the Lukur elect, few of whom were permitted so deep inside her sacred walls.

As Kinar reached the top stair, the doors of the chamber ahead burst open and Uruna stomped out and halted, her face contorted with fury, breasts bared, feet spread apart to reveal the cause of her rage. She flung an arm back toward the room behind her and pointed a damning finger at the humbled form crouched on the floor inside.

"Get him out!" she spat.

Ku-Aya peered around Kinar's shoulder with a timid peep. "Is he dead?"

"No, the fool lives on because the gods would not have him!"

"Did he—did he spill—?"

Uruna's fists clenched at her sides. "It is plain to see, madam, he failed on the first Step. We had barely begun. It was a waste of the god's attention and a foolish amount of money, just as I warned."

Fearing all was lost, Kinar nevertheless hoped for a reprieve. "But he came so highly recommended, passed all the tests."

Uruna abruptly calmed herself. Her chest heaved, her grey eyes flashed silvery venom as she spoke in a manner only slightly more in keeping with her station.

"If you please, Lady Kinar, remove the offender before he is indeed taken. The longer he languishes, the more apt they are to snap him dead just for spite."

She turned on her heel and strode briskly from the hall.

Kinar turned around and took stock of her retinue. By now a good-sized tribe of Lukur had gathered in their night smocks to attend the commotion. She spied the yellow-headed girl hovering at the back.

"You, Retha, come at once!"

Ku-Aya's aging face crinkled in a frown. "But she's not—"

"Hut!" A stern look from Kinar cut the old woman short. "She may not be Sumerian," she said in a hoarse whisper, "but she's the only one can move safely among the snakes. We cannot have the suitor returned to Azziz a corpse."

The girl was tall for fifteen, a half-breed throwback to an invading clan of giants who had ravaged the frontier two centuries ago before being subdued by a cunning feat of tactical ingenuity. Apart from prominent muscle definition and overpowering strength, a full-blooded Nord male was characterized by his height. The girl's own father stood six inches above six feet, easily head and shoulders above the tallest Sumerian. Most remnant Nords were employed as smiths. Kinar had heard rumors that the queen of rival city Uruk had armed small groups of them to hunt down marsh-dweller slaves for her ambitious ziggurat. Arming Nords was a flagrant breach of law. The prevailing opinion in Ekur was that any Nord not behind walls was an arrow aimed at one's neck, although the ladies were happy enough to post the giants as unarmed sentinels throughout the city to deter crime.

Retha moved quickly to the doors and made ready to close them. Kinar barred one door with her arm and crowded past the girl, muttering so that only Retha could hear. "I must be Inanna's witness."

"You should live so long."

The girl's sharp tongue had gotten her in trouble often, but Kinar knew her well enough to let it pass. "Go about your work, and tell me when it's safe for the suitor to take his leave."

The huge chamber measured fifteen paces by twenty and lay empty, save for a stone dais built against the far wall and the four erect serpents coiled on the floor. Scant light from candles placed at each corner of the dais cast the figures in soft shadow. Beside each serpent sat a reed basket for safe transport to and from the serpent lair. The man's clothing lay in a heap near the door.

Kinar watched the girl walk up to the first cobra while the young tailor crouched naked on the floor, still as death, his gleaming, lithe body caught in the candle glow. His name was Apilsha, and he was the comely servant of a wealthy priestess in Azziz to the east. As Retha approached the cobra, Apilsha raised his head ever so slightly, eyes wide with terror, his beautiful body trembling. Gone was the bravado displayed at yesterday's interview. His alleged years of preparation had ended with a single moment's loss of control. The serpent god Enshiggu offered no second chance.

For her part, Retha went quietly about the business of enticing each cobra into its basket, speaking not a word nor showing any gesture except to open each basket lid for its occupant. Uruna had confided the nature of serpent communication to Kinar—a silent, invisible sensation that was felt rather than thought. What disturbed Kinar more than her own lack of the mysterious affinity was the diffident ease with which the Nord girl had acquired it.

When all four serpents were safely put away, Retha returned to the center of the circle, hiked her skirt, and sat cross-legged before Apilsha with her eyes shut, arms outstretched to her sides. She held that position for several moments, and when at last she opened her eyes, it was to speak in a voice almost too soft to be heard.

Kirith azzeh manna Enshiggu,
Ama, 'Nanna, abilum,
Kiri-gah lu, kiri-mah nu, Apilsha-tum,
Sigah, selah, selashum.

"Enshiggu, thou guardian of the serpent way, we bid thee forgive Apilsha his trespass, that henceforth he may live, love, and prosper."

Kinar staggered back a step. Great gods, the girl spoke the old tongue! First a rapid ascent to serpent keeper, now mastery of a forgotten language? What next? How much of the girl's education had she missed?

And forgive the failed consort? Not strike him dead for his offense? What manner of serpently compassion was this?

And coming from a Nord girl not yet inducted as a priestess. If Uruna had trained more acolytes like her, Serpenthood had established a greater foothold than anyone imagined. Regardless, Kinar had heard nothing about it, an unforgivable lapse for a woman of her station. She made a mental note to question Uruna further.

"Rise, Apilsha."

The command that should have come from Kinar came instead from the girl again.

Apilsha stood, head hung, unable to face either woman. Now Kinar moved to his side.

"Come, my friend, let us offer you rest and refreshment, and we'll get you home. The ordeal is past."

As she guided the hapless man into the hall, she cast a backward glance and met Retha's unforgiving glower. The ritual had failed, Uruna's bid for Sight nipped in the bud once more. Defeat did not rest well with the women of Ekur. Apparently it suited the Nord girl even less.

But in her heart of hearts Kinar knew the girl's unspoken censure was directed not at the tailor from Azziz, nor at Kinar for choosing him out of desperation. They all knew too well the real problem. Their aspiring prophet Uruna was in trouble and running out of time.

CHAPTER TWO
Mission To The Ghana

On returning to her bed chamber, Uruna latched the door and threw the bolt. The Mothers would respect her need for solitude, as they had on dozens of prior occasions. Gods, so many she had lost count! The follow-up routine had become nearly as familiar to all as the rite itself.

She bathed and dressed in haste to be on her way without further delay. She had decided before embarking on tonight's ritual that if either she or the tailor failed to perform, she would go to the house in the desert. She had tried the god's way. She had allowed the Lukur to blunder through one hapless suitor after another. Now but one chance remained, and she was taking it.

A trap door beside her bed led down into the bowels of Serpenthood. Uruna threw on a shawl and lit a candle. Then she lifted the door, climbed down several steps, and reached back and closed the lid behind her. If all went well, she would be back before dawn.

At the foot of the stair she paused before a small door that led to the serpent lair. She turned the other way and followed a narrow passageway that ended at an ancient wall of clay bricks. A gap at the far end marked the intersection of bricks and broken tunnel wall. She had discovered this path to the river walk years ago and told no one of it.

Moving quickly, she squeezed through the opening and descended further into the dank cavern below. The tunnel mouth was low and narrow and stank of river muck. She doused the candle to crouch in a duck waddle and drag her hem over the slime until she emerged in the deep shadow of Shutu Gate. The buttress of the abandoned relic would hide her from view, should a sentry happen to glance eastward. She continued on to Nunbirdu Canal, then struck off down the levee road in dim starlight.

She was scarcely halfway to her destination when a lone figure appeared out of the night gloom carrying a walking staff.

"You!" she said to the woman she sought. "How did you know I was coming?"

"Don't ask foolish questions," said the desert crone. "Not far ahead I've set up a tent—with tea and biscuits!"

"You are ever full of miracles."

"Aha! Only for my faithful Uruna. But come, let's save our breath and step lively before the tea grows cold."

Moments later they arrived at a roadside stop long out of use, since boat taxis now plied the canal by day with regular frequency. At this hour the two women had the canal's entire length to themselves.

Uruna knew her hostess only as "Nashi." To farm folk in the hinterland, Nashi was the ghost of a legendary witch. To Uruna she was the flesh-and-blood personification of serpent lore, a kindred spirit in a wasteland barren of the old wisdom.

As for Nashi's view of Uruna, she had always been outspoken. "Thou art the wellspring of my hope, a flower cherished by seers past and present."

She had added the lament that she was herself the last and only "present" one.

Nashi struck a flint and lit Uruna's candle anew, then opened the tent flap. Inside, Uruna was treated to a low, linen-covered table with two cushions. Gardenia scent wafted from a petal pot.

Nashi must have fetched it all from her house miles away. Surely such preparation had consumed hours.

"You knew the rite would fail before we even started!" Uruna exclaimed.

"Perhaps so, perhaps not. Does it matter?"

"You might have warned me and spared Ekur all the arrangements for nothing."

"But that would have left nothing for the people to wish for. Or you."

Uruna shook her head. "You're right, it doesn't matter. I need your help."

"Oh, but I'm far past helping anyone, even myself. These old bones—"

"Just tell me what to do, Nashi, and I'll do it. I'm surrounded by feckless hypocrites without an inkling of serpent sense. This pretty boy they presented hadn't a smidgen of self-control. We're losing what little remains of the serpent way. I thought I knew the key to prophecy, but obviously I don't."

"Maybe a fresh look at the whole thing."

"Exactly, but where to start?"

The old woman sipped her tea and watched Uruna's face in the candlelight, her eyes crinkling with pleasure at some inner secret among the thousands she kept.

"You must go a-hunting," she said.

Uruna heaved a sigh, suddenly aware of a great weariness. "Please don't speak in riddles. I'm so exhausted I can't think straight."

"No riddle here. I mean what I say. Take yourself down to the *ghana* for the hunt."

"Augh! I last sought boar with my step-father when I was ten."

"Pigs won't help with the Sight, Uruna. You need a man."

"I think I've quite used up the world's supply of qualified—Oh, no! Not on your life! Not the lion hunter! The one they call Tezu-Mah?"

"Seems your mind is quite capable of straight thought after all. Consider how he might fare better than a shirt maker from the provinces."

"Oh, to be sure, why not a wild stalker from the swamps! So much more adept at serpently matters. He spears them and eats them raw. Uck!"

"Does no such thing. He's nearly quit of animal flesh."

"And you know this how?"

"Same as I know other things. Such as how a vanquished queen will leave by Shutu Gate tonight, but not without a taper, so I need not bring one."

"Nashi!"

"He's fearless, he's strong, his spirit speaks to the animal world. He's lived at the edge of existence for nine years."

"You're certain he's not one of the dead who walks? Or a spirit who roams the bogs, filling marsh-dweller heads with claims of miracles?"

"Is it a miracle to kill a raging lion with aught but a spear? Or is that courage at work? Perhaps the best course would be for you to find out for yourself."

"I? Go down to the marshes?"

"I believe that's where he's to be found most days. The *ghana* is a more likely hunting ground than, say, a temple bower or a barley field."

Uruna studied the black eyes that regarded her. The playful twinkle was gone, the amused half-smile replaced with tight-lipped conviction.

"You really mean it," said Uruna.

Rather than answer directly, Nashi abruptly switched topics.

"This girl," she said, "this Retha who tends your chambers and speaks the old tongue and holds her counsel wisely while elders prattle. Does she strike you as trustworthy?"

"I trust her more than I trust myself, as you must know, since you seem to know everything else. Let's say I go down to Larsa, or Burum. Say I leave my post, my duties as judge of the court, my daily altar celebrations, all that. Just abandon my life and hie me downriver to prowl the rushes for a mythical huntsman. How does my trust in Retha fit such a scheme?"

"Who else should know what you're about when you go?'"

"I haven't said I would yet."

"You don't need to. We both know you're going. The question remains how that settles with those left behind."

"Well, it'll give them plenty to gossip about."

"And speculate. And scheme and maneuver."

"Why, Nashi, I believe you do walk the temple disguised as a spirit. Are you suggesting I leave my duties to an untried *kadishtu*?"

"Nothing of the kind. Simply let her be your eyes and ears while you're away. The girl has a Nord nose for subterfuge and foul play. It's in her blood line."

"That would be trust on a very large scale."

"Does it bother you?"

Uruna pondered a moment. "The inconspicuous attendant at the door. The drudge who lingers in the next room after her sweeps. That's how she learned the old tongue from councilwomen."

"And how she picked up serpent lore—from *you*."

Uruna sipped the last of her tea and nodded slowly. "I like it."

"Thought you would. Now to another matter. The Hanza are set against the Seddua as never before. The clans will bring ruin if their feud continues unabated. There's talk of murder, and where one finds talk, one encounters plotting and planning, until all that remains is for the deed itself to be done. And then the host of Hades will be loosed among us. Tell me what you know of Gunzeks."

Uruna twisted her head with a jerk. Nashi's train of thought darted about like a house mouse through rooms.

"All I've been told is that they straggled down from the north a few years back. Rag-tag refugees without gods or rules, but mainly without shirts on their backs."

"They were tent people, wanderers without roots, struck down by famine. Now the Uruk temple gives each man among them a house for his family and food and clothes."

"That's what every temple does for the poor."

"Note I said each *man*, Uruna."

This sounded like the work of the apostate inside Eanna temple at Uruk.

"Enguda," she said.

"Yes, the Bull Priest who hates women."

"I've heard the stories. If true, he would replace every temple woman with a man and rule the lot by the lash and false promises."

"All true and then some. Have you met the man?"

"No, I haven't had occasion to."

"Take care you're in plenty of company if ever you do. He sets these Gunzeks upon the marsh dwellers to make slaves. And he's up to something else down there, but that's a brick unbaked as yet. Your hunter knows more. That's the ally you need, Uruna. An ally Ekur needs when the worst comes to pass."

"What could be worse than the Hani enslaved?"

"The death that knows no end."

Nashi pinched the candle out and swept the tent flap aside, indicating an end to their nocturnal tea talk. Uruna rustled to her feet and with heavy heart followed her hostess outside beneath the stars.

Nashi had chosen a euphemism rather than voice the prospect every Sumerian dreaded: Mankind once again girded for war.

CHAPTER THREE
Larsa's Streets

Larsa's crowded streets offered rootless humanity both blessing and curse, sanctuary and snare. Betrayed by the river's meander ages ago and bereft of gods or a temple to put them in, she lay hostage to the open desert, a destination for refugee and renegade alike. Time and misfortune had cast her as a stronghold for cutthroats and brigands. Treachery lurked round every corner, abided in her deepest shadows. It was said: Better to embrace a lion than bed down with Larsa.

At an open tavern on Street of Wayward Women, a hunter in loincloth and leather collar broke his fast with a merchant of his acquaintance. His naked torso stood out in the throng like a plum in an egg basket. With stories abounding of a mad lion stalker prowling the cities, his appearance in Larsa gave rise to speculation and drew attention he could ill afford.

For years he had roamed Sumer's great southern marshes, commonly called the *ghana*, home to the diminutive Hani aboriginals. The frequency of his visits to Larsa had dwindled as the city's offense to his senses grew. Returning from only a few weeks in the bush, he would smell the town long before its raucous din reached his ears. He would tolerate its urban excesses only long enough to obtain provisions and see to his affairs, then hasten back to his wilderness retreat. With a bounty on his head raising the likelihood of betrayal from any quarter, each stay heaped anxiety on annoyance.

Thus, by the narrowest chance had he learned moments ago of a lion's rampage near tiny Kudu Mahti, a miserable outpost on the southern extent of Larsa's branch of the Euphrates.

"The rogue took two at once," Lamech told him, wiping juice from his beard with a swatch of linen. The wine peddler wore corpulence as proudly as the gaudy raiment that caused him to sweat in Larsa's muggy heat.

The woman at his side was not Lamech's wife, but a harlot. In shameless Larsa she had reason aplenty to announce her trade with painted face and heavy scent. Her eyes roved hungrily over the hunter's muscled body, taking appreciative account of the shaved jaw, the sleek black hair swept back to a warrior's knot, the scars marking limb and torso. He felt uneasy before her brazen stare.

What those eyes failed to detect was the toll taken by a lifetime spent tracking game in the wild. With approaching middle age, the hunter's body had begun to slow by a hair here, a sliver there. Each loss went unnoticed by all except himself. But the tally was growing, a deadly accumulation in an enterprise that forgave not the slightest imperfection. In the hunt, the god would know—and the lion. In the hunt, timing was everything. In the final moment, nothing else mattered.

Careful to avoid the woman's eye, he fixed his attention on the merchant. "How long ago?"

Lamech had put his hunter onto enough lions to know the importance of speed, and he brimmed with propitious news.

"Not two days yet. My sources raced from their village and got here only last night. Your arrival is timely. I don't see you for months on end, and here you show up on the very heels of an assault."

"I've been away."

The hunter's response was deliberately vague. He'd been dodging slavers and bounty hunters. The scoundrels seemed to multiply each week in the fen. Worse, for him, their adaptation to swamp hazards was approaching his own.

Lamech's mind stuck to business. "No matter. My contacts are most anxious to be rid of the beast before their field hands panic and abandon the produce of their labor."

"My friend, the rest of the world doesn't always view life as a matter of money. They're terrified, and rightly so."

"You will recall our bargain? Ten minas of silver for telling you first."

"Your greed matches your gluttony. That's two years wages for a laborer. Five it was and five it stays."

"But I must cover the rising price of grain and housekeeping."

"I haven't been away that long. Five will become four if you keep this up."

"Ah! Very well. For a wealthy man, you bargain like a market hawker. No, don't deny it! You're no swamp rat, though you may dress like one. And why you would prefer a muddy bed to the charms of a Lukur princess or, say—"

The hunter slapped a coin on the table in front of Lamech to shut him up, and nearly lost a knuckle as the merchant's hand snatched the object with the speed of a shell gamesman.

"You'll have the rest of your money if I decide it's worth it," said the hunter. "Now show me to these fellows of yours before they fall prey to a worse impostor. This wretched hold is beginning to make me ill."

Lamech turned to the woman. "See? I told you he speaks like a high-born."

The woman eyed the hunter with an ingratiating smile and a leer meant to invite a more fleshly morning pursuit. He deliberately ignored her and put his next question to the merchant.

"Tell me what news you have from Nippur."

Merchant and harlot exchanged glances as an unspoken message passed between them: Bush-beater doesn't know. Well, let them think him an ignorant throwback. It served his purpose.

Lamech bent forward with exaggerated confidentiality and his stool groaned beneath the shift of his bulk. "You sequester yourself too long, my friend. All of Sumer is abuzz with talk of the woman up there."

"The queen?"

Lamech glanced about at the other customers in an effort to add import to his news, but the harlot dropped all pretense of sophistication and scooted her stool closer to the hunter.

"Did you know her?" she asked. "They say you once attended."

She referred to the temple practice of attracting comely male adolescents to make babies with equally attractive girls, thereby perpetuating the upper ruling class. He'd hated the conceit of it then and still did.

"I was too young," he said, and steered the conversation back on course. "What's the excitement about?"

A smirk twisted the harlot's rouged mouth; she had managed to rouse the hunter's interest.

"What else but serpent business?" she said. "This time it's more intense. Her last suitor was a tailor from Azziz. He was too quick to the peak. Some say the cobras finished him off, but I'd be surprised he didn't die of fright first. Now Temple Ekur probes the four corners of the world, seeking the next to bring her the ecstasy." She arranged her features in a haughty look. "Personally, I think the notion of a woman's heat is wasted. A few moments of intense passion and a man's urge is spent."

He let the challenge lie untouched, having never in his life needed to buy a woman's favor. He was a hunter, and his business was bringing down lions, not women.

He spat onto the dirt floor. Uruna! Every time he heard she was with a new mate his throat burned and he tasted gall. For days afterward he would rove the marsh in a black mood. Ridiculous waste of energy, pining like a feckless boy.

You gave up your chance for that long ago, and gladly. You have your life. Move on.

The merchant had more to say. "Couple days ago she was sighted on the Uruk channel headed for that town down there on the river mouth, Burum. Where the sea-goers land. Something's up, something big, but can't be a consort in that mud hole. There's none there fit to give what she's after, you get my meaning. Word has it she likes to—"

"That's enough about it."

"If you say."

The harlot at last gave up her pursuit and stood up to scan the crowd for another prospect. He paid the tavern keeper and stepped into the street. Lamech rolled through the gate after him and drew closer to confide another matter.

"I can get four minas for the trophy hide. We split two and two."

The hunter regarded Lamech with tightlipped disdain. "*If* I find the rogue and kill him before he kills me, and *if* the Hani do not prise him away to a desert burial, and *if* I should ever find reason to visit this god-forsaken hold again, then maybe I'll recall who deserves reward and deal with him justly. All right?"

Lamech watched his benefactor carefully, unsure how to interpret the hunter's meaning. "Fair enough," he agreed with a tentative nod. Then: "They were here again last week, you know."

"Doing what?"

"The usual. Nosing around, asking questions."

Bounty hunters, looking to collect ten minas from Uruk's Bull Priest by ending the hunter's liberation of Hani slaves. "How many?"

"I saw only three but there may have been others. The Slave Soldier from Uruk was one of them."

So, Captain Borok had dragged his sorry ass farther afield than ever. Persistent buzzard, but a buzzard nonetheless.

"Did he question you?"

"No, I—er, kept my distance."

"By which you mean his purse is still smaller than mine."

Lamech lifted a brow. "He's Nafti, you know, not Gunzek. A warlord, they say, came out of the west. Runs that Gunzek rabble for Uruk. Now he closes upon you, hunter. I am seen with you today, tomorrow he appears and yanks on my tongue. I must talk, purse or no, for I cannot endure pain."

"You also cannot endure a day without profit."

"The demands of my nature," the heavy man smiled and patted his ample stomach, "and my endowment."

For now, the hunter would suspend judgment. Lamech would discover soon enough how the gods dealt with misery's profiteer.

He found Lamech's informants at a potter's shed on the edge of town. The fools tried to pass themselves off as a pair of lowland grain farmers, but it was apparent to the hunter's keen eye they were slavers. A roving lion would drive the marsh dwellers deeper into the *ghana* than any slaver dared to go and shut down his trade in the blink of an eye.

The first "farmer" proffered a large sum of silver.

The hunter looked the man over. "You had a bumper crop, I see."

A knowing leer. "We did all right."

The second man snickered with a gap-toothed grin. "Do a lot better, you put that lion away. Maybe something in it for yourself after, you know?"

This was the part of his life he hated. Such men as these were interested only in money. They cared nothing for Hani lives, as long as they themselves prospered. The only reason he dealt with them at all was to use their lucre for the marsh people. No amount of lion-killing could make up for sons and fathers lost to the harsh rigors of digging and hauling dirt from sunup to sundown. A woman left behind with children to feed was forced to rely on her neighbors and whatever the hunter could provide—if he knew of her plight. It was never enough.

The lion had been spotted heading north from a place called Za, but the village of Kudu Mahti lay directly in the beast's path.

"He's a big fellow," said the leader of the pair.

"You saw him yourself?"

"A footprint, but it was enough." The man spread both hands with only his thumbs touching.

"Just one sign?"

"He's in and out of the shallows, would be my guess. Looking for shore folk. Those on the rafts are too much trouble for him. Caught the last two as they worked their field. Animal knows what he's up to."

Spoken like a predator, not a farmer.

The hunter finished his business with the two reprobates and set out from the town without further delay. He found his boat and weapons where he'd left them and gave silent thanks to the gods for one more reprieve from brigand avarice.

As he pointed his swifthull downstream, he figured he might make Kudu Mahti by the following morning—provided he poled all night.

And provided the Slave Soldier wasn't lying in wait along the way.

CHAPTER FOUR

Disaster and Rescue

Uruna had never in her life undertaken a more ill-considered venture than her so-called hunting trip to the *ghana*.

First, the secret of her expedition was out before it became fact, leading to wild conjecture and fear-borne objections from the very people she had hoped to avoid. When at last she pushed off in her swifthull, it was not the silent, solitary escape she had intended, but a ragged departure orchestrated by a company of bickering, contentious women clamoring over authority. Council had thrust upon her two oarsmen for her craft plus a pair for each of two fast escorts, in all a host of six men, together with their armament and provisions. Kinar would have added an *udalla* anointing minister to each boat if Uruna hadn't nearly come to blows with her.

Then, during the stopover at Isin, her strident appeal for solitude on the final leg had probably cost a friendship. Holub, the young *galla* soldier who took her safety as his sole purpose in life, had departed with a hurt look and a remark about fools questing for trouble being sure to find it.

So what had she done once she was finally on her own? Hired a shady guide who stole her boat and kit the first night in the marsh. The thug had left her bow and quiver only because she'd wrapped her arms about them in her sleep.

On her sixth day out of Nippur she was weak from hunger. The barley cake in her tote had turned a mottled green from the thick moisture. Yesterday she had caught and eaten a small carp she could not keep down. Larger prey could smell her a mile off. To add humiliation to defect, she had lost her bearings in the farthest reaches of the great southern marsh while chasing a dove for breakfast—a futile blunder that only increased the likelihood she would starve before a predator caught wind of her.

But catch her he had.

Now she stood stock still in blood-soaked barley, the body of a child at her feet, while a black-maned lion watched her through a screen of rushes at the edge of a reed brake. He was finished with the babe's carcass. In fact, he had already started back into the reeds when she'd blundered onto his killing field in desperate haste, seeing only the dove. She felt the lion's steady gaze as he bided his time, silent as the wind, nostrils flared to catch the new stench, alert for the slightest crack in her resolve.

She had stripped to the skin for the *ghana's* steamy heat. No lance, not even a sword, just her bow and quiver and a skinning knife, plus hunting skills borrowed from faulty childhood memories. Her exposed back and chest were bug-bitten raw, her limbs nicked by grass blades. A wise lion would deem her unfit prey and leave her for vultures to pick.

The beast remained oddly wary. Uruna felt his feral mind sizing her up, considering the larger trophy, weighing the meaning of this new situation. Her own mind locked up, blocking out will and thought. She had faced death many times before, but always with a cobra and assurances from the divine. Never one-on-one barely twenty paces from a rogue killer with a taste for human flesh. She could only hold her place and wait. The next moment belonged to the lion.

"Ease left and mind the child."

She hunched her shoulders and nearly shat herself.

A man behind her! On cat feet! She wanted to turn around for a look, but she shifted aside as directed. Her foot brushed the tiny ruined body, and she felt the man move as well. The lion stayed rooted in place.

She held her position as the man stepped forward into her field of view, a beardless hunter as naked as she, wielding a heavy cedar lance tipped with copper, the spearhead as long as his forearm. Black hair swept over his ears to a knot at the back. His smooth skin was a deep bronze and the muscles of his arms and torso gleamed in the sun like armor plates.

"If he takes me, try for deep water," he said, and planted his left foot. His left arm was already extended in a throwing stance.

"Shuh," he said to the lion, his tone understated but assured of getting the animal's attention.

The big cat answered with a hideous bellow that shook the air like a peal of thunder, flinging his rage ahead as if sound alone might knock the faint of heart from their feet.

In an instant he was out, a lord of imposing immensity, feet braced upon his domain, the ivory menace bared for all to see. His head was as broad as a bullock's hindquarters and came level with the hunter's chest. Forepaws the size of meal platters crushed the reeds like barley chaff. With bold confidence he bounded out of the brake and charged.

What happened next would remain with Uruna the rest of her life. Her mind registered every detail.

The hunter's arm swept down, the lance flew outward.

A ringing sound filled the air, like a male voice in song.

The lance struck the lion's chest square on and drove straight in, burying the spearhead in the heavy mane.

The hunter remained motionless, implacable in his launch stance.

The lion stumbled and slid to a stop, its nose less than a human stride from the hunter, the shaft protruding from its chest.

So close was she to the beast that its hot breath brushed her face.

But the lion's ordeal was not finished, for it clung to life with stubborn defiance. The hunter pulled a shorter boar spear from a sling on his left shoulder and backed away from the dying beast.

"Move back, slowly," he said to her, but her legs quivered like a hooked fish. She couldn't have moved to save her life.

"Will he die?" she heard herself ask in a tremulous voice.

"Gods willing, soon. Or I'll have to use this." He brandished the short lance.

The great shaggy head lay inert on the ground. As Uruna looked on, the hunter approached the animal, watching the rib cage heave in shallow, uneven grunts. With the tip of the shorter spear, he prodded one shoulder. A lip twitched but the rest stayed still. He dragged the tip across the ribs and poked the flank. Nothing there either.

Without warning the lion rolled onto its belly and faced straight ahead, muzzle dark with blood, gulping heavy breaths while it gathered strength for another move.

Uruna back-pedaled furiously, awed by the animal's incredible reserves of strength and the abrupt return of her own. After a brief pause, the lion's forelegs levered up and he sat upright. Six feet of lance haft bobbed from his chest as the hindquarters responded reluctantly to the lion's will. The huge beast struggled, grunted with a mighty strain, and staggered upright to face the world once again on all fours.

The hunter retreated quickly, lifting the short-shafted spear for a strike. The lion tottered a step forward, the ugly shaft pushing him awkwardly off balance.

She marveled at the animal's courage. He was as undaunted in death as he was in life.

The hunter nodded as if attuned to her thoughts. "A worthy king driven to madness, unwilling to quit. But watch him now."

When the lion fell a last time, the hunter raised the spear high and held it ready, but the lion coughed blood and closed its eyes, the protruding shaft mocking its feral beauty and incredible stamina. With a final groan, the lion expired.

Uruna realized she'd been straining every muscle in her body as she shared the animal's death agony. Her legs buckled and she collapsed to her knees, drained of energy as if it had been she gasping a last breath on the barley mat.

A sound from the hunter brought her out of herself, and she turned to see what further work needed doing.

Prayer, apparently, for he sat nearby on his heels, hands folded on his bent knees, head bowed as he murmured a quiet requiem. His shoulders shook, whether from grief or emotional release or physical exhaustion, she didn't know, but the sight moved her deeply, and she felt obliged to speak her own thanks. Still on her knees, she began a quiet homage to Great Mother, to the hunting god Shumu-gan, to her personal god, Kumta.

When she was done she looked up. The hunter was standing now, watching her. She got to her feet and noticed for the first time a small crowd gathered at the far edge of the field. They were Hani, the marsh dwellers known in the cities as "Old Ones." How long had they been there? Had the hunter brought them? Had they witnessed her hapless thrashing after a bird?

They came forward now, and as they neared the hunter, he spoke to her in a low voice.

"Scouts from Girsa picked you up at dawn. Out on the Silla stream. Said a huntress had come to find their missing child. And here you are."

Huntress? She who had lost her bearings on four occasions and stumbled onto the ravaged babe in reckless pursuit of her first meal in two days? She who could barely fit an arrow to a bowstring or strike a target?

She stood now before an entire village, clad only in a loincloth, her face and limbs smeared with swamp mire. Sweat dripped from her chin. She smelled like a slaughter pen. The stalker's crimson arc on her face only aped the real thing. She felt trivial and inconsequential, a shiny flower adrift in their life-death world, yet the Hani forsook ridicule to include her in the hunter's honor.

A handful of men sprang forward to greet the hunter, each striving to be at the forefront. Two of the men moved to the still form of the dead girl and reverently wrapped her remains in a blanket and carried it off. The nearest introduced himself as Jabali, headman of Kudu Mahti, and addressed the hunter by name.

"Tezu-Mah, Inanna be with you."

Uruna's hand fluttered to her chest. The legend himself! The very one she sought! Not a god, but a flesh-and-blood human being. Fearless, strong, powerful. And so much larger in life than in fable.

The hunter engaged Jabali in a warm hug, symbolically embracing all of Kudu Mahti and honoring their pain and hardship and loss. The two men clung to each other for several moments, and in that single act of love the hunter won the people, for they gathered close to touch him and speak their faith and receive the warmth of his heart.

The group retreated back to the edge of the field, sweeping Uruna along with them and leaving the lion in their wake. She cast a glance back at the dead beast and the hunter leaned close.

"The Hani will take care of it. He belongs to them now."

"But your lance..."

"I'll get it back—or have another made."

A fire was set onshore near the hunter's moored boat. Three elderwomen performed an ancient dance of thanks for an end to their terror. Someone brought ale in an earthen jug and the dancing soon turned into a subdued celebration of Tezu-Mah's appearance and his vanquishing of the lion.

Uruna felt she was intruding on a sacred ceremony. The hunter and the people of Kudu Mahti shared a bond more intimate than any she had known. They were his children, and he was their savior. The release of anxiety charged the air with palpable energy, a great deal like the serpent's song but mellower and more masculine. Uruna longed to be included, but she belonged elsewhere. These were not her people. Kudu Mahti was not her place.

A Hani woman sought the hunter's embrace and he held her close, letting her feel the security of his protective power for as long as she needed. When she was satisfied, he released her, and Uruna realized she longed to take that woman's place, to drink from the same fount...

Gods! He was coming her way.

She was all alone, standing on the beach in her besmirched skin, as conspicuous as a gull in the desert.

Now that he was close again she saw the rough edges, refinement coarsened by the wilderness. Scars on his chest and arms attested to his brushes with death, and under his gaze she felt the same fierce intensity he reserved for his quarry. He was all game-stalker, raw and hardened, a killer under tight rein. Certainly not one for the likes of her.

He glanced down at her bare bosom as though noticing for the first time. "Where is your boat? I'll send for your things. I assume you brought more than an archer's kit."

She felt her face color. "The heat here is beastly."

Wrong word!

The man who was Tezu-Mah smiled, then gave her a perplexed look. "You're the serpent queen."

Uruna tossed her head. "Why would you think such a thing?"

"The serpents on your back."

Oh, feathers, the tattoos! She'd forgotten the sinuous emblems she'd had pricked into her skin over the years in the belief they would aid her quest for prophecy. In Nippur the designs were always covered by gowns and robes of office. She had no secrets from this man.

"They symbolize aspects of temple ritual," she said.

"They're quite beautiful, really, although I doubt you need further adornment than you give to the world."

She swallowed hard, not knowing what to say, and he took her silence as a signal to press further.

"They say you lie with serpents, speak to their spirits, that sort of thing."

"Stories. It's really not that way." Why couldn't she catch her breath?

"Indeed?"

"Well, some of it is, but only when Memet and I are alone."

Why was she divulging so private a matter to an utter stranger? The lion business must have rattled her daft.

"Is he your consort?"

"Snake. Cobra. From Meluhha. Eight feet of magnificence. Such wisdom in his eyes, and oh, what an armful..."

She cut her babble short. Another secret slipping from her tongue before she could think. He must believe her an utter fool now.

His eyes glowed with some inner discovery. "No cobras around here. What are you doing in the *ghana*?"

Looking for you!

"My, um, my uncle was a temple hunter for Kish. I learned from him."

And forgot every last trick of the hunt.

"This place is nothing like the Akkad. Your uncle and his lot rid the northern hunting grounds of lions years ago, chased them all down here. Lion gets your scent and *f-f-ft*, no more serpent queen."

"You're trying to frighten me."

"This place belongs to the Old Ones. The *ghana* is all they have left. Before long they'll be used up by slavers and frontier farmers. Your place is in your palace with your fine lady friends."

"You're being unkind."

"Yes, I suppose. I haven't been in decent company for a long time. Out here you learn not to trust people from the city. They only know how to take. Tell me, how did you come upon the lion—or the girl for that matter?"

"I was chasing a bird and I nearly fell over the body."

"Truly?"

"I wouldn't make up a story like that."

"You weren't tracking Death Maker?"

"Is that what you call him?"

"That's what he becomes when the demon gets into him. So you didn't track him."

"Please don't make me feel worse. I did nothing to merit Hani respect."

"They believed you would find the girl, and you did—in your own way. Give yourself that much for ending their doubt and worry."

"Yes, but if not for you I'd be lying in the grass as dead as the girl."

"Maybe we both heeded the gods. Where is your boat?"

"I lost—it got stolen. My guide left with it the first night."

"One of those brigands from Lagash?"

"Um, he came recommended."

"You don't hire a guide out of that town unless you plan to lose your kit. How much did he take?"

"A lot."

"Tell me."

"Everything. But a man there said I might find you in Kudu Mahti. That's why I came out. To see if you were still here."

"You came to see my shame and report it."

"Your shame? How about your courage, how you gird the Old Ones in honor. Your exploits are all anyone talks about. By most accounts, you're immortal."

He looked away into the distance, his jaw twitching.

"No boat, no kit, no guide, yet you came anyway..."

He pondered the notion in silence before looking again at her. "Tell me, where did you plan to spend the night?"

"Same as last night. On the ground. Maybe beside one of the huts?"

"These people guard their doors all night through. The lion smells your hot flesh, he comes. He's all nose and mouth, his senses find you across miles of swamp. It's a miracle you're alive. This one is gone now, but there are others."

"You must think I'm a fool..."

"No, I'm simply telling you how it is out here. You don't know what you're up against. Look, I'll take you to an island tonight. You'll be safe in my boat. Tomorrow, one of the boys here will fetch you in a fishing skiff and take you back to the main channel."

"Where will you be?"

"I don't know, there's talk of a new track."

"I see. I should have said this before. Thank you for saving my life. You're right of course, I shouldn't have come down."

His perfect teeth formed a most beautiful smile. "I've heard of your way with the cobra. Powerful *meh*, worthy of great respect. But see, it doesn't work out here. Leave in the morning, and allow the Old Ones to get on with their lives."

And let you get on with yours.

She understood now.

He abruptly turned about and strode back to the dancing, leaving her alone and feeling wretched.

She was trying to form a plan for her return to Nippur when a woman approached from the crowd and without warning wrapped her arms about Uruna's neck.

"She was mine," the woman said into Uruna's ear before she pulled back, her cheeks wet with tears.

At once Uruna realized she was embracing the mother of the dead girl, and she pulled the woman closer and whispered her own grief.

"Inanna keep you."

The woman pulled away, her eyes still glistening. She had something to say.

"I saw you stand before the lion, defending my baby, protecting her until Tezu-Mah could come, and I was struck by your presence. That you, a great queen, should travel so far to find her, to be here for our day of need."

I'm not great at anything. I was driven by other reasons, selfish reasons...I stood locked in fear for my own life...

The Hani woman wasn't finished. "You were the same with the cobra at the feast of Haran."

"Oh! You were there? But that was my first—I was just a child then."

"So was I. You showed everyone your courage, just as you did today." She glanced upshore to where the hunter had joined a group of men. "He is quite taken by your bravery, but I think even more by your beauty."

Uruna felt hardly a trace of beauty in her filthy, smelly skin. "Oh, I doubt that. Anyway, he's the brave one..."

"He could not take his eyes from you. He is afraid to speak what is in his heart. This a woman knows."

"You're very kind to say so."

"It is the gods' work."

"Do you think so? Such things are so hard to–"

"You are meant for him."

"Are you a seer, perhaps?"

"I see with a heart that has beheld such a wonder before, many times. It was so with me and my Balulu. Now he waits at the pyre and I must go to him. Inanna with you, always."

She blew a kiss and walked away.

Uruna stood in place without moving, her thoughts a turmoil of confusion. Nothing had gone as planned. She had no idea what she was doing in Kudu Mahti. An odd combination of fortune and misfortune had brought her to this moment, an accidental savior, a hero without a prize. What was she to make of it?

A while later Tezu-Mah returned with a small reed skiff. Working in mute silence, he tied the craft to the stern of his swifthull and helped her in, then leaped onto the stern plank and pushed off. Uruna crouched in awkward silence as he guided the swifthull over the black waters and sank the prow in a patch of reeds.

With darkness closing round them, she stood in the center of the boat, clutching a cushion to her chest, and made a feeble attempt at a farewell.

"I hope you find what you want."

He stared at her without speaking. Several long moments passed while her heart pounded a beat so loud she was sure he would hear it. Then abruptly he hopped into the little reed boat and pushed off. In seconds he was gone.

CHAPTER FIVE

Diversion to Burum

Uruna spent the twilight in the swifthull listening for threats from this quarter and that, but nearing only the pervasive surge and retreat of locust song. Soon she became absorbed with the boat itself, running her hands over the rails polished by years of the hunter's grasp. Her fingers reported each bump and groove, as his must have done on similar nights. She imagined the thousand touches of his hand where hers now followed.

Here was his sanctuary in the fen, his refuge from death and peril. Bestowed upon her for the night despite her offense, a token of his generosity and concern in full measure. A night bird called, and she sent her thoughts across the water to him, willing the same song to reach his ear, wishing it were her voice lulling him to sleep.

When at last she lay her head on the cushion, she felt her cheek brush the hollow pressed by his face on countless nights past. Low on the eastern horizon, her birth star, at least the one her childhood self had chosen to signify her origin, twinkled its familiar greeting. She longed to show it to him, to whisper the night through of stars and dreams and favorite things...

Her dream was broken at first light by a call from the water, a boy in a small reed skiff. With a terse remark about no room for belongings—as if she had any—he proffered a bean cake and a beverage in a goatskin flask to ease her hunger. His news surprised her.

"Your people were sighted yesterday on the channel below Larsa."

"My people? I sent for no one."

"Two Nords on the paddle, a pair of fine ladies dressed in white. They asked after you."

"Who brought this news?"

"Not important. We'll hook up with your friends later in the day, get you home safely. A woman alone on the water is a sure target for Gunzek patrols."

He bent to the pole and set out for Girsa without another word, leaving Uruna to squat by herself in the prow, mulling her tally of shortcomings.

The hunt had proven too much for her. She had not paid her respects to Jabali. The dead child had passed through her life without receiving her tribute or her blessing. Instead of consoling the bereaved mother, she had accepted the woman's praise and affection. The whole outcome made a mockery of her quest.

As for enlisting the hunter to her cause? Lunacy! Sheer arrogant folly, born of her abysmal ignorance of his life and her obsession with her own. She had embarrassed him and humbled herself.

And poor Nashi! She had dashed her mentor's hopes for an ally on the rocks of unmitigated stupidity. Far from winning the man's favor, she had offended him, and he had spurned her roundly. He was wild and rude, his earthy manner alien to her temple-bred sensibilities. Yet his approval meant more to her than all the Lukur pledges of a lifetime.

She straightened in her seat and faced forward. Regrets were not in order. Her fortunes lay with the serpent and her return to Nippur. Her place was in Hall of Sacred Union. A hunter might spear his lion to save a tribe, and thereby win a place in their hearts. But she was bride to a whole nation. A woman served the purpose for which she was intended, and hers was prophecy.

So, why did that seem less significant than before?

𒀭 𒁹 𒆠 𒌋𒌋

The foursome in the swifthull were indeed from Nippur: plantation overseer Eduanna and Retha, plus Retha's father, Arn-Gar, and a younger Nord from the smith village of Na-Purna. After hailing one another from afar, the two parties put in at a strip of bare shoreline. As Uruna waded into the shallows, she looked up and found all four still sitting their boat, mouths agape.

Retha was first to find her voice.

"You're brown as a beetle—all over," she said, adding the reminder of Uruna's near-naked state.

Eduanna gulped and gathered herself for the welcome, but drew back quickly from the stench emanating from her queen.

"The river for you, madam!" she exclaimed, struggling for Lukur composure. "I brought your things. Get out of those rags and dress appropriately for your station."

The Hani boy and the men walked a little way upshore while Uruna bathed in the river and Retha dropped a white dress over her head and shoulders. Thus refreshed, Uruna accepted a dried beef strip from Eduanna's kit and gnawed voraciously.

When the men returned, she asked what had brought them down from Nippur and learned the entire trip was Retha's doing. Eduanna seemed content to let the girl speak for the group.

"Council wanted to make an expedition of it. You know, the royal barge and twenty women. It would have raised too many questions, so we sneaked away in the night."

"As I tried to do. I hope you succeeded where I did not."

Retha pointed at Uruna's escort. "This stout Hani lad can't be the great Tezu-Mah," she said. "What happened? Did you lose the man's favor to a comely boar sow?"

Eduanna drew herself up in a huff. "Do not address your queen with such impudence!"

Uruna couldn't help but smile. "Why not? It's how she and I talk between ourselves. I've no pretenses left, if I ever had any." She turned to Retha. "He's smitten with the Hani people. I could no more wrest him from their midst than pull your father from his beer bowl. How are you, Gar?"

"Well enough, madam, now that you're safe, but we should save talk for later and make haste for Nippur—that is, unless...."

He glanced at Eduanna, who took his cue to give her news.

"A herald brought word of a serpent recently arrived near Ur, from Meluhha. Its keeper is reportedly a snake adept."

Retha chimed in. "Fellow's also befuddled by beer most of the day."

Uruna wondered aloud what significance this news brought to the situation.

"The serpent is a king cobra," Eduanna answered. "The idiot in charge of him doesn't know what to do with him and asks if we might be interested."

Uruna shifted her gaze back to Retha. "You cooked this up. Where is he?"

"Burum," the girl answered.

Uruna addressed her Hani escort. "How far?"

The boy pulled his chin, considered the southwestern horizon. "If you go straight through this day and all night, probably get there at daybreak. If you stay over at Bushiba…"

"There isn't time enough to stay over anywhere. Gar, we'll make way for Burum."

"But madam, the Lukur await in Nippur."

"For what? An empty-handed huntress? That slothful bunch can wait another day or two. If this king cobra is half the measure of serpent I require, we cannot delay another hour. Boy, can you guide us there?"

"My name is Pana."

Uruna shook her head at the lad's spunk. "Pana, please forgive me. I should have asked your name before. Can you take us to Burum?"

A small smile played about his lips as Pana nodded his answer.

Gar took no pains to hide his exasperation, placing his hands on his hips with a silent glare for his daughter.

Uruna pointed out the obvious. "She serves her queen well."

"And her own interest in the bargain," he replied.

Retha frowned. "How is that?"

"Time for that later," he replied.

Before they set out, Eduanna pulled the Hani boy aside and arranged a man's wage for his efforts. While they were busy, Retha approached her queen and quietly slipped an object into the pocket of Uruna's dress.

"What's this?" Uruna said.

"For tomorrow morning," the girl said, "and not before."

Uruna rode with Eduanna and the men while Retha sat Pana's skiff. For the first time in days Uruna gave in to exhaustion and napped sitting up in the sun with her back against Eduanna's knees. The going at night would be slower.

So, she considered, if not the better man, perhaps a better serpent. She would press on for Sight, knowing the gods worked in mysterious ways and trusting that Inanna's hand was at work here. Otherwise, she would heap greater folly on a poor design, and take loyal friends into danger with her.

CHAPTER SIX

Tracking Death Maker

As the sun's first rays brightened Kudu Mahti, Tezu-Mah stared across the water at the palm-fringed island where he'd left the serpent queen. She was gone, of course, had fled to rid herself of his strident warning. He'd given her no other choice. Surely matters of greater importance awaited her in Nippur.

Gods, what a vision! She had nearly taken his breath when he'd discovered, too late, he was dangerously close to that smooth perfection of skin, those wide-set eyes of silver grey dancing with promise, the soft hollow of her neck, the arched bow of her upper lip begging his own…

She would kill him. The lion would catch him staring at a phantom memory and strike him down before he turned his head. One did not cloud the mind with lust on the eve of a hunt. Shumu-gan dealt such a fool but one hand—slow, agonizing death.

Yet, her parting image bloomed in his mind even now, as fresh as any flower, and his throat burned with a pang of regret.

"I hope you get what you want," she had told him, clutching the boat cushion like a protective shield.

What he wanted, he had realized in that moment, was standing right before him, waving him away. Her words had driven a lance straight to his heart and destroyed his cold resolve, filling his mind with doubt and raising a host of long-forbidden feelings that threatened to undo him. He shook his head, desperate to clear his mind before it became filled with useless sentiment.

He took a borrowed skiff to the isle and tied it to the swifthull's stern. As he climbed aboard, he nearly stepped on her gift, a small mat woven of thin strips sliced from a rush blade. He looked closer, saw the pattern, and a lump rose in his throat. In the dark of night, working only by touch, she had fashioned the fronds to resemble a lion's head.

He poled back to the village in a mindless daze, unaware he'd pushed the prow ashore until a man's voice dragged him back to the present.

"Slave Soldier camped in Girsa last night."

Jabali stood a few feet from the boat with a Hani longbow in one hand while the other idly twirled the slender shaft of a script arrow. The only reason bounty hunters hadn't claimed Tezu-Mah yet was the expertise of Hani messengers armed with arrow shafts marked by clever scratches only they could interpret. The mystery exasperated the Bull Priest, and he was killing them off as fast as his men could find them.

Girsa was a mere two hours away by swifthull. That put the Gunzek chief, Borok, dubbed "Slave Soldier" by the Hani, directly between himself and the lion. The hunter set his mind to plotting a course around Girsa yet close enough that he wouldn't lose the lion's track.

He noted that the villagers had returned his weapon. Its shaft and that of its mate pointed aloft from their stanchion in the stern of his swifthull.

"The boy," he said to Jabali, "the one whose family the slavers killed last month. What is his name again?"

"Pana Huta. No longer a boy, but a man now, eh? I sent him after the fine lady this morning."

"Tell Pana if I do not return, the boat is his."

Jabali regarded him with a fierce look. "You will take this lion, Tezu-Mah," he said, pointing an emphatic finger at his feet. "You will take him down."

The hunter nodded, hoping his courage might soon match the old man's conviction. Then he pushed off, propelling the sleek craft past the scrawny tip of land, away from Kudu Mahti's refuge and last night's forbidden reminders, trailing his dread of the lion into the *ghana* wilderness.

He might not outrun the demon fear quickly, but he would let the vast reed expanse soothe him. He had shared its fish with sea fowl and swamp birds. He had spent gray mornings watching egrets stalk the shallows on tall spindly legs, while overhead, pelicans cruised inland on the early drift of salt breeze. The sweet melding of wetland and bright sky nourished his soul and body. He could dwell there the rest of his life and be happy, yet he sensed an impending closure. His spirit was adrift and fading. Was his stay drawing to an end?

A puff of wind riffled the stream's surface, turning the sun's dusky gold reflection into the haunting stares of a thousand lions. One did not ignore such an omen. This was the river warning him of Death Maker's return.

He might last another twenty years if he simply went back to Nippur and made babies with some clucking hen from the temple fold. But far fewer if he kept stalking killer beasts in the wild. He wasn't sure he had the will or stamina to take a lion anymore. Could he bring down another raging cat while standing like a stone with his limbs locked in fear?

Once again he would have to find the answer or yield further Hani lives to the lion. If he fled the marsh, the city-softened world would hold him blameless. But could he live afterward mourning the fate of the Old Ones?

Pole on, he told himself. Get back to the task at hand and don't stray again. Yours is not the only life at stake.

A glossy ribbon of inverted sky streaked the channel ahead, and he looked up and saw a great white heron moving on the wind with masterful, easy grace. Not far ahead, the bird alighted in the mud shallows and stood for a while, watching him. Then, as he drew near, the heron lifted lazily into the air, flew a short distance, and stopped to watch again.

They traveled that way together for some time, bird of promise, man of hope.

He found new track toward midmorning, a paw print wide and deep indicating the monster described in Larsa. This lion was headed toward dry ground. He slid the boat into a patch of reeds, shouldered his weapons, and struck off overland in the lion's wake.

Neither plan nor direction governed the next two days. He would plow through thick sand for hours, find track, lose it, and find it again. To keep his spirit pure, he abstained from food. He spent each night on the ground among crawling things. He arose at dawn, bowed to the four winds, and entreated Shumu-gan, master of animals, for permission to take the crazed lion. Then he prayed to Utu-the-sun for strength and asked Nanna-the-moon for humility. He made a small *mushakku* offering of incense before setting out each day.

Toward evening of the second day he wandered into a small pocket between two hills and immediately encountered spoor. The lion had returned to the reeds. The thrum of insects filled the sun-soaked air. Sweat poured from his face in runnels. He nearly gagged on the heavy musk all around, declaring the lion's domain.

Such a reckless, uninspired trespass was not the god's work. He had merely stumbled into the animal's lair, and now he stood inert, no idea what to do next. Soon the flat twilight would transform the green brake into a confounding mass of gray. If he retreated for the night, the animal would surely follow his scent and take him in the dark. But he hadn't yet seen...

The lion coughed once.

In a heartbeat, the locust song ceased.

The hunter stopped and held his breath. Yellow eyes had followed him into the fen, confident, serene, hungry for human blood.

A deep growl. The marsh shook with a bottomless rumble.

His heart leaped in his chest and he froze in place, senses rattled.

He was sure he hadn't made a false step. Had someone less sure of foot intruded? Another hunter? Slavers?

Stay focused on the lion. Anything else and you're a dead man.

He brought the eight-foot lance to his shoulder and checked the shorter spear lashed to his back. Armed and ready, he awaited the first nuance of shape and shadow, knowing he must seize the least advantage that came his way and make do with it.

He sensed the lion's attention shift to himself, and imagined the small ears cocked, the simple mind abruptly intrigued with the intruder, the jaws aquiver with anticipation. A cold shiver of dread crawled up his spine and pricked his scalp, and the mighty pounding started in his chest, racing faster, accelerating to a gallop, until the *thrum-tum, thrum-tum* was a violent drumbeat demanding attention.

The sound would betray him! The lion would hear!

Hot energy exploded through his entire body, searing his nerves like molten copper and filling every fiber with a visceral fear that screamed at him to run-run-run like a deer. He fought to keep his feet rooted in place. If he so much as shifted his weight right now, Death Maker would charge. His mind knew as much, yet the terror continued to grip him, and he felt a high-pitched keen start in his throat.

He squeezed his eyes shut and swallowed hard, and the voice of Shumu-gan, god of all hunters, rang inside his head:

Seek him! The heart of the lion is mine!

He heard a soft whisper, and a settling peace fell over him like a mantle of softest wool, damping down the animal terror and taming the raging fear. His strength returned. His limbs felt charged with new energy, as once again he became grounded solidly to the earth.

The enclosure remained undisturbed by his ordeal. A fly buzzed close and touched his sweaty brow, bringing him back to hard reality. He ignored the insect and focused on the leafy vegetation, willing his vision to penetrate the uniform green-on-green everywhere. Where was the lion?

He lifted a foot over a clump of bracken and pivoted slowly, wielding the heavy lance as a counterbalance and keeping the sharpened copper head out front and low to prevent a charge underneath.

Nothing stirred. The fly had disappeared, driven off by a primal sense of danger and the odor of musk. Only hunter and lion existed. Now each belonged to the other.

There! A spot of dun behind the green brake, maybe twelve, fifteen yards away.

But now it was gone. The lion had shifted even as he watched, soundless in its passage, its heavy mass bending not a single reed.

Where are you now, Death Maker?

He sought gaps in the broad-leafed foliage, strained to catch another glimpse of color, any color but green.

There! To the left, between those broken reeds. A patch of animal flank. If he sent the lance in there now he'd lose his best weapon. But further to the left, that large mat of crushed reeds. The animal had lain there earlier.

He needed maneuvering room for the lance.

He edged his left foot toward the clearing and held still.

No sound from the lion.

He stretched his left foot outward, barely touching the broken reed matting, and shifted sideways, pelvis level, knees bent, weight centered. In gradual, steady steps he put space between himself and the lion. Two yards, four yards, six, the soles of his naked feet soundless as he advanced. Now he was one with the fen, covering ground on cat paws of his own, inching leftward.

He came upon a narrow defile and stopped. Directly ahead, the lion lay sprawled on a patch of bent rushes, still attending the hunter's starting location. The hunter stood locked in awe as he took the measure of an animal more immense than any he had known.

Body twice the length of a boar lance. Forepaws larger than a man's head. Hindquarters as broad as a bull ox.

He hefted the lance to his shoulder, and twenty pounds of hardwood settled evenly astride his ear, balanced, level. Now he was ready. He was the path to the lion's heart...

Crick.

A footfall off to the right. A mate? Impossible. The rogue was finished with his own kind. Another man, then!

Lion ears twitched forward to attend a small brown patch that flicked into view and out again. The hunter's practiced eye saw it too, a block of tan between the rushes to his right.

Whoosht!

He flinched as an arrow buzzed past his neck and slapped the reed thicket behind him

Then a loud *thwock*, as a second arrow stabbed the ground just inches behind his left foot.

He crouched and gave the shaft a yank. The tapered head came out like a sodden weed. Not a game head, but the narrow tip of a military archer whose targets were human.

At once Tezu-Mah understood what had caused the sudden hush over the fen. While he had trained his senses on the lion, he had become quarry himself.

Bounty hunters had found him.

CHAPTER SEVEN
Introduction To Kukhmet

Only in Sumer could news of her impending arrival have reached Burum while Nippur's queen still plied the river. By the time her crew drove the boat's keel onto Burum's mud pack, a great multitude filled the quay from end to end. A cordon of exuberant locals waded out from the bar, thrilled by the spectacle in their humble lives—the appearance of three white-garbed priestesses emerging from a swifthull.

None of the crowd seemed to know the proper greeting for a queen. The men stood in place and gawked, the women crossed their ankles and folded hands over bosoms, but what held their fascination was not her perfection of face, nor the fine fabric clinging to her form, nor her luxuriant hair.

They saw only the totem bespeaking her power: a carved cobra mounted on her headband. Ketha's thoughtful reminder of Serpenthood's power.

Upriver a hundred yards, in deeper water, a barge from the north was just putting in at the quay. A pennant atop its passenger box signified it as belonging to temple Ekur. Uruna started at the sight.

"What is the royal barge doing here?" she said to Eduanna.

"I've no idea, unless news of the cobra brought half Ekur's council out. I'd wager they figured out their queen's mind before she did, and left Nippur two days ago in our wake. Took the Uruk channel instead."

"Gods! No wonder the crowd showed up. They'll make a festival out of this."

"There's more."

Eduanna tilted her head away from Uruna to indicate the approach down the beach of a tall woman on the arm of a slightly taller man, leading a retinue of several white-clad ladies. Udea Seddua, high priestess of Eanna, had earned the whispered scorn of her peers for her unapologetic use of slaves to erect her sprawling temple complex, and for her indifference to the lives lost in the process. The man was her consort, Enguda, a self-ordained priest who had done the unthinkable by installing men on Eanna's council with Udea's tacit approval.

Although Udea's once-high beauty had faded over the years, she nevertheless maintained a regal bearing, taking position at the front of the crowd as though they had come to see her.

"Looks like the Bull came with her," Eduanna pointed out.

Enguda had adopted the bull god Guda Abzu as his personal deity, and upon his ordination had earned the nickname "Bull Priest" among the people. He was reportedly as callous toward human life as his queen.

"Why do you suppose they showed up here?" Retha wondered aloud.

"Because by now half of Sumer knows about us," said Eduanna. "He'll be displeased that we slipped past his guardposts in the night. Were the situation reversed, he'd have an army lying in wait just over the horizon, so he suspects the same of us. Besides, he opposes our pursuit of Serpenthood. Probably looking for a way to discredit whatever happens today."

Uruna felt the situation slipping rapidly out of her control. "Do you think he knows why we came?"

"Of course he does. He has spies just as we do, but he doesn't know how we will use it and he wants to find out."

At that point, the ladies from the barge closed with their queen: temple treasurer Ku-Aya and chief counter Lub-Sunna, with Shua Kinar in the van. Uruna spoke before Kinar could utter a greeting.

"Do I detect a seer in our midst?"

Kinar inclined her pretty head. "Whatever do you mean, dear?"

"I only decided to visit this mud hole myself yesterday. It would seem we already have a surfeit of foresight."

"Hah! Would that it were so. After we got word of the cobra we had to take the chance, even if you'd decided you had your fill of these wretched swamps."

Uruna leaned in to brush cheeks. "I'm thrilled to see you, Kikki."

"It was the girl's idea. She talks with such ease to serpents, as you know. You trained her well."

Uruna pulled back. "What gave you that idea?"

"The way she got them to go back into the baskets without a spoken word."

"When?"

"The other night. After the tailor botched it."

"Kikki, I taught Retha no such thing. We trade jokes while she does her sweeps in the hallway, that's all. Are you sure?"

"She returned each cobra to its basket, then she did the Selashum benediction in the old tongue. I assumed you taught it to her."

"This is absurd. She does scrubs in my apartment, folds laundry…"

"The girl spoke a most appropriate prayer for the unfortunate shirt maker. I thought it was your schooling. It was she placed the serpents on the altar before the ceremony."

"Kikki! That's always been Niccaba's job! You can't be serious!"

"Never more so. But here she comes. Ask her yourself."

Before Uruna could speak, the mystery girl took command of the situation as she had, apparently, the entire journey.

"I sent Pana to fetch the man who sings to cobras, or whatever he does. Haven't seen him—wup, here he is now."

Uruna and Kinar exchanged a "we'll talk about this later" look before turning where Retha pointed.

The crowd parted as Pana emerged with a stocky, black-skinned fellow in tow. The man was groomed in the southern fashion of indigo vest with matching linen kilt, indicating a temple peer of high station. A beaded yellow kufi topped his head in the Indu tradition, although his kohl-rimmed eyes and shaved jaw marked him as Nubian. Both regions were renowned centers for serpent adepts. The man's muscular arms and deep chest portrayed a common laborer, but the arresting candor in his eyes told Uruna he regarded himself as her equal.

Pana proceeded as self-imposed envoy. "Madam, before you is the cobra master of whom you spoke. May I present Gula Gusar, of Ur. Sir, Uruna Kumta, Entu of Ekur, chief magistrate, and high priestess of Serpenthood."

How had a simple lad from backwater Kudu Mahti learned such information? From the hunter? If so, had Tezu-Mah's disdain only been an act? Or was he tracking her even now through his little not-to-simple Hani agent?

Uruna took a moment to clear her thoughts before offering her hand to Gusar. "You are from Ur? But what has that unfinished town to do with serpents?"

Gula Gusar hastened to explain. "Ur is my home today, but I spent my youth learning the serpent way from the Mohenjo priests of Meluhha. I am honored that you traveled so far—"

"Thank you, what is his condition?"

The man gazed at Uruna transfixed, his face blank, his attention completely absorbed with her endowment of high bosom and shapely hips, the head of raven hair, the flawless face, the delicate mouth.

Kinar stepped between them and whispered low for Uruna's benefit.

"Poor bloke has the manners of a field hand. You've thrown him. Let me handle it." Then, to the snake man from Ur: "Shake yourself loose, man, and answer the queen's question!"

Gula Gusar gave the ladies a startled look. "Um, condition, condition. Ah, the snake, of course! He is the picture of health, madam. A right sturdy animal and a willing performer."

"We'll see about that," said Uruna. "If you please, show us what you have."

Gusar clapped his hands and a pair of burly dock workers came forth carrying a slatted crate between them. Gusar pointed to a spot before Uruna and the draymen placed the box at her feet.

"Bring him out," she said, for she was already feeling the serpently probe that indicated the god was aware of her presence.

"Ah, madam," said Gusar, "shouldn't we move the container away from the crowd first? To your apartment, perhaps?"

Uruna continued staring down at the box. "I have no apartment here. Use your knife. Just snap the lashings."

Gula Gusar demurred, then spread his hands in an appeal to the ladies of the Lukur for help with this errant woman of theirs.

"What is he called?" Uruna asked.

"Erm, Andababa, after an Indu god of some sort."

"Some sort. You did not inquire of his master which sort that was?"

"Indeed not. Never laid eyes on the man. We never spoke."

"But you found him in Industan?"

"No, madam, he was brought thence to Meluhha before I acquired him."

"I see. And what is your business with him today?"

"I entertain the people."

"Show us, please."

"Well, I'm not sure. I usually prepare myself first. The danger, you know."

To Uruna's view, the man was wasting time. She slipped her dining blade from the sheath at her waist, stepped past the fool, and, snip-snip, the lashings were on the ground. Someone stirred behind her and Gusar gasped in astonishment as a corner of the lid lifted an inch.

"Look out!" he shouted, and the crowd reacted by scuttling away, so that Uruna stood inside a cleared area surrounded by her ladies and the citizens of Burum.

As everyone watched, the lid crept upward. Uruna spoke aloud. "My, but you're a curious soul, Andababa. Couldn't wait to come out and see everyone, could you?"

The first hint of color showed through the opening, and then the cover slid off and the magnificent cobra head lifted clear of the rim and continued up.

And up.

Someone in the crowd screamed, and Kinar barked a warning. "Be careful, Uruna!"

He was indeed a king in every sense, and he rose up on his thick stalk of scales like the regent he was, peering around grandly at his human subjects, wideset black pupils nearly filling the round gold irises as he regarded the world from the confines of his compartment. His head and back were the deep brown of oak bark and the flat jaw formed a clean break above the breastplate of creamy yellow. The cape of his flared ribs was narrower than that of his bolder cousin with the eye on its back. He finished his survey and his eye registered Uruna and stopped. He remained in the box. He was asking to be released.

She backed away in the direction of the town, all eyes focused on her and the cobra. He needed a small amount of encouragement to surmount the top of his box and make contact with the earth again. The crowd parted as Uruna extended the distance between herself and the deadly king. She squatted on the quay matting, crossed her legs, and tensed her abdomen, letting the serpent heat flood her limbs and rise through her core.

To the gasps and muffled shrieks of the crowd, the cobra lifted his trunk over the rim and down one side of the box. His compact head came erect again, and with a flick of his tail, the animal flashed across the mat and stopped just short of Uruna's face.

The crowd gasped again, but Uruna stayed perfectly still. In words long out of use and unheard by all save herself, she bestowed upon the king her name for him—that of a serpent god worshipped in far-off Egyptum.

Henceforth, thou art Kukhmet.

The head flattened and reared back, blazing hostile energy as the black fork lapped the air just inches from her chin. The hood moved laterally to the right, then slid slowly left as serpent senses registered the human contour, scanned blood warmth, read the alien vibrancy to confirm friend or foe.

Uruna responded to this display of barely restrained menace with a light shrug. If he had refused the name, she would be dead. It was time to confer his office.

Thou art no more a creature of the land, but a prince of Serpenthood. Thou shalt obey my command and give me Sight, that I may lead my people.

The beast in him cautiously attended her, then as she urged him forward, he dropped his head and relaxed before her. Now he was indeed Kukhmet, blessed emissary of Enshiggu, god of Serpenthood. The meeting was complete. Her will was his will. He would answer her quest for the unseen.

She suppressed a thrill of triumph. On a muddy bar where river met sea, all had transpired according to myth. The voices that had called to her all her life were not imagined. She had not been beguiled by false promises from raving demons. The messages were from the divine, bequeathing wisdom and courage, ministering to her.

She now saw the great king cobra as a magnificent creature of regal bearing, keenly aware of his surroundings, a sharp-eyed, intelligent being worthy of respect. "You look quite lovely today, Kukhmet," she chimed aloud in a soft voice. "So handsome in your lovely yellow cape."

She inclined her head and brushed the top of the brown death head with a soft kiss. The crowd's collective intake of breath might have upset a lesser creature, but Kukhmet accepted the off-hand affection without so much as a ripple over his heavy twelve-foot body, splayed out on the straws like a length of deck hawser.

Uruna gestured with an expressive turn of wrist. "See the fine people from across the land, your guests for the day."

The cobra was interested only in the woman before him and kept his attention fastened on Uruna's countenance. The crowd around her stood in shocked silence. Had she overplayed her hand? Kinar and Lub-Sunna, Ku-Aya and Eduanna, all stood mum, their prolonged search having culminated in a humble peasant town with an impromptu snake-kissing ceremony.

The townspeople stared transfixed, either witness to a marvel of startling significance or struck speechless with terror, as a deadly snake surrendered to the Lukur queen from Nippur.

The introduction complete, Uruna slowly got to her feet, made a little half-turn and glanced over her shoulder at the great king cobra from Meluhha, whose head reached nearly to her waist.

"Kukhmet, come dear," she said to him, and the crowd parted willingly as the queen and her serpent king made a solemn procession up the beach toward her royal barge.

CHAPTER EIGHT
Clash With The Bull

Burum's crowd milled about, unwilling to leave the site of the greatest wonder in their lives, a story they could now pass down to child and grandchild:

I was there. I beheld her magic with my own eyes.

Kinar took charge of negotiating the cobra's purchase—for an amount Gula Gusar could not refuse—while the other ladies paid obligatory respects to the Entu from Uruk. Kinar made a point of asserting her temple's good will, while Retha stood by, soaking up the art of diplomacy firsthand.

For her part, Uruna was anxious to depart Burum and be on the river before the full heat of the day descended. With the great cobra safely in her possession, she hiked upshore to the barge and instructed Gar and the crew in how to secure Kukhmet in the large palmwood basket brought down from Nippur for his final transport. She then turned her attention back toward the crowd to signal Kinar and the others for departure.

The quay was still thick with people, and though she scanned the throng for a patch of white among the drab browns and grays, she saw no sign of her ladies. A tall pile of crates and bins obscured the far end of the quay. Most likely they were behind it.

She wove her way through columns of stacked cargo, careful not to snag her hem on the raw wood slats. But something caught and held her skirt, and she stopped to see what it was. A tiny monkey had stuck its arm through the slats of its box and grasped the white fabric tight in its little fist. Before she could bat the hand away, a much larger hand appeared from behind her, grabbed the slender arm, and twisted. The monkey screamed and jerked its arm back into the cage, whimpering piteously.

The Bull Priest loomed above her. Curved buffalo horns on his leather helmet framed a weathered face and added an ominous aspect to his towering height.

"Lady Uruna, how good to see you again," he purred, placing a proprietary hand on Uruna's forearm.

"You hurt that poor little ape!" she cried.

"Not terribly. Filthy thing won't try that again, I assure you."

"I must leave."

Cargo boxes enclosed her on three sides, Enguda blocked the only exit. His bearded face broke into a mirthless grin as his long fingers encircled her arm, his stare impassive beneath a heavy brow. "But we missed your stopover at Eanna."

"We traveled by another channel. Really, I must find the others."

She moved to withdraw her arm, but the Bull held her fast.

"Pity. Days and nights on that dreadful river must have done insult to your lovely skin."

"We camped in adequate comfort, thank you. The objective was to make good time, not indulge our own pleasure."

"Quite an impressive little performance you put on today. I'm sure the common folk were enthralled and the experience only added to your popularity. Very clever. The fools are easily persuaded by myth and fable. And fear, of course."

"We were not here to entertain, sir. What you call a performance was, if your eyes would be opened, a demonstration of Serpenthood's power. We have not lost our will to recover its blessing in full measure. Will you please unhand me."

Instead, the Bull shifted his grip higher and clamped it about her upper arm as he bent forward slightly at the waist, closing the distance between them in a near-embrace. The smothering aroma of thyme in his beard clotted her nostrils. He shifted his weight so that his heavy linen robes swirled about them both, blocking sun and sky. She was alone in a wooden maze with a brute known to hate women.

Enguda pushed his face just inches from hers and spoke in a quiet voice only she could hear.

"You speak of power as if you know it," he said. "I'll show you power, madam! You see before you what a man can be—a real man, not one of your simpering temple lackeys or those field drudges who bend their backs in the sun. You see this man's power, you feel it now, and you fear it!"

"Please release your hand, sir," she said slowly and firmly, glaring at him to show her contempt rather than the fear he sought.

The Bull's grip only tightened with bruising force.

"The Kurg savages are camped but three day's march from Nippur. They won't stay there long. You've no defense when he bursts down your gate. Gods, woman, you're near enough to kiss his foot! Do you know how little it would take to plunge the whole land into chaos and anarchy? And how many generations to recover, if ever? We cannot stand by and watch Sumer sent into that oblivion! You know it, every temple woman knows it.

"But rather than build an army, you swoon before serpents. Rather than grant a man the right to choose his own destiny, you would prophesy the extension of female dominance in every walk of life."

"You are wrong, sir!"

"Rather than forecast a path to salvation, the Lukur would have you strengthen their grip on power, quash any threat to it, until a savage rips it away by force. Well, know this, my serpent-kissing queen. Yagga-Tor cannot escape my power, which is mightier than any god. That Kurg savage will bow down before me. You will see, for I have mastered the will of men. If you would protect this land and all the people in it, forsake this serpent lunacy and join us at arms. Against a united Sumer no Kurg can stand. We shall drive him back so far he will never return."

Uruna twisted her head to one side and tried to break the Bull's grip, but his lank iron-gray hair fell across her face, and his full-length beard spilled onto her bosom. He was clearly enjoying his thinly disguised display of physical superiority, yet, with all the intensity in his voice, his face remained an emotionless mask of serenity. Only the snapping black eyes betrayed the rabid hostility seething just beneath the placid surface.

"Let me go!" she demanded, trying to send her voice outward to the crowd, but it came out as barely more than a whisper.

A stack of crates suddenly scraped against the quay matting and crashed into the water. At once, Enguda stepped backward and released her, his face ashen, his eyes wide with shock.

What had happened? What had she done?

Nothing, it seemed, for the Bull heeded not her command, but instead a pain inflicted by a force greater than his own. There beside him stood Gar, feigning an amiable grin as his massive fist clutched the Bull's left bicep with overpowering might. The Bull's mouth gaped as excruciating pain shot through his arm, but his eyes fastened on the Nord giant with hard rage.

Gar hauled the priest backward out of the forest of crates, crafting an air of deference for the benefit of witnesses as he rasped a quiet threat through his brilliant smile.

"If you value keeping your balls above your knees, goat-sticker, you will never, ever, touch my queen again."

He released his grip but kept his eyes locked on the Bull.

Enguda flexed his arm to restore circulation, his black eyes blazing hatred at his attacker. "You will die for this, Nord," he said through bared teeth. Then, with a twist of his shoulders, he spun about and stalked away.

Gar rushed to Uruna. "Did he harm you, madam?"

She rubbed her arm where the Bull had gripped her. "I'll be all right, Gar. Thank you, my friend. I was warned how dangerous he can be, but I never got a taste of it until now."

"It was my fault for not staying at your side."

"No, it wasn't, you were loading Kukhmet as I told you to do. Let's forget it."

"Uruna, the council must know."

"Please, I want you to tell no one, lest the Bull have his way and create a greater rift than already exists between our two cities. Gather Kinar and the others. I want to leave this place while we still have what we came for."

"Very well, I'll ready the crew at once and we'll put a proper end to this trouble."

Uruna set off toward the barge, with Gar immediately behind. He would not allow her to be left alone again for a moment. Her arm still hurt, and her mind spun with confusion, but she was determined to show none of it.

Hours later, as the barge slid upstream past the Eanna ziggurat at Uruk, "trouble" did not begin to describe the raw fear that possessed her. In spite of the midday heat, she huddled in her travel box like a waif against winter cold, arms hugging her torso, knees quaking, her left hand covering the swelling purple bruise on her right arm.

Gone was her pretense of affronted contempt. She felt neither brave nor defiant. The Bull knew how to intimidate a woman. For years at Eanna, he had preyed upon each councilwoman until she assented to his demands without a whimper. He must have caught them all by surprise, each woman trapped alone in an unguarded moment, the same as she. The accounts of atrocities in the warrens of that temple were not the product of overzealous imaginations. She shuddered with revulsion.

But overriding her disgust with Enguda's abusive excesses was the humiliating truth he had spoken. While she pretended to guide the leaky craft of Lukur legacy, she clung to a declining regime dangerously close to losing power as it increasingly entrusted to godly magic matters that demanded mortal choice and action.

Far more severe, however, was her own blind belief in prophecy as the consummate defense against aggression. As the Bull had pointed out, forecasting doom was merely a prelude to disaster if not acted upon by leaders able and willing to mobilize a fighting response. Such unswerving assertion of the collective will called for the authority Sumerians had denied themselves throughout centuries of undisturbed isolation.

Sumer needed a king.

CHAPTER NINE

A Price For Victory

For a single, brief moment, the presence of three foes at once confused the lion and caused him to hesitate with his body fully exposed to view.

Tezu-Mah retreated a step in spite of himself. Never had he seen a beast so enormous, so completely daunting. The head was as broad as a door and came level with the hunter's chest. He was magnificent, an imposing lord of his domain, but further appreciation was impossible, as in the next instant the lion charged his nearest enemy, an archer who, in his zeal to fell the hunter, had placed himself squarely in the lion's sights.

To the man's credit, he stood his ground and calmly brought his bow around to take aim on the bounding head. Too little too late. With a single leap, the lion drove into his foe and was upon him.

Thwock, thwock! Two arrows struck the lion high on the left shoulder.

The archer's comrade had not hesitated.

The lion responded by lifting his head to snarl, nothing more. His prey was down, and he was already drunk on the elixir of blood seeping between his claws.

"Take him!" the second archer shouted at Tezu-Mah as he bolted and ran for the reeds, having spent his last arrow as well as his lust for killing.

The hunter heard a snapping sound, and the first archer screamed as his ribs buckled beneath the lion's ponderous weight. The man continued to yell in a cracked voice, begging the gods for release, but his torture had just begun. In a few moments, the animal would begin the grisly work of tearing apart the outer casing of flesh, and the sobs of inconceivable agony would start.

The hunter's lance was already up. A step forward, a glance at the target spot, and the big eight-foot weapon flew across the short space.

He watched the lance enter the animal's ribs just below the two arrows. The tip cleaved innards and vessels and ran out the other side. Amazingly, the lion stayed up for a few seconds to regard his killer with indignant disdain. Then his wounds took full toll, and he toppled onto his right side with the spear shaft pointing skyward. He twisted around and blinked benign resignation at the victor, accepting his fate.

So you're the one, his eye seemed to say.

The lion was finished, but not by any victory Tezu-Mah wanted to claim. The Bull's henchmen had struck all honor from the place, imposing human terms of combat on a man-to-beast contest. He had not faced his lion.

He yanked the short spear from his shoulder strap and moved to dispatch the soldier without prolonging the fellow's ordeal. The one eye that remained in a face like red cabbage now began to roll away from the world for the final turn inward. The man's lungs pulsed rapidly in shallow breaths. Blood pooled beneath the opened rib cage and stained the reeds a dark crimson.

With a swift motion, the hunter stepped to the man's side, drew the spear upward and plunged down with all his might. The weapon went in clean, split the heart, and came out in his hands again, ready now for the worthier victim.

The great shaggy head lay inert on the ground. Still, he approached the animal at a distance, watching the rib cage heave in labored, uneven grunts. With the tip of the shorter spear, he prodded one shoulder. As with his kill in Kudu Mahti, he dragged the tip across the ribs and poked the flank. Nothing there either.

Suddenly the lion heaved. In a flash it rolled onto its back, panting its final throes in shallow breaths.

He should have backed away more quickly, for the death pain sometimes caused a twinge of limb or spine. Instead, he hovered over the animal, feeling an odd mixture of fear and remorse when the lion bellowed a final roar. A hind leg twitched awkwardly, and he felt a slap on his left thigh.

He floated to one side, vaguely disturbed by the laggard response in his leg. He looked down, and in an instant felt red-hot pain, an unrelenting stab like the forge iron that had marked his arm when a boy. A scream wrenched his mouth open and he staggered sideways a few steps, lost the horizon in a spinning blur, and plunged headlong into the lion.

He blinked and saw soft golden sky rimmed with jagged spears of bulrush.

Roll away from the lion.

When his limbs refused to obey, he looked over at the shaggy head stretched out beside him as though asleep. The half-closed yellow orb watched his plight with waning interest.

What will you do now, man?

The pain came in waves now, beating him like flagellating vulture wings. Better have a look at the damage, do something about it before he fell senseless. The effort to roll onto one elbow seemed to take hours, but he got an arm under his body and lifted himself enough to examine the wound.

It was bad. A claw had raked a gash in his left thigh from hip to knee and blood welled the full length of the opening. He would have to bind the flesh quickly or die tonight in the jaws of scavengers.

The swimming sensation in his head came and went as he dragged himself over to the edge of the rushes. He got out his knife and managed to cut several spears of the thick grass, then snipped a few hide thongs from his quiver. His body shook in violent spasms and he feared his hand might slip, but he bound the rushes tight to his leg, closing the flesh until the edges met, growling through the pain like a madman.

He would never make it back to Girsa in his condition, and he was days from the nearest road. Little likelihood of rescue out here, but his chances of being found would improve if he got himself onto the rise of one of those hills. The jackals and birds would find more of interest with the lion and dead archer, or so he told himself.

The base of the hill was not far off and a shallow ravine cleaved the short rise. He dragged himself several yards into the thicket of upright reeds and rested, looking back at the swath he had cut. The wound was draining blood and he was weak. Was the night coming early or was he losing consciousness?

He looked up. The hill cleft was no closer than before. What had looked like a short walk took much longer to crawl. He hitched up his nerve for a sustained effort and elbowed forward, dragging the damaged leg behind like a tote, forcing pain from his thoughts and blinking the sweat from his eyes.

First make the ravine. Then think about the top.

He moved forward, an insect scrabbling across the cane floor, every inch an agony, penance for the life he had taken. So be it, he was a man and he would live tomorrow by the grace of lives he had spared today.

How noble. Now be a lizard and just survive.

He heaved himself onto the hilltop as the last rays of sun dipped beneath the flat horizon in a world gone distant and fuzzy. The arduous crawl up the ravine had raked skin from his arms and chest, and his soil-caked bindings made a fire in his leg. But he was alive.

And an easy mark now for more soldiers. To be sure, there would be others in the area, perhaps as close as an hour's march, and certainly within a day of their fallen comrades.

He rolled onto his back and felt the smooth breast of hill beneath his spine. His eyelids grew heavy and fluttered closed. A light breeze caressed his crown and he lay motionless, letting the wind sift through his hair and tattered skirt while his mind drifted in and out of lion space—dun-colored fur, white fang, razor claw, dark blood pool—again and again visiting the instant of the lion's slash. Another step to the side and he was spared, a step nearer and his vitals would have spilled onto the ground. Death had lost by the narrowest of gaps.

There was a lesson in the experience. Wellspring of knowledge from every escape. He would give the matter close consideration, but later. Right now the light was fading…

Too tired to think. Maybe in the morning…

He'd have to make a new lance, talk to the weapon maker. When he got better.

And what would become of his beautiful boat?

Hope the boy…Pana was his name.

Pana, take good care of my boat. She glides like the heron.

CHAPTER TEN
Terms At Nippur

A rigid ultimatum was hardly the reception Uruna expected upon her return to Nippur. Nevertheless that was what she got, and she could come up with no better word for it.

Of course the hour was late—nearly half the night gone. But the strange quiet pervading the shoreline carried none of the peaceful drone of a city asleep.

Gula Gate was tended by a solitary watchman. Not a soul stood ashore to greet the landing party, so Gar ordered his crewmen over the side into water up to their waists to haul the heavy barge ashore themselves. Off-loading Kukhmet and the baggage went likewise. The ladies debarked from a ramp into ankle-deep water.

A lone fisherman came out to start his day and showed surprise at the sight of six burly Nord oarsmen doubling as dock hands.

Uruna started trudging up the river bank toward the gate and looked up at the sound of her name. Chancellor Niccaba, once an Entu herself, met her at the sentry station. She was alone, and she faced her queen in the brazier's warm light, firmly assured of purpose, a gleam of triumph lighting her eye.

"You will see Ensi Marduk from Aramdan first thing tomorrow."

If she expected a glowing response, Uruna offered none.

"After a week in the wilderness, a brief welcome might have sufficed," she said.

Niccaba proceeded unabashed. "He's been here three days awaiting your return. We sent word downriver but I guess you weren't where you were supposed to be. Did you get the snake?"

Uruna recalled now why Niccaba's reign had been short-lived.

"We got the cobra, he's immense and powerful and just what the gods ordered and we're filthy and exhausted and I would so appreciate a night's sleep in my own bed before we talk about visiting dignitaries."

"He's a serpently man. The best yet."

"Good. I'm glad. We'll see what he brings to the table. Now may I go home?"

"The Uzba decided."

"You involved the whole Uzba? All forty?"

"It's that important, Uruna. The best chance we have, and I wanted you to hear it from me before you're swamped with entreaties. It's all anyone can talk about. Everyone is terribly excited."

"How nice for everyone. Now if you'll excuse me, I must attend to the other half of the bargain."

"Other half?"

"His name is Kukhmet, and I think he's had his fill of a travel crate. Good night."

She made a sharp whistle for Gar, and the big man quickly came to her side. "This way," she said. "I'll show you where to put him for the night."

Gar gently inserted his bulk between the two ladies and Niccaba was left to stare at their backs in bleak amazement.

Let her stew, thought Uruna. So a male—a Nord male, no less—would breach the female sanctum of Serpenthood House to ply the Gipar dormitory by night. She imagined the voices of reproach she'd hear tomorrow.

Unheard of. An outrageous intrusion. Most unseemly.

Unqueenly.

She spent the night as she wished, alone with a twelve-foot king cobra sprawled on the floor beside her bed.

𒐓 𒄿 𒆕 𒈫

The Uzba decision was more far-reaching than Uruna had realized, for it had necessitated a large dose of political convenience. What shocked her sensibilities more was the universal presumption that a wholly secular organization should dictate a religious decision.

"The wedding will take place within a fortnight," was how Niccaba broke it to her over a breakfast of tea and cakes. Kinar had joined them, as was her custom, and Uruna had asked for further explanation of the visitor quartered half a week already in an area previously reserved exclusively for women.

"Whose wedding?" Uruna asked.

"Yours."

"Preposterous. I have no intention of marrying anyone."

Kinar confined her attention to the formidable task of spreading plum jam with the sharp tip of her dining blade.

"I told you last night," said Niccaba. "The Uzba already decided. Nuptial preparations began two days ago."

"Niccaba, prophecy is not gotten by edict."

"The vision would be a blessing for all, and we hope for it with all our hearts. But there are other issues at stake."

"Mine has always been Sight."

"Yes, and you have made a commendable effort that will be rewarded in time. Meanwhile, our immediate survival is at risk. The horde above Kish is ready to move and neither Kish nor Nippur has sufficient defenses. Uruk has come forward with an offer of troops."

"Uruk? The Bull's Gunzeks? You must be out of your mind!"

"Uruna, be reasonable. We have no recourse."

"And this marriage everyone's arranged for me will in some way assure our safety? Please explain how that works, as long as we're being *reasonable*."

"An army cannot move on empty stomachs. We could not meet Enguda's terms for support funds, so he accepted our offer."

"I still don't see what he gains."

"You will become the bride of his son, Ensi Marduk."

"His what? Where did he get a son?"

"You will reside with your husband at his home in Aramdan."

"Never heard of Aramdan. Where is the place?"

"Above the Anatol."

"Above? There's nothing above those mountains but clouds and rain. And snow. Or do you mean farther north?"

"You will find your accommodations most pleasing. You will be safe there to pursue the Sight."

"You mean safely kept out of the Bull's way."

"Uruna, it's not what you think."

"Gunzeks in our streets, rapping on our doors, tramping through our fields. Gubna priests roving our temple and braying sacrilege over sacred relics. Enguda's minions everywhere! That's what he wants and that's what your pack of fools gave him. Uzba, indeed! They know nothing of the human spirit, they no longer hear sacred songs or carry Great Mother in their hearts."

"That's a terrible thing to say!"

"You didn't stop them, did you?"

"I was one voice. They were extremely difficult to persuade."

"You didn't even try."

"Uruna, please, the tide of consent was overwhelming."

"Your fear is greater than your good sense, madam. You've become like them. I didn't want to believe it, but I see it in your face even now."

"So you refuse to marry the Ensi."

"I haven't met the man, Niccaba. I've been promised to a man I know nothing about. If there's a chance he can bring me the Sight, if he's merely willing, I must take it. That will be my reasonable choice. Not the promise of protection by a lying murderer."

She rubbed her arm where the Bull's bruise was now but a nagging memory.

Kinar pressed a cake crumb beneath her finger and made it disappear on her tongue. "Really delicious cakes today. The new baker is to be commended."

Uruna wrinkled her brow. "What new baker?"

"Part of the Bull's offer, in advance. Fellow was trained by a baking mistress in, of all places, Aramdan."

Of all places, indeed. Good for Kinar. At least one of Ekur's staff still possessed the art of political subtlety. The Bull's insurgency had begun without a whimper of contest. At this rate, Uruna could expect an Aramdan manservant to draw her bath by bedtime tonight.

Time to turn the discussion to the vaunted Ensi himself. "Tell me what you know of this man I'm to wed."

Niccaba leaned forward with eager indulgence as she gave her account of the proceedings.

Uruk's courtship of the serpent queen had come in a rush of mad impetuosity characteristic of the Bull Priest and not entirely unexpected by the ladies of Ekur. What would have amounted to brash impertinence under other circumstances was overlooked in the interest of making up for fourteen frustrating years entertaining unworthy suitors.

A visit was arranged. The supplicant presented himself to *naditu* and Council. Forty Uzba ladies sat in the open as Ensi Marduk sang in a high-pitched strangle to a small, round basket.

A monocled cobra climbed out of the basket.

Ensi sang some more.

The cobra went back inside.

Niccaba waited for something more significant. The Uzba considered the feat significant enough to stamp their feet in applause.

The gentlemen of Uruk took their leave.

Smiles and nods in their wake.

"And that was it?" Uruna asked.

"No, we drank wine and congratulated ourselves afterward. The decision was unanimous."

"Five ranking members from Ekur Council were absent on temple business. How do you derive unanimous out of that?"

"It was unanimous among those present."

Uruna fought for patience. "The man is a mere snake charmer. The monocled breed is small and vicious, inclined to bite first and ask questions later. Totally unsuitable for the Sleep of Serpents. But nevermind, I understand what's happening here, and while I don't like bowing to fear-driven country bumpkins, I won't oppose the audience."

Niccaba frowned. "What audience are you talking about?"

"The next step in a queen's betrothal. First step is done—you selected the consort. Next comes the audience. That's how it works according to tradition. What day have you scheduled?"

"Why, I haven't scheduled any audience."

"Fine, see to it and give me time to prepare for it."

"Uruna, there's no need for an audience. We've begun readying the hall. We already sent heralds with the invitations."

Kinar was looking askance at Niccaba as if suddenly finding herself in the presence of an idiot. Time to close the discussion before her two counsellors got into it.

"Don't worry, Niccaba," Uruna said. "Audience is just a matter of formality. How handy that the Ensi is still here and won't need to travel. That should expedite the matter quite nicely, don't you agree, Kinar?"

Kinar The Lovely responded by stuffing her mouth with the last cake. Whole.

At day's end, shortly after returning from Evening Devotions, Uruna heard from Niccaba: tomorrow evening, Serpenthood arbor after supping hour.

To Uruna's great relief, her bedtime attendant that night was one of the girls from the Gipar.

CHAPTER ELEVEN

Bedu Refuge

Bright colors overhead. The aroma of cooking oil and garlic. A voice blossomed into existence, word images unfolding slowly, like petals opening in the sun.

"...small hunting party marching up the river."

"...turned west a few miles away."

A man talking to him. No, reporting to someone else. A male voice in a thick, guttural accent.

The hunter could not see who was talking, so he moved his head to get a better view and immediately felt sick to his stomach. Stabs of pain wracked his lower body, but he couldn't tell exactly where because his mind refused to focus.

His legs? Had the lion—?

"Head them off," said a woman's voice. "And keep them away. I have more work to do here."

A face loomed above him, distorted like a squash gourd. He blinked, closed his eyes.

"A-a-ah, we are back among living," crooned the woman. "Such shame. Such beautiful body to be treated like that. You belong in temple harem or queen's bedchamber. Or in garden with me. Ha-ha!"

Tezu-Mah smiled in spite of the pain. His lips were cracked and dry, his swollen tongue felt like a huge boiled egg in his mouth.

"Plath," he said.

"If that is best you can manage, perhaps I send you back to the lion. Oh, stop your flirting now, man comes back."

He wanted to ask who the man was, but drifted off instead, swimming among visions of the river, faces in firelight, a dark-haired woman who danced in and out of sight. And the lion, golden eyes sizing him up, measuring him for a feast, leaping forward, mouth agape.

She was there again. The talker.

"Now you must sit up and take broth. Here, I help you. Oh, much better, now sit, sit. Take it, take it. Oh, such a wound he gives you, the lion. I do not stitch so much flesh since I stuff the boar for the feast of the new year at Faw Haran. They bring you in, you look nearly as bad as the pig, but not quite, for he is dead and roasted and you are, hah, quite alive, oh yes. More? You drink more?"

The effect of the broth was miraculous. He could feel the strength coursing through his body, clearing his mind, returning sensation to numb limbs...

OH GODDESS!

He sucked his breath and bellowed involuntarily.

"Pain is good," pronounced the woman.

He shuddered. Good or not, the pain would not leave his leg; it refused to subside. It would turn him into a bawling baby.

She shoved a stick between his teeth.

"Bite!" she ordered, and he bit down and grunted. "Now look at me. Look at me!"

Roaring behind the stick, he opened his eyes. A pair of long-lashed almonds rimmed with the indigo tattoo of the Bedu women returned his stare. The heavy brows were drawn together in a frown beneath a fringe of long black hair. He realized she was trying to see how conscious he was, whether he had sustained a head injury as well. He noticed her hands, soft and wise to the response of a man's body.

"You are better. And I think your friends come this way." The dark eyes examined his own, weighing the effect of her words.

"Freth?"

"Yes, your hunting friends. Man from village tell me so."

"Nhoh!" Damn the stupid stick to the demons, he could not speak!

"Is all right, they carry you to safety." Again the close look. Was she a slaver spy?

"Noth freth. Thlaverth. Noth thee me heawh."

"More broth, or I never understand a word you say."

She pulled the stick away neatly and brought the bowl to his lips. He took it in desperate gulps to avoid drowning in the stuff. She was sturdy and strong in the hardy Bedu manner, and so she had her way with the broth, letting it dribble down his chin and over his chest but making sure it went down.

"What ith it?" he asked when at last she paused to give him respite. His swollen tongue still refused to cooperate, even without the stick jammed in his teeth.

"You cannot understand if I tell you."

"Ith working."

"Of course. I make it."

"Thank oou."

"Akkai."

He slipped into a troubled sleep, uncertain whether hours or minutes passed between more sips of broth, the soft touch of a cool hand on his fevered brow, the murmured rise and fall of voices, sometimes distant, sometimes close at hand.

When he could sit up long enough to focus, the sun was angling west and his litter sat in the long blue shadow of a Bedu tent. The woman's husband introduced himself as Mechem Zaheer, and his bride as Lasheen. They were newcomers to the delta, having traveled day and night for fourteen days from Martu in the western steppe lands. At dawn two days ago they had topped a rise and beheld the river.

"I do not see anything like it before. So much water. So much green."

The hunter decided to be his mortal self, Anu, again, having submitted on several accounts in the previous hours to levels of indignity unworthy of Tezu-Mah.

"You should see it at full flood," he said. "Water covers the land between the horizons."

He seemed to have regained his tongue, as well as the ability to experience a mortal's anxiety at being discovered by his enemies. Bad enough that he was outnumbered, but to be helpless before the Bull's soldiers was to put oneself at the mercy of the merciless.

"So, where are these others?" he asked, affecting a tone of nonchalance.

"Several miles to southeast. They arrive soon in time for the midday meal. I must help Lasheen prepare as proper host."

"Help me out of here instead."

Mechem Zaheer eyed his guest warily. "You in no condition to move or be moved, my friend."

"It doesn't matter. There's money for you if you get me down to the river."

"I have no need of money."

"My everlasting friendship, then."

"Ah! Now there is value."

"You are both fools!" Lasheen gave her husband a scornful look. "I just finish binding wound." Her dark eyes flashed to Anu's face with an expression of grave concern. "If it open again, I cannot—"

"If I am found here by these men, I shall be returned to their people and that must not happen. You must believe me."

"They seek you because you kill the lion?"

"Yes," he lied. The simple Bedu wouldn't understand the mad rationale which drove the Bull's minions to prey upon hunter and frontiersman.

"That is bad?"

"Yes."

"Where I come from is good to kill lion."

"It is good also for the people down there. But to the people in the city, it is bad."

"Where this city is?"

"Three days upriver."

"Is large, this city?"

"Probably none larger in Sumer."

"Then, all those people, at such great distance, how they can find you?"

"They can and they will."

"I think I do not like these people very much."

"They don't understand the way of life out here."

"But they make rules for us anyway, ah?"

"Yes."

"I see. And for you to return to the place of such rules, you are punished, ah?"

"You get the idea."

"Ah, why you didn't say so?"

Lasheen pushed forward.

"Mechem! We must not move him!"

"From where?"

"From here, you dolt!"

"But we not here."

"Ai, I married imbecile. Of course we here."

Anu interrupted the insane discourse.

"What are you saying? That you will send them away?"

Mechem shrugged. "Lion live here. He eat people. No one know where he strike next."

Lasheen grinned. "You are brilliant!"

"You just call me dolt!"

"I change my mind."

Mechem shrugged, gave Anu a resigned look. "You want her?"

Lasheen clapped her husband over the head and bit his ear, then looked triumphantly at Anu.

"Do you see why I marry him?" she proclaimed.

Mechem Zaheer slipped from his tent and departed with a song on his lips.

"Now that we alone..." said Lasheen with a frivolous waggle of eyebrow.

"Aren't you two ever serious?" asked Anu.

"Never!"

She was a delight, this woman of the desert—playful and full of mischief, yet adept and capable and wholly self-assured while she served her husband in his own tent. How unlike his sisters and the temple women he had known, who sheltered their frivolous sons and husbands from duty and conflict.

How unlike his mother. Sooner or later he would have to face Heganna, who totted up filial obligations like grain stores. Nine years of neglect damaged the pride of a woman whose estate holdings ran second only to the temple's. Heganna would interpret his leg wound as due penance for resisting her will. He and she had always differed over her plans to install him in Nippur's upper echelon, and the schism had driven him into the *ghana*.

Differences of another kind awaited him at home. The late years were usually the hardest on a woman, when her flesh betrayed her and she turned for compensation to a venerating family—obedient, loyal offspring who brought babies to her knee. And the only son of her life had run off to go hunting.

She might forgive him. She already possessed three daughters with prolific wombs, unswerving devotion to duty, and the Hanza acumen for sharp trading. But the family fortunes depended on temple influence, and Heganna had calculated on Anu's to forge alliances with his charm and fair face. That much wouldn't have changed in his absence, but one look at her scarred, sunburnt renegade just might change her implacable mind.

He was unsuited for the genteel life—a misfit who might never learn to cope without causing offense. A few moments behind closed doors made him uneasy; an hour inside any structure drove him frantic. He might sleep under a roof one night, perhaps two, but then he got desperate for a clear path under open skies. He would snap awake at the slightest flash of light, start like a deer at the crack of a twig. For days at a time he roamed nude without thinking about it.

Something may have killed the hunter god within, but the wild thing the god had made was still alive and very much in control. Yet, for some reason the *ghana* wilderness was rejecting him.

What would a wild man do in tame Nippur?

On another day Lasheen came to him with a smirk.

"While you are asleep like the dead, a boy comes," she said. "One of the Hani. His name is Pana and he steals your boat."

"Steals it? I bequeathed it to him!"

"Bequeath? What is this bequeath?"

"I gave it to the boy."

"Oh, I do not say it right. He hides the boat in the reeds where the soldiers cannot find it."

"Smart kid."

Lasheen fished in her apron pocket and pulled out a shiny object that caught the late sunlight. "He give me this for you."

She slapped the object down on the tray beside Anu and spun about. "I make bread now. 'Bye."

And she disappeared inside the tent.

Anu looked down at a lion's claw, neatly excised just below the knuckle and shorn of hair. Its ivory hook formed a crescent that fit the palm of his hand. Had it come from the very lion he slew? Perhaps the Kudu Mahti huntsmen had prised it from the carcass before they disposed of it—and thereby deprived the Larsa merchant of his trophy share.

So be it.

He spent the rest of the day working the claw into an amulet, figuring when he got well he would purchase a ring for it. For now, a rawhide thong would have to do. As he worked the claw, he grew familiar with every curve and crevice, the arc shape, the texture of bone.

After the evening meal, he stopped Lasheen on one of her many cook's errands and pressed the amulet into her hand.

"What is? Oh!"

Her eyes begged the question and he answered. "For you."

She clutched the amulet to her chest in both hands, then kissed his forehead.

"It is like moon. We are bound to this moon, you and I."

He thought it a beautiful way to finish with the lion.

CHAPTER TWELVE
Power Consolidation

The great minds of Uruk, at least those belonging to the male gender, had assembled in the Senarib, a large block building set to one side of Uruk's administrative compound. Inside its buttressed walls, a great commons sixty yards square marked off a full quarter of the enclosure. The square itself was also called the Senarib, or seat of agreement, where Lukur authorities contended with Uruk's hegemony on matters of secular oversight.

Enguda, the Bull Priest, was the first in memory, male or female, to bridge the two groups.

The crowd was on hand to pay homage to the extraordinary man who had set a bold precedent by assuming priestly office. The fact that he was neither ordained nor pious by nature detracted not at all from his appeal tonight, for he had withstood nearly two decades of censure and ridicule since that first leap. His latest audacity was to create a brotherly order calculated to crack the Lukur monopoly by sharing with the ladies such privileges as Inanna conferred on those in Her service. Few in the audience dared entertain a similar ambition, but every man present held in awe the Bull's capacity for claiming rights that made the women squirm.

Enguda patiently indulged the fawning multitude in order to glean the self-possessed few. A small but vigorous corps served his cause, yet not one of those sworn to secrecy enjoyed the priest's confidence. To speculate about his plans was dangerous. The slightest breach of security invited eternal banishment from the priesthood. The Bull's every tactic encouraged competition, rewarded treachery, and fomented distrust—always to his own advantage.

Tonight's special guests were the two male elders he had managed to place on Eanna's council. Aradegi already commanded Uruk's constabulary with an authority most men only dreamed of. He needed no priesthood to enhance his position. Imgua, a venerable aristocrat reputedly more than seventy years of age, collaborated daily with Lukur overseers to steer a course for Uruk's teeming burden of humanity. Neither man required aught but his own power, nevertheless both were essential to the Bull's plan and each had showed up in the earnest belief that he could dissuade the priest from further dividing the city against itself.

The Bull dealt with Aradegi early on as the crowd peaked at nearly a hundred men, each vying for a chance to see and be seen by the "great man." He was entertaining the disinherited son of a leading female landowner when Aradegi strode up with a brace of aides and a scowl to indicate both his distaste for the occasion and his intent to engage the impudent priest quickly and get on to other business. The planter took one look at the newcomers and beat a hasty retreat.

"Welcome Aradegi," the priest offered. "I trust you find our little assembly orderly and proper?"

"You know I'm not here officially. I was curious to see what you're up to. You're a freak and nothing more, but right interesting to watch."

The Bull Priest glanced at the pair of constables at either elbow of the commander. "I didn't know I was under surveillance."

"These fellows are my personal guards. Dangerous business we're in, you know, keeping the peace. Got to be sure where you step."

Aradegi was unpracticed in the art of innuendo and thus his attempts at clever double-talk were usually as heavy-handed as his dealings with street offal. His brutish dark brow belied a keen intelligence but served to intimidate the ruffian fringe it was his lot in life to control. In genteel company such as tonight's, Aradegi covered his social shortcomings by affecting an abrasive demeanor and keeping his stay short.

"No risk of any kind here," the priest assured his guest. "Just fraternizing with my friends of the *gubna*."

"Yes, I heard that's what you call your priesthood. Strange word, I don't believe I know the meaning."

"It's Old Chaldean, a Hani word for the spirit guardians of the underworld. You ought to feel right at home with the term, Aradegi. Like the *galla* constables who watch over the souls of our own ancestors."

"I'm more comfortable leaving that job to Inanna and the Mothers."

"I'm sure you are. After all, they still bake your bread, so to speak, don't they?"

Aradegi didn't miss the implication. His nostrils flared beneath a hostile stare that plainly spoke his sentiments about male priesthood. Not surprisingly, Aradegi stood firmly with the Lukur and would stay there until ousted. Too bad, for he was a formidable force and the sort of leader needed for the brotherhood. Perhaps he would come around later as the movement gathered for the run at kingship, but by then it would be too late for him. If Aradegi failed to grasp his chance tonight, so be it. The Bull Priest had no use for last-minute opportunists.

Aradegi frowned with almost comical effect as his low brow contracted to a narrow furrow above the glint of hatred.

"You put us all at risk, Priest," he growled. "The gods have been patient with your disbelief so far. Now you bring these Gunzek vultures to crowd around the carcass of beloved Motherhood. Mark my word, man, you have more to fear than the mortals you offend. Once it looks like you speak for Sumer, we'll all suffer the wrath of demons."

The Bull regarded his self-made adversary with equable good nature. "I never realized our city was defended by the god-fearing rather than god-loving. A danger to us all if superstition gets the better of our good sense. I bid you well, Aradegi, with a prayer that Inanna will share her grace with man and woman alike, and love us despite our differences."

The burly features confronting him suddenly lifted with a beatific smile. "Save your sanctimony for the rabble, Priest," said Aradegi, gathering his two witnesses for departure. "If I thought the sword was any kind of answer, I'd have struck you dead where you stand. You're just another man, not as terrible as many believe. It's a relief to me. I thought I might have to take you seriously."

He made as if to go and turned back with an afterthought. "Don't hurt yourself playing soldier."

The city warrior gave the priest his back and left.

"A right clumsy fellow when it comes to words."

The age-mellowed voice came from Enguda's left, and he turned to find Imgua standing a few feet away by himself. The familiar robe of office was gone from the bony frame and a simple frock of gray wool fell just short of his knees, revealing a pair of skinny, grizzled shins sticking out of well-worn leathers. The white beard was trimmed square and curled to match Imgua's full head of hair. With his bushy white brows raised in characteristic open-faced wonder, Imgua inclined his head in acknowledgment of the Bull's attention.

"*Gubna*, did I hear you say?" he continued. "You're calling yourselves *gubna* after the Hani swamp elves? Hardly a fortunate choice, I'd say, but better than naming yourselves after those Nazim monsters tried to steal the Sight from the Lukur."

"That childish tale from ages past? Gods, the whole business is better left forgotten."

"Well, you're almost right, but there's a lesson in it for all of us—Lasori's legacy of mixed blessing and curse. Of course the rumor goes to this day that a dedicated few secretly practice Nazim rites of sacrifice and debauchery."

"Rumors founded in Lukur suspicion."

"Or prudence. Nowadays nobody knows the difference, what with the old ways disappearing as fast as the Old Ones themselves. So the Mothers try to scare us into good behavior. Where'd you hear this *gubna* term, anyway?"

"I have the definition from a Hani chieftain," the priest said, pleased to switch his exchange with the old wizard to a more trivial matter.

"Then he was playing with you. No matter, the joke's lost on anyone below the age of fifty, which leaves me to bear the lance alone. How is your boy?"

"He's up in Nippur and doing well. I think by now he's met nearly everyone on Ekur's council."

"You'll never dissuade the Mothers at Ekur from their course," said the elder man. "Chancellor Niccaba has the whole temple seeking a serpent mate for the queen. They're combing the world for a man who can send her into the ecstasy, and they'll find him, mark my word."

"Of course they will, Imgua. We've seen to that ourselves."

"Well, how remarkable! Did you aid them with this brotherhood of yours?"

"Nothing so elaborate. A much simpler solution lay readily at hand: a young man of, should I say, intimate acquaintance."

"But when did this fellow learn Serpenthood? I thought every male in your order was busy with religious instruction."

"Imgua, use your wits. The whole affair boils down to a single hour of the most ridiculous fantasy. See, here's how it supposedly works. Husband goes in to wife, helps her mix venom with strong wine, and she quaffs the potion. They couple on the floor while deadly serpents stand watch. Thus inebriated and pleasured, the woman reaches her peak and wondrously gets transported to the serpent realm, from which she will discern events to come. Now I ask you, how can either mate maintain coitus, with a half-dozen unpredictable, unrestrained cobras poised within striking distance? Does this sound like the path to sacred prophecy, or is it the rash invention of a demented woman on the brink of insanity?"

"The Entu is one of the most respected—"

"I think the poor woman's lost her mind."

"Gods sakes, man, the Sleep of Serpents isn't Uruna's invention! The ceremony has a tradition going back hundreds of years. She merely inherited it from her predecessors."

"None of whom succeeded in the preposterous charade. Imgua, how many men—*and* women—do you suppose perished from the ceremony without the world being told?"

"You're accusing the Lukur of conspiracy!"

"I'm merely attributing to them the great practical sense for which they are renowned. Why else the elaborate secrecy surrounding the ceremonial participants? Why the great aura of mystery surrounding the whole business, except to perpetuate their elevated station by obscuring the sad truth?"

"And that would be?"

"That there never has been and never will be a serpent prophet."

"Blasphemy, sir!"

"Of course! Runs straight against all temple teachings, especially those dispensed to us by the feminine power regime. But my *gubna* priests have discovered facts that refute their contention of a Lukur prophet line."

"But everyone knows the great queen Lasori restored Sumer by Serpent Sight!"

"So said the Mothers of her time. Who knows with any certainty after generations of retelling? Indeed, she was a great leader, and no doubt she vanquished her enemies as soundly as reported. But a prophet? More likely that tale was invented to raise her office a little closer to the gods."

"Enough! I'll countenance no more wild allegations of this kind. It's time you ceased this scandalous heresy if you value your head."

The Bull lowered his voice and bent closer to the old man. "It's time, my friend, to unmask the Entu as impostor. Naturally, we'll be kind about it, for she's obviously the tool of others in high places, easily influenced because of her troubled spirit."

"This is all highly irregular, sir," Imgua mumbled, casting a nervous glance around the room. "None of it true, of course. I've met the lady in question. Numerous occasions. Be assured she's neither weak-minded nor meek of spirit. Quite the contrary."

"Her very strength attracted the demon in the first place," said the priest with air of injured piety. "She's not to be blamed for her affliction. Gods, how could she be any different? The Mothers have had her under their thumb since she was seven. Now she can be relieved of suffering by a gentle, understanding husband more fit for leadership."

Imgua's mouth dropped open as he regarded his host with disdain. "Your intentions are quite clear, Priest, and none too subtle, if you ask me, which I'm sure you will not. Let me warn you to tread lightly where Serpenthood is concerned. You've managed to get where you are by exploiting mortal fallibility. The gods are another matter, and quite beyond your powers of persuasion."

"I couldn't agree more. But Sumer languishes under female rule while rogues and brigands march upon her door. The gods will intervene as and when they see fit, helping those of us who take bold action rather than become entranced by a drunken stupor."

Imgua's eyes hardened like black agates as the wizened features froze in a mask of reproof. "You're not the first of your kind, you know. I should have stopped you when I could. But you were young and full of vitality and I hoped you would acquire wisdom. In that I was wrong. Your development stopped with the mastery of craft and deception. Oh, wipe the smug look from your face, my friend, I knew my appearance tonight would give you the endorsement you want. You don't need my concurrence, willing or otherwise. Council hasn't enough resolve to stop you."

"Then why not join us?"

"Because I'm from the old way. I revere the women in my life, I don't abhor them. I'm part of the culture of peaceful rule, something you don't understand. You don't want me along except to blame for your failures when the splendor you crave turns to ashes."

"We're headed for a new day, Imgua. You could share in the new rule, you know. You're more fit for it than I."

"I'd be too old even if I agreed with your cause, which will never happen, not as you foresee it. Oh, you'll have your share of triumphs, and the way will look clear for a time. But what you don't understand about yourself will become the first obstacle, and your misunderstanding of Sumerian manhood will be your downfall. That is, if the serpent queen doesn't get to you first."

"She's no threat. She'll be the first to go."

Imgua gave him a long look, arrived at some private conclusion, and gave a short shake of his head. "So like your namesake, the bull, you'll charge ahead anyway. Pity."

"I don't need your pity or anyone else's."

"I didn't mean you. I was thinking of the lives you'll waste before you're stopped. Lives of precious value."

"The few must die that the many may live."

Imgua spat to one side. "That borrowed saying was never meant to justify the course you're about to take. I know it's not your nature to confer favor unless repayment is obvious, but grant an old man his wish. It's simple enough."

The Bull felt magnanimous. His strongest adversary had just removed himself from the field of play. "Certainly, if it's within my power."

The elder lifted his chin and squinted along his nose. "Remember tonight when you die. As the tide suddenly turns and you're swarmed over from the least suspected quarter, just remember what was said here."

"A word of wisdom from the councilor, is that it? Go ahead."

"Lasori sent it down across the ages, and where she got it nobody knows. She said, 'The mighty shall fall, and the least shall be risen up.'"

The Bull grinned at the familiar proverb, a trite prayer of squalid hope dredged up by the weak and defeated to justify their plight. How sad that a man of Imgua's brilliant achievement should fall back on that useless dreck. He would have believed the man had more backbone.

"I'll keep it in mind," he promised. "And Imgua, thank you for your concern."

A sadness crept into the bleary eyes as Imgua swung a shawl over his shoulders and pulled his pouch to his side. "My concern for you, priest, is greater than for your victims to come. For their suffering on earth is brief, whereas your pain will be from everlasting to everlasting."

𒈫 𒉿 𒅗 𒐖

The Bull was far from disappointed with the evening when he repaired to the catacombs beneath Eanna Temple. Both men had shown their colors in the arrogant belief that they were beyond his reach—true enough for the moment, but an inequity he would soon rectify.

His small prize from the swamps awaited him in a cramped compartment lined with unplastered brick. Borok, the captain of his guard, met him at the captive's door with torch in hand and wordlessly pulled the latch away for him to enter.

"Keep that fire outside," he reminded the Nafti soldier. "We don't give him the slightest excuse for a weapon."

He had to stoop under the low ceiling as he waited a few seconds for his eyes to adjust to the darkness. On a clay bench built up from the floor, the Hani elder sat with his back propped against the back wall. The old man stirred his small frame, lifted an eyelid to regard his captor, ran a tongue over parched lips. A bucket of water stood in the corner for either drink or waste containment. By the absence of excrement on the floor, the man chose not to litter his habitat. Two days without water had taken a toll. He ought to be softened up by now.

"Where is the hunter?" asked the Bull without any preliminaries. They had started each visit the same way.

"I don't know." A hoarse whisper.

"He was in your village last week to chase the lion."

"He came to kill it. I assume he did so and moved on."

"Which way did he go?"

"I already told *him*." The Hani pointed feebly at the Gunzek.

"Tell me, again."

"He went north and east after leaving his boat for the boy."

"Yes, Pana is the lad's name, I believe. Do you know where Pana is now?"

"No. I have seen none of my people since you took me."

"Aren't you curious to know what's become of him?"

"He is in the care of the villagers."

"No longer. He's in my care now. Living on the other side of that wall behind you."

The Hani's eyes widened.

"Yes," the priest affirmed, "but we have no wish to harm the boy. You could make it easier on yourself and Pana if you persuade him to work with us."

"I don't understand."

"Sure you do. You're a Hani chief, not a simpleton. Talk to the boy, tell him to take us to the hunter, point him out."

"And if I cannot persuade him?"

"Then you both die here."

"The lad has committed no crime."

"He's Hani. That's crime enough by my rules. Now, you're the boy's last hope, but you won't make it another day without water, and the boy won't listen to anyone else. Tell him to cooperate, and he lives. That's not so much to ask, is it?"

"You think you will kill Tezu-Mah this way, but he is a god."

"Maybe so, maybe not, but either way we intend him no harm. We just want to talk to him."

The Hani squinted at him, gave the matter a few moments of thought. "Bring the boy," he said.

"Good man, you're doing the right thing."

The Hani nodded. "Yes, I am sure of it. But you will need to treat the boy well or he will not last. The swamp is harsh."

"Don't worry, my men know the swamps well enough."

Outside, he turned to Borok. "Bring the boy to me when you're sure he's convinced, then get rid of the old man. And make sure the boy is fed tonight. I want him fit to travel. This could take weeks."

"We won't need that long."

"You've had a year to catch him and all you've come up with is a tired old Hani swamp rat and a kid. Don't make a promise you can't keep, just be sure you come back with the hunter."

"I'll have ten of my best Gunzek hunters, in two groups. No Sumerian can slip past those lads."

"I'm well aware of your fierce reputation, Captain, but you're forgetting one thing."

"What's that?"

"This Sumerian kills lions."

CHAPTER THIRTEEN
Serpenthood Initiation

Three weeks after Uruna's return from Burum, the autumnal equinox signaled the beginning of Sumer's cooler season of *Enten*. Uruna's frosty mood matched the weather, and she was seldom to be found except at Morning Call and supper with the ladies. She spent the remainder of her waking hours locked away with her serpent companion, doing what and to which purpose none could divine.

So it was with great surprise one afternoon that Retha found herself smack in the middle of the temple's greatest mystery.

Having seen Uruna at work in Burum, she tried to ignore the stories circulating among her *kadishtu* peers—tales of the queen's erratic behavior, her obsessive preoccupation with the cobra—offset by accounts of her ability to know things before they happened or were said. For both reasons most girls were uncomfortable in her company. Retha began to understand why, and to form her own misgivings, on the day Uruna suddenly opened up to her.

The day had started out normally enough. By midmorning she was already chore-weary when Kinar took her aside with a "request" that she substitute at the well for a girl who had fallen ill. After that, Retha had worked up a healthy sweat hauling double pails of water to the commissary and back. The sun was nearly overhead when she stopped in the shade of the arched entry to House of Decrees and propped her back against a column to bathe her neck with a wet cloth.

She felt a nudge at her shoulder. Uruna's shadow blotted out the sun, a playful smirk decorating her lips as she looked down at her junior-most colleague.

"Not enough that you should neglect my tubs, Retha, but to loll about in plain sight at the busiest hour of the day is to risk one of Lub-Sunna's sternest reprimands."

Retha struggled to get her feet under her, but Uruna pushed her back and plopped down beside her.

"How did you learn to handle cobras?"

Uh-oh, trouble coming.

"I watched you."

"I'm almost always alone."

"I'm almost always sneaky."

A mild chuckle. "And serpent talk? Kinar says you got the serpents back inside their baskets without speaking a word. How did you manage that?"

"More sneakiness. I listened to you talk to Meret and Silim."

"Dear, I don't speak aloud to any of the cobras."

"Well, I heard somebody talking."

Uruna gaped. "You're serious."

"I couldn't understand any of it at first, of course. Sorry, but I've been listening since I was thirteen."

"You hear serpent talk."

"More like a soft voice-thing inside my head. Well, you can explain it better, I'm sure."

Uruna's heel started bouncing on the step. "Retha. Dear Retha," she muttered over and over.

Then she buried her head in her arms and her shoulders shook. She appeared to be sobbing, and Retha reached out a hand to apologize for her transgression. Instead, her queen came up laughing.

"You rascal! You blessed, beloved yellow-headed rascal, I love you!

Do you know how long…?"

Retha could only stare back in dumb confusion. She had crossed some sort of a line, but couldn't imagine what measure of penalty she had incurred.

Uruna loved her?

For several moments Uruna didn't seem to know what to do with her hands. She placed them on her face, wiped her skirt, folded them about her knees, scratched her scalp. At length, she turned and peered at Retha, stone sober.

"Are you finished with your chores?"

"I'm doubling for a sick girl. But I can do her scrubs later, if that makes any difference."

"Scrubs." Uruna bobbed her head like the word answered an imponderable enigma. "Scrubs for the mistress who converses with the divine. Of course. Perfect. Why not?"

Uruna pushed to her feet and skipped lightly down the stairs.

"Come with me," she called over her shoulder. "I've got something to show you at my place."

"But I have to tell Lub-Sunna where I'm going."

"Not today. Maybe not ever again. Come along, Retha—no, leave that scrub bucket for a drudge to fetch."

They stopped by Uruna's quarters to pick up a strange contraption that looked like a music clapper.

"For our scaly friend," she explained in answer to Retha's unspoken question. Now it became clear that Uruna had only serpents in mind. Apparently, little else held interest for the woman.

"Two times never to go into the garden," Uruna now cautioned. "In the early morning he comes out to hunt, and also at late evening before dusk. Never both, you understand, and not every day. You just can't be sure when he's in and when he's out."

"Would he attack me?"

"Not unless you crossed his path, which is easier to do when he's scurrying around after food."

"What does he eat?"

Uruna's answer was nonchalant. "Whatever we put in the garden. Rats, lizards, voles, frogs, sometimes a fish. The garden is his lair and we put prey inside just for him to hunt."

"Oh."

That would explain the temple's accumulation of writhing creatures, in particular the small cobras in Retha's own custody. Had she erred in her duties that night with the tailor from Azziz? Was today a further test? She was not curious to learn more of Kukhmet's habits, personal or otherwise, but Uruna pressed on.

"Thing is, he takes one and then scurries away and doesn't eat again for several days. The gardeners aren't convinced how safe it is, won't go near the place."

Well, at least the gardeners exhibited good sense.

"Then who tends the plants?"

Uruna beamed. "It's one of my greatest pleasures. Of course, I have to be careful at all times, but I get to see to my flowers and share a bit of casual time with my friend."

"Still sounds dangerous. Why not just keep him in his room and toss in a carcass or two?"

"Wouldn't do. He needs the light and air of the garden. And he must hunt his prey and kill it himself. Won't touch dead things."

How civilized. A veritable prince of good taste.

The walled vestibule abutting Serpenthood's west wing was dank and foul with the smell of death, a fitting redoubt for its deadly master, but hardly hospitable to humans. Ordinary humans, anyway. Retha fervently hoped the king had retired to the expanse of garden beyond. She had always disliked dark corners, but sharing the shadows with a serpent was a disturbing thought.

No, "terrifying" was a better word for it.

A low door led to the outer enclosure where Uruna's garden caught daylight. The fading sun touched only the buttress tops high above Uruna's balcony. The grounds lay in deep shadow and looked quiet enough. Only cobra prey lurked there, trying to be as unobtrusive as possible.

The door opened onto a platform raised above a sunken floor. Uruna beckoned to Retha to stand close to her while she closed the door behind. A rope and stanchions marked the visitor boundary and two steps led down to the floor from either end. Above the wall directly opposite, a clerestory admitted diffused light onto the unfinished bricks.

Uruna pointed at the dark corner to the left. "He's down there."

A large lump of coiled flesh rested against the wall.

"Is he asleep?"

"I don't know, let's find out."

"Uruna!"

"Do you think I'd let anything happen?"

"Well, no, but he doesn't know me."

"That's why you're here."

"What should I do? I mean, how do I act?"

"Well, you can't walk up and take him by the hand, ha-ha. Just follow me and do as I do. If you must move an arm or a leg, do it slowly."

"Uruna, I'm scared. What if he bites me?"

"He won't harm you while I'm here. In time, he'll come to accept you and then you can approach him on your own. Come down with me now. He's really a beautiful creature."

Uruna pulled aside the rope and quietly put a foot on the first tread. "S-ss-sah!" she sang out to the dark interior. "He can't really hear anything I say, of course. Just feels the vibration of my voice. He lives in the world of scent, which he sniffs with his tongue. Yours will be of great interest to him."

Not exactly words to gladden the heart! Retha recalled again the episode on Burum's dock and did not envy the experience. It was one matter to have spent your life with the things, but quite another to have your first encounter.

Uruna bent to a crouch about six feet from the object against the wall and tapped the floor twice with the clapper she'd brought. A dark shape lifted in the murky light, twisted on the heavy stalk to find the source of interruption.

Retha stayed where she was, afraid to move. Uruna extended her hand palm-down, about six inches above the floor. The thing suddenly unwound from itself and slid toward the hand in an eager, graceful movement. Uruna's outstretched arm became a ramp onto which the cobra lifted its body for support. She bent her elbow and hoisted him as he continued up her arm and across her shoulders. Kukhmet now stopped and peered around at Retha.

"He's watching me!" she shrieked.

Uruna straightened and turned around slowly. "We'll go outside in the garden light so you can see him. Of course he can sense you just as well in here as out there, but today you're our guest. Kukhmet, come now. Come outside with Uruna."

As Uruna ducked beneath the lintel of the small doorway, the lighted garden illuminated her, and Retha's breath caught at the sight of the twelve-foot brown body, banded by a black stripe around the neck and riding the bare-skinned shoulders of Nippur's high priestess like a long-tailed family cat.

She followed slowly at a respectful distance and emerged in the green jungle compound. Serpenthood's outer walls formed three of its sides and the city's higher redoubt closed the back. She had seen the garden from above while cleaning rooms, but standing on the floor was infinitely more pleasing. Lacy tamarisks arched above fan palms set out in pots on the grassy floor. A winding narrow brick path led back to a rock garden with a small pool fed by a clay pipe. Baskets strung from a reed lattice dripped golden alyssum that fell nearly to the upraised tips of pink and crimson hollyhocks. But Retha had little time to appreciate the surrounding beauty, so tense was she in the cobra's presence.

Uruna turned around on the walkway so that she and the cobra faced Retha squarely.

"He's just dying to know who you are," she said, whereas Retha could see no appreciable change in the severe cast of eye trained in her direction. "See how he's fixed his nose toward you. If he didn't care, he'd be down off me in a flash and away into the shrubs."

"Sh-should I approach or stand fast?"

"Oh, come right over, he's fine."

Fine for a mistress, but what about a jittery Nord priestess with rag knees?

"Why are you doing this?" Retha asked. "Does everyone have to make friends with Kukhmet?"

"No, just a few are invited," Uruna said in a matter-of-fact sing-song. "I believe you're the first to come this far."

"You didn't tell me."

"Oh, Retha, move over here closer and stop being so silly."

She took a tentative step forward, more to test her balance than to avoid danger. The small head watched intently, then moved slightly to the left away from Uruna's head for a new angle of view. The black tongue flicked at her once, twice. His look had the inquisitive aspect of animals she had known in the barnyard at home, craning for the better angle of view.

She felt bolder and took another step.

Kukhmet truly was magnificent, much more of a presence than she had imagined. His creamy jaw made a flat arch over the blue-black flare and lemon underside, and the diamond rows of scales along his body were the dark earthen color of new dates. Twin polished obsidian beads sought her out as the head moved forward in a tentative inspection, retreated, advanced again.

"Look at him!" exclaimed Uruna. "He can't get enough of you! I've never seen him like this before, he's absolutely charmed by this lovely lady he's meeting for the first time, aren't you, Kukhmet? Yes, you're quite smitten, I believe."

"Maybe he knows I like him. I do think he's beautiful, and so vital and alert. He truly is kingly, isn't he?"

"Oh, yes, and he loves to hear you say that!"

"How can he understand? I thought you said he couldn't hear our voices."

"He hears what's in your heart, Retha. Draw nearer, let him catch your scent, and don't worry. He's ready to make friends."

Now she was close enough to touch Uruna, which put her terribly close to the flat stalk rising right up beside Uruna's right ear. Retha felt an irresistible urge to reach out and touch the cobra, to run her fingers over the braided length of body and experience the texture of those marvelously smooth scales.

"Give him your hand," said Uruna, quietly sober all of a sudden. "Slowly raise it to him and keep letting him know your desire. He wants to know your touch."

"What will I do with him?"

"If he wants to, he'll move onto your arm and take your shoulder. Just give him good support and don't drop him. It's really a pleasant experience."

Retha let her arm come up from her left side, her hand amazingly steady, her will going out with it as she watched a bridge extend between herself and the regal shape. The head dipped slightly, the body slid from behind Uruna's neck, and Kukhmet took the short journey from one human to another.

The body was heavy and much stiffer than it looked, and she was aware at once that the beast was all muscle and bone, and warm as well. With decisive grace, Kukhmet moved steadily past her ear, around behind her neck, and came to rest on the other shoulder.

"He's sniffing your hair," said Uruna. "Oh, Retha, this is delightful. You've no idea what this means to us both. I was hoping for maybe a tolerant nod in your direction, but this is far more. I wish I'd brought you before."

"Will he know me the next time?"

"Do you mean you want to come again?"

"If he's interested."

"Well, I think he'd be disappointed if you didn't. He hasn't any friends except me. There, did you feel that? He presses himself closer to your neck. That's a very good sign. Oh, Kukhmet, what does it mean, this affection for Retha? Will you tell us some day?"

The weight suddenly shifted right, and Retha reflexively brought her right arm up. Kukhmet quickly took the arm and she sensed that he wanted down. She bent her knees slowly and dropped the hand and watched the sleek body slide down to the earthen floor and away through the grass.

"Did I do anything?" she asked Uruna.

"No, he just decided he's hungry and went off to find something. All done, I'm off now. That's how he is. And quite at home with you, Retha. I'm dying to discover what he sees in you."

"Well, maybe he just likes me. What else could it mean?"

Uruna stared into the waning green light of ferns and palm canopy splayed along the wall in a lovely private glade, her sanctuary now open to another. She looked round at the scenery once more, as if recording the surroundings in her memory, and as she turned to go, she brought herself up short at the sight of Retha standing in the way.

"Oh, sorry," Uruna said. "He does that to me sometimes, pulls me away to a corner of his realm and plants something in my mind. I'll dig it up later. Remember what happened just now between you and Kukhmet. It's extraordinary and special. He's locked you in, and for you there's no turning back. You're part of us now."

Part of whom? Retha wondered. The Lukur and their traditions? Had she suddenly joined the ranks of the privileged who shared Uruna's special little retreat?

"I don't understand," she fumbled.

The wide grey eyes simply stared back, and for a moment Retha thought she was in for a fit of the "mad Uruna" the other girls talked about. But Uruna shrugged a shoulder and lifted her brows in light-minded dismissal.

"Serpenthood," she said, and she turned about and vanished through the small opening.

CHAPTER FOURTEEN
Gunzek Attack

The weeks following his deliverance by Lasheen's expert stitchery gave Anu plenty of time to consider his prospects. He could get about on the leg for several hours at a stretch most mornings. His first steps away from the campsite were always the most painful, but rather than sit and lie about, he endured the arduous process of forcing the limb past the point of agony, eager to restore strength to his disused limbs as he ventured farther into the desert each day.

"We should move," he said to the Bedu.

"You're not ready."

"I may not have the chance to get ready if Gunzek slavers find us."

"Inallah handles such vermin for us. But you're right, in a few days—"

Mechem was interrupted by a distant shout.

"Tezu-Mah!"

Anu tensed. The cry sounded from the low ridge that ran above the ancient dry riverbed in which they were camped. A boy bounded down the rocks like a wild goat and broke into a run across the hard flats.

It was Pana, from Kudu Mahti. And he had company.

Farther upslope behind the boy, six men carefully picked their way down the rocky talus. Four of them carried arrow quivers and the other two had lances tied across their backs. All wore a fighting man's loincloth and leather armor, protective plates of ox hide that covered upper legs, groin, arms and torso with sweat-polished surfaces that gleamed in the sun like a beetle's hard-shelled carapace. A seventh man lingered on the top of the embankment, his attention focused on the progress of the two lead men, who by now had unslung their bows. Only after his men had reached the bottom did the last start his own descent, at which point Anu got to his feet.

They were military. Battle-hardened faces surveyed the camp with predatory intensity. Lithe bodies moved with easy, cat-like agility, wasting neither energy nor distance. They carried no provision packs, which ruled out a hunter band or even a squad of lion soldiers. Stripped for action, they boldly asserted their dominion by approaching camp without calling out the universal hail to show friendly intent. One by one, in leisurely but steady progress, they filed onto the flat and fanned out, closing to within twenty paces to stare at the camp like buzzards surrounding prey.

"They mean no good," he told Mechem. "Be careful."

Mechem shrugged. "A band of huntsmen, and empty-handed from the looks of them. I'll ask Lasheen to put something together."

The primeval beast stirred inside. Wait and watch; they only ready themselves for danger.

Pana ran up and wrapped his arms around Anu's waist, and he cradled the back of the boy's head with one hand while he watched the men approach. Pana pulled back and looked up at him with a wide grin.

"We found the lion you killed, with your lance still buried in its chest! The whole village has seen it now. I gave the claw to the lady here."

"Who are these men, Pana?"

"Hunters like yourself. They seek the lion's mate."

A rogue took no mate but left the pride and shunned his own kind for life, which was the very reason for his name. Any hunter would know. "Did they tell you where they came from?"

"The one who leads them is captain of the guard at Uruk. Look, he gave me a knife!"

"I see."

Anu examined the captain, who by now had arrived at the bottom of the slope. He was dressed in armor like the others but a helmet of polished bronze wrapped his head over the crown from ear to ear and flared in back to cover the nape of his neck. Shoulder-length black hair streamed from beneath the helmet, and his beard was barbered trim and square, unlike the scruffy shag of the others. Anu saw black eyes above scarred, pitted cheeks, and a slash of cruel mouth—the face of a tyrant who held the world in contempt. He had seen the face before in Lagash.

The Nafti slave soldier, Borok. Uruk's butcher.

Mechem pushed aside the flap of his tent and strode forth with a goatskin bag.

"Welcome to the house of Zaheer!" he announced. "We are humble but we offer what little we have. Draw near and share wine with me and my friend. My most excellent cook will join us soon."

The soldiers neither answered nor stepped forward to accept Bedu hospitality. A warning signal flashed in the hunter's mind as the old premonition of disaster sank in his gut like cold stone. The visitors had no interest in the Bedu. They waited for a signal from their leader before making the first move.

How could Mechem be so trusting? Was he impervious to the aura of danger that now permeated the encampment? The smell of death was on the air. *Too late!* cried a warning voice in his head.

Borok came to a halt several steps in front of his men. Mechem marched forward and extended the goatskin to his guest, who ignored the friendly gesture and set his eyes instead on the bronzed figure near the tent.

"Pana!" the man called to the boy. "I would meet Tezu-Mah. Point him out."

Anu clenched the small hand in his fist. Pana winced and stirred at his side. "Captain says I may become a hunter like these. It was I who told him I knew Tezu-Mah."

"These men do not hunt game, Pana. Now go inside and help Lasheen."

"But Master told me—"

"Pana!" the man shouted with a stern glare to indicate his temper was not to be tested. Pana started forward, but Anu planted his feet square and resisted.

"See?" Pana called out to the pock-faced warrior. "I told you he was like a god. And Tezu-Mah is my brother."

"Yes, child, you spoke well."

The response sounded tame, but Borok was eager to close with his quarry, and with a rude sweep of plate-strapped arm shoved the boy aside, as though ridding himself of an annoying insect, and advanced on the hunter, sights narrowed. He stopped short of striking range and the deep-set eyes took in his catch with possessive pride.

You're mine, the look said. Your head will make a fitting trophy for my wall.

"So you're the lion-slayer bush people brag about. Eleven kills, if you actually took that fellow down in the marsh." He pointed at Anu's ravaged leg. "Looks to me like you let your guard down, my friend. Happen often?"

A glib retort came to mind and slipped away as the hunter-god crowded out all other thoughts. Borok, emboldened by the hunter's silence, aimed a chuckle over his shoulder, but his men saw only the lion hunter who had acquitted himself with awesome effect upon their feckless comrades.

To Mechem, the gap in conversation was an awkward pause requiring his attention, and he reappeared at the captain's elbow with his goatskin held aloft.

"Have a drink to cool your throat," he offered.

Borok locked eyes with the hunter as he grabbed the wine bag from the Bedu's hand and poured the precious contents on the ground. His teeth flashed a vicious grin as he regarded the smaller man's dismay with sordid appreciation.

"This is the blood of the Bedu," he hissed with a defiant lift of his chin. "Like wine it will be spilled upon the desert from here to the western sea. Get aside, monkey, while I deal with what I came for."

Anu locked eyes with the fierce warrior. In a soft, quiet voice he addressed Mechem. "Take the boy inside, my friend, while I speak with this man."

"He talks!" Borok feigned amazement. "The swamp rat has a voice. And such fine diction—I'll wager he's a runaway brat from the household of a rich Sumerian whore. Not a real soldier, right lad? Just a spoiled temple singer gone wild."

"Take the boy, Mechem. Now."

The Bedu made a move to comply, but the captain snapped a straight-arm brace against the Bedu's chest.

"No, don't take the boy, Mechem," he countermanded. "Leave him here to see a man's work done."

Anu gestured with a hand. "This man has no issue with you. Why not deal with me and let him alone."

"Yes, why not?" The captain swaggered as the mirthless grin on his face slid into a sneer. "I'll tell you why. Because I decide who I leave alone. You apparently need a lesson in the use of power. Calum-Dug!"

An archer stepped forward and halted beside his master. The captain pointed at Mechem.

"Bind him!"

Pana dropped the hand of his erstwhile hero and piped an objection. "But the Bedu helped Tezu-Mah! You've no reason to harm him."

"Oh-ho, little Pana, I shall harm him and more! Run back to Kudu now, before you get hurt."

"Why should I be hurt?"

"Run, monkey meat!"

A cold voice spoke from behind Anu. "Give the boy to me."

Borok scowled at the intruder, then beamed. "Why, Mechem, you had a woman in there all along. And a fine-looking one."

Mechem jumped to his wife's side and placed an arm around her shoulders. In a placating voice he clung steadfastly to the role of unoffended host.

"You've not tasted my wife's cooking yet. Perhaps if you'd care—"

Borok smashed a fist into the Bedu's face with a hard blow that sent the smaller man to the ground with blood spurting from his nose and a bright purple bruise on his cheek. Mechem stared up at the sky and tried to focus on Lasheen, who crouched at his side and moaned.

Anu lunged at the offender but the archer moved in quickly and sent a fist crashing into his head. Stunned but still on his feet, Anu instinctively staggered into his attacker instead of away, and jerked the man from his feet with a single thrust of his lance arm. His fingers found the throat and squeezed. The man's hand made a feeble attempt to bat away the deadly grip as the face at the end of his arm turned red, then purple. He heard a shout and a bellow and he was struck from behind by something heavy. The ground came up at him and he felt a sharp pain in his ribs.

The captain barked orders to his men. "Get a thong on the hunter, now!" He spied the litter lying in the shade of the tent awning. "Truss him to that frame and do it well. You over there, I want two of you on him so he can't break loose!"

Anu felt a taut cord bite into his wrist. Before he could warn her to silence, Lasheen turned from her husband and screamed at the captain.

"Coward! Do your own work if you've the strength for it!"

The soldier turned on her.

"I've strength enough for you, my lovely."

Mechem struggled to his feet and a knife appeared in his hand. Lasheen shouted at him to stop.

"Mechem, in Inallah's name, no!"

Faster than anyone could think, the tip swiped across the captain's chest and put a line across the armor. A thin weal of blood oozed from the gap of skin exposed between the two leather plates. The captain looked down at the Bedu with disgust, pulled the sword from his belt sling, and without word or warning plunged the blade clean through Mechem's chest.

Lasheen screamed and threw herself at the man, clawing his face and driving a knee against his groin plate. The captain grunted and swung a wild blow that missed, then his hands found Lasheen's wrists and held her at bay.

Anu bucked and two archers landed in the dust. He got one foot free and clouted his nearest abductor in the head with it, then arched up from the ground, litter and all, and slammed his head into one man's face. Several bodies pounced and he went down beneath the weight of four men. Pinned to the ground, he watched the Uruk captain pick up Lasheen and carry her screaming and kicking into the tent.

He bellowed his outrage to no effect. The hide thongs only tightened the more he strained. Suddenly the screaming from the tent went silent and Anu stiffened. The only sound in the camp was the archers huffing to catch their breath. Then from the tent came a soft, rhythmic squeak, as of leather scraping across flesh.

Pana staggered tearfully around one corner of the tent and stood with his mouth agape at the horrid debacle.

I didn't know, he mouthed silently as his eyes fervently sought forgiveness from his beloved hero.

The knife, child! Anu raised his chin and closed his eyes to sign the weapon, but the boy was too young to understand the gesture, and he staggered out of sight behind the tent.

Presently the captain emerged, wiping his nose on his forearm. His cheeks were ravaged by deep marks: Lasheen had exacted her small price for what the monster had taken, but his attention had shifted back to the hunter.

"Carry him inside and put him next to the woman," he told his men. Then to Anu: "You'll watch her suffer again before we kill you, lion-hunter. You're about to see how the mighty take what they will."

He followed the litter into the tent and waited while his men secured the litter frame to a support pole. Then he sent them outside and crouched beside his victim with a triumphant grin.

"Look at me well, " he said in a voice quiet with menace. "I am the new Sumer. Look at me and behold power that controls. Look into my eyes and see death for the pot-bellied heathen who eat swamp offal. See the end of their pride. We take the boy's people from Kudu to the temple at Ur this very day. They're going to build a new one, E-kish-nu-gal, make her the greatest worship center of all. Look at my hands, Sumerian, and see power that scourges the land you hold so dear. My loins will issue sons to rule instead of the temple hags. Kings will stand at the altar, men who know how to put the land to proper use, how to build great cities, how to conquer backsliders with the might of their great armies."

"And who know how to violate a woman. That is unmanly, and yet you boast of conquest. Great Mother will turn you over to demons for your infamy."

The man prodded Anu's chest with a finger. "Save your concern for yourself, hunter. Your day is done, as surely as we take your life within the hour."

There it was, right before him! The man took the very light of day from the world. When he looked at you, your heart went cold.

He was one of the godless, neither human nor demon, but half of each with an extra ugliness added: death-worship. You heard the stories and listened to warnings from the time you were little, yet you always wondered if such people truly existed, because everyone you knew lived for Inanna and strove to preserve the precious gift of life every way they knew how. Nothing could touch a man who was so far removed from his gods that he would embrace death with abandon. Only implacable logic could steer a course through that wasteland of cold, unforgiving edict.

"You work for the priest at Uruk," he told the godless one. "I saw you once in the street with him."

"He would be here to kill you himself if he could. Doesn't matter, I'm paid to do the job for him."

Keep him talking. There was more to learn from the man than his boast that he could kill well.

"Your ways are nothing new. You think by force you can control Sumer? An age-old folly. Kill me and a thousand take my place. Sumer puts her traitors to the torch. Nords were the last victims."

"This time we shall win."

"We'll see."

"No, not you, because you won't live long enough. A pity you have to miss the pain about to pounce like a lion on these soft-hearted people."

"The Bull Priest, is that it? You hope to take Sumer at his command? He hasn't the heart for it, no understanding of human life. You're doomed."

"We're blessed, you fool! It's serpent vision that leads us! I've seen it myself! I know! That's why the second son went out from Eanna to Nippur, to finish the work of serpent sight." The black eyes gleamed as the soldier's remark registered with Anu. "Oh yes, you understand my meaning well. With the sacred coupling comes ultimate power, the sanction of the gods themselves! With a prophet in his pocket, the Bull can take Sumer by the sword with help from the almighty war god. We'll take lands from here clear north to the Akkad, and nothing will stand in our way."

"Then why am I so important? I'm just a lion-hunter. I haven't seen the inside of a city for a year. No one knows me, I won't be missed if I stay out here."

"Aha, you would be missed indeed. Oh yes, people everywhere clamor, 'Tezu-Mah, Tezu-Mah.' That's you, isn't it! All this outcry for their beloved hunter sucks their will to work, makes them cling to the old way of dreaming but not doing. With you out of the way, my master will put their backs to better use."

"The Bull Priest isn't the first to try it, but he may be the last. The Hani have a great heart, but they're also Inanna's favored."

Borok spat on the ground. "I was right, you're nothing but another breeding boy! Temple women filled your mind with that rot, didn't they! Goat dung, all of it! Endless peace! An empty promise to keep a man shackled to his plow and sucking tit so he can live in a woman's house. You're less of a man for going along with them. If it were my choice you'd watch Nippur's streets run with blood while my whip scourges Lukur backs!"

"Then spare me now, to suffer later."

"Don't take me for a fool. No, you must be removed, like all the other tools of the old way."

The Nafti straightened and gave his girth a hitch as he addressed one of the men standing outside the open tent flap.

"Prepare a fire. This man's wound will open soon and have need of cleansing. The lance head that took the lion ought to be about right for the job."

Borok whisked out of the tent and left Anu lying on his back, still strapped to the litter and looking up at the bright stripes of Mechem's tent glowing overhead.

Poor Mechem! And Lasheen! Was she still alive? More the pity if she was.

Almost in answer to his thoughts, Lasheen whispered across the tent to him.

"Is he gone?"

"Yes. Inanna in Heaven, are you badly hurt, Lasheen?"

"I don't know, I suppose so."

"Damn, he's a fiend! I've got to get my hands on him!"

"His blood does not bring back Mechem. Oh, my husband! Why you did not listen?" She whimpered softly in the corner, a widow now with only grief for a companion.

"They'll all die for this. Somehow, I swear, every one of them will pay."

"Anu, listen, I have blade in my clothing. I cut you loose."

"Lasheen, no! If they catch you—"

"What can they do that is worse? If they kill me, I am spared whatever else they plan."

"Don't talk like that."

"Shush. This take some time."

Anu lay silent while the obsidian sliced and gnawed against the heavy rawhide thongs. Progress was slow because she had to work in short, tiny strokes to avoid making a sound. Her work was doubly hard for the stiffening of leather caused by his struggles. She had been working for what seemed hours when she suddenly stopped.

"Someone comes," she whispered.

"I think a cord just pulled loose. Quick, finish now."

He felt the bonds slacken beneath his back as a thick voice called from a few paces outside. Lasheen rolled away and huddled against the tent wall. Anu kept his freed hands crossed beneath his buttocks and waited.

A hand yanked the tent flap aside and abruptly closed it. The first archer grinned at Lasheen's supine form in the corner and gave her a kick in the ribs, then squatted beside Anu.

"Fire's hot," he said. "So's the blade. You're going to yell like—"

His last words ended in a gurgle as the obsidian blade opened a clean slice across his throat from ear to ear. The archer stared at Anu wide-eyed, the thin red line on his neck suddenly welling dark crimson. He gurgled once more and toppled over sideways. Lasheen stared down at her bloody hands and the blade fell from her fingers.

"I kill him."

"Calum-Dug!" Borok's voice from outside had a hard edge. He was impatient.

Anu's fingers flew, unraveling the thongs like a weave master. He leaped up, threw open the tent flap, and bolted outside. The nearest man spun around at the sound of racing footsteps, but he was no match for the wild thing that piled into him with the force of a charging bull and pinned him to the ground. Before the man knew what was happening, his own dagger appeared in his assailant's hand and jabbed a hole under his jaw. The hunter shoved hard, the tip entered the soldier's brain, and he was dead.

The rest were a good ten paces away. The captain screamed orders at his men, and two reached for their swords while the other pair fumbled at their quivers. Brandishing only the dagger, Anu flew at them without caution. The boy appeared at the edge of his vision, dragging the huge lion spear from the fireside. Pana flung it upward with a single flowing motion of arm and wrist, and for an instant the spear seemed to hang in the air for him, waiting to be grasped. He caught the haft without breaking stride and danced to his right.

The brutes gaped at him in wide-eyed terror, their unworthy cowardliness keeping them slow and uncertain. He trained on one of the men and his senses locked. The arm came down and the spear sang through the air straight into the man's chest. The hot tip shattered his spine and cleared his back by a foot. He fell onto one side and lay there, one leg feebly pawing the ground.

The archer on the left fitted an arrow to his string and started to bring the bow level. The hunter charged directly at him and the archer flinched and dodged away—a fatal mistake, for the hunter closed too fast for the eye to see. Before the archer could react, his arrow was snatched from its bowstring, flipped end for end, and plunged through his right eye. The archer screamed and fell to the ground, where he writhed in mortal agony.

The hunter rolled away just in time to avoid the next man's arrow, which struck the ground inches from his foot and glanced away. He bounded up and tilted toward his attacker. The man turned and bolted for the desert.

Suddenly Borok was himself in peril. Drawing his sword, he barked at the two remaining swordsmen to do likewise.

Anu darted to the archer felled by the lance, pressed his foot against the man's back, and yanked the haft clean through with a single heave and a roar of effort. Wheeling away from the ruined carcass, he pushed the gory thirty-pound weapon aloft like a child with a prize and took aim on the officer's chest.

"Charge him!" the man yelled frantically to his two minions. "He can't take all three of us!"

The other two were brave but not stupid. The hunter was obviously in command of the situation, and they braced their weapons for defense instead of attacking.

Borok's expression changed from terror to craft.

"Take me, and these two will cut you to ribbons," he boasted. "Go for either of them, and my sword will roast your heart over the fire tonight."

The two swordsmen wavered. Slack-jawed, eyes bulging with terror, they were more in fear of dying than in serving the screaming fool who dallied with the hunter demon. One lowered his sword and stood aside.

"I yield to Tezu-Mah," he said.

"No!" Borok screamed. "We can take him!"

"Yield," said the second swordsman, also dropping his sword tip.

Borok was suddenly caught in the unenviable position of standing centered between two turned henchmen and a deadly killer. The bloody tip of the lion lance pointed unwaveringly at his heart. He backed away slowly, sword tip high.

"I leave now only because I have cowards on my hands, but I'll find you again, Sumerian."

The effort to hold the lance steady forced a growl from the hunter's throat. Calling up his last reserve of animal strength, Anu exhorted the weapon to obey his will. The lance tip lifted and advanced, its message plain:

Now is not the time for idle threats.

The three remaining attackers back-pedaled until they reached the talus slope, which they rapidly ascended, taking far less heed for their footing than earlier. Only when the last head had disappeared over the rise did the lance dip slowly and touch the ground.

The hunter of lions felt nauseated and weak. He began to shake violently and the lance tumbled from his hand and fell to the ground. The leg had opened up and the wound throbbed. Blood covered both thighs, some his own and some from the slain. He slumped to his good knee, propped himself on both hands, and heaved.

"Anu! I'm coming!"

Lasheen's broken voice called to him from somewhere behind.

Then she was at his side with Pana, kneeling with him, and he felt the world turn crazily and he went over onto his back, where the bright sun flashed from behind Lasheen's head. She wept uncontrollably as strands of dark hair fell across one cheek, but she reached a hand behind his head and pulled his face into her shadow.

"Water!" she shouted to the boy. "Go fetch jar from tent. And bring litter. We must drag him back inside."

"No," Anu objected weakly. "We need the boat. Pana, where's my boat?"

"After you left I hid it in the rushes."

"Get it back."

"Anu! He only is boy."

"Not anymore. Pana fed me the lance and it ran true because he had courage. Put himself at risk. Now he's a man."

He turned his head to face Pana and shook off a wave of nausea.

"You told me once you wanted to do a man's work. I sent you away. Today I give you a new chance."

Lasheen bent closer. "Anu, this crazy!"

"Lasheen, those men will come back tonight. They know I can't last. The boat's our only chance."

"I can't leave *him*!"

Mechem. She wanted to bury her poor husband.

"We'll put him to rest here, beneath the stars," he promised her. "He'll be watched over by the eyes of the gods. Save yourself, Lasheen. He fought the attacker for your life."

Lasheen got up and looked back at the tent. At the sight of her dead husband stretched out on the ground under the tent wing, her face crumpled in a spasm of grief. She pressed the sides of her nose with her fingers and drew her palms hard across her cheeks, willing her features into a mask of composure.

"First, Pana, get water," she said. "Go!"

The boy sprinted away and Lasheen spoke to the tent in the distance, gathering her strength in small amounts as she listened the sound of her own voice.

"All right, Anu, we fight. We get away and go to river, and we find boy's people where you are safe for a time. But first we bury...our dead. And I want look at your leg, great warrior. You dash around on it like you are deer. You attract carrion if it go bad, do you hear? You do not listen to a word I say. Men never—"

She looked down. The lion slayer was sprawled on his back in the hot sun, his eyes closed, his mouth slack, sleeping the dreamless sleep of the exhausted.

"Men never do," she sobbed.

CHAPTER FIFTEEN
Nord Priestess

Temple business ran according to tradition. There was no written record, since no one foresaw the need to scratch marks in clay for purposes beyond trade accounts and stock inventories. Therefore it fell to the empowered to perpetuate tradition through verse and song. And thus did Uruna dredge up from her prodigious memory the obscure precedent that inducted Retha into temple service upon the close of her sixteenth year.

Convened without notice to join hands in holy communion before Ekur's sacred altar, the three senior ladies were unprepared when Uruna presented the Nord acolyte for induction.

Niccaba frowned.

Kinar smirked.

Ku-Aya gaped open-mouthed.

"Shall we begin?" Uruna said with all the aplomb of her office. "Niccaba, the invocation, if you please."

Niccaba stammered an objection. "Un-unheard of."

Uruna rejoined with stern disapproval. "May I remind you, madam, of the invocation for Deliah, begat of Shu-gula, begat of Imbelulu, begat of Lamesi before Tara Seddua unto the third generation of your own line. Deliah was fourteen years and ten months and she served Kish well for one and forty floods. Selah."

"I, er, do seem to recall…"

"The invocation, then?"

Niccaba bowed her head as Uruna squeezed Retha's hand and got a heartfelt squeeze back.

Kinar joined in the celebration with unquestioning joy and no little humor. Ku-Aya stumbled through her benediction, then finished with a little flair.

"May the Nord gods Adin and Toth rejoice in our new daughter."

When the ox-blood sipping ceremony was done, the five of them made Inanna's hand star, touching heads at the center, then sang the Alla Manna and paraded onto the platform above the city, where Retha stepped to the forefront and chanted Morning Call.

The girl was radiant, and on seeing her joy, Uruna's heart leapt to her throat, for she saw in the Nord girl a fleeting memory of her own great moment in what seemed ages past. She peered over the platform's edge for a glimpse of the proud couple on the street below, now witnesses also to their daughter's remarkable achievement.

In the changing room afterward, Uruna grinned as Retha spun on her toes in a little dance of ecstasy.

"No more pots for you, dear," she said. "Now the real drudgery begins."

Retha stopped spinning but the broad smile would not leave her lips. "I know, and I welcome it."

"Good, because I have your first task already in mind."

"Oh, really?"

"As you know, I am to meet the Ensi for the first time. Each of us requires a chaperone. If you will do me the honor, we'll meet this Marduk fellow and his temple escort."

"But Uruna, I'm only sixteen."

"Yes, isn't it wonderful! See that you remember everything said, by whom and to whom. I want you to wear your politician's hat. Other ears may hear differently and I'll need a reliable witness. Are we clear, madam?"

Retha smiled at the honorific, then sobered. "Quite, madam."

"Good, now run down to your parents and share your joy. Oh, and ask your father to tell you about the monkey at Burum quay. Then share it with no one else."

Retha gave her queen a puzzled look, then remembered she was dealing with the royal iconoclast and dashed away, giving vent to a girlish enthusiasm that would soon vanish beneath the ponderous weight of duty.

𒈨 𒂡 𒆜 𒌋𒌋

The sneak thief from Uruk watched the Nord girl embrace her parents in the street across from his position. Thus assured of her identity, he retreated into the cleft between two buildings and made for deeper shade. Just before the alley opened onto the back street, he turned abruptly into the house of a pottery vendor. The potter was not at home, but the thief continued down a hallway to a back room where his employer lurked in shadow.

"It's done," he reported. "Girl took her vows."

"What about the queen? Was she there?"

"Got only a glimpse of her up top 'fore she went back inside."

His employer slipped a silver piece into the rogue's hand. "Well done. Now get yourself back to the alley and make haste to the river before the barge leaves. I don't want you anywhere near this town for a while."

"Wasn't nobody supposed to know she was getting made priestess today, that it? How'd you find out about it?"

"That's none of your concern."

"Them Nords. Whatcha fixin' to do, kill 'em?"

Nabi Gahn brandished a sharpened metal rod that gleamed in the scant light from a shuttered window. "Shut your mouth, fool, before I sew it tight as a penny purse. Now begone!"

Nabi watched the frightened thief take to the street, then waited a hundred count before he climbed to the rooftop door. He'd arranged a beer party at a park across town and made sure the potter was invited. None would know he'd used the premises.

Several houses away he dropped down to another alley and took it to a crowded street. He loved crowds and hated them for the same reason: tight quarters afforded an easy disappearance but limited escape options. Right now, he just needed to disappear.

He found his own swifthull waiting for him, manned and ready. He'd be halfway to Adab before the informant left the quay, no connection to him.

He had the information he'd been sent for, but no idea why the installation of a sixteen-year-old girl in Nippur carried more importance than a hired murder. In all his years of plotting and deceiving and deadly deeds, he'd never once envied the prowess of another, never met one more deviously clever than himself. But the machinations this man could dream up and keep straight in his head were beyond Nabi's admiration.

They terrified him.

CHAPTER SIXTEEN
Naked Crescent

On a muddy stretch of beach below Adab, shapes of fire dancers shimmered above a flaming pit as a migrant Bedu band paid homage to a fallen Hani. Lasheen's tribe had found Jabali's body floating in the river and laid him to rest on a shore far from his home. Pana and the hunter Tezu-Mah kept their distance as Lasheen joined the throng.

Anu felt the fire in his leg and bit down hard on the hazel nut in his cheek. Lasheen had given him the tough shell when she tired of hearing him pepper the air with grunts and groans the day long and most of the night. Her hero's image had become tarnished as the harsh reality of forced cohabitation revealed him as simply human after all.

A dancer lurched by and peered at Anu from eyes stupefied with drink, one of those who took strong libation in an attempt to forget lion-fear and one's temporary loss of manly pride. The clan around the fire were not Jabali's besieged Hani, but a ragged bunch of Bedu refugees Pana had stumbled across in his haste to lead Anu and a catatonic Lasheen away from the desert killing ground. As Anu looked about at faces in the firelight, he saw none to whom he had pledged his life, save for Pana. He had struck an uneasy truce with the boy after his raging slaughter of the Gunzeks nearly scared the boy off.

He watched the mourners without feeling. With Mechem Zaheer only two days in the grave, he was unable to dismiss from memory the brave little Bedu who had been his brother and protector for a full month. Twice had Mechem saved his life, and he had not returned the honor. Worse, his own messy reprisal had redeemed none of the man's virtues, but instead compounded his widow's terror and jolted the stricken Hani boy with yet another example of man's inhumanity to man.

To be sure, Lasheen refused to hear his recriminations, recalling the magnitude of the threat.

"I too take a life, if you remember," she said when he lamented his butchery of the soldiers. "They force us on killing path. You take lives to save me from torture, and if you do not, we are all lying dead back there in the desert."

A haunted expression had suddenly shaken her composure, and for a brief instant Anu had feared for her soul. He hoped she was better now, although he hadn't seen Lasheen since he and Pana had placed her in the care of the camp women.

He stirred and got to his feet with effort. Pana was instantly at his side.

"I cannot find Lasheen," he said.

"She's not in the tent where we left her?"

Pana shook his head, his eyes luminous and grave in the orange light. "The woman there said she just got up and went out."

"How long ago?"

A shrug. "About when the dancers started, she said."

He felt a nervous twitch of apprehension and tasted bitter gall.

"Where did you look?" he asked.

"I asked at every tent."

"Did you look inside?"

"They all said she was not there!" Pana twisted his fingers in mounting despair.

Anu placed a reassuring hand on the boy's shoulder. "You've done well, Pana, don't worry. Come with me, we'll find her."

Word of the search quickly reached the headman, and he personally threw open every tent to inspection.

They learned she was in an outlying tent where she had found Mechem Zahir's family. A black-headed man with fierce eyes stepped outside to talk to Anu in the dark.

"I am Bakhar," he said. "Mechem was my brother."

He went on to explain Bedu tradition, wherein the brother of a fallen man was obliged to care for the dead man's wife. Bakhar would take Lasheen into his household, and after a proper interval of mourning, would marry her so that she would not be left to wander Sumerian streets in poverty.

Had she told Bakhar of the Gunzek dishonor? It was not Anu's place to reveal an incident that might ruin her welfare. Instead he spoke only of Lasheen's honorable rescue after saving his leg.

Bakhar then clasped Anu's hand with both of his own. "Inallah with you for avenging my brother," he said, and then he lifted his arm for the object in his grasp to catch the distant firelight.

The ivory hook made a bright crescent shape in the flickering light: Death Maker's claw.

"She cannot keep a gift from a man who is not her husband. She weeps when she asks me to return this lion claw to you. She says it is for the woman you love. It is also to remember who you are."

Anu reached for the claw and rubbed its smooth polish between thumb and forefinger. "Tell her I love her as I love my own sisters."

He then thanked the Bedu man and took his leave.

Pana led the way back to their camp.

"Will you keep it?" the boy asked.

"Yes, as a tribute to a good woman."

"I shall miss her."

"I, too. We only knew her a short time but we both love her."

Next morning, the people gave Jabali a Bedu burial and then left the two of them alone with him. Pana helped him fashion a small shrine of mud brick, and then they each made a pledge of faith to the courageous Hani chief. They loaded the boat and took quick leave of that dreary spot, following the estuary up to the main channel and spending the rest of the day in slow progress up the near shoreline, with Pana on the pole and Anu seated in the stern.

He couldn't answer the boy's questions about where they were headed or what they should do. He was spent, the world around him as devoid of meaning as the events that had brought him to such misery. The river offered no help; each bend looked the same as others before it.

No heron for you today, hunter, the empty sky told him. See what a ruin you make without godly counsel to clear your path. Learn how lost a man can be without his heart.

They paddled upstream on the Shat-al-Hai, heedless of the sun's passage overhead. Whenever Anu tired, they would put in at one of the meander's eddies. Pana would lean against the pole with listless indifference, satisfied to watch pools for fish while he waited for the hunter's strength to return.

On their first night afloat, Anu slipped into an introspective mood to wrestle the demons of self-contempt. With the last passing of the spear from his hand, the god had left him and fled to Eternity. He wallowed in despondency, as listless as the fattened carp suspended in the boat's shadow, unable to summon the will for one more go at the river. Adrift between realms, he languished, half-asleep beneath the canopy of stars.

So it was with astonishment that he awakened in the middle of the night from a disturbing dream in which he had stood to his hips in swamp mire, utterly unable to move as the soft silt dragged him deeper. A woman had stood on shore watching him, waiting for him to leave the mud, but he was stuck fast and sinking. At length she had turned her back and walked away, leaving him alone in the muck. He called out, or thought he did, but she kept walking, and he was overcome with a deep despair as the night and the mud and a sense of doom closed round him, until all was darkness.

Now fully awake, he saw the dream's meaning with astonishing clarity. He was stuck in the past, while the world with its woman of promise moved on. It was time he changed and took charge of his life. If he clung much longer to the old, the new would move beyond his grasp without another look back.

He got to his feet, intending to call for Pana to pack up, they had a journey to begin. But instead, his head went into a spin, and he looked up and saw the stars reeling crazily overhead. His head struck the ground hard, and he felt a jarring impact, but no pain. For several moments he lay on his back, watching patches of stars wink out. And then he saw and felt nothing more.

CHAPTER SEVENTEEN

Courted By A Ghost

Anu's next opportunity for discourse with a woman was shrouded in mystery, and took place under circumstances he would not have imagined possible.

He came to his senses standing upright, both journey and destination lost in oblivion. His hands propped his weight on a crumbled railing overlooking a ruined courtyard. To loosen the stiff muscles of his lower back, he eased forward slightly. Strange, he felt not the slightest pain in his leg.

Perhaps he had died after all, and this was the afterlife of legend.

"Get thee here, hunter."

The hoarse, croaking sound came from behind him, a warble that cracked with age but rang with firm tone and authority. Anu spun around and peered closer, prepared to fend off a demon attack.

Instead, an old woman stood at one end of the courtyard, braced in the shadow of a clay brick arch. Her clothes were the drab gray of parched soil, a blend of bleached wool and dried membrane tied at the top with a dusty brown mane. Her shape mingled with the ragged outlines of broken brick. She might be real or an apparition, but she resembled no demon effigy known to him. His heart leaped with hope.

"Who are you?" he inquired in a voice softened with awestruck wonder.

With surprising agility the old woman stepped away from the arch and skipped down a low flight of broken stairs into the sunlight.

"We are one and we are many," she replied as she approached him. "We are Great Serpent Lady of the Desert, Mother of Wisdom, Keeper of the Songs. In other times we are Entu of the Akkad and Heavenly Mother of Edin-On-Tigris, the Blessed Serpent Princess to whom wisdom comes through the eye of the viper. We are the fabled mystic of old and last in our line to possess the ancient secret of prophecy. We are Rahnee of Edin."

Impossible! The great Rahnee of legend and folklore? He caught his breath and tightened his grip on the rail to keep from toppling. How could it be? Edin had been reduced to rubble before his grandmother's day.

His hunter's eye swept his surroundings. Were these ruins a remnant of fabled Edin? The windswept temple concourse before him was empty except for a fractured fountain set in the center. Beyond the fountain, a broad staircase littered with debris ascended to what had been the temple proper but was now a shell scoured by wind and winter rain. Clumps of dead cassis weed poked through the broken surface of foot-worn paving stones, the stalks beaten flat by blowing sand, dark tendrils shriveled by drought. The roof was gone and the beams had fallen in. Sand-filled corners of two rooms showed dung left by wild animals.

The ruined sanctuary resembled the abandoned residue of battle, not the living quarters of a renowned priestess. Blank walls stared back at him. The platform where once Inanna's statue might have received abundant garlands now sat empty. Everything was gone, the effigies, the candles, the tapestries. Edin had been stripped of her religion as well as her past. Yet Rahnee, abandoned by the river and her people, had stayed on, sustained, according to some, by her own magic and the grace of Inanna. She must be a hundred years old, if indeed she was a living soul.

As if to remove all doubt, she approached him, her spine straight, her keen eyes undiminished by age as she took his measure. She was magnificent in spite of her destitution. Her bearing transformed her tattered smock of coarse wool into the robes of a royal princess. A length of cotton cord bound her slender waist, and in her left hand she wielded a shepherd's staff with the sturdy grip of a Hani oarsman.

But the face stopped his heart. As Rahnee narrowed the space between them, Anu caught a remnant blush of the captivating beauty that once had obsessed all Sumer. Now wizened and leathery from the sun, her features were nonetheless charged with serene confidence.

He heard a crack like a bull whip, and in a trice the sordid surroundings fell away, and he was caught in the spell of that fabulous countenance. For an elusive moment he glimpsed magical depths of beauty past, a perfection of form transcending human loveliness, reaching for him, tasting of him, mingling his essence with divine elixirs of which mortal men only dreamed.

The haughty arch of brow traced a skeptic's mask begotten by loves and betrayals beyond counting. Emerald eyes gazed longingly, lovingly, beguilingly from heavy lids lowered in sultry appraisal. His will fell before a siren who could lure any object of her affection into unquestioning obedience, adoration, worship.

All this passed in the blink of an eye, and then his vision blurred, and he was back amid Edin's ruins, facing the venerable temple queen, amazed that she was unchanged from moments before.

She stood before him as full of life and power as any tale told. Soft hair as full as a Nubian queen's and as dark hung past her shoulders. Nimble hands floated gracefully from her sleeves, the skin remarkably supple in spite of time's ravages. Her eyes gleamed with pleasure at his wonder and twinkled to each discovery. Transfixed, he stood mute before the woman of mystery and waited for her to speak.

"Come to me, hunter. These old eyes would see thee closer."

Old eyes indeed! Rahnee had not lost her charm. She spoke to him in the old tongue according to the temple custom of her day, when a woman pledged her life to preserve sacred tradition. Her people were gone and her temple dissolved to dust, but her legendary exploits still captivated any Lukur who aspired to her perfection of heart and her wisdom in the ways of Inanna.

She stepped closer and looked the hunter up and down with keen scrutiny.

"Thou art most fair of face," she said, running an appraising hand over his bare chest and arm, "and becoming of limb, son of Heganna. Do come inside. The day grows hot."

How did she know his mother's name? Had he babbled it in his delirium? Or did she possess a power so great that such knowledge came without effort?

Just beyond the arch she led him into a chamber lighted by a slot cut high in the outer wall. Dust covered the floor. A stone dais and a row of pots lined the base of the left wall. In the center stood an altar of white stone. Rahnee stopped before the cube and stood for a moment as if waiting for some event to pass. It was said among men that the high priestess took her consort upon such a throne, but none of his acquaintances could speak from experience. Was this the fate Rahnee had in mind for him?

Before he could imagine the horror of such a notion, she spun around and fixed him with a gaze both fierce and compelling.

"You are a rogue as deadly as any you slew, Tezu-Mah," she declared.

He took a step backward and collided with the wall. She barely took note of his reaction as she stalked him like a lioness.

"At heart a rebel, you are every woman's worst nightmare, a man who thinks for himself, whose soul is his own, whose life is beyond her reach. For that, no temple can forgive you, no woman can but love you."

His breath grew still. Every word was an arrow striking his heart, affirming a truth he had not known until that moment. Ancient wisdom sprang from eyes that devoured him, as the woman of mystery went on.

"You are the agent of change in a world gone stale. Your fate will be more painful than the wound you carry. But though you live a thousand lives and die a thousand deaths, yet will you stay the course before you, for you are an implacable force. And so we set you free to establish a new order. For this time and times to come, you are the sire from which all being proceeds. You are the blade we thrust into the heart of man."

Rahnee lifted a brow at his look of astonishment and cocked her head. She was waiting.

Anu was stunned. "As usual, my fate is given to me by a woman."

"Perhaps for the last time, to your utter pleasure, I'm sure."

"No, I would not pass through life without sharing a woman's counsel—or at least her opinion."

"How generous! But that is your first task if you are to meet your fate before death overtakes you and condemns us all to another generation of human stagnation. Tell me, do you expect to find such a woman abiding in the swamps with the wild animals you hunt?"

"No, of course not."

"Then where?"

"The city, a woman of broad experience. A leader of some sort, but not temple-born."

"Udea of Temple Eanna fits your criteria so far. She's clever, ambitious, likes strong-willed men. Pity she's chosen one of shallow character."

"Enguda isn't called the Bull Priest for being weak."

"To be sure, but his strength is confined to his brawn and a penchant for cruelty. I spoke of character, Anu. Do not be obtuse. But back to this woman of wisdom whom you would not find wallowing in swamp mire. Who might she be?"

"I-I can't imagine."

"Oh come now, she's waiting for you, she's a woman of power, perhaps a bit too bright for her position. Must I introduce you myself?"

"I'm a hunter. I'll find her."

"Please do so before she sacrifices a husband to her obsession with snakes."

"Oh my god, not the serpent fanatic!"

"Why not? She's perfect."

"Yes, perfectly crazy. You tell me to seek an intelligent woman of power. I'll grant you there's none higher than the Entu of Ekur, but Uruna's been trying that snake-charming trick since she was ten."

"Twelve, actually, she didn't have her flow until then."

"That's beside the point."

"What she does is not a trick, it's a very arduous spiritual process fraught with danger. Anyway, it's not every male who can face four cobras while coupling with the most alluring woman in Nippur, and keep his seed."

"And rightly so, lest he be found as dotty as she."

"My, my, how we have misjudged our Anu. I fear we shall have to endure your slumber until the next lifetime. Pity the poor Lukur, murdered in their beds. Pity poor Sumer, reduced to smoke and ruin while the Bull plays god. And pity poor Anu, condemned to watch it all unfold because he missed his turn with fate."

"You are an exasperating, conniving woman, just like all the rest."

"Thank you."

"I will not be badgered into committing a fool's errand."

"I quite agree. You should find your own reason to unite with her."

"I doubt she'd have me, anyway. As you pointed out, I'm a renegade. I left my family to prowl the swamps, rejected my father's good intentions, risked my life for a few thrills. They'll laugh me to scorn."

"But didn't you know? You are venerated in Nippur. Your mother defends your name proudly at temple. And your father tells his friends stories of your prowess with lance and arrow."

"I'm not a very good archer. And I probably just threw my last lance."

"Anu, do you hear anything I'm saying?"

"All right, I'll go!"

The wrinkled face broke into a radiant smile, and Anu's irascibility vanished. "You're a blessing, did you know?" he told the venerable queen.

She nodded. "Yes, I've been told that before."

"Well, I'm not known for my originality."

The smile widened. "Give it time, hunter, give it time."

As he gathered himself to leave, she stopped him with a touch on his arm. "One promise, Anu, just one."

"Name it."

"Be kind to the hearts you break, and cherish those you keep."

"That's two," he chided, brushing her cheek with a kiss.

"Not so, hunter of hearts," she said. "With love they're one and the same."

She reached up to his face with a gentle caress. "Close your eyes."

𒀭 𒈾 𒆠 𒌋𒁹

Morning sun and shadow rippled over his face, and he jerked awake. He was back on the river, with Pana at the pole, the boat's prow pointed into the current.

"Why are we headed upstream?" he asked.

Pana's brow wrinkled in a frown. "You told me to, after the lady left."

"Which lady?"

"The one who brought you out of the desert at dawn."

"I don't remember."

"She said you wouldn't."

Another of Rahnee's illusions?

He sat up. "I'll take the pole today, Pana."

"Your leg hasn't mended yet. Lasheen's not around anymore to fix it."

"Then you be nursemaid as well as navigator. I'm poling."

"It's your boat. Just don't do anything foolish and die on me. I'm tired of burying friends."

Anu smiled at the plucky jibe. The boy was thinking like a man and spoke his mind with a man's forthright assurance. Perhaps they were both on the mend.

The pole felt light in his hands as he pushed the tall prow north. The surge of current swept round the slender hull, bearing a promise of sustained resistance all the way to Nippur. He dug hard into the stream and turned for home.

THE TEMPLE

CHAPTER EIGHTEEN
Audience With Marduk

Galla constables were the only semblance of military organization available as Nippur's defense. Upon her elevation to office as Entu at age eighteen, Uruna had taken one look at their disordered ranks and tarnished reputation for debauchery and had charged their leader with a wholesale overhaul of discipline and combat readiness. The grateful response had shocked everyone, as well as the speed of *galla* improvement.

To a man, the regiment's respect for their queen was an overwhelming outpouring of loyalty. Their devotion to Uruna stopped just short of worship. Broken spirits mended, they vaulted into new roles of self-respect and dignity, discharging their duties with the calm assurance that they embodied the Sumerian mandate for masculine power with restraint. Forced to deal with humanity's lowest, they kept their own spirits high and enforced Sumerian law with righteous enthusiasm when necessary. In the first year of her reign, Uruna saw public respect for *galla* emerge and take hold. Today's force was the pride of Sumerian manhood.

In service to their queen tonight, the First Squadron of Nippur was put to the test the moment the Ensi from Aramdan arrived for his audience towing a squadron of his own, Gunzeks carrying armament in flagrant violation of city law, their smug grins confirming an immunity arranged by temple accord.

Sensing a brooding hostility between the two forces, Uruna vetoed Niccaba's arrangement for the shadowy arbor's confines by ordering both enclaves to convene on the open Aniginna concourse.

Under the full light of a dozen torches.

Before Inanna's enthroned statue.

With Uruna's temple party seated atop the fountain wall, four stair steps above concourse level, forcing the Ensi and his all-male party to crane their necks in order to address the ladies.

Niccaba started off with an attempt at a grand presentation.

"On this momentous—"

Uruna cut her off in mid-sentence.

"Come forward, sir," she said to the man who would be her husband.

Niccaba backed away as Marduk took a step and stopped. A robed male at his side started to follow.

"No, not you," Uruna said to the false priest. "I mean this fellow here. Marduk is your name?"

"I am he, madam."

"Strange name. I don't believe I've heard it before."

"After a faithful attendant at my birth."

Marduk had his father's tall frame but the more muted features of another in his line. His hair was shorn to the ear and his clean-shaven jaw bespoke a strong character. The man's brown-eyed gaze met Uruna's with forthright candor. He was older than she'd expected. She sensed he perceived his age to be a disadvantage, so she probed across the space between them, felt the man's trepidation, absorbed the answer: One and thirty years.

A considerable age for any suitor. Possibly the product of a youthful dalliance on Enguda's part. She saw no sign of the father's harsh manner in the son.

"Tonight we forgive your ignorance of temple protocol. You come to us a stranger—a most unusual wedding arrangement."

"Madam, I am here at the request of the Uzba."

"Uzba does not rule here. You should know that after three days in our midst. Surely you were instructed in temple protocol?"

"Perhaps. I don't know for sure. Have I committed some obscure offense?"

"Obviously you were not. A serious lapse on our part, for which I apologize. Appropriate disciplinary action will be taken. You see, an audience is just that and no more. A chance for you, the suitor, to be seen by me and your betters, the ladies who live in Great Mother's care. Prior to any marriage arrangement, not after. Tell me, sir, in whose care does Aramdan abide?"

"I beg your pardon?"

"Aramdan, where you live. Or used to live, I'm told."

"It's just a city, like yours."

"Nippur has no equal. We are the lap of Inanna, the home of Inanna. We do all things for Inanna, whom we worship and adore. Which god do you worship?"

"This is most irregular. I was not told…"

"Perhaps you bring us Shumu-gan, host of all hunters. Or is it your father's? What is it—Guda Abzu? After a dray animal? I'd never heard of it before he put those ridiculous horns on his head. So, pray tell us whom you worship."

"It is a private matter."

"I fully understand. Do you pray to your private god as you approach the Agabzu Mina."

"Aga-what?"

"First Door. First Door to Serpenthood, in the prophet's rite—oh, nevermind. You don't know anything I'm talking about, do you?"

"I'm afraid not. Nor would you know anything I might say about the home of my clan."

"Tell us, then."

"It's a small city far to the north."

"Snows a lot up there, I'm told."

"Eight months of the year. We do not have such elaborate

accommodation as yours, so I'm not surprised you take me for a country lout."

"I do nothing of the sort, sir, you speak well. Say more about your home." She lapsed into Old Ki-engi. "*For such purpose did we grant thee audience.*"

"Eh?"

Gods! He didn't know that either.

"I'm sorry. Go ahead about your homeland."

Marduk shrugged and spread his arms in a gesture of futility.

"There's not much more to tell. We spend months at a time indoors shivering by the hearth, wrapped in animal skins. We share the lodge house with dogs and goats, lest they be lost to wolves. I like it here much better."

"The cobra cannot live in snow and ice. Where did you learn to charm the ringed one?"

Marduk brightened and seemed to come alive for the first time.

"I was seventeen when I ran from home—Uruk at the time. Spent three years in Meluhha with a serpent adept named Vu Sant. We worked with simple asps at first, then the cobra, and then a black one I loved especially. Not a cobra, but he would seek me out often for affection…but I ramble. My master said true knowledge would come from my inner soul, not the snake. He died before I could learn the secrets you possess."

So, a softer side to the Bull's male bloodline. Too soft for Enguda? A gentle character unsuited to his rigid schemes? But suited for some faraway keep where none might witness such dreadful weakness?

"Hear me, Marduk. I possess only such knowledge as Enshiggu bestows. None of it is to be kept from the world, for all is freely given. I am truly sorry you lost your master. One never stops grieving for the great ones."

"So true—but how did you know?"

Instead of answering, Uruna turned to Niccaba with a disapproving look that told her, You could have done this. You could have brought out this man's need, his quest that was cut short, his loss that disqualifies him. But you left it for me to do.

"We are not ready," she declared aloud, and stood up so that she looked down on the assembled gathering. "Thank you all for coming. You may go home now."

The small crowd turned and ambled off into the evening by twos and threes. Her own Lukur left, followed by Uruk's gowned neo-priests—even the Gunzeks, baffled by the proceedings, their spoiler role thwarted—until only Marduk remained. Retha stood locked at Uruna's side, unable to take her eyes from the man. Was it a girl's infatuation or a woman's keen inspection that held her in place? She had told Retha to pay close attention to every word.

In answer to Marduk's puzzled frown, Uruna smiled for the first time. "You were brave to come," she told him. "You're doing your father's bidding, but I sense a deeper purpose."

Marduk's shoulders drooped and he lowered his eyes.

"I'm no longer a young man, as any can see, but I've so much to learn. He has no idea what it's like. He can't see what others see, or feel what they feel. I'm not sure he feels anything."

"You've more to offer the world than you realize, Marduk. Give yourself a chance. We all must walk the path we're given, not knowing where it leads."

"Then I must warn you."

"About what?"

"About the path you've taken, the path of a prophet. I met such a man in my travels, a seer. He would stare long and hard into the firelight, until he became lost in it. He told me his gift was a curse, for he couldn't share what he saw. No one wanted to hear their death spoken. Eventually he could only foretell doom, and watch it befall others. Soon after he told me this, I learned he'd killed himself."

Uruna felt her pulse quicken and realized she had descended from the fountain to Marduk's side without an awareness of it.

"How sad. Who was this man?"

"The same who taught me the serpent song. Vu Sant."

CHAPTER NINETEEN
Advice For A Queen

The morning after her audience with the Ensi, Uruna was more confused than ever. Apparently, minds were made up. The Lukur were clearly steeped in fear. Niccaba's dogged insistence on Ensi Marduk was proof that they were afraid to continue the search, to test rigorously any suitor, to prolong the interval without prophecy. Heaven might wait an eternity, but the Lukur could not. The Bull's offer might be the last reprieve they ever saw.

Nashi's idea had sounded promising, until she mishandled it and plunged into catastrophe. Her temple councilors were finished with her. She had no family of her own. Her best friend was a cobra. Who might she consult now?

Better to seek secular counsel, or so she reasoned as she stood before the cool fountain at Hanza House, having presented herself to the sentry at the gate. She was not accustomed to calling on the ladies in town. Usually it was the other way around, but she was running out of ideas, and the Hanza woman's practical resourcefulness might prove out.

Her hostess appeared quickly, beaming at her all the way down the corridor.

"What a delightful surprise!" she called ahead, rushing forward with her arms wide. She hugged Uruna close and gave her arm a light squeeze. If the woman had always been so affectionate, Uruna didn't remember it.

"How long has it been?" Uruna asked. "A year, two?"

"Much too long if you ask me, dear. I spend most of my time in the provinces, so I'm so glad you caught me at home. Is Kinar with you?"

"I left her to her temple work."

"Oh." An awkward pause, then: "To be sure."

"The two of you are quite close, I understand."

"Yes, we're dear friends."

Heganna was worried about confidences, about Kinar's tacit deployment as the Hanza envoy at temple, an insider privilege quietly overlooked, as it suited all concerned.

"I came about a personal matter," Uruna said. "I know it's unusual, and I hope you'll forgive me. I'm rather impulsive sometimes."

"Yes, I know. It accounts for some of your more surprising successes. Come, Uruna, and sit with me in the garden. The poppies are a riot of color this time of year."

They sat beneath a cork willow and chatted over trivia while they waited for tea to come. Yellow fish swam in a shallow pond at their feet. Pink alyssum bordered a path between beds of red and orange poppies leading back to a shrine. A shady alcove sheltered a glazed statue of a boy, no doubt the work of Heganna's husband, the master sculptor Sebbu. Something in the boy's stance struck Uruna as disturbingly familiar…

She expressed a mild envy of the flowers. "I can't grow them anywhere except indoor pots. My garden is really for the serpents' pleasure, and the gardener isn't willing to dig with a cobra lying about."

"The man has good sense. Pardon me, but I'm only telling you what you know—most people give serpents a wide berth." Heganna sucked a breath of anticipation. "So, tell me about your trip to Burum. I heard it went well with the serpent."

Uruna smiled and plunged ahead. She explained her meeting with

Gula Gusar, her introduction to Kukhmet, the surprise overture of marriage upon her return. She was careful to leave out the incident of Enguda's ugly entreaty.

Heganna listened to all with interest. "So, this Ensi fell short of your expectations," she observed.

"In a manner of speaking, yes."

"Uruna, how long has Niccaba been trying? Really trying—sixteen, eighteen years?"

"I'm twenty-six. The Mahut prince was the first, a boy brought out of Egypt when I was twelve, but they had started the search five years before that, when I arrived with Meret. The Ensi is my twenty-second suitor."

A flicker of pain crossed Heganna's features and vanished.

How much did the world's richest woman know about Ekur's search for a royal husband? Heganna had to be privy to the desperation driving the Lukur. Kinar would have seen to it, might even have volunteered Hanza resources somewhere along the way. In all likelihood, Heganna had been persuaded or even instructed on occasion to fund Lukur travel. And if so, what of it? What was the expenditure of a few talents to a woman reputedly worth a tenth part of Sumer's entire wealth?

Heganna regarded her queen with a candid eye and a rueful smile. "Don't tell me," she said. "Let me guess. The ladies have panicked."

"Kinar's been here before me. She told you."

"Not this time."

"They would ship me off to Aramdan and seek another for prophecy in my place."

"Uruna!"

"At least, that's my assumption. I don't expect them to act right away."

"How could they do such a thing?"

"With a unanimous vote, the same as they did selecting the man in the first place. As it stands, I'm still chief magistrate, and none want to replace me at worship."

"Of course. You can't be replaced in those offices without severe consequences."

"But the Bull won't be so circumspect."

"He's behind the whole business. He's got them all cowed. What a pack of ninnies!"

Of course Heganna was astute enough to divine for herself the flaw in Lukur temperament. One didn't have to walk Aniginna hallways to feel the tense apprehension that rode with the faithless everywhere. But Heganna was careful.

"So much for their choice of husband," she said. "I don't suppose they deliberated long."

Uruna shook her head. "They bargained for security and just wanted it done, whether the man was right or not."

"And what do you think?"

"I don't know. That's why I came to you, I guess."

"But could you love him?"

"Who, the snake-charmer?"

"Sounds like you couldn't. Wrong man for the job, eh?"

"Well, love is important, but having the Sight is crucial…"

Heganna took Uruna's hands in her own. "My dear, love is everything. Love drives the world. You know when it hits you because you can't think of anyone else. He totally consumes your attention when you're with him."

Uruna took a long breath as the hunter moved across her mind. The air inside the garden was suddenly stifling.

Heganna continued.

"This Ensi Marduk. What happens when he looks at you? Does your spine tingle? Does he tie your tongue in knots, make you want to please him…what's the matter, what did I say? Your face is as bright as a poppy."

"Nothing, I just realized what a rare gift you have, that you can speak so eloquently of love."

Heganna studied her guest closely, silent for the moment. "Uruna, tell me. Does a queen lead with her head or her heart?"

"Her head, lest we be dashed on the rocks of her conceit."

"Nicely quoted. Is that your conviction or a palliative the Lukur drilled into you?"

"I know when to use my head and when my heart. The quest for prophecy is no place for romantic emotion."

"Is that what Enshiggu-god says?"

Uruna stared in stunned shock. "How do you know his name?"

"It's a little-known fact that I was a priestess for two years."

"Just two? But how did you learn the canons? It takes years before his name is so much as spoken."

"I and my sister studied in a small place. We learned the canons from an adept who took us rapidly through it, until I realized I didn't belong there. I left before I turned sixteen. But the point, Uruna, is your heart. Always with Enshiggu it's the heart. Nothing less will do, and you know it."

Uruna watched a yellow carp glide out from under a lily pad, flick its tail, glide back into the shade.

"You're saying I should wait."

"My dear, I'm not telling you anything your heart doesn't already know. You just have to discover it and follow. Yours is the way of the heart. Mine is the head. We're each of us made for a purpose."

Uruna continued staring at the fish.

Then Heganna said a strange thing. "Who is he?" she asked.

Uruna looked up, startled. "Who is whom?"

"When I speak of love, he makes your face burn. He makes your eyes search the water, steals your tongue. You've already met the man, haven't you?"

"I don't know."

Kudu Mahti had hardly been what she would call a meeting of hearts. More like a battle. He had told her to leave. He had pushed her away from himself with deliberate, brusque intent. He belonged in the wild freedom of the *ghana*, not locked up in a world full of women. He had moved her, and she had felt drawn to him as no other in her life, but she would never attract a man like him, and hoping otherwise was a waste of time, a sure way to get hurt.

But Heganna had struck her mark.

"If he shakes the ground you stand on, you must take no other. If he stills your soul, wait for him. The gods have bound your spirits, the gods will bring you home."

"But I mustn't keep everyone waiting. They've gone centuries without the Sight."

"Still your mind, Uruna. Silence it. Stop being a Lukur and start behaving like the marvelous woman you are."

Uruna rose to her feet and thanked Heganna. She left her offering of cakes at the foyer shrine and followed the doorman out to the gate. She gave the sentry a prayer seal from her pocket, then stumbled into the high heat of the midday glare, heedless of the shaded refuge along one side or of the track her bare feet took over the hot stones.

Her mind wandered from Burum along the river's shallow turns to Kudu Mahti, to shapes dancing in mute triumph, a fire along the shore, a boat's upswept arc defining a sentinel for the night. And a woman encircled by a man's protective strength.

Then out beneath the *ghana's* silver sky she flew, along the flanks of wetland mire to the uniform curtain of green, where the stain of death lured the eye to certain treachery, where the air rang with locust song one moment and seized with terror the next, as a lordly rumble shocked the earth. She felt the reassuring answer from Tezu-Mah, Seeks-With-No-Fear, tasted again victory's redeeming power, and her heart at last found voice and sent a silent call:

Hunter, are you out there?

CHAPTER TWENTY
Arrival In Nippur

The bargeman from Adab cleverly maneuvered his craft ahead of two others and put it dockside where the largest body of workmen stood ready to off-load goods. As he threw down the plank, he made a bow of courtesy to his esteemed passenger, a rich merchant from Uruk, but his fare barreled past him without so much as a *good-day*, his eye on the road and the outstretched hand of the cargo chief.

Anu drew alongside the disgusted sailor and spat into the water. "Tight-fisted peddler," he muttered.

The barger squinted hard at the merchant's receding backside as though committing it to memory. "He'll lose a day getting out of here for that. I cut off a friend back there whom I'd hoped to stand to a drink from the favor."

Anu pawed inside his pouch and came up with a clay token. "Well, take this instead."

"I don't want a good man's money, hunter, you paid your fare. But thanks just the same."

Anu pressed the token into the man's hand. "Go on, take it. For the good talk and friendship."

The man accepted the gratuity with a curt nod. "Them's fair that labor with their backs and brawn. It's soft-livered takers like him that ruin a man's spirit."

Anu took note of the laborers and hawkers crowding the quay. "Nippur seems larger than when I left. Did I forget so much, or has the city grown?"

"Oh, she's grown, but not for the better if you ask me. Every winter the rabble pour in from the north, planters tired of fighting sand and salt leach, eager to try weaving or hawking wares. The ones who fail at it join the *nazli* beggars, and they all squat together in those pens along the outside."

"You mean the awnings over there against the wall? That used to be a date grove, but I see the trees are gone now."

"Chopped up for *nazli* cookfires or else chewed down by their flea-ridden goats. Gotten to be like a second city, but rank-smelling and dangerous. A place to stay away from. I don't know, there's an ill wind brewing up there in the Akkad. Sometimes in the night you can feel it in your bones, the same as when the tiny spirits sing their sad songs in your head—"

"Say, I have to be off. But thanks for the warning, and enjoy yourself tonight."

"I'll do that. A good day to you, friend."

He negotiated the slight gradient from the waterfront to Uruk Gate on his own, putting his leg to the test and finding the result encouraging but tiring. He considered hiring a litter for the trek through Nippur but quickly rejected the idea as likely to draw unwanted attention. He trudged on between the sculpted lions at Uruk Gate and up the wide Avenue of Lasori, mingling with the throng who wore a path between the city's southern entrance and the temple marketplace.

After five minutes on the street his leg complained, and he stopped at an ale shop to buy a mugful. Two blocks from the Aniginna gate his leg declared a revolt and forced him off to one side. In the declining shade of the old Exchange building he propped himself on his good leg to ease the soreness. A girl passed by and he caught himself watching her backside sway up the street.

"Careful," a voice at his elbow warned. "You're not up to that yet."

Nabi Gahn! How had the hunting master learned of his arrival so quickly?

How indeed—Nabi made it his business to know such things. His upturned face now watched his full-grown former apprentice with the disapproving look that kept students endlessly striving. You never outgrew lowly status with Nabi Gahn. You only grew away from him after you discovered there were things in life more important than the master's approval.

Nabi stood under the awning in his peculiar one-legged stance. His angular frame added to the effect of a heron fishing. He hadn't changed much, hair a little grayer, shoulders more stooped, but the fire was intact and so was the danger. You always kept your guard around Nabi Gahn.

Nabi pointed at the boar-sticker slung over his former student's shoulder. "Won't take any lion with a fire poker like that. You didn't learn much, did you?"

"No, I started taking naps after the third day of your droning. Actually learned to kill from a Hani woman that stuck lions with one hand while she stroked my backside with the other."

"Obviously the lady was blind and took you for her goat. How are you, Anu? Your leg looks like crow bait."

Nabi Gahn's eyes made a sweep of the street, taking in rooftops, shoppers walking by, stall tenders. To Nabi, the world was full of foes seen and unseen.

"Right now I feel like my leg looks," Anu replied.

"Not smart to parade around the city looking that way. Fellow doesn't like you can pick you off without a fight and walk away clean."

"I left a few of that kind back in the *ghana*."

"What? A few rascals chased you from your happy home?"

"Not exactly. Most of them fed jackals afterward. Who are you thinking of sending in my place?"

Nabi Gahn's black eyes grew sharp, then swept the street scene again. He said nothing.

It was not a satisfactory parley and they both knew it. The street banter was forced, their miserable attempt to resume brotherly accords an embarrassment. Another fire from the past had died while he was away. He would miss Nabi Gahn as much as he missed the god.

"I need a good lance," he said to break the impasse.

"Go where you got the last one."

"That was in Uruk. The old man has died since."

"You didn't come to Nippur to find a new lance."

"That's right. I came to find my center again. I think I left it here with the family who raised me and friends I could trust."

The look sharpened again. Nabi held his gaze and answered. "Ask for the red man in Na-Purna."

"Red? A Nord?"

"Get back on your feet fast, hunter," said the teacher who ignored stupid questions. "This isn't the wilderness. The man next to you may be your enemy."

"Who would want my heart, eh Nabi? Who gains from taking down this wreck?"

The uplifted leg came down and Nabi Gahn moved suddenly toward the alley's mouth.

"We're each of us stalker and prey," he said, repeating the familiar phrase from a time long ago. "Watch your back, hunter."

Then Nabi Gahn stepped into the street and was gone.

CHAPTER TWENTY ONE
Conscripted To Court

Anu knew his leg needed further mending. His outer thigh muscle had stiffened and required an expert's attention, so he gave up roaming Nippur's streets and sought aid at House Of Abundant Life. One look at his leg and the head surgeon commandeered a litter and a bevy of *kadishtu* maids and sent him to the wards.

She might as well have consigned him to hell.

The infirmary drove him nearly mad. So many voices going at all hours of the day and night. Women bustling in and out of his room, swabbing his parts and clucking over the wound. A different one each time, as though they were taking turns with him. Try this poultice, and that. Now turn over, don't be shy, let me see your cheeks. Let us have a look here, and a look there. How's that feel? How about this when I press here? And the mortifying business of relieving himself in the presence of a strange woman. As if he were a helpless little tot.

Three days was all he could stand, and then he got up and took to the streets. Inanna's beard! He was on the mend, wasn't he? And getting better, no thanks to them! No more languishing on the porch, and no more being propped up in a sick bed either. He wasn't sick and he wasn't going to let them have any more of him! They just wanted to truss you up and put you on a leash. Not at all like

Lasheen...

He fingered the claw inside his pouch. The feel of the talisman pulled up good images and bad. Lasheen was among the best. The claw would keep her memory close, remind him of what was important.

When he returned to sick bay, he learned his thoughtless escapade had caused a great deal of anxiety, consternation, and time wasted searching for him.

Anu told them thank you, but he simply could not spend another night in the infirmary.

The ladies understood but were not placated.

He was contrite. He owed a great deal to Lukur generosity, but wasn't he a greater burden if he grew weaker for lack of rest?

A compromise was reached. Until he mended, the hunter would be ensconced in the *kadishtu* dormitory where he might be within reach of a qualified physician—as well as forty teenage girls practicing sexual prowess to prepare for the day they would provide Ekur's newborn nobility.

Forty *kadishtu* eager to tame the wild hunter in their midst.

Forty young women with pulsing, ripening flesh, black-headed with dark eyes and dusky skin. Each chosen for her bulging breasts and fecund vitality, each fairly bursting to demonstrate her fitness as the embodiment of life-giving abundance.

After two days of loud chatter and snickering and broad adolescent jokes, Anu was ready for a bed in the curing wards again.

He was just climbing up from sleep when a dorm monitor entered the room towing a golden-haired girl.

"This is Retha," she said simply. "She will be your escort."

The Nord girl was obviously distressed, for she regarded Anu with a look of alarm bordering on panic.

The monitor ignored the girl and addressed Anu. "We've got to get you out of here fast."

"What's wrong?"

"A farmer has appealed to the temple court for his dead wife's land.

A mob clamors at the gate, demanding his rights. The queen will hear him within the hour. It would be best if you leave."

"I must have been in the marshes too long. Have I committed another offense?"

"If being male can be considered offensive, yes. Under the circumstances it's probably best if we get you to a house in West Quarter."

"Across the river?"

Retha bridled. "That shanty town is no place for this man."

"Not for you to say, Retha."

Anu was growing uncomfortable, and not from the pain in his leg. "I'm in the way here," he said quickly. "Thank you for the hospitality."

"Follow Retha, quickly. She'll see you out safely."

Anu snatched up his vest and quiver and followed Retha down the hall at a trot. Women in white were running everywhere as the entire temple prepared for the trial event, but Retha dashed nimbly among them and plunged down a broad staircase. He struggled to keep up.

"Why the rush to trial?" he asked, out of breath and acutely aware of the disturbance his hurried exit was making.

Retha answered without breaking stride. "Council thinks a delay will inflame the citizens more. Reports from the outside are ugly."

She paused to let a string of white-robed Lukur pass. Their hostile stares drove Anu to the wall as he tried unsuccessfully to diminish his size. A male in the Gipar was an affront to womanhood. Even if he was a tall, husky looker.

Retha took off again, and he hurried behind, nearly losing her in crowds, unnerved at every turn as she perversely guided him through the busiest part of Abundant Life. Crowds of Lukur thronged the main corridor and jammed every meeting room. Coiffed heads turned at his passage. Eyebrows arched appreciatively at his comeliness, then dropped in scorn for his gender, creating a wake of lingering looks that were neither flattering nor encouraging.

He spied an empty corridor to his right and fled into it. Any diversion was better than his one-man parade. He would apologize to his escort later.

A shout from behind stopped him in his tracks.

"Anu of Hanza!"

The familiar voice rang through the hall, causing heads to turn and still more stares to lock onto his tall frame while he stood in full view above the throng. A hush fell over the women as he looked in vain for the caller, mortified by the attention. Then the wall of white linen parted, and a woman he recognized headed straight toward him.

Lady Niccaba.

His heart stopped with a rush of juvenile fear and a fleeting memory of pain and humiliation. She had once tossed him out of the temple for leering at a priestess seated in prayer. The top of Niccaba's head barely met his shoulder, yet the woman still intimidated him.

Niccaba quickly took account of his scarred torso and dropped her gaze to the fresher line on the leg.

"Great Mother in Heaven, look at you!" she exclaimed, running her hands over his arms. "We're blessed to have you in Nippur once again—and whole. Will you stay long?"

The cold eyes said she was more interested in how soon he might leave. For no reason he could discover, Niccaba had always disliked the Hanza clan, but she had reserved a particular contempt for their single male offspring.

"I've no immediate plans," he returned, adding with suitable self-deprecation, "except to remove myself before I add further offense."

"Then you've heard," she declared with customary bluntness.

"A little. I'm not sure what to make of it."

"A farmer from Adab asks for his wife's land after she died. He was denied in provincial court and somehow got his appeal pushed up. We will hear his case within the hour, but as you are aware, the law requires the presence of public witnesses. There's a mob in the street clamoring for male rights. Since we've sealed off the Aniginna, we're short of secular visitors. Your presence would be helpful."

She was expert at making a demand sound like a polite suggestion.

Anu glanced about at the forest of sober faces and aimed a solicitous smile at Niccaba. "How could I refuse, madam? You honor my house by asking."

Niccaba had little time for civilities. "Good. Show yourself at the Chamber of Laws when the call goes out."

She abruptly turned on her heel and the throng swallowed her again.

Retha reappeared at his elbow. "You lead a charmed life, sir. I was beginning to think the lady intended to have you put out on the street."

"Better to suffer that crowd than this. Where will I find the Chamber of Laws?"

"In House of Decrees, where else?"

"I've never been inside."

"Don't worry, I'll take you there."

Before he could move, another voice called out from behind. "Not so fast, you rascal!"

He would have known Kinar's voice anywhere. He turned about slowly to prepare himself for the unkindness years usually worked on attractive middle age, and was shocked. Kinar still possessed the striking beauty that once had been the talk of every male in Nippur. She gazed up at him with an expression of rapt interest.

"Are you an imposter, sir, or does Anu still live in the flesh?"

He smiled at the well-deserved jibe and spread his arms for her. "Kikki," he said, using his pet name for her, "you look wonderful. It's good to see you."

She leaned forward for a kiss, offering only her cheek in a gesture of cold reserve. A lifelong absence was not quickly forgiven.

"How unsettling to learn of your return under these trying circumstances," she said. "Have you been with us long?"

"I've been—repairing."

Kinar glanced down at his leg and stared at him with a reproving look. "I thought you were impervious to the call of duty, but I saw your wound from across the room. Did the *ghana* take a price from you? How else do you account for your return, Anu?"

"The life is harsh," he admitted. How did one explain endings, when the attempt always met with disappointment?

"And you've had enough," she concluded, "or is it the other way around? Did the *ghana* chew you up and spit you out? The leg looks serious, Anu."

"Not permanent, thanks to the labors of a good woman."

"M-mm, your debt to womanhood increases with each escapade. It's a mess, Anu, such a waste of excellence. I hope you appreciate the concern your absence has caused at the home front."

He shifted his feet restlessly, aware of a new crowd attracted by their dialogue, watching Kinar corner the hunter like a fox at bay. He wanted to bolt and run as instinct dictated, but he wasn't in the swamp anymore and he regarded the lady too highly for that.

"Quite contemptible of me, to be sure," he admitted meekly. "Look, I've got to rush off—not the way to treat a good friend. May I call on you soon?"

"Perhaps after you've paid your mother a call."

"Yes, as soon as Aniginna gates reopen."

The lovely face hardened in unforgiving scorn. "Heganna deserves better."

"A better son? Yes, I've thought so for years."

"Don't be self-effacing with me. You know what I mean. Spend some time with your mother. She's not getting any younger."

"May I convey your respects?"

"Good heavens, you're brash. I see your mother at least twice daily, Anu. She hardly needs word of her closest companion from an occasional son."

He ducked his head. "Guilty as charged."

Kinar's stiff composure cracked suddenly and her face crumpled as she wrapped him in a lingering embrace.

"We miss you at home," she whispered in his ear, and then she tore herself away and fled into the crowd.

He turned and found Retha gaping at him with wide-eyed awe.

"Get me out of here!" he demanded.

Retha raced him out of the building and down Abundant Life's broad stairs onto the wide concourse. She crossed the pavement ahead of him and skipped lightly up the steps to the tall opening through which women were pouring into House of Decrees. Anu caught up with her on the landing and leaned against a column, wincing at the sharp jabs shooting up his thigh. A call to court rang out from inside the hall.

Retha doubled back and bent to examine the leg. "Can you make it, or should I find a litter?"

"Don't be smart, there wouldn't be time. I just need to catch my breath."

"It's inside and down," she explained. "More stairs."

"I can manage."

He did manage, but with considerable effort and an agonizing moment at the bottom when he wasn't sure he could make the last few paces under his own power.

The court chamber was small, about twenty-five feet square, with a low ceiling and undecorated plaster walls. A dozen men and two women stood at the back, facing a raised dais that spanned the other end. The ladies of the court had not yet made an appearance.

Retha started to leave, her duty done, but he grabbed her by the hand. "Madam," he said, to honor her position as he brought her hand to his lips and smiled. "I am in your debt."

The girl swelled with pleasure and blew him a farewell kiss before disappearing into the outer hall.

CHAPTER TWENTY TWO
Stolen Moment

Anu moved to a position at the rear of the gallery in case he needed the wall for support. Except for a tapestry and a stone stela painted with strange symbols, there wasn't a lot to see.

Several Lukur filed into the room and took positions along the front wall, where they faced the gallery and waited for the procedure to begin.

Two matrons arrived next, followed by the queen. As she took the dais with regal self-possession he grabbed at the wall behind him, nearly overcome.

The *ghana* huntress!

She stood solemnly before the gallery, arms at her sides, two lustrous dark braids clasped beneath a plain gold band of office. As she spoke, she ran her eyes around the room to observe how her words weighed with everyone present. They stopped on him for a faltering moment, then swept on.

Had she recognized him? Did she remember that day with the same earth-shaking impact?

"These proceedings shall not be reduced to spectacle," she announced. "Forget the clamor outside the gates. Forget hearsay and rumor. In court we observe decorum and hear all sides with fair judgment. Conduct yourselves accordingly. Inanna bless us all."

She turned from the gallery and nodded to a guard posted at the side door.

Anu expelled air from his lungs and realized he had been holding his breath since the moment of her entrance. This was not the haughty priestess he had banished from the marsh, whose high color had stood out stark against Kudu's bleak monotone. This was not the serpent visionary who had followed his every move, judging his imperfection, mocking the sordid field where he played god. In Ekur's hall of judgment, she was simply Uruna, a woman quietly going about the business of being a judge.

Even as she took absolute command of his senses.

Gone was the stain of the *ghana*. Her skin was clearest perfection, a flawless setting for graphic, dark features that commanded attention. Raven hair of blackest black fell straight from crown to shoulder, reflecting gleaming blue ribbons of light. Long lashes framed a pair of wide-set, luminous gray eyes that measured the world with frank, level assessment. Her full-length robe of office failed to obscure a luxuriant form and graceful carriage. As with their meeting in Kudu Mahti, the spectacle of Uruna's utter loveliness held him transfixed. He could not imagine a woman more desirable, more compelling by just her presence alone.

But it was the mouth that took his heart away, a full and generous mouth with a small tuck at each corner that hinted at latent good humor. The upper lip arched to a small cup that begged his finger's touch. In profile she showed a barely perceptible pout, the lingering hint of little-girl charm that summoned forth a man's urge to protect and defend.

She was far shy of thirty years of age, and therefore an unlikely prospect for elevation to her rank. A priestess usually became Entu only after a lifetime in the order. How then came this youthful freshet to Inanna's throne? Most likely Council had found in her an extraordinary trait or talent. Perhaps she would reveal her special abilities in the proceedings.

The judicial council stood behind Uruna, eight matrons bearing various objects of religious significance. Painted wands crossed above the breast, scepters and pikes of gleaming hardwood. One woman cradled a small brown cushion on which rested a gleaming gem.

Lady Niccaba took the position of honor just behind the queen's right elbow. The gray-haired matron of awesome respectability claimed a line of heritage directly from the Mother of Mothers in old Persa, Hursag of Azerabad, from whose loins had sprung a dynasty lasting six hundred years. It would be Niccaba who had drafted the tokens of conduct, who would bring particulars of law to the queen's attention, whose wisdom and experience would guide the court to a verdict. Directly or indirectly, the room would hear from Niccaba today.

"Let us close our eyes in prayer," she pronounced.

The queen immediately shut her eyes and joined the rest of the room as Niccaba launched into a lengthy benediction. Anu waited several moments, trying to follow verses he had hadn't heard since childhood, but it was no use, his mind folded up and went blank.

He fidgeted.

He opened his eyes to steal a look at the queen.

Uruna stared back at him, her eyes wide with unflinching examination. The candor in her open gaze was unsettling. She had caught him, yet he was unable to tear his eyes from her face.

She engaged him! Uruna, Entu of Nippur, conspired with him against the entire room, against Niccaba and the council, against the prayer to Inanna! For an instant of time they existed apart from the world, two souls intimately connected in a stolen interlude, sharing their spontaneous encounter against the mutual risk of discovery. She seemed as surprised as he, unable or unwilling to break the moment, and in that simple lifting of the veil, Uruna revealed her heart in the purest conveyance of feminine surrender.

A flush of warm excitement filled Anu with a sense of completeness he had never imagined. Whatever transpired henceforth could only pale before the bright promise enfolding him. He was smitten.

𒈨𒁹𒆠𒌋

Niccaba finished and the audience lifted their eyes. Uruna struggled for composure as she tore her eyes away from the hunter. She turned to the sentry of the court and gave the order.

"Breeg—"

Her voice caught and she cleared her throat.

"Bring the appellant forth."

A gangly farmer shuffled through the doorway, stroking the gilt frame in wonder as he passed. He stopped where Niccaba pointed and stood hugging his torso in an awkward pose, apparently stunned by his surroundings.

Niccaba pronounced the trial open. "All gathered here, stand fast before Uruna, beloved of Inanna, Enshiggu, and all herein assembled."

Uruna addressed the hall without ceremony.

"This is a hearing, not a trial. Nevertheless, the court expects the same decorum and respect for the parties involved, as this is a place of law. So be it."

"So be it," the ladies echoed in unison.

"Let us address the appellant, Lipit-Enlil."

She then broke the first precedent of the day by stepping down from the dais to take the farmer's hands in her own.

"Lipit-Enlil, please know that we also grieve for the loss of your beloved wife, Sabit."

The man's astonishment mirrored the faces surrounding him. "I-I thank you, madam."

To the sound of feet shuffled in agitation, and still holding his hand, she turned with him to face Inanna's altar. "Shall we ask once more for wisdom in silent prayer."

She closed her eyes as the hall fell silent.

"Thy will," she intoned to close the benediction.

The hall contained no chairs. All proceedings were conducted according to tradition of standing erect before witness, advocate, and judge alike. Rather than return alone to the dais to resume her high station, Uruna broke further precedent and stood in place beside Lipit-Enlil.

"How are you called at home?" she asked.

"You mean in the house?"

"Yes, by your wife now deceased, your children if you have such, your family and friends."

More foot shuffling. This level of intimacy breached protocol. Unheard of.

"Um, just Baba."

"May we also call you Baba?"

"Well, of course, you're the queen and all."

"Tell us, dear Baba, what brings you today."

"My wife died, you see, leaving me no daughters."

"She was a priestess here at Ekur, correct?"

"For twenty-two years she served in the nurseries."

"Did she give you sons?"

"Yes, two. They are grown."

"And do they live at home?"

"Yes."

"Tell us your appeal."

She knew very well the farmer's request, for she had been briefed the day before and spent an hour with council arguing whether the issue should be brought before Judgment Hall. She had won that argument.

The planter answered: "I have worked the land all my life. I was blessed to marry Sabit very young, for the barley is all I know."

"I see. And with your wife's death, the land would normally pass into the hand of your eldest daughter, if you had one."

"Yes, but I don't, and so it passes to the temple."

At that point Niccaba stepped forth. "It is both custom and law, as he says, for ownership to pass to the temple in the absence of a female heir. However, the man need not own the land to continue working it for income."

Uruna nodded at her fellow Lukur. "Thank you for the interpretation, Niccaba." She turned to the farmer. "What say you to that, Baba?"

Lipit-Enlil glowered at Niccaba. "Indeed, I can work it, but for temple wages, and under a temple overseer who knows nothing about barley. Where was the temple, I ask you, when the dike broke in the night, and I and my sons went out in the winter cold, and my son Kuda lost a finger locking the weir? The land is mine by right of working it my whole life."

"You are asking the court, then, to grant ownership of Sabit's lands to you?"

Lipit-Enlil drew a long breath and gathered himself as he turned and faced the Lukur assembly square on.

"I am asking the women who have kept to themselves all ownership of house and land and enterprise for a hundred years and more, to endow me, Lipit-Enlil, with these forty hectares, that I may pass those lands to my sons when I am gone."

His little speech sounded practiced to Uruna's ear, and she imagined the others in the room picked up on the same tone. It was time to put the matter to a test of commerce before these women of enterprise.

"Lub-Sunna," she said to her chief counter, "step forth and account for Lipit-Enlil's production."

Lub-Sunna consulted a clay tablet and rattled off a litany of five years of barley production from the Sabit lands, then gave her summation. "In just the past five years, the appellant has exceeded quota by a fifth portion. Actually, he's done much better than that on several occasions according to record."

Uruna then asked the counter for an assessment of temple-run fields.

"Of the past five years we have made quota in two," she replied.

"And what is the penalty for coming up short?"

"Well, there is no penalty. We don't dock our own wages, for pity sakes."

"How many surplus loaves are we talking about?"

"From Lipit-Enlil?"

"That's whose appeal we're considering, yes."

"Um, roughly, er, five hundred loaves."

"In total?"

"No, per year."

A murmur passed through the Lukur and quickly became a clamor. Uruna glared at Niccaba to rap for order, and at the sound of stone on stone the assembly quieted.

"We shall have no further outbursts or the room will be vacated except for appellant and advocate."

She turned to tiny Ku-Aya, at sixty years of age the farmer's nominal advocate by dint of her council seniority. The woman had uttered not a word during the whole proceeding.

"Has counsel anything to add?"

Ku-Aya blinked and stepped forward.

"Under temple supervision Baba, that is, the appellant, would have no incentive to produce beyond quota. Nor would he be punished for achieving less. As his grain allotment is set by each prior year's production, he would produce approximately five hundred loaves less each year."

Ku-Aya had prepared well. Uruna nodded her approval.

"Now tell us where this man sells the product of his field."

"Four parts to the market and one part he gives to the temple."

"And what does the temple do with his portion?"

"They bake loaves for the orphanage."

Uruna had heard enough. "The appellant will face the court."

Lipit-Enlil turned his gaze on his queen and set his mouth in a firm line. He was ready to hear his fate.

"Court finds for the appellant. Niccaba, see that the record shows

Lipit-Enlil inherits all fields and equipment and water courses from Sabit."

"But, Uruna, court hasn't voted. You can't force judgment."

The hunter stepped forward to address Ekur's chancellor.

"Please, who is magistrate here?"

Niccaba whirled on him. "Witness may speak only when asked! Anu, what's got into you?"

"I seek only understanding. Since this is a hearing and not a trial, and your honored magistrate has pronounced judgment, how must I bear witness of your call for other opinions?"

"Your insolence is tolerated, sir, only because of the Hanza family's repute."

"Thank you, madam, but the matter here appears decided regardless of my presence or my family's absence."

"See here—"

"So be it!" Uruna cut off her chancellor's diatribe before it could begin. "Adjourned!"

She turned and strode briskly from the room, fighting back a smile of triumph as the farmer raised his voice in praise of Inanna, his queen, her court, and every little god he could think of. His single voice was drowned in the ensuing clamor of Lukur outrage and confusion.

Anu of Hanza!

Heganna's own was here in Nippur! Not bounding about some bloody fen contending with death and mayhem, but standing in her own court, near enough to touch. Sharing secret eye contact and reaching out to her, defending her before Niccaba's ponderous rectitude.

At the outer hallway she was beset by a crowd of onlookers, all talking at once and begging for news. She pushed her way through the throng and quickened her pace, hoping to make the doorway into Hall of Serpenthood before the joyous rapture left her.

She wanted to savor that moment with her hunter, that precious unity of spirit she knew in her heart was right and true. Had to be, for she had caught his look of delight just before she dashed away. Had felt his heart—

That was it! She was feeling again what others felt! After so many years burdened by duty, her lost childhood "touches" were returning, just as surely as she had felt the planter's yearning for the land, had heard the fearful desperation in his voice so clearly that she could render no other judgment.

All because *he* was here. She had his name now: Anu! Near enough to feel, near enough tell him she was his for eternity.

Near enough at last to belong.

CHAPTER TWENTY THREE
Launched From Home

Lilla's eyes sparkled with cheer as she filled her brother's cup to the clamor of voices raised in boisterous fest. Anu reached up from his chair and gave her swollen belly an affectionate pat before she moved off to serve the others seated around the table. She was happy and satisfied, which, along with the wine, made him feel good.

The harp and drum struck a lively *zumpa-zumpa* beat and he ducked to avoid a neighbor girl's whirling sash as she danced close to flay him with her scent. Uncle Obi winked at him past the young woman's play for attention and raised a speculative brow, puckering his mouth around a beer straw with a knowing leer. Nobody had changed in his long absence. It was good to be home.

But it was even better to be a short walk from Serpenthood—and Uruna.

While friends and family gathered to celebrate his return and the impending arrival of Lilla's second child, he struggled to take part in the joy around him. His mind unerringly drifted back to those smoky eyes regarding him across the courtroom. Everyone's unqualified acceptance of his nine-year separation was gratifying, but he wanted to be in a bower with those eyes, that face, probing the mind he knew he could never fathom in a lifetime.

He got up to give the leg a stretch and almost immediately encountered Samurra-Lada, a neighbor from across the lane and his father's closest companion. Samurra wanted to reminisce, and Anu, in a relaxed and charitable mood, indulged the old gentleman. While they were talking, a hand slid through his arm and he looked down to find Auntie Gaya's clear gray eyes beaming up at him.

"Gayalla!" he exclaimed, taking up his mother's sister in a warm hug as, behind her, Samurra's grin slid away into the crowd. Gayalla's spare little body squirmed in his grasp.

"Auf, you'll squeeze the date juice from my old veins. Dear Anu, how good to see you at home!" She radiated the sincerity that reminded him why Auntie Gaya had always been his favorite.

"So often I've thought about you," he told her, "out there in the *ghana*, or up on Tigris with the tribes, when the nights were long and the way back seemed impossible, and I would go to Gayalla, my steadying point, my refuge."

"I would have believed perhaps a lovely damsel instead of an old desert crone with one foot in the grave."

"Not true. After enough time out there, your heart goes toward those dearest to you, and you top my list."

"Lovely to hear you to say it. We've had a difficult time guessing your whereabouts for so long, you simply must come up to Demshalla and tell me all about it. I've thought of you often, wondering if you were cold, fevered, rejoicing..."

"Alive?"

"Well that, too, goodness yes! But by the look of you, nothing has got the better of you. I mean it now, I want a visit so we can talk."

"You shall have it. How about next week?"

"Done! Do you think you can remember the road to Demshalla?"

He laughed. "I know it better than my own street."

"Good, but come by yourself, without all these people. You were always with the whole family, whom I love dearly, but this time I want you to myself. I've grown selfish in my dotage. Your mother will have plenty of time with you before then."

He smiled to hide the sobering reminder that he still had neglected Heganna. "Speaking of whom, I haven't seen her for a while. Have you?"

"Try the longroom. A gentleman from Ezzub province was there a while ago with her. And Anu..." Gayalla gave him a glower of reproof.

"Yes?"

"Take it from one who knows. She's missed you terribly, and she's elated to have you back."

"Elated?"

A grave nod. "I know she hides her feelings from the world, but a sister can tell, and so I'm telling you. She couldn't be more pleased."

Strange that he'd taken twenty-six years to create that effect.

He found her, as he might have expected, holding discourse with a merchant. Anu swept the room clear of the intruder with a single black glower.

Heganna patted the divan cushion beside her. "Come sit. I'd like to hear from my son how he spent the last nine years. From the looks of your leg, you got careless at one point."

She wanted it all, the bad with the good. Heganna of Hanza would be satisfied with nothing less, but he knew before trying the futility of putting into words what it was like to run with the gods.

"He hooked when he fell. I was saved by a Bedu and his wife but we were set upon in the desert. The man forfeited his life and the woman was assaulted. Afterward, I brought her out of the wilderness with a boy orphaned by the lion. She saved the leg."

"In a single breath you cover long years of time. Tell me what became of your attackers."

"Tezu-mah drove them off."

"Your god. How many attacked? Two, four?"

"Six."

Heganna put aside the loom and examined her son with a close eye. She swung her feet down and turned her body toward him, the better to take in her son's breadth of shoulder, the definition of musculature, the calloused hands and feet. Her gray eyes gleamed with keen appreciation for his robust physique, the latent power beneath the placid exterior. She felt of his arm the way she might test melons at market.

"You turned yourself into a warrior," she said in a tone of mild reproof.

"I have given myself to Tezu-Mah. I am one with my god." Or so he wanted to believe.

Rather than press the point, she went another route. "Tell me how you found food, where you lodged, what it's like to see dawn on the *ghana* and know you might not live to see the sun set."

Well, she had a certain appreciation for it.

"For six years I lived with the Hani," he told her, "and before that, three with the Kurdeshi. To hunt and forage safely, I learned to think as an animal thinks, see what he sees, feel what he feels. My first winter in the Anatol mountains I slept with a swine to keep from freezing. I've eaten wild grass rather than starve, squeezed dew from my cloak at morn to cross the next dune."

"So, you enjoy the enduring gratitude of primitive huntsmen and a lovely split up the side of your leg. What else has it gotten you, this life?"

"I have a boat built by my own hand from cedars grown near the western sea. I learned to forge my own weapons for the hunt. Merchants are pleased to trade the pelts I take in exchange for food and necessities."

"Which you willingly give away to needy frontiersmen."

"When I can. I work to protect the people, as I was taught in this house. Tezu-Mah does not seek advantages from men. He's made me fit to live day-by-day in the wild."

Heganna's eye strayed to the red scar above his knee, returned to lock his gaze firmly. She would appraise her manly son differently after this, but she was stubborn.

"Our choices make us who we are, Anu," she said. "Not the gods."

"Well then, I guess I chose to put my fate with the *ghana*."

She shook her head slowly. "You set your mind long before."

"When I left Baba's shop to take up the hunting life. I know, you were disappointed."

"Before that. Before you found that weapons master, what was his name?"

"Nabi Gahn."

"Six years with the man, and not one day did you have for the temple."

So there it was! She was still clinging to that old clap-trap about vying for the attentions of priestesses.

"They wanted pretty boys to make babies."

"Oh, Anu! Attendance is more than bedding *kadishtu* maidens. But that's not my point. You chose to remove yourself. You took your attention away from the temple and gave it to the ones who keep to the old ways."

"Is it so lowly of me to protect the Hani? Surely you don't mean I should fulfill my destiny by serving ladies in their beds."

"There's so much more to it than you saw in your short time there. You were only fourteen when you left. You'd hardly set out on the road to your purpose when you ran away. Everyone held such high hope, the Mothers, Kikki and I, the Council. But we couldn't compete with the excitement of the hunt."

"I didn't go out there just for the thrill of facing wild boars, Mother."

"Boar hunters can be found in dozens! The same for silly temple petitioners! Oh, why must men be so dense? You were so different from the other boys, Anu, you were always special, from the very first. Not simply because you were mine. This goes way beyond maternal pride. Council came to me. The mighty Lukur came to this very house in your twelfth year, begging and wringing their hands. He's the one, they told me, he's the one for her! And so we sent you along. But if you think we groomed you to parade around like a peacock, you missed the whole point!"

He got to his feet and strode rapidly to the other side of the room to escape his mother's push-push-push, the same way he had done as a little boy. He was never enough for her, could never measure up to her expectations. Now he commanded rooms and made people stammer, and she was talking about someone he couldn't remember having been.

"What *was* the point?" he said to the plastered wall in front of his face.

"Gods, you're twenty-six! You should have figured it out by now!"

He spun away from the wall, feeling the heat rise to his face as his voice dropped to the same menacing tone as when the soldiers had appeared at Lasheen's tent.

"Well, I'm dense, as you so aptly put it, so tell me. What could I have done better than any other man in Sumer?"

Heganna, oblivious to his change of mood, supplied the answer with uplifted chin. "Served your queen!"

"My queen? Who?"

"Uruna! You must have heard the woman's name, for gods' sake!"

His knees suddenly refused to support him, and he grabbed for the wall bench and lowered himself awkwardly. "Well, uh, of course I know her name," he fumbled. "Knew it then, sure."

"You oaf! She's the diadem of the world, the very center of temple life, the meaning behind everything they do. Did it ever occur to you to inquire about her?"

In truth, no, he hadn't once asked, and the magnitude of his oversight swept over him in a floodtide of resentment: Why hadn't any of them told him? He had been just a love-struck adolescent at the time, a young rake who pumped weapons by day and maidens by night, too infatuated with his girlfriend of the moment to care about the workings of Ekur's higher echelon.

"What should I have done?" he asked. "I mean, what could they have wanted from me?"

"The Mothers put no designs on anyone, Anu. They simply hoped, since you had already entered service, that you might make your own place among them."

"A man's forbidden to enter sacred ground."

"Don't talk that rubbish! There's been a priest at Uruk for twenty years! A man, the right kind of man, is crucial to the plan."

"I don't see how. I mean, I was fourteen and untried, so what could I possibly have brought to the temple?"

Heganna lowered her head and bent forward to gather patience for the slow son who had difficulty with the rudiments of personal affection.

"Your courage, your compassion," she said to the floor. When she looked up at him again, her eyes were filled with tears. "They perceived it early on and hoped you might approach the seat of serpent knowledge. They hoped you might learn how to give Uruna the Sight!"

He swallowed hard. "Instead, I went hunting with Nabi."

"The Council was deeply disappointed when you left, but they wasted no time in resuming the search. Now they're at it harder than ever. And failing at every turn."

"I never knew," he said. "I never saw any of it. The hunting god gave meaning to my life. He made me an instrument for his people, and saved them from scattering to the wilderness. Tezu-Mah gave more than the Hani ever asked."

Deep furrows creased Heganna's brow as she opened her hand to him. "It's a mark of your goodness, Anu, for which I love you. But you were born to even higher purpose."

Should he tell her of the high purpose to which he'd pledged himself for nine years? Was any Nippur woman strong enough to bear the retelling of Gunzek atrocity? Could she understand her son's need for vengeance in kind? Or his vow that a certain Gunzek officer would die screaming the next time they met? He knew too much of things that needed destroying lest they kill again and again.

Heganna broke the impasse.

"These temple concerns must seem petty when set beside your world. "

Anu ceased thinking of Gunzeks and Hani and the broken vows of city dwellers. His mind raced back to something his mother had said earlier about failed hope and a woman's dream of prophecy, signs that pointed to a score of missed opportunities, and more recently, to dreamt wisdom bestowed by a desert wreath urging him to follow his heart.

And then yesterday, the precious gift of love in a glance from the very diadem herself.

Was there anything to be done now by a man who had tarried over the minutiae of snares and animal dung while the massive tide of human events rolled past him?

Across the garden a raven wiped its beak on the back fence. The iridescent shoulders gleamed rainbow hues, the way Uruna's hair had caught sunlight in the aftermath of the rogue lion kill. He recalled her frank inspection at court, reaching for him, completely engulfing him in a look that touched him like a caress, soothed his restless stirrings like the softest blanket. On each occasion her keen scrutiny had found something to worship and adore.

Heganna spoke his thoughts as if she'd heard them.

"She could make a difference if she got the Sight."

Did mother and son at last think alike?

"It's an imperative now," she continued. "We've much more to lose this time. Entire cities, fertile plantations, the law from Lasori that keeps us whole. Every precious gift from Great Mother would disappear, not just a village or two but people and livestock beyond counting. We won't recover the way we did last time."

The raven brought its head around with a quick flash of beak. Its black eye regarded him for a moment, then swooped away out of sight, alone and free on the wind.

Heganna got up from her seat and stood on tip-toe to kiss her son. "Now go see your Auntie Gaya again," she said to him gently. "She'd like more of you before she returns to Demshalla."

Anu tucked a stray lock of silver hair behind her ear. "If I could make you see..."

"Shush! Be happy awhile with us, is all we ask."

"I love you, Mother."

"And I love you, Anu. I hope you know that now."

He stood in place for several moments to soak in that new warmth. Then he took to the hall in search of his aunt.

CHAPTER TWENTY FOUR
Uruna Defies Death

Anu had given himself a day off from family visitations. Hoping for another view of Uruna, he had joined the throng in the temple square to watch a feat of Sumerian engineering. Today Ekur would receive a new altar stone.

Ox teams were harnessed, the dirt ramp had been tamped into place, the draymen waited for the signal to begin. Bearers stood ready with urns, some to cool the drag ropes with water, others to oil the skids. Six heavy hawsers wrapped the load in a web of hemp. Chocks had been laid up along the course, positioned to prevent the burden from retreating on its rails. The only sound was the occasional stamp of an ox hoof.

It seemed to Anu that half of Nippur had turned out to see Inanna's new altar of stone hoisted from the street, dragged up the ramp, and maneuvered inside the temple. Common folk weren't allowed to watch the masons carve runes in its surface. The meaning of the marks was known only to the holiest of women, another of their despised secrets.

But the crowd didn't care. They were on hand for the action and excitement. It wasn't every day you got to see forty oxen teamed with twice as many men.

Anu was there to watch Uruna. He had learned of the hoisting only yesterday and hadn't considered going until he heard on the street that the occasion called for the queen's presence. He stood near one of the ox drivers and scanned the crowd for signs of Lukur gowns, but saw not one. If she was there at all, she must be up on one of the rooftops or, more appropriately for a queen, behind a window in one of those rooms overlooking the street.

The sound of the break rang in his ears like a thunder clap. He looked up as six men on his side of the stone flew through the air, propelled by the hawser's first whip. Like angry reptiles the loose ends thrashed through more men, cutting them down four and eight at a time.

Now the weight of the stone was too much for the remaining lines, and they too squawked and groaned and then snapped apart with explosive might.

Several men jostled Anu from behind, and then people started screaming and shoving in their panic to get away. But Anu kept his eye on the ramp above as to his amazement the drag lines upended the last rank of oxen and the big beasts went sprawling.

Suddenly the stone was loose.

Now the greasing went to work in reverse, helping the stone gather momentum rapidly. First to go were the splinter chocks. The stout oak stubs snapped in two and the stone rumbled on. His eye sped forward to the base of the ramp and he cringed in horror.

A tiny black-headed tot stood directly in the stone's path, stranded behind the rampaging crowd. Anu tried to move and couldn't. People jammed against him from every side.

He heard the rumbling roar of the stone and watched in frozen horror as the little girl spun around in confusion.

Run, child, run! his mind screamed, but it was no use, the babe was too small to understand if she heard. She was doomed and he was helpless to save her.

At that moment a small figure emerged from the sidelines and sprinted for the child on a dead run, her skirts flying as she lifted her knees high and pumped her arms to cut the distance. She kept her eye on the child as the stone crashed down, snapping chocks and sending splinters flying into the crowd with lethal momentum. Anu ducked, and when he came up, the woman was flying through the air, her arms outstretched for the babe. In the instant before contact he glimpsed her face, the grey eyes calm and focused on her target, her black crown of hair wrapped in a gold band, and he heard the life-to-life song, for she was a lance going straight for the heart. She was Uruna.

She struck the child with both hands and the tot sailed out of harm's way into the crowd on the other side. And the stone sped on, headed straight for Uruna where she lay on the pavement.

Roll! he shouted, knowing his voice would never carry to her in time, watching immobilized as the stone struck the first brick course, crushed several more, and kept on going, unstoppable, unredeemable as on it flashed toward Uruna, filling the air with a terrible grinding and scraping.

She was rolling even as she looked up at the huge mass bearing down upon her. Rolling, and then up into a stance with majestic grace, dancing nimbly away as the ponderous leviathan ground to a halt less than a step to her side.

She hovered over the great slab now at rest, looking down at it. Her hands hung limply at her sides, her shoulders sagged beneath the weight of her accomplishment. He couldn't see her face, but he knew what was going through her mind, and he rejoiced.

Uruna had won! She had risked everything and lost nothing. The hunter's greatest thrill was hers now. They shared the same ecstasy of life conquering death, and he had to tell her. Even as the crowd milled around her and she disappeared from view, he knew that somehow he must reach Uruna and tell her that he too had heard the song.

Uruna released the hands of another grateful woman and moved a step closer to the gate. The thrill of victory spent, she answered the mawkish throng from a sense of duty, the whole business having been reduced to obligatory response. She longed to get away to the sanctuary of her chapel where she could reflect on what it all meant.

She sought out Kinar and grasped her friend's arm for assistance.

"It's time for us to go," she hollered above the clamor. "See if you can work us over to Aniginna Gate."

Kinar nodded assent. "The crowd is thickest there. I'll summon a few burly men to make a wedge for us. It'll take just a minute."

Uruna turned to watch for the next well-wisher and was nearly bowled over by a man who suddenly lurched at her from the crowd. His handsome face demanded attention and emitted such an exuberance of wild delight that she feared he might be one of the deranged she had overlooked.

"You are a lioness!" he proclaimed.

"I beg your pardon?"

The hunter! Anu was here! Standing with her beside the sacred stone in the dusty road.

"The lance song. I heard it as your feet left the ground. It's the same as with the lion!"

His bronzed shoulders loomed before her like the burnished horns of a bullock. Piercing dark eyes explored her face with passionate entreaty. His long black hair was swept back over his ears to a knot. Uruna had an impulsive urge to touch the scar on his rib, to feel the pulse in his neck, to run her hands over the sinewy arms that could sweep her up like a lamb. Instead, she reached for Kinar in a grasp for solid logic.

"Kinar, do you know this gentleman?"

Kinar turned her attention from the other direction and her face beamed as she took in the hunter.

"Why, Anu, how good to see you again! Twice in a week after no sign at all for years! Uruna, this is Anu of Hanza House—or was before he went off to live in the wilds. He used to attend princesses."

Now he attends lions, with a spear I am told."

Eyes that sparkled with earnest approval never left Uruna's face but enveloped her, lifted her above the chaos and beckoned her with promise of a shining brook, a leafy glade, a secret interlude in a peaceful hollow. His smile broke upon her with the brilliance of sunlight, fracturing her placid surface as she felt her composure disintegrate.

"Pay no attention to me, lion mother!" he told her quietly. "Just let your heart race with the larks and go straight for the face of the sun."

Kinar inserted herself between Anu and her queen. "Anu, please, this sort of talk is most inappropriate."

Anu ducked around Kinar's head and lifted a mighty fist.

"Feel again the pulsebeat when life was in the balance, die or prevail, and you blinked"—his hand opened like a flower—"and you were alive! It's because your heart was pure, and the sound proved it."

"Sounds? What next? Do stop talking in riddles, Anu!" Kinar's irritation was a pebble in his way as Anu brushed aside her remark.

"The lance song. I heard it too. You know what I mean. It's the same as with the lion!"

Uruna flushed and pressed a hand to her chest. He knew! He voiced with astounding clarity feelings no one else could possibly understand! But did he truly see into her soul, or was he only a raving lunatic?

Kinar shoved against his arm, a moth fluttering against a towering tree trunk. "Anu, I shall have to call guards if you don't leave this moment."

He pushed Kinar gently aside. "Yes, Kikki, in a minute. Listen to me, Uruna. Now you share the pinnacle with Tezu-Mah. Take life's doubling of reward, for today you have won life besides your own."

Uruna stared at him, feeling a deep silence open inside her at the sound of her name on his lips.

"For you, Uruna, there is no turning back. You tasted the elixir of life's sweetest grace. You will hunger for it again."

The weight of his words drove like a lance thrust straight at her center. The huntsman took the measure of his shot, nodded satisfaction, and disappeared into the crowd.

Kinar took it upon herself to fill the gap that followed.

"I'm sorry, Uruna, I had no idea he had become so strange. He used to be a nice boy who fairly dazzled the temple with his presence. We haven't seen him in years."

Uruna was busy with her own thoughts. "He hunts lions, you know."

"Yes, that's the rumor."

No, I saw it myself. I was there. I felt it then.

Kinar had her own take on the matter. "Pity his poor mother who waited for his return."

As Kinar carried on about Heganna's distress, the sound of her words faded into the hum of the crowd. Uruna heeded the hunter's voice.

Lion mother, he had called her! He who faced the lion's yellow-eyed stare had called her lioness! He who had chased her from the *ghana* had just now warmed her with flaming admiration.

It was an omen, a sure sign clearly affirming her right to Serpenthood. Just as Heganna had said the other day.

Always with Enshiggu it's the heart.

Had the mother known at the time it was her own son they spoke of? Had she asserted her own will to influence the outcome? Or was this more of the gods at work?

It didn't matter. She must never again doubt her course, for she and the hunter were somehow connected by the invisible thread of fate. Three times had their paths crossed, but this time he had come to her. Scorned at first, she had next won his honor at court, and today she had won his esteem.

She prayed that his heart would be next.

CHAPTER TWENTY FIVE
Child Of My Dreams

Uruna sat in Serpenthood's east wing and waited for the god essence to flow as her shadow flickered over the back wall of the shrine. Beside her, Kukhmet watched patterns only a serpent could see. The spice offering jar lay at her knee. A pair of oil lamps lighted the tiny room.

Child of my dreams, she began, letting her prayer flow up among the coils of harmony rising in song from cobra heat. Your mother wishes for you the sweetness of Inanna's kiss. If I could hold you in my arms, you would feel the surge of my heart, but it is not given to me to bear my own, as I am endowed with a multitude of children from Inanna's womb. To lead them is to be their servant. To be so bound is to be blessed. Nevertheless, I love you as if you were alive and mine.

This man. You saw him through my eyes, you heard his silent pledge, you heard my heart answer. I think he is the one. I think I have finally found my Enshiggu man. But I am unsure why I cannot rejoice in this precious revelation, this gift of greatest measure.

What is wrong with me? Why am I more doubtful than ever? The possibility should restore my hopes, vindicate my pursuit of the serpent spirit, but instead I fear he will be too good, his love so ardent that he takes me beyond myself and carries me out of trance. I shall forget some minor step in the potion mix, or a line from the chant. For want of a grain, Enshiggu will cast away the whole bushel, and though I push and strain at the door, it will remain shut, and I shall go down to everlasting slumber in the arms of my lover.

But hear how heavily I protest failure, when my worst fear is that I shall succeed, and the door will open. The hunter will make it happen, I know it. He will take me to the Sight because he is without fear and thus he makes all things possible. He knows his god, but I'm not sure I know mine, for I often wonder if I have done truly all I can. I fear I cannot be both wise and humble when I prevail, and knock on the Sixth Door of Heaven, and I am answered.

Yes, my worst fear is that I shall gain the threshold, realize my every ambition, and stand there paralyzed and confounded, dumbly gawking at a prize too great to accept. I shall look into the holiest of holies and see only my own mortal soul, and return to my people empty-handed.

What shall I do, daughter of my heart, when the door pulls wide and shows the way to salvation? What will become of us all when at last it is my turn to act, and I cannot?

She heard a drumming in her ears and welcomed the heat of serpent will that flowed upward from the spot behind her navel. Hot charges rushed up her spine like molten metal and shot outward along her arms to sting her finger tips. The surge of heat lifted through her abdomen to her heart, her chest, but halted at her throat. She threw back her head, opening to the flow and giving, giving to the expanding energy. But it was no use, she knew it would rise no further.

She could not do it alone. She needed the power of masculine passion to ignite the flame and push the Sight to a soaring ascent.

Anu of Hanza, she prayed. Listen to your hunter's heart, and seek the serpent track. Come out of the ghana, and hunt with me.

In the Hanza compound, Sebbu Hadrach stepped back from his latest handiwork and appraised the four-foot likeness of an Uzba lady landowner. His son then watched in horror as the master sculptor took a crude gardening trowel and plunged it again and again into the clay carving.

"It was no good," Sebbu explained.

"But it's a perfect likeness of Nindada!"

"That's the problem. Too much meat, not enough soul."

"Well, I'll grant you the woman's ample of bosom and belly, but all that work! To just destroy it…"

"I'll make another."

"Baba…"

"And better. The same you must do with your life."

Anu rapped out a tattoo with a pushing reed he'd picked up from his father's bench. "Because I came back too late."

"Never too late, Anu. Don't let the women put that on you."

"But it's true."

"Tell me, did you ever miss with the lion?"

"A few times. It was messy."

"But this situation is not?"

"Baba, please."

"It's the same. You finish the job. You do not stop and feel regret."

"With the lion it's different. You have no choice. You don't leave an animal wounded for others to torment. If you only graze him and walk away, he'll get up and chase you down."

"As I said, it's the same. Your mother says this woman is intended for you, and you for her. The old woman in the desert said as much."

"That was a dream."

"All the more reason to follow it."

"She's promised, Baba. The council made a pact with Uruk."

"What did they give for the word of a scoundrel? Kicked her out of Serpenthood. What a sham, what hypocrisy. Unworthy of respect or obedience. Your mother says so, her friends at temple say so, we all know what's going on. None would blame you for at least making an approach."

"I couldn't get inside to speak to her if I tried. They're holding everyone hostage in there."

"Then let's find an excuse to get her outside."

"Good, let me know when you come up with something."

A voice called from across the garden. "How about Springfest?"

It was his mother, stepping down from the house.

"Nobody goes anymore," said Sebbu.

"She does. Every year."

"Is it the same dull ceremony as ever?"

"Probably. Haven't been to it myself in ages. But Anu could make the trip. Sikkim's not far."

Anu looked from mother to father.

"How soon?"

CHAPTER TWENTY SIX
Festival At Sikkim

Each year after the spring rains ceased in the north, Kalumma-Dalla, Nippur's high-priestess of the *nigenna*, would venture abroad in search of planting sign.

She would examine the water markings on a holy staff chucked into the left bank of the Euphrates, and decide if the river was ready to charge the canals. She would study the soil in fields the men had ploughed, harrowed, and broken up with hammers for ten days by sunlight and starlight. When she had divined the conditions to be auspicious for the first sowing, Kalumma would send word to her queen that Enbilulu, god of agriculture, was ready to receive the prayers of the people.

Early the day after receiving the hunter's praise in the street, also the third day of the first week of *emesh*, the summer season, Uruna departed Nippur in response to Kalumma's summons. She traveled afoot southeast to Sikkim, the village where the Shrine of Enbilulu was erected, taking with her twenty *udalla* anointers and a dozen seed bearers laden with sacks of barley corn. A short column of faithful laity trailed along to observe the celebration and report home.

The outcome was uniformly optimistic: a ceremony performed flawlessly, a fortuitous auguring by the village seer, manifold signs of bounty along the way, a pleasant celebration and meal before the party returned. Each year the pilgrims were fewer in number, the reports more banal. Life consistently sprang from Sumer's rich blanket of silt and continued to produce a tradable surplus year after year. Why endure a hot trip just to watch the queen wave her hand over the ground? Why spend one's holiday in Sikkim's meager accommodations when one could visit old friends close by, or spend the time with relatives?

In his youth, Anu had never gone to Sikkim. Holy Planting Day was usually an occasion to seek worldly pursuits, and this day would have been no exception had he not burned to see Uruna once more. An hour after rising he was following her troupe like a happy puppy, hanging back half a mile to avoid being recognized, and losing ground because of his leg.

The going in the first hour was comfortable enough, but by the end of the second he was sweating, badly in need of drink, and far behind the procession. When at last he staggered to the edge of town, visitors and townspeople already filled the marketplace to the gutters.

Anu found the communal well easily enough and helped himself to a draught from the pail. As he straightened from returning the vessel to the bottom he felt a light tug on his arm and looked up. A pleasant smile greeted him from the dark-eyed vision of beauty he had come to watch.

"We meet again," Uruna said.

Her hair hung straight to her shoulders, her skirt was immaculate, the smooth skin of her neck and shoulders showed not a drop of moisture. For a woman who had just passed two hours on the road she was remarkably fresh. Where were her attendants? How had she escaped the press of the people?

"You catch me at a disadvantage," he said, fumbling for words. "I've not yet recaptured my strength."

Her gaze fell to his scarred leg and her brows drew together with unaffected concern. Her disarming candor touched him, adding to her enticing beauty a human warmth he found altogether irresistible.

"A serious wound," she remarked with appreciation. "You walked with us all the way from Nippur?"

"I fell behind, couldn't keep up." He hurried away from that line of discussion. "Did I miss the ceremony? I wanted to see how you do it."

She shook her head. The light sound of her laughter was a delicate melody, her jaw line a graceful arc that begged his caress. She was close enough to touch! For a moment the rest of the world receded from view as every detail of her skin, her hair, her clothing commanded scrutiny. His eyes couldn't get enough of her perfection!

"Everyone's just resting from the journey," she assured him, "revisiting our Sikkim friends. They have some wonderful cakes over there by the tent if you're hungry. And some wine. It's really a very informal affair, one of my more pleasant obligations, if you can call it that."

"I'd love to watch."

"Good. I'm glad you came. I was hoping to see you again."

"You were?"

She abruptly sobered and averted her eyes, a little girl caught with her hand in the honey jar.

"I only meant—"

He charged ahead recklessly. "Will you have time afterward? A place where we can talk? I realize you're terribly busy with the celebration and all..."

"Not too terribly."

Her hand caught his arm and he was stopped by the thrill of sensation that raced along his skin. She must have felt his response, for she flinched and recoiled as though she had touched a flame.

"I can make the time if you feel it's important."

"It's important to me. I hope afterward you'll agree."

A woman called to her from the crowd. Uruna leaned toward him with a conspiratorial whisper.

"Ask for the house of Shu-alla. I'll meet you there after the feast."

"There's a feast too?"

"Oh, they always cook up a marvelous roast. Help yourself, make friends. I have to go."

He watched Uruna walk away from the well. At the edge of the square she turned and glanced over her shoulder at him before melting into the crowd.

He stood for several minutes arrested by the impact of that small picture of perfection, neither questioning nor analyzing the bliss he felt, but instead basking in the rapturous feeling that he owned the day. Then, charmed by the musical echo of Uruna's voice in his head, he floated through the tiny marketplace, stopping to feed his ravenous appetite and smile with benign ecstasy at complete strangers.

Each delicious morsel was Uruna. Every radiant smile was Uruna. The sky was brighter, the earth was richer, because of Uruna.

She had told him yes! *I was hoping to see you again*, she had said. Great Goddess, he was a love-struck boy! He would never be the same.

He ranged through the tents, raking juice from a ripe plum, snapping a rotund grape in his teeth. He swashed through the crowd in great strides, laughed and bantered with sweet wenches who giggled and slapped each other in mock rivalry for his attention. An old woman selling clay effigies plied him with a ragged smile and he purchased one for twice its worth. He clowned for a group of small boys playing tow-the-barge. At a game ring he squatted with knot-muscled planters, happily singing fatuous boasts and exchanging good-natured gibes when he lost.

Sikkim! What a glorious spot! What charming people to share in his happiness!

Sumer's farming stock were a far cry from the Hani swamp people. Leathery skin weathered by the harsh sun clung to their slender, wiry bodies. The skirted men were taller and not as heavy-muscled as Hani hunters, and their soft-eyed women tended toward a quiet beauty. Sumerians were clannish, and the family rated first above all, but land ran a close second. The entire community doted on the children, in whom lay their hopes for continued good fortune. Daily life embraced tradition and religious culture; prayer drove the life cycle as it moved the heart. The annual visit from the temple was the pinnacle of a year's hard work and an opportunity to share the bounty with guests from far away. For a single day of the year, the entire planter community focused attention on the township of Sikkim. Everyone turned out, all participated, none was a stranger.

A shout went up heralding the start of the sacred sowing. At the edge of a field bordering Sikkim's flanks, the crowd opened a clearing around a brick pillar set in the ground on a wide base and narrowing toward the top. Here stood the Shrine of Enbilulu, decorated with flowers and spring boughs of fruit blossoms. Four elders from the town escorted Nippur's queen and her high anointers to the place of honor before the Shrine as everyone gathered round with gleeful expressions to watch the ancient rites.

A small boy and his smaller sister approached Uruna, each bearing a tidy bouquet. She stopped and bent to her haunches to accept each bouquet in turn, favoring its bearer with a broad smile and a kiss. Still kneeling, she chatted quietly to her two diminutive hosts as her fingers deftly wound the flowers into a band for her hair. Had she applied the same dexterity with flowers to her woven lion's face that night in the *ghana*?

With her new crown in place, Uruna stood, took each child by the hand, and faced the shrine. The women with anointing vials encircled her and the two children and the townspeople closed in against the ring. A dark-skinned, grizzled farmer broke ranks with a plough which he set before Uruna. She neatly put a small foot to the tool and shoved it into the soil, then said a benediction.

The anointers took up a chant and began tossing seeds into the circle. Barley might never sprout from the random piles strewn inside the circle, but the deed was symbolic. Tomorrow the men would return to the blessed field with seed corn basket and seeder plough. Today, Uruna sang psalms from the people and asked Enbilulu to protect canal and water flow and send his children, Lahar and

Anshan, down from Heaven—Lahar to bless ox and goat, and the goddess Anshan to bless plough, yoke and crops.

What she did next was a remarkable stroke of instinct.

Uruna bent her shoulder to the plough and pushed a short furrow two feet, three feet, and stopped. The ploughman gave her his hat, which Uruna proudly donned as an emblem of honor to polite applause. The farmer then took up the traces and prepared to haul the plough.

Uruna spat on her hands, spraddled her feet like a peasant, and heaved against the plough as the man pulled. The blade dug a full yard, then two yards more as the earth fell away on either shoulder of a clean furrow.

Suddenly the plough skipped over the surface and slid away, sending Uruna down on her hands and knees in the dirt. She came up laughing with dirt on her arms and elbows and feet, and in wiping her brow drew a dark smear across her forehead.

Now she had the people with her. To hearty laughter, she hauled the plough back to the furrow, whistled to her "ox," and dug the blade firmly into place again. She finished the furrow in a good straight line and crossed the circle to the other side.

The crowd stamped their feet and roared approval, and Uruna answered with a victorious fist above her head and a grin of heartfelt triumph. The hem of her white dress was smudged with grime, but her beauty was undiminished by the dust of her beloved land.

Anu's cheer was as loud as any. None could but love her earthy good humor and profound appreciation for their labor. She belonged to them, and they to her.

Anu joined the return to town, where the men put on games of skill in the square. Young and old alike tested athletic prowess as strong arms chucked rakes and sickles at straw targets. A foot race followed, starting at the market square and progressing through town, around the foundry, and back along the Nippur road. The object was to run as hard as you could and yet salvage enough energy to cross the finish line. Each participant triumphed as family and friends cheered home their own gasping, staggering champion. Spirits were raised even higher when the women came out from their houses with platters and pots of food.

A matron in green linen sidled up to Anu and spoke in a soft voice. "She awaits you now in the house of Shu-alla. I shall tell no one."

CHAPTER TWENTY SEVEN

Grape Arbor Tryst

The sun was well past meridian when Anu passed beneath the lintel of a large house on the east end of town set back from the road in a grove of palms. Shu-alla was a tiny woman of indeterminate age with iron gray hair and black eyes that shone with perpetual mischief. She took the measure of Anu's towering figure and nodded hearty approval.

"Take your leisure in the garden out back, young prince," she said.

Uruna awaited him on a bench beneath a grape arbor, miraculously cleansed of any evidence of her earlier toil, and ceremoniously announced by Shu-alla, who lingered only long enough to set out wine and a fruit bowl.

"How did you find such an idyllic spot?" he asked when their hostess was gone.

"I'm a queen," Uruna stated, as a matter of simple fact. "People seek out the best for me. I've stayed with Shu-shu every year since I was thirteen, when I did my first Holy Planting. She's become a dear friend."

"You wield the plough like a planter's wife. The people loved it. The men boasted of your exploits. Your love of earth brings the gods closer to the people, they said."

Uruna glowed with satisfaction. "Really? They said that?"

"Inanna's truth," he told her.

She hunched forward, elbows on knees. "I started that business only a few years ago to relieve the monotony of *nigenna*. The ceremony alone was too much to endure any longer. Nippur used to come down here by the hundreds and just take over poor Sikkim. Now it's like so many other things we seem to be losing."

"It's easy to see why the gods keep coming back. The people love you, Uruna, and I can hardly blame them."

Anu took her hands from her lap and brought them to his lips.

"I touched a doe one morning while she grazed," he told her. "Her surprise was the high point of that day, and ever afterward I thought she was the most beautiful thing could ever happen to me. Now I look at you and I cry inside because you are so beautiful."

Uruna looked at his hands, his lips, his eyes. She swallowed hard and her eyes glistened. He held his breath and bent closer, wanting to take her in his arms, to plumb the depths of her being as a thousand questions rushed to his lips and away.

How would he ever take the measure of this woman? With the swiftness of a cat, but harmless in her pursuit, she went straight to the truth and emerged with triumphs of the human heart. He wanted to be the breath she inhaled, the water sliding between her lips and running over her tongue, the first sound to brush her ear on wakening, the song ringing joy in her heart.

"I must tell you—" he began.

She pressed a finger gently over his lips, a soft caress of tantalizing intimacy.

"Anu, I know," she said. "I feel it too."

Her finger continued across his cheek and traced a line to the back of his neck, a light exploratory stroke, flesh to flesh, life to life, a tentative, wondering probe for possibility as her eyes widened with delight at the discovery of each new shape.

"Did I tell you and forget?" he said, his mind in a spin.

"One look at you and I know what's in your heart. That's enough for me."

He bent and placed his mouth on hers, felt her soft lips yield and reach up for him, eager to drink from the same cup, willing and wanting the same melody to sing from both their hearts. The sweetness of her was a pain too precious to bear, urging him beyond the barricades of flesh to taste the breathtaking reward within.

They parted lips reluctantly and Uruna gently leaned her hands against his chest to watch him up close through languorous, smoky eyes that spoke her complete surrender.

"When do you suppose it first happened?" she asked, the lightness of her breath an exhilarating sequel to the kiss.

"In Kudu Mahti," he said without hesitation.

"But you sent me away."

"Only because I'd see only your face instead of the lion."

"But that moment in the court chamber, when we stole glances."

"I was yours—you knew it then."

"I wanted to believe it but I wasn't sure. I didn't know your name."

"And then the day they lost the sacred stone and you caught that child..."

"Kinar gave me your name then, and I knew I could hope."

"You were magnificent! A huntress sure of her target! How my heart sang for you, Uruna!"

"Do you know what it means to hear you say my name that way?"

"Uruna!" he said again. "A song on my lips. I'm like a child. I say foolish things and I don't care."

"Your words are wonderful to hear. I could spend the rest of my days listening..."

She stopped, as if hearkening to a sound he hadn't heard.

"Something is wrong?" he asked. "Something I said?"

"No, no. It's, oh, I don't know! I've never felt this way before, not about anyone. Anu, I want it to last between us. It has to. I couldn't bear to lose you to them. This time I want someone for me, but they always take him away, and I don't want that to happen to you!"

"Who are you talking about, the Mothers? Are you saying they'd take me as Damuzi? The temple wants to claim an aging lion killer for their sweet prize?"

She looked away, suddenly estranged, detached.

"No, it's worse," she said with a wistful, husky voice that tore his heart. "I took an oath. Long ago, years and years ago. It seems forever that I've lived with the promise. I can't break my pledge, or else I'd betray the trust of a host of devoted women and destroy their spirit. I cannot take a king."

"I have no use for kingship, Uruna. Only put me by your side to love you and share your dreams."

"If only you could."

"What, share your dreams? Is that so difficult?"

"It's more than a romantic wish, Anu. I mean it in the most literal sense. The temple has an ancient tradition, that if a man shares with his anointed queen the dream she seeks, she will receive a vision. Nippur needs that vision most desperately. I promised the council to seek the vision for our survival."

"I know, I was told."

"What do you mean?" She edged closer, her eyes begging to hear more.

Did he dare speak of Rahnee? Or had he dreamed a fool's delusion while slumbering?

"There was a woman," he began, then stopped, unsure how to proceed.

"Tell me her name."

"Uruna, I'm not sure of any of it."

"Just tell me."

"She said she was Rahnee of Edin."

Uruna clasped both hands over her mouth and looked at him with eyes that brightened with some inner response.

"She told me to seek you," he went on. "Said I was finished with the *ghana*. Well, any fool could see that much. But she wouldn't hear of anything else."

Uruna dropped her hands to her lap, a radiant glow to her cheeks.

"Say more."

"I told her I know nothing of serpents, and she said it's not a trick, what you do, that a man is needed and his part could be learned if, if..."

"If love was deep between them. Oh, Anu!"

"Is it difficult to accomplish, this dream?"

"I've spent my life preparing, trying. Every day, nearly every hour, always readying myself for the god. The task is arduous and dangerous, but I can't do it alone because it takes the doing of not one soul but two. A couple united in love and prepared to endure death."

"There's more you're not telling me. Are you saying love alone is not enough?"

"M-mm, perceptive of you. Yes, to aid the queen through the process, her mate must have a mastery of three aptitudes. You are qualified in two: the art of love-making, according to your temple reputation, anyway, and fearlessness before death."

"The god of no-fear lives in me. Or did. What else must I know?"

"The Lukur have many names for it, but I know it as the Secret of the Doors. Only a person specially trained through years of study can understand it."

"What's it got to do with serpents?"

Uruna's eyes widened with alarm and she slipped out of his arms and retreated a step. "How did you know? Who told you?"

"My temple friends, Uruna. You haven't been compromised. I know nothing more than the common rumor that you're friendly with serpents and you've spent a lifetime studying them."

She turned away and walked to the edge of a shallow pond. A shadow darted toward her feet and paced the waters holding her reflection. Uruna ignored the fish and trained her eyes on a grove of palms in the distance.

"Study. Yes, I suppose you could call it study, although I'm never sure in his presence who is the subject and who the object of such enterprise. I speak of Kukhmet."

"A god?"

"A cobra. He sleeps at my feet." She pivoted and faced him with her chin lifted in challenge. "Did they tell you that also? Does it offend you? Revile you perhaps? Can you imagine a man entwined with a woman while she's wrapped in the coils of her other lover?"

"Uruna, stop."

"That's what they say!"

He quickly drew her to him, surprised by the ease with which she yielded to his touch.

"If you slept with a lion, I would gladly share your bed. The lion enjoys company in his slumber. Now a cobra?" He widened his eyes expressively.

The haughty chin came down and Uruna chuckled softly. "Your timing is wonderful. I was getting morose."

"Uruna, listen to me. I don't care what others think. I will do anything for you, go to any lengths to share your life, whatever may come with it. Show me how to learn from the serpent. Teach me how to help you, and I will. I once gave my will to the hunting god. I will do the same for yours. I will be your helper to the gate."

Uruna closed her eyes and drew a deep breath. When she opened them her face showed hints of pain and defeat.

"It's too late for us, Anu," she said. "One has already been found, just a week ago. The council is preparing our marriage."

Anu felt cold fear reach into his heart and shake it. He released Uruna's arms and stood, sure now that he was losing her the way he'd lost the god. Something in him was unworthy, slowing his stride so that he was late to the mark.

Suddenly he felt the weight of the day's labors as the leg shivered, and he leaned against a pillar for support. In the pond, a squadron of slender shapes milled in his shadow and darted out of sight beneath the bright green pads.

"Who is the man?" he asked her listlessly. "Where did he come from?"

"I've met him once, in the Aniginna with the ladies and his priests and soldiers. He spoke a few words and I—"

"You agreed to marry him?"

"No! There were supposed to be tests and then the Mothers would ask me—but it didn't happen that way. While I was away in Kudu Mahti with you, they convened a council and decided he's the one."

"Tell me his name."

"He's called Marduk. An emissary from Ekur learned of him in a land far to the north, but he was living near Uruk all this time."

"How strange. Does he know these rites of the serpent?"

"He's demonstrated a certain, er, way with vipers."

Anu leaped into the breach. "You're not convinced!"

Uruna shuddered and shrank away. His explosive outburst had frightened her, a most unforgivable dropping of guard, but Uruna was wrestling larger demons, for she went on.

"Of course I'm convinced. I-I have to be. We haven't found anyone in fourteen years of searching the four corners of the world. Marduk has the best chance to lead me to a vision."

She seemed hesitant, unsure, but he was just learning about her, and if he kept pushing too hard he might lose any chance with her. Still, the words spilled out of him before he could think.

"Do you love him?"

Uruna stiffened her elbows at her sides, her small hands doubled into fists. "Love? Anu, these matters take time."

He stepped closer and drew her to him. "Look at me," he commanded, feeling her heartbeat pound against his chest as he probed her soul for the tiniest weakening of resolve.

"Could you give him the best of your heart and trust him to return the same?"

Doubt. A tiny frown of consternation. "It's too soon to tell."

"But soon enough to plunge headlong into a marriage arranged hastily by a desperate council. It's madness, Uruna."

"I must do it! It is my duty!"

"You're avoiding the issue. What about the man? Tell me what's wrong with the man!"

"Nothing is wrong, exactly."

No defiance, no indignant resolve to defend a promised husband. She was strangling on hopelessness, her light dimmed by doubt and fear. The hunter in him strained to drive the dark intruder into the open and chase it down.

"You hesitate, your eyes are clouded when you answer me. The mention of the man does not bring joy to your face. You look left when you should look right. What do you feel in his presence?"

Her eyes closed. "Don't," she pleaded.

"Tell me what you feel when you're with him!"

A sob wrenched its way past her throat and her eyes snapped open. "Cold!" she cried. "I feel coldness and I'm afraid!"

"The man is craven! How could such a beast put fear in your heart? How could he have gotten past the Mothers? In what way did he threaten you?"

Uruna shook her head.

"No, no. He says nothing unkind. He's always well-mannered and solicitous. It's just a feeling I get." She looked to one side and straightened to full height. "But I must put my own feelings aside for this purpose. I must do the will of the council."

He traced a finger along the smooth curve of her jaw line, seeing the inconsistency of her reason, loving her for being so dearly flawed.

"Uruna! Love! Listen to yourself!" he whispered to her. "What you're doing is denying the warning of your inner god. He signals danger and betrayal, and you must listen. Your heart, Uruna, is the drumbeat of the land. By your heart you judged the planter with honor and truth."

"Only because you were there for me."

"In your heart you've seen my love and you know I worship you. Give me time, give Sumer time, and together we'll capture your vision."

She caught his hand and pressed it to her lips.

"Dear heart, if I had met you years ago we might have worked on it together. But there isn't time anymore. While I waited and searched in vain, I let Nippur slip to the brink. We're betrayed by allies, my council is driven by fear. We don't have years to prepare, nor even months. I must accept Marduk's offer."

"Uruna, you're listening to the voice of doom. Tezu-Mah hears it as he stumbles upon the lion in its lair. All he sees are great sinews ready to launch the beast six yards in a single leap, claws that can shred a man's skin from his bones in a single swipe. He smells the beast and he smells his own fear and he hears the voice telling him to run, run or be killed, which is exactly what he must not do. And then he remembers to listen to his heart, and he is quieted, and he sees possibility, opportunity, the slender thread by which the lance will be guided to the beast's vital spot."

"This isn't the same. We're dealing with immortal gods, not hunting game."

"Yes, it's exactly the same, and you know it. You knew it when you stood in the road with the stone bearing down upon you, no chance of escape, only your own annihilation if you failed. But you leaped for the child and won."

"Your confidence is greater than mine. Sumer needs a sure will and strong hand like yours. Would you become a king for Sumer?"

"When she has you? I couldn't acquit myself half as well. You've governed for your entire life, and you command the will of the people. The power is already in your hands, not mine. Besides, it's not for a man to rule. We're unsuited to the purpose."

"Oh, hogwash. Women have produced their share of unfit rulers. Gender has nothing to do with one's qualifications for office. When I look at you I see a man who accepts his fate without fear and plunges straight at the obstacles."

"That's faith."

"It's more than faith, it's courage. And wisdom."

"By whatever name, it amounts to a trust in action. Each day is a new test of resolve. Act now as you acted with the child. Show no restraint, move without concern for the consequences to yourself. Make your stand with me."

Her eyes wavered ever so slightly, a fawn seeking the route to safe cover. He swept her reluctance aside with bold assurance.

"Uruna, I give you my love now, here in Sikkim with the sun shining and Shu-shu's flowers smiling at your beauty. If your god accepts my heart and I work hard enough, I can give you whatever you require. There has to be a way, there is a way. We just don't see it yet!"

Uruna watched him, bearing her hunger for him openly, her eyes liquid ovals of love drawing him irresistibly forward.

At once a flash of golden light flared, illuminating the space around them, and he felt the essence of Uruna reach for him, surround him, until he was immersed in a delightful soothing glow. A kindred spark within him ignited, reached outward to meet her, connected and bonded. Uruna's features blurred and became a river surface, bright water shining in the sun, and a woman's voice, not Uruna's, spoke to him in dreamy-soft tones from a distance:

The sign of Heaven's door is cast in stone.
When the full moon shadow meets her hand...

The voice abruptly faded on the air. Anu shook his head clear and the water image sharpened and became Uruna's face again. She blinked once, a languid drop and lift of sinuous eyeline over dove-grey disk, then shivered and brushed away a strand of hair as she looked aside in distracted confusion.

"Did you..." She stopped and stared up at him, like a child awaiting her parent's direction.

"I heard it too," he said.

"You heard? Oh, yes." She drew a deep breath and shuddered.

"What happened?" he asked.

"He was here."

"The god."

"Yes."

"I see no serpent about."

"He doesn't show himself to mortal eyes. To follow the serpent way, you first have to look past the obvious, then see life through...serpent eyes. My part is done. My appointed mate will help to complete the cycle."

"What do the words say?"

"The riddle waits for each of us to answer, but only if you bring the god your answer before Sumer is swallowed in oblivion."

"Where do I start?"

"It's too late for us, Anu! You can't imagine how much there is to learn, the preparation, the concentration. It's too much for any human to compress into the tiny time left. He is already chosen. He will be waiting for me when I return to Nippur."

"There has to be a way. Just promise me, Uruna, not to marry this man until I return."

Uruna raised a hand to his face. Her lip trembled as she traced a line to his chest and laid her hand over his heart.

"I can't do that, Anu. I can't make a vow with the likelihood it will be broken in a single night. Our future is in the gods' hands now."

"Uruna..."

"The others are waiting in town. I have to go."

He grabbed her hand and pressed her palm to his lips, and her eyes followed the hand, went out to him, and he saw that she was helplessly bound to his touch, unable and unwilling to give him up. He had to be the one to do it. He must release her.

On a sudden impulse, he snatched the knife from his belt, snapped the thong around his neck, and shucked the beads off the end. Into Uruna's open palm he placed the ivory crescent. She looked down at the claw, curled against her flesh like another part of her hand. The shape fit perfectly around the base of her thumb.

"Let him protect you from harm," Anu told her. "He is a quarter moon. Look for me on a full moon night. I will come for you and I will please your god, and you will have your vision."

Uruna clutched his gift with fierce delight and bit her lip, her eyes brimming with emotion as they lingered on his face. She took a last drink of him, then turned and dashed from the garden.

Anu walked home that night by a different route, taking the path that followed the slender ribbon of the Shat-al-Ama canal, alone with his thoughts and the silent, star-swept sky. He had a new quest. His tired body bent happily, eagerly, to renewed purpose, to a cause worth more than all the lions of a lifetime.

He had a woman to win.

CHAPTER TWENTY EIGHT
Two Blows Foretold

A gentle breeze rose up from Euphrates to sweep the evening clean of dust as Uruna walked the Sikkim road home. Silhouetted against the reddening horizon, Nippur spread her ramparts like a great billowing skirt beneath the temple's bodice, caught in the sun's afterglow. Uruk Gate and a world of duty awaited her return, but she was still drunk with the sensual profusion of the arbor's sweet balm and Anu's exquisite touch, and she wanted to savor the experience as long as possible.

For perhaps the hundredth time she fingered the lion's claw at her neck. Ignoring half-heard snatches of road talk around her, she floated in a realm apart, suspended by the magnitude of promise contained in the naked ivory, a token as raw as uncut lapis, but to her, utterly beyond price.

Uruk Gate was alight when she arrived with her *udalla* priestesses. Flames towered above the twin oil tureens mounted atop the gateposts to cast a welcome in all directions. As they entered Street of Humble Need, Kalumma-Dalla pulled Uruna aside to mention a concern that shouldn't wait till morning. Uruna surprised herself by agreeing without hesitation.

"Freshen up in your apartment," she said, "and then come to my place." She lifted her tote from her hip. "I sneaked away some cookies and cream. We'll have to finish them off before they spoil."

She was humming a planter's ditty to herself when Kalumma rapped on her door. The *nigenna* chief's guarded expression warned Uruna against appearing too lighthearted for the discussion ahead. Nevertheless, she was determined to let no news smother the resurgent joy inside struggling for release.

Kalumma sat herself before her much younger queen and arranged her flounces with great care before she spoke.

"In the tenth season of Gudmalla's reign..."

"There came a great flood," Uruna finished.

"Er...yes. How do you know of such a thing?"

"I was told in my preparation for induction."

"Good heavens, that was more than a decade ago."

"Fourteen years, seven months, to be exact."

"But how can you remember...?"

"It is one of the traits for which I was chosen. You wish to warn me of an impending flood, but you couldn't say anything in Sikkim. Prudent thinking, to be sure. How soon?"

"Uruna! My gods, how could you know already?"

"The color of your eyes, your immaculate preparation for this meeting."

Moreover, the return of my "touches" by which I see what you see.

Also of use might have been reports from her own sources abroad. She smiled to encourage the woman further.

"Go ahead, dear, I need your keen mind to clarify the muddled tales from farm folk. Tell me, how bad will it be?"

Kalumma's eyes cast about furtively. She had expected to create a much greater impression with her findings, but scarcely any news escaped the queen's notice these days.

"I have consulted the tablets from that time. Ours will not be as devastating, for we've learned a great deal since then about levees and soil conservation. But the Anatolian snows are much deeper than usual. Next spring the flow will not abate as early as usual. This past winter a weir above Karka burst and caused a diversion of the river's course. The *nigenna* priestess up there sent word the river plowed a new furrow."

"Meaning what?'"

"It's running faster over harder ground. A new branch has become the main channel. Another wet season like this one will push our levees past their limit."

"How do we prepare for it?"

"The same as Gudmalla did, and Lasori before her. With prayer and fasting."

Why not add a little old-fashioned manual effort?

"How reliable are your reports from the field?"

Kalumma's head quaked with pride. "My men are the very best! Such devoted souls! They feel the land, they move with the water, sense every shift of wind. No beer bowl for them at night, they're out checking weirs, rodding channels, testing every ditch and furrow. They know, madam, and I am proud of every one."

"I am sure they're a credit to us all. So you would interpret their findings to mean danger ahead."

"I would, for I believe we've done all we can to insure containment on temple lands. However, I cannot say the same for our private landholders. Hanza planters guard their own tallies from Seddua eyes with jealous fervor. But as you know, the other *nigenna* temple lands lie downstream from us. Nippur will be struck first and hardest, after Kish and Kutha, of course."

"And Mother Tigris? Will she too cover the land?"

"I cannot say for certain. Our emissary to Aramdan did not...did not..."

She broke off and struggled for composure. It was well known that Puabi Dalla had not returned from her gallant expedition to the far north, and was presumed to have perished. The loss had hit Kalumma Dalla particularly hard, for Puabi was her only child.

Kalumma tried to hide her grief behind her hand, but her eyes welled up, and Uruna got up and went to her and took her in her arms.

"My good and faithful Kalumma. Bless you. Great Mother keeps you and yours in her heart."

The older woman recovered with a mighty effort and gave Uruna a short nod.

"My greater concern is the feud between our two largest secular landowners. Uruna, we cannot prepare for flood in such a divided state. Only a united effort will succeed. You know it, I know it, the Mothers in the northern provinces know it. But I cannot say the same for Udea Seddua and that clan of hers. Nor really for Heganna. I saw her son in the Sikkim market today, and I was tempted to try his reason, but he's only been back a week."

More precisely, four days, thirteen hours...where did she get that? Were her senses returning after so many years? Had the hunter done something in the arbor? Could a single kiss release so much...?

"If you wish, I'll approach the man," she said.

The discussion then moved to the particulars of crop preservation and damage control. With the cookies and cream consumed, and satisfied she could learn nothing further from Kalumma, Uruna closed the conversation.

"It goes without saying, but I'll say it anyway. This must be kept between the two of us."

"I quite agree. The *nigenna* workforce will await your word and maintain the current state of things. But Uruna, there's already suspicion abroad in the hinterland. Planters may lead simple lives, but they are not stupid. They can read the signs as well as I."

"Understood. We'll have to take swift action, but I need time to marshal resources from the other temples. We must unify our efforts."

"Good luck on that score."

As she prepared to leave, Kalumma stopped at the door.

"Uruna, despite that debacle with the consort from Azziz, I cast my lot with you."

"Thank you, my dear. For that and for today."

Once she made sure Kalumma was gone, Uruna crossed to the window and gazed down into the lighted courtyard before speaking over her shoulder.

"You can come out now."

Retha slipped out from behind the drape where Uruna had hidden her from Kalumma.

Uruna pushed her new ally toward the door, but Retha turned with a puzzled look.

"Shouldn't we talk about the flood? Where are we going?"

"Fetch your cloak," she told the girl. "The river gets cold at night."

𒀭 𒁀 𒆠 𒌋𒌋

After first checking her garment and then Retha's to be sure the hoods obscured their faces, Uruna struck off through a warren of Nippur's darkened back streets. The sentry at Exalted Gate was more concerned with outsiders seeking their way into the city, and the two of them quickly slipped past him and turned the corner outside.

The moonless night closed round them as stark and opaque as a tomb. Uruna hugged the base of the west wall as Nippur's reassuring torchlight vanished. And then they were out beneath the stars, Retha feeling naked in her flimsy robe as each step took them farther from the city haven.

The air was indeed cold where Uruna picked her way along a narrow path at the base of wall near Gate of No Shaking, and Retha was thankful for the extra wrap. The gate's ancient opening was bricked over, closed off a hundred years ago when an earlier regime had moved the harbor farther downstream. Against the taller ramparts of the new wall, its squat posterns crouched like dwarf sentinels. Uruna slipped into the shadow of the gate's declivity and drew Retha brusquely to her side.

"Stay out of the light," she whispered, and pointed up at the wall top where sentries were likely to walk the thick perimeter. You could march a yoke of oxen atop the wall's wider parts. Farther down the parapet a single torch struggled in a rush of cool river air.

Uruna immediately began whispering from the other side of her face, and Retha flinched as she realized there was a man standing right beside her. He had stolen in behind them without a sound, a large man by the elevation of his response.

"Tell us about Kish," urged Uruna, and when the man demurred, she vouched for Retha. "This is Retha. We're sisters in Serpenthood tonight. She keeps a keen mind and a tight tongue inside her head. Go on, Suba."

The man hesitated before starting, as if gathering his thoughts, but when he spoke it was with clear-voiced intelligence.

"As near as I can tell, there's a regular flow of grain stores coming downriver out of Kish, all according to covenant with Nippur. But the whole lot goes straight past Amaninda Number One, past Number Two, and right past Nippur under our very noses, all the way down to Uruk. The tablets with the counts change hands at Babyla, a tiny poke across the river from Kish. A scribe there duplicates the symbols—your ladies know the meaning of those scratches, I don't—and sends the fake copy back with the courier."

"Are you absolutely sure of this, Suba?"

"I was courier myself on one occasion."

"You diverted tablets?"

"I was entrusted with them, yes, and I returned the fakes as directed, to avoid suspicion."

"Who gave and who took?"

"A different man on each end. I operated by a password given to me by an unfortunate lackey who died as he slipped the tablets to me."

Retha was puzzled. "How did that happen?"

"He fell on my knife."

"Oh," she said, shaken by the man's casual euphemism for murder. Suba, however, had more to tell.

"A fellow they call Borok runs it all up there. He's half Gunzek, half something else, and he hates everything that walks upright and thinks."

"What's he look like?" asked Uruna.

"Tall, heavy build, pocked cheeks and a scarred furrow down his left cheek, like a woman raked him well."

Uruna shifted her weight in the dark. "Why do I think I've heard the name before?"

"Because he works for the Bull. We ran across him down in Uruk a couple years ago, remember?"

"I believe you told me at the time that he was running slaves for the Bull."

"Exactly, and your council claimed it was impossible."

"They insisted no Lukur would condone slavery, and when I explained that Eanna's old women no longer controlled Uruk's affairs, and hadn't for years, they shut up fast."

Retha crouched in the dark with her back against the cold bricks, trying to fit together what the two were saying. Suba provided his own answer for both women.

"The Bull's playing for keeps. He needs strong Hani backs for his public works, but now he's ready to do something more aggressive."

"Like make a move against Nippur?"

He paused in the dark. "I thought you knew. He has two hundred men camped downriver from here."

"Two hundred! For what purpose?"

"To occupy Nippur as a defense force."

"Means he'll turn our city into a satrap for Uruk."

"Yes, and before the Kurgs make a move, would be my guess."

"We have to round up every *galla* soldier from the provinces. We'll head them off before they cross the river."

His silence signaled Suba's assent. Before she could think, Retha felt his powerful hand on her shoulder.

"Make sure this lady doesn't suffer from a slip of your tongue. Our fate depends on what we do in the next few days. We can't afford a single false step."

"You have my word," Retha vowed with a swallow.

Suba's hand released her and swept around Uruna's shoulders in the dark. The two lingered in the embrace, and then the big soldier slipped away into the darkness of the palm grove.

Retha rubbed her shoulder where the touch of gentle strength had reminded her of her father's caress. From such men came the purest affection, a rare balance. She had thought her Nord race held a monopoly until she saw the same trait in Uruna's soldier. Oddly, she was pleased to know it reposed in another.

"Where did you come across such loyalty?" she asked as she and Uruna trudged back to Exalted Gate.

"He's part Nord," she said. "Surprised?"

"Not much. More like delighted. Do you know his line?"

"A grandmother back in Lasori's time took an invader as her husband. Other Lukur did the same to quell the Nord hostile heart. Now we've no ally more steadfast than our enemies of old."

"But how did you find Suba?"

Uruna waited a few paces before replying. "I was married to him."

"What?"

"He was my first consort. We were very young and very much in love, and when the Mothers came to take him for sacrifice, I couldn't bear to lose him. So I slipped him down the back wall from my bedroom. We've conspired together ever since."

"You still love him, don't you?"

"Yes."

"Why didn't you take him for a husband? Wasn't he fit for Serpenthood?"

"He wanted children."

"And you don't, is that it?"

"Oh, Retha, you don't understand. It's the life I've chosen."

"Sorry, I've got so much to learn. Is there some rule that forbids the high priestess from rearing a family like any other woman?"

Uruna stopped in her tracks so abruptly Retha nearly crashed into her.

"No one's told you."

"Told me what?"

A great sigh and heave of shoulder, like a dray-woman shrugging off the day's burden. "Preparation for the Sight requires regular ingestion of cobra serum. Very tiny doses, never enough to endanger the supplicant. But it kills the life within. I've partaken of the venom since age nine. I cannot bear a child."

Instinctively, Retha reached for Uruna's hand and drew it to her face.

"I'm sorry," she whispered softly. "I didn't know."

Uruna's wry chortle was a surprise. "Neither did I, sweet," she said, turning her back on the river and continuing up the path. "Neither did I."

CHAPTER TWENTY NINE

Duty and Ceremony

As Uruna trod Nippur's streets in the pre-dawn darkness, her thoughts stayed on Anu, causing her to miss several turns on a route she'd taken daily for half her life.

Weeks before, following her return from the *ghana*, she had called for improved attendance at Morning Honors, with the added insistence that everyone greet Inanna's new day with as much joy and enthusiasm as they could muster at that hour. This morning she was hard pressed to be prompt for her own mandate.

Twenty faithful lined the sanctuary in two rows when she reached the top of the stairs. She continued down the tiled path strewn with fresh rose petals and joined Eduanna ten paces from the altar. The congregation waited while a small girl approached with flowers and salt on a plate. The two ladies accepted the gifts with loving embraces and turned around to address the slender ten-foot obelisk above the altar.

In spite of the morning chill, both women doffed their robes and stood before the Inanna shrine in their white linen smocks. By the light of dawn, each priestess raised her voice in the familiar chant, and the celebration was underway.

Take this fragrance, O Inanna, to your sacred lips.
Receive the salt of life from your humble servant.
Cleanse my heart and make me pure.
Make me pure and worthy, Loving Mother,
Make me pure and worthy of your blessings,
O Inanna-Tum.

Uruna finished sprinkling petals from the wicker plate and reached for the goblet Eduanna held outstretched. Still facing the altar, she sipped, lifted the vessel high and turned it, then sipped again. The ritual done, she passed the goblet back to her partner and stood silently for several moments.

Everyone waited quietly until the sun caught the tip of the obelisk, and a temple woman sent two small children forward with a calf, giving the little boy an encouraging nudge when he balked. Uruna smiled as she bent to kiss each child, then winced with good humor at the calf's soft lick as she did the little ceremony with the garland. Then she led six acolytes in the Alla Manna, turned and retraced her path to the stair.

Today, instead of retreating to her private shrine, she took the stairs and quickly descended to the street and on to her assignation.

In the market square she pleased a company of urchins by buying each a ripe plum, and then she turned down a side street and entered the narrow alley where the flower vendors set up shop every day.

Each seller occupied the same stall and offered the same flowers day in and day out—one vendor, one flower, one place. If you wanted red poppies you spoke to the black-faced man with the gold ring in his ear. For white daisies you visited the exotic young woman with the orange spot painted between her brows. Uruna stopped before the tiny old woman who sold "yellow faces" and brought a petal to her nose.

"Is the mother of Luppi as fresh as these lovelies?" she inquired.

"Oh, it's you! My heavens, yes, child, I thrive yet another year as my daughter brought forth yet another child to me."

"A son?"

"Another daughter!"

"Ah, Great Mother favors you. Then I must have twelve of your 'faces' for luck."

The old woman quickly selected a bouquet. "You must go inside for tea and dates. My treat."

The clear signal. "You're very gracious to offer. I can't stay long."

"Please, you'll sweeten the day."

Against the bright summer morning's heat, the brick-walled interior stood dark and cool. Uruna passed through the anteroom and followed a short hall to the room in the back. The *galla* soldier waited on a low bench set along one wall, cradling a male toddler in one huge arm as he used his other hand to push a stick through a broth bowl. He looked up as she entered and furrowed his dark brow.

"You're lovelier than ever," he pronounced. "The city of Kish has no maiden half as fair."

"And you've tried them all," Uruna responded lightly.

A narrow smile momentarily broke the heavy features and vanished abruptly. Humor came uneasily to Lemdu. He took his daily bread from the harsh realities of intrigue, combat, and deprivation. The few pleasures in his life came from a rare but well-earned furlough. He would be in the city long enough to bed his wife and provision for the next venture. He gave Uruna a significant look.

"I have the confidence of their queen," he said.

As the full weight of his words sank in, Uruna's mind reeled. Great Hosts! Their best hope had been for him to gain a few tidbits of information before being found out. How had a brute like Lemdu won his way straight into Kish's lap?

"What is she like?" Uruna asked.

Lemdu's face darkened. He put the boy down and gently patted the tiny behind, sending the child on his way.

"You don't want to know," he said. "I can tell you she's in league with her neighbors, Kutha and Sippar, little more than cattle holds. She feeds the Kurg army. I know how the sheaves are diverted even before they leave the gate, how the money changes hands, all of it."

"Did you get the Kurg count?"

"That's the strange part. No one seems to know, although they're close enough to see for themselves."

"And you were not?"

"That's why I must go back."

"No."

"Uruna, it's vital." The huge chest heaved. "There was news of a disaster north of the Akkad—an army or a plague, and something to do with crop failure. Whatever it is, I have to find out."

"No, you've done quite enough."

"There won't be another chance, there isn't time. I have her complete trust. If I'm not back in three days she'll become suspicious."

"Let the witch fret! Leave her to her miserable hold, she will not involve you further! Lemdu, she cannot have you!"

"But what about the threat? We can't just sit here and wait for death to come dancing down the valley and strike us!"

Uruna placed her hand on Lemdu's forehead. "I discharge you," she said.

The hard lines around the mouth softened. "And if I do not accept?"

She smiled. "Then I shall have you chained in the keep, where your cruel wife will visit daily with pomegranate and wine. And when you've suffered enough—"

"Don't jest, Uruna. We're talking about the welfare of our people."

"Let me take care of it."

"But they'll perish!"

"Lemdu, trust me. Believe that your queen has more than one resource at her disposal. You've done more than I would have asked, much more. I want you home now, with Luppi and the children and Na-Na."

"You're the queen. I can't put demands on you, but you must promise to put me with the first force you send out."

"Lemdu, you have my word. We'll use all the powers of Heaven to defend ourselves. We're Inanna's favored. We are Nippur!"

The small mouth tightened, the head nodded once. Lemdu was appeased but not satisfied. The warrior in him yearned to do battle, his heart was ready with the sword, but the Sumerian revered his queen and yielded to her command.

"At the first sign of trouble," he started.

"You have my word. I'll call upon you, my precious friend. For now, be husband and father. Enjoy life and put Kish behind you. I'm going directly from here to *disikku* where I shall say six prayers for you."

She hurried away down the hall and outside, desperate to hide her misgivings from Lemdu's penetrating scrutiny. She forced a smile as she patted Na-Na's shoulder affectionately and tied the bouquet to her wrist, and held herself to a slow pace while her heart begged to race ahead to the seclusion of her room where she could hide from Lemdu, hide from judgment for the hopeless sham she had concocted for his benefit.

If only she had the confidence of her own words! She had used empty promises to dissuade Lemdu. If he really understood the meager extent of her resources, if he even suspected that she had no ally but himself and Suba, he would rush off to danger heedless of the consequences and get himself killed. Matters were getting too complicated to bear without benefit of other informers...

"There you are! Time for *disikku*, Uruna!" Niccaba's sing-song voice broke her reverie.

She was at temple! How had she gotten inside Ekur so quickly? What had she said to the sentry? She didn't remember passing the reflection pond or hiking up two flights of stairs or squeezing through the tiny entrance behind the altar.

Niccaba bathed her feet with oil, helped her don the holy vestments. How vain and shallow of her to deceive Lemdu that way! Only a fool would have sent him off alone in the first place. What was she thinking, putting the fate of thousands in one man's hands?

With stately measured steps she marched the length of Ekur's sanctuary. At the dais, she lifted the hem of her gown and mounted Inanna's sacred platform, made her turn, and faced the hall while the children set out bouquets of flowers around the altar base. She was supposed to be meditating. Instead, she pleaded forgiveness.

Inanna, why am I not with you at this sacred hour?

Did the Mothers notice her distraction? Had everyone noticed Uruna-the-fool stumble awkwardly before Inanna's very nose, forgetting to do her part, forgetting verses she had repeated a hundred upon a hundred times? She couldn't remember, but the faces turned toward her gave no evidence she had faltered back along the way.

She needed a plan and the forces to carry it out. Moreover, she needed answers to problems before they grew into crises that demanded action without forethought. Here she sat in the very lap of Inanna, the country's shining hope for prophecy, and she doubted. Was she indeed Inanna's chosen, or a feckless impostor? Would Council's choice for the miracle of Sight go unanswered while she sat immobilized by questions?

Niccaba bumped her elbow. Oh yes, the benediction. She really must put personal matters aside and concentrate on the rite.

With calculated deliberation, she measured out the ground emmer flour and sprinkled it over rose petals scattered about the polished surface of the altar table. Niccaba took the plate from her and placed the golden vial in her right hand. Uruna lifted the lid and poured the blend of date wine and ox blood into the golden chalice. She sipped once from the rim, rotated the cup a half turn, sipped again, then focused on the middle distance as Niccaba took up the chant.

Ox blood. She was pouring meaningless libations down her gullet like a swill, when she knew very well what truly captured a god's attention: Sight! The ultimate risk, an offer of life in exchange for a glimpse of eternity.

The gift within her awaited liberation. She had experienced its ripening presence in the garden with Anu, like a child flowering in her core. Yet, she would never bring forth the Sight if she chose wrongly now.

Indeed, was Marduk as unfinished as the others? Every experience told her she'd chosen unwisely in the past. Would she now place her own longing before her duty to Goddess and the faithful?

No, the untried hunter from the wilds was brave and devoted, but he wasn't ready for the ultimate act of her life. She needed a man sure of the serpent way, and such had been found despite Heganna's insistence that she must love such a husband.

Her mind went back to Anu. Was his presence a sign for the future or a test of her resolve? Did the gods hold a hunting mate in store for their serpent queen? Or had they guided the Lukur to the more practical choice?

Lemdu's findings only stressed the urgency for armed protection. The ladies had negotiated the first step in that direction and she must follow with her part of the bargain. Sumer was out of alternatives. As ever before, she must do as the god demanded, be Enshiggu's willing instrument.

She remembered to ask six prayers for Lemdu before she left.

CHAPTER THIRTY

Treachery At Hand

On his return from Sikkim, Anu spent a restless night in his mother's house, rehashing his conversation with Uruna. Nothing seemed to go as foretold. Rahnee's assurance was a myth of magic and nothing more. Uruna's love promise was subverted by her duty to a vague tradition. His own baseless vow to leap Serpenthood's boundaries had only intensified her doubt. He'd failed her in the arbor as badly as he had in the *ghana*, and tomorrow would prove his worst fear, that her love for him was an illusion, like all the rest.

When at last he fell asleep exhausted, it seemed only moments had passed when his eyes snapped open, a habit from his hunting days of popping fully awake at first light. He grabbed a few plums from the dining table and took to the streets with the Hanza household still locked in slumber.

The sense of impending doom that preceded every lion kill daunted his hunter self now. The Bull had orchestrated an armed occupation in exchange for a meaningless ceremony that fooled no one. But he wouldn't stop there, always several steps ahead of everyone else. The wedding terms had no binding precedent, but the Bull would contrive to make the matter appear otherwise. Nippur's streets already rang with anticipation of a festival. Anu struggled through the clamor, one goal in mind: to convince Uruna not to marry.

The Aniginna was quiet and nearly deserted when he finally pushed through the gate. Everyone had left to celebrate.

He crossed the concourse and slipped inside the unguarded Gipar. Encountering no one inside, he found the Ensi's quarters by dint of his hunter's sharp ear.

Two men were talking just inside the doorway to the Gipar suite. He crept into the vestibule for a view of the interior. A tiny vial on a table between the two men captured their full attention. He held his breath for one's answer to the other's question regarding its contents.

"Enough to drop an ox," said Nabi Gahn.

"Will it kill her?"

Was that the Ensi himself speaking? Anu craned to hear his old mentor's reply.

"You'd like that, wouldn't you? Your eyes tell me so. But no, her death would ruin everything."

"How long before it works?"

"A thirty count, no more. I assume you can count that far?"

The insult was ignored. "And until she wakens?"

"Two falls of the sand."

They went on a bit more, but Anu had already begun his retreat, recalling Nabi Gahn's uncanny ability to detect a foe's presence without benefit of sight or sound.

What astounded him later was Nabi's failure to pick up his tail as Anu followed him through city streets toward the river. Anu kept to the shadows, a precious advantage he'd seldom enjoyed hunting in open flatland, and watched his old mentor go straight for Gula Gate rather than take evasive maneuvers.

As the fight master approached the river, Anu knew one of two possibilities was in place. Either he had gone undetected by Nabi for an unheard of length of time, or he was himself being followed by an expert tracker. He ducked behind a buttress on the outer wall and checked in both directions. No one trailed him.

Nabi continued on down to the river's edge, where he joined two men with a swifthull. After a brief discourse, Nabi hopped into the boat and took himself downstream.

Toward Uruk.

Heganna had figured rightly. Nabi had long been in the priest's pay.

But to what end, this caper with the Ensi? The Bull had shoved his marriage scheme down Uruna's throat and won Lukur favor in the doing. Marduk's place as husband to the queen was secure regardless of the serpent rite outcome. What need for further duplicity now?

The bull had another board peg up his sleeve, and Nabi Gahn was part of it.

Regardless of temple rules against trespassing, he must warn Uruna. If she went ahead with the rite tonight, there was no question it spelled ruin of some kind.

The guard posted at the gate was not in uniform and had four louts for company. Anu was quickly surrounded and hustled back through the gate and inside a corner house in deep shadow. Rough hands shoved him into a tiny room, and he realized his mistake and began his turn, but not soon enough. A Gunzek stepped behind him with a club.

"Sleep tight, hunter," said another's voice just before he felt a blow to his head and the world closed down upon him.

CHAPTER THIRTY ONE

Trance or Drug?

Long after the sun was gone, Nippur's ubiquitous brick and mortar extended the summer sun's baking process. Uruna stood inside her apartment, miserably hot in her wedding costume, and waited for an assistant to remove the tall headdress of hammered gold and the gown that flowed over her sandaled feet.

The wedding ceremony had been a perfunctory affair conducted by a few and witnessed by even fewer. She had stayed her post throughout, a creature of obsession with duty, her thoughts absorbed with the hunter and not with her betrothed at all. Now, at the Bull's insistence, she would endure his pretentious attempt to invite prophecy at the hand of his appointed heir.

With the gown removed, Lub-Sunna began anointing Uruna's entire body with oil. A girl sent from Uruk tended her hair, working the thick shocks at her temples into tight braids. A third stranger daubed ceremonial paint on her chest and abdomen. When she thought they had done enough, Uruna sent them away.

Her will was spent, her desire dissipated, her mind dwelling on each moment in the arbor with Anu. None of tonight's contrivance touched her. She moved through each step of preparation with neither intent nor care. She could only hope the rest of the night belonged to the serpent god.

Niccaba's need for pomp and spectacle would not be satisfied by Sacred Union's stark confines. For the first time in ages, Hall of Consecration was opened for a ritual other than dusting and cleaning. One entire half of Serpenthood House had sat out the centuries, empty and waiting, and now the enormous sanctuary received the two supplicants.

Bride and groom approached each other from opposite ends of the main passageway and joined hands before twelve-foot carved double doors. Hidden attendants pulled the doors inward and Uruna stepped into Inanna's most sacred interior. She had viewed the interior several times before, but tonight's ceremonial splendor nearly took her breath.

The massive walls along its length were bathed in a soft yellow light from oil sconces hung from six huge supporting columns. Set into the floor at the other end was the sacred stone, a round, flat dish three yards across and carved with intricate runes whose ancient meanings none alive understood. A ring of votive candles decorated the stone's rim. Glazed jars of ointments and scents were arrayed in symmetric patterns behind the stone.

The raised dais supported a clutch of five serpent baskets, Kukhmet's larger than the other four. Beyond, a crimson altar drape formed a backdrop trimmed in gold braid. Halyards strung with fetishes of carved palmwood festooned the periphery of the hall like spangled fish nets drying in the sun. Every aspect of the chamber was calculated to entice the god's pleasure with embellishment.

Uruna's stomach clenched as she stared, horrified. Such excess was a ghastly affront to the god.

Her sense of doom increased as she spied a square table covered with a blue cloth rimmed in gold. The sand timer had been placed on top in a gesture of Lukur optimism. Cups on the device would fulfill their purpose only if she and the Ensi persuaded the god to open the Sixth Door. Six lethal hurdles and long hours of arduous work must pass before that instrument could come into play.

Her only adornments were a narrow loincloth and a beaded choker. She displayed her firm breasts proudly for the god. Her black hair hung straight to her shoulders, gathered by a braid at each temple. The scented oil on her skin caught the light of the wavering candles, making her body a gleaming encasement to house and nurture the new god.

As wifely duty commanded, she approached her husband and took his hand. The contact carried none of the charged energy she had felt from the hunter, but she continued holding Marduk as she explained the procedure.

"We must begin with the potion," she reminded him. "Help me prepare it before the god."

"Of course," he said, "Where's the vial?"

"It should be over there on the floor, next to that blue jar with the stripes."

He left her and went to the jars, obviously grateful for something to do with his hands, and retrieved the vial. She quickly poured its contents into the crystalline flagon.

Marduk took immediate interest in the object's rare translucence. "I've never seen such material."

"It comes from a stone found in the heights above the Nile. This item found its way to Nippur shortly after I was installed at Ekur in my twelfth year. Now, if you please, the brew."

He lifted the pitcher of strong ale and dribbled it expertly into the flagon. Someone had trained him well, for he examined the level closely against the light, continuing the even flow until it reached the score mark.

"Will it make you drunk?" he asked.

She thought it a strange question, unless one had a particularly low regard for the solemn occasion. Perhaps Marduk was more rattled than he looked and trying to mask a deeper disquiet.

"Not drunk," she answered evenly, holding up the small vial he had fetched for her. "But with this I shall become removed from myself."

Marduk chuckled. "What's in the vial, stronger ale?"

"No, it's cobra venom," she answered simply.

His baleful gaze was almost comical. She hesitated to explain how the mixture induced a light trance, how it lifted her above care and swept her toward the first realm. He might mistake her state for catatonia and ruin the whole ceremony.

She squatted cross-legged and began sipping the concoction. Marduk joined her on the floor and observed her progress until she had drained the vial.

"You will notice a dilation of the pupils in my eyes," she explained. "When they are quite large, I will not respond to this." She held up the palm thorn.

"You want me to test you with pain?" he asked, a strange light in his eyes.

"Press it against my fingertip. If I wince, I'm not with the serpent. Otherwise, you'll know... Oh, um, it's starting to come on..."

The room got hazy and Marduk's features blurred. "One more..." She faltered. "One more step." She was already feeling thick and loose from the drink. "Arrange the bash...baskets at the four corners before—"

Marduk gently eased her onto her back and bent over her. A corner of her mind told her something was wrong, that it was too early for his advances. She tried to resist, but he was too strong for her. *Wait, Marduk*, she started to say, but her tongue was caught in the grip of serpent will. His hands coursed down her ribs and over her hips, really marvelous hands actually, and she felt herself responding although she didn't want to start just yet. He was in such a rush.

"Fetch baskets now..."

The sensation of the potion was almost too much for her. She wanted his flesh and she wanted the sweet singing in her limbs to go on and on, but it became a numbing, dull bliss. She felt stupid, her husband looked stupid, the whole ceremony was preposterous, a ludicrous excuse to indulge sensual pleasure...so silly.

She tittered as Marduk rolled to a sitting position. As he regarded her, his features writhed about his face like snakes on a pillow...

That was hilarious…snakes on a…

Wait—what was he doing?

Standing now, hovering over her supine form and speaking, his words failing to make sense through the fog of confusion.

The stupidness abated somewhat and she rolled her head to one side. Kukhmet above her remained still, his attention following Marduk's receding form.

Was he moving away from the dais? Was it done?

She didn't remember any of it. Done so soon?

Marduk parted the first rank of curtains and murmured to a woman standing watch. Then, without another word, he left his bride and walked out the door and into the hallway.

She lifted a hand to stop him, or thought she did. The thing had not gone well, she decided in a faraway corner of her mind.

Her head suddenly crashed against something hard and unyielding. Had she gotten up and fallen?

The lamps flickered and went out.

Foolish attendants, forgot oil. Teach them a lesson, first thing tomorrow.

Yes, lesson. Show who's in charge here.

First, have to sleep…

CHAPTER THIRTY TWO
Unraveled And Undone

Uruna came awake kneeling on the floor. She could not lift her hands and knees. They seemed pinned in place by an invisible force. The echo of her own incoherent scream rang in her head as she groped for an anchor, any support to keep Serpenthood's enormous consecration hall from sliding around.

The nearest pillar looked oddly distant, like a tower on the far shore of a brown-tiled sea. The floor tilted, the walls leaned at crazy angles. Part of her was still adrift in the dream, the rest knew the dream was finished and she was lost.

A wave of grief seized her body, already weak from the potion's effect, and shook loose a torrent of anguish from darkest corners of her soul. She choked on hot pain and her eyes stung from the watery cascade that rushed down her face. Gasping for air, she surrendered to silent, wracking sobs.

She had nothing. A lifetime of hard work, and the path to a vision was as far from her as when she had started. She had reached for the prize, had tried with all her soul, and the window on Sumer's fate had actually opened to her for the briefest flash, then snapped shut, leaving her empty-handed, the prophecy denied.

Which part had she done wrong? How could she fail again and

again? It was too unfair, too cruel, so unlike the gods to encourage her all her life and suddenly dump her like a sack of refuse.

A hand reached down and hoisted her by the arm—firm like Kinar's and full of the same dependable strength, ready to gather her fallen ward. She looked up, expecting the familiar vessel of sympathy that received all her woes, but the face was youthful and light-skinned and fringed with gold. A disapproving frown wrinkled the fair features, and the lovely mouth turned down as Retha prodded her luckless queen with a foot.

"Get up."

The Nord acolyte in Hall of Consecration? Council only admitted ranking Lukur. How had the girl got in?

Uruna straightened her spine and looked around, unsure of her balance. The curtain was drawn, the snakes were back in their baskets—Retha's doing probably. Rose petals lay beyond the altar in scattered piles where a careless foot had kicked them off the sacred path. Slender smoke plumes rose up from votives snuffed out by a draft from the open doors. Marduk had knocked over a gold vase in a fit of pique on his way out and sent the vessel into a row of standards which lay scattered like hay threshings on the polished floor.

Again the toe in her side, this time a little harder.

"Everyone's gone now, so get a hold on, Uruna. You'll just make yourself sick by crying."

The mild shock to the ribs pulled her head up. How bold of the girl to speak to her queen that way, but Nords held a cold disdain for any weakness. The girl probably knew about her failure already.

Uruna pushed with her hands and sat back on her heels. Where was good Shua Kinar, faithful friend and mentor? All those years a shepherd and not beside her lamb in her darkest hour?

She was getting maudlin, the potion playing her emotions like a lyre. The girl still towered over her, dressed in her perfect white smock with the gold shoulder clasp of the Lukur.

"How could you do this to yourself?" she said. "You're drunk, you know, from the wine. You were supposed to sip."

"I dith—I did. It was mush too strong." Her head swam with confusion. "We measured care-flee, ver-r-ry carefully. I entered the Door, I think. I entered…and then he stopped."

"He says you swallowed enough wine to stun a docking crew and slumped over dead drunk."

Uruna didn't think so, but what could she say? The details were lost in a fog of blissful pleasure and half-remembered scenes of cobra heads rising from the floor, Marduk lifting himself over her, the patterns in the ceiling turning slowly overhead. An exotic interplay of venom and wine and other elements still swam through her veins, distracting her, making everything slow to a crawl.

The potion! Where was it? She turned her head to look for the tiny drinking cup, but the room went into a violent spin and she crashed against Retha, caught the girl's sleeve, and hung on in a frantic attempt to stay upright. Her mind was a jumble of colliding images but she forced it back through time. For some reason she felt it would be important later.

She hoisted herself off the floor and tried to sit up. The serpent essence had not left altogether, but something else was pulling her down, down, something very heavy.

She rolled once, saw the floor rushing up to meet her face, and blacked out again…

…but now she was moving, Retha helping her onto her bed. How had she gotten to her apartment? She collapsed on the mat, looked about for her Nord companion, but saw only a closed door.

She was alone in her room. Alone with defeat.

𒀭 𒌍 𒆜 𒈦

Stale bedcovers, the taste of copper, a fading memory of lost hope and remorse. A ray of sunlight made the world red behind her eyelids, and the pounding in her head started again. Uruna turned away from the light and reached up to push the shutter closed. Too late, she realized her mistake. The nausea hit fast and she retched on the floor beside the bed.

Gods, what a mess down there. She must have coughed up wine venom half the night.

"Shedah!" she bellowed to her morning attendant. The shout bounded around in her head and she winced with agony. Everything was exaggerated: the room was too bright, the chairs and rug looked oversized, her toes resembled bulbous tubers as she swung her feet onto the floor.

Ugh! Watch your step there!

She stood and took a tentative step. She was no longer sick and the dizziness from the night before had dissipated, but her bedroom surroundings looked oddly intensified and misshapen. Potions had never had this effect before.

It *had* been four doors, hadn't it? Obviously the fifth ingestion had been too much for her. Four doors were miracle enough, but with Sight it was all or nothing. You either had it or you didn't, and it was clear she did not.

Don't think about that right now, she told herself. Deal with it later, after you get your strength back.

She was much improved in one respect: she wanted to eat—craved a meal. She would go down to breakfast. She would have jam and cakes and drink a whole pot of tea, and then she would suck the juice from a ripe plum or two. The thought of food propelled her out of the room and down the hall before she knew what she was doing. The outer door was jammed shut and she plowed into the solid planks.

The door was barred from the outside. Who would do such a thing?

"Shedah! Where are you?"

No answer. Strange, no sign of the girl who was constantly underfoot and had the obnoxious habit of being punctual.

Uruna ran to the big arched window in her longroom. The sky outside was unusually bright, the garden shadows shallow, almost as if the sun were directly overhead.

Gods, it was high noon! She had slept through Morning Honors—she always performed the service, welcomed every new day. Who had done it this morning? Niccaba? Kinar? Anyone at all?

She went to the basin and drew a cup of water. Sloshed it down and drew another. Probably a side effect of the potion, but she couldn't get enough water. The gnawing hunger was another matter and quickly becoming an obsession. She had to have something to eat.

She heard a sound in the garden and leaned out her window.

"Retha, is that you?" she called down.

"Oh, you're awake. I'll be right up."

"Bring me a cake and some tea, I'm starved. And why is the door barred?"

"Orders."

What was going on? She had more questions, but Retha had already ducked inside.

Retha returned with a small feast. The cakes had sat for hours but they tasted delicious and the honey-laced tea was sweeter than nectar. She gulped and chewed like a ravenous hog.

"Where's Shedah?" she asked, licking the last crumbs of her demolished pastry.

"Reassigned. But forget about her. I think you should get over to Decrees and find out for yourself what's going on."

"Will you be forgiven if your prisoner escapes?"

"I was joking. It was my own idea in case you awoke and weren't yourself. But you're fine, so go on, I'll clean up."

The mall outside was vacant. Uruna dashed across the lawn and up the steps to House of Decrees. A dozing sentry popped awake when she poked him in the ribs, then stood with a sheepish grin as she passed through.

A throng of white-garbed Lukur jammed the hearing hall as Uruna threaded her way to the council chamber. She was just about to enter when Marduk stepped out of the crowd and quickly closed with her.

"No matter what they say, I'll stand by you, Uruna."

Hardly the self-serving defense she had expected from the man who had abandoned her. She gave Marduk a quizzical look.

"What should I expect to hear?"

"Well, it's all speculation, nothing to it. I told Niccaba and the others that it wasn't your fault."

"Of course not, it was yours."

"Forgive me if you can. I was utterly irresponsible to let you go on after you were so completely overwhelmed."

"I was not over—"

"Shush, they're coming now."

"Marduk, that's not how it happened!"

"Quiet, dearest, it'll be all right if you remain calm."

Dearest? Where had that come from?

A quartet of gray-headed ladies approached and gathered around Uruna in a tight circle. Galba kissed her noisily on the cheek before Ku-Aya and Kinar each stepped in for a quick squeeze. Niccaba drew her close in her familiar bear hug and whispered her love.

"We've been talking," she said, as if the obvious needed explaining. "Came to a decision late this morning. I guess you were still asleep, poor dove."

"Decision about what?"

Marduk put a protective arm around Uruna's shoulders. "A terribly hasty decision, ladies, although I guess you don't want my opinion. I think Uruna ought to have had more time."

Niccaba glared at him but answered Uruna instead.

"Last night's misfortune set us back considerably, dear. We took a vote."

"But we got inside the Fourth Door," Uruna objected. "You know what that means, Niccaba. We're almost there."

"Yes, and I know how much you want to give it another try, but we considered every aspect of the matter and came to a conclusion. The vote was unanimous." She took a deep breath. "We're going to look for another."

Uruna exploded. "This is insane! After twenty-eight suitors, it took my whole life for you to find this man. Now we're on the brink of victory, and you want to look for another husband?"

Niccaba's eyes teared as she clasped her hands to her mouth. "Not another husband," she said.

Suddenly the world dropped from under Uruna as the meaning became clear: her friends had given her a vote of no confidence. The search for Serpenthood was on anew, but not for a husband.

Temple Ekur wanted another seer.

CHAPTER THIRTY THREE
Male Counsel

A *galla* constable's blunt shoe prodded the drunk sleeping it off in the alley behind Sin-gamil's tavern. Disgusting, the state some people got themselves into. Handling lizards like this one was the least desirable part of his job, but it saved him from threshing barley.

He gave his toe to the bloke once more.

"You can't sleep here. Get up and move along. Come on now, up, up!"

Anu felt another hard jab to his ribs and rolled away from the stench of beer and vomit. The movement sent a pounding in his head and he winced and pressed a hand to his temple.

The *galla* backed off a step and brandished his club.

"We'll have no trouble from the likes of you, now."

The man hovered above him, blocking the sun and forcing Anu to squint in the harsh light. A row of shop buildings lined one side of the narrow street. His back was pressed up against the wall opposite.

Where was he? And why did he stink of beer? He hadn't had even a sip the night before.

"What day is this?" he asked.

"On your feet. I haven't all day to answer questions."

"Was the royal wedding yesterday?"

"Yes, and you celebrated too much. Do as I say now."

Anu struggled to his feet and before he could stand caromed into the tavern wall.

"Ow."

"Can't loiter, goomba, or I'll be showing you to the gate."

"That's where I got bumped." Anu pointed at his crown. "Right here."

"Sure, and you'll get bumped elsewhere if you stay in my sights."

"All right, just let me…get my bearings. Is that Tradesman Street down there?"

"Yes…phew, you need a good cleaning, you do."

"Did they take…?" Anu felt for his tote, found it intact and his money with it. "No, I guess not."

"Say, you're a big one. Not that hunter fellow they talk about, are you?"

"No, I belong to a rich widow in the Darma."

"Oh, sure y'do, an' I'm the queen's housekeeper. Well, then, get a move on to your rich lady."

"Any word about the queen and her dandy?"

"Nothing came of it, 's what I hear. If she'd got the Sight the whole town'd be jamming every street."

Anu nodded his respect for the constable and thanked him for not hustling him out of town.

He made his way to a cistern where he washed off the beer stink as best he could, then on to the Aniginna gate. But the sentry there sent him away with a terse "nobody gets in or out." As he turned around to consider that unusual development, he nearly bumped into Kinar, ploughing ahead with her face down, lost in some pensive rumination.

When she glanced up and recognized him, he put his question to her. "What happened last night?"

She looked away. "I'm forbidden to say."

"She was drugged, wasn't she?"

Kinar continued to avoid his gaze. "What do mean by such a

thing?"

"She got slipped a potion that knocked her senseless. I overheard the planning of it. That son of a whore she married did it."

"Anu! That's a terrible accusation!"

"Then tell me it isn't true."

"He defended her at—no, I can't talk about it."

"Don't you think the time for secrecy is well past? What did they do to her? Tell her the whole thing was her fault?"

Kinar went cold. "Good day to you, Anu."

"We who respect her haven't done much in her defense, have we?" he said to her back.

His mother's best friend pressed on for the gate.

"Don't let the Bull win this one, Kikki," he called after her.

She whirled around, her cheeks hot with fury.

"He won the whole contest long ago," she shouted, "on the very day you chose the hunt!"

She left him standing in the road with his face burning, his hands squeezing invisible necks.

𒈫 𒐊 𒐕 𒐼

Back at the big house in the Darma, Anu sought his father and found him drawing clay from a fresh sculpture. Sebbu took one look at his son and nodded with a sideways grin.

"Looks like you took a licking," said his father. "Get into it with Gunzeks again?"

"In more ways than one. I need your help."

"Anu, my fighting days are long past."

"Not what I meant. I'm in a hurry. The Bull is already running this city and just removed Ekur's latest chance for a prophet."

"What do you mean?"

"Uruna's on her own. The Mothers dropped her like a hot coal. I think I can help her, but I need to learn the serpent way before they choose another."

"Another what?"

"Another woman for prophecy."

"That's mad. It took ages for them to get this far with Uruna. Starting over would mean none of us would live to see the day."

"So you agree with me that Uruna's the only hope to foretell how to bring down the Bull Priest."

"I suppose you could put it that way. What's it got to do with you?"

"We love each other."

"Anu! That's wonderful!"

Sebbu started to embrace his son, but Anu pulled back.

"It's not enough. I need to learn Serpenthood. I need to be the man she needs for the serpent rite."

"Don't look at me. I don't know anything about that business."

"I was hoping you wouldn't say that."

Sebbu tossed aside his trowel and wiped his hands with a rag. "Come inside and have a talk with your Auntie Gaya."

"Baba, I love her dearly, but I don't have time for that."

His father laid a gentle hand on Anu's shoulder. "She'll tell you all about snakes and seers and the witches who work with them."

"I'm not looking for stories."

"What are you looking for?'"

"A ghost."

"Anu, come now."

"Or maybe a witch. Maybe she's both, or a demon, for all I know. But she once told me my path is with Uruna. She knows things, Baba, and whether she's real or not, I've got to find her."

"Then you must put your quest before Gayalla Hanza. We men of this house are blessed with the most precious of women. If anyone knows anything of this woman you seek, it is she."

"I can't believe such an answer might come so simply from so close at hand."

Sebbu smiled. "That's the way of the gods, sometimes." He sniffed the air. "I believe she's just pulled something from the oven. I'll have to join you, lest such treasure fall into your mother's wasteful hands."

CHAPTER THIRTY FOUR
Plan of Action

Uruna wasted no time on self-pity. Marduk had drugged her. Not a shadow of doubt about it. Through some sleight of hand the Ensi had neutralized Enshiggu's wrath and escaped the cobra's penalty for treachery. She struggled to recall a question that had crossed her mind as she watched Kukhmet's gaze follow the man's exit, but the answer was lost in drugged oblivion.

Enguda was moving fast, his eye on more than Nippur. Negotiating the marriage had been just the first step. Now that he had unseated Uruna, the curfew was lifted and she was free as before to rove the land. She would take steps of her own to slow the Bull's progress and hope she might stop it altogether.

What irony, she thought, as she rang the goat bell at the smithy gate and watched Arn-Gar's dusky Sumerian wife leave the house. How perfectly incongruous for the sacred city's queen to seek its salvation from the scion of a once and daunting enemy.

Milsah knew her queen by sight, but the reverse was not the case. Uruna found the woman's polite reserve a far remove from Gar's bold assertion. It was obvious Retha favored her father's brusque demeanor and her mother's looks and acumen. She liked the woman immediately.

Gar saw her from the forge and came over as they approached the house.

"To what do we owe this honor?" he asked.

"To your loyalty and the Ensi's complete lack of it," she replied. "We've much to talk about."

A small smile lighted the Nord's heavy countenance. "Wondered when you'd get to that point. But you needn't have walked all the way to Na Purna to tell me."

"On the contrary," she told him. "There's no place more fitting."

She delivered her proposition in the dining nook over tea. When she was finished, she looked over at Milsah, who had propped an elbow on the window sill to gaze across the grassy lea behind her neat plastered brick home.

"I had hoped it wouldn't come to this," she said to the smith's wife.

"So had we all, but there's no other choice."

"You're sure?"

"I have too much faith in you both to think otherwise."

Gar scooted closer to his wife on the dining bench and drew an arm about her shoulders.

"All right, now I have news of my own. We already began training at arms just days ago. The Hanza woman anticipated your decision and commissioned her son. Her intent was to defend her southland fields. I like yours better."

Uruna was reeling. Anu had already started!

Gar sensed her surprise and spoke the inevitable.

"You see why Nord and Sumerian can no longer be enemies. We share the same soul. We meet fear and danger head on."

Uruna answered with a grave stare. "We want you to come back to us, Gar, safe and whole. All of you."

"And the men we leave back here at the forge?"

A handful of Nord smiths would not accompany their fighting brethren on the trek north.

"They'll join you at arms with weapons they fashion in your absence."

"Are you sure the *galla* soldiers will follow a Nord?"

"I can command it while I'm still their queen, but I don't think that will be necessary. Suba will convince them. He's part Nord, you know."

"No, I didn't, but it makes sense. You've taken quite a departure from Lukur tradition. Some would call it treason, or even blasphemy."

"They toy with words while others act. Let's do what they cannot and forgive them even as we save them from their own fears."

She got up from Milsah's spotless table and took her cup to the basin, ignoring Milsah's look of alarm and returning it with a rueful smile.

"I'd cook my own porridge if they'd let me," she said, "but I doubt it would be edible."

That earned a chuckle of momentary relief from the tension surrounding their hastily-conceived ploy. All three sobered quickly from the realization they were headed for a long stretch of anxiety. Uruna hoped it would not involve grief as well.

At the gate, an unspoken concern hovered over Gar and Milsah like a portentous cloud: how would their daughter emerge from this?

Uruna directed her conclusion to the girl's mother.

"Retha lives by her wits. She leads and others follow. She'll outlast us all."

On the walk back Na Purna Road, the truth of her own remark astounded her. For the first time in her life, she pitied the Bull Priest of Uruk. Not for the defeat an army of Nords or Kurgs or even mutinous Gunzeks might bring upon him.

The greater foe was a young woman with golden hair and the courage of a lion.

CHAPTER THIRTY FIVE
Gaya's Sendoff

Auntie Gaya was being difficult. Anu knew he was an exasperating nephew, that she had really wanted to be told stories. Instead, he plied her with a host of questions, all having to do with the woman who ran the temple.

It didn't help that Lilla had stayed over with her baby, and that Heganna and Sebbu wanted to be included.

Gayalla scowled at each mention of Uruna.

"Why are you doing this?" she demanded over scraps of the midday meal. "You're gone for years and the first time you show up, you're in a hurry to run off again. Why do you insist on discussing serpents?"

Anu leaned across the table to emphasize that the discussion was between himself and his aunt.

"Uruna desperately needs a mate," he told Gayalla, "one who knows the serpent's secret. I wanted to be that man before she married a mistake. Now that the temple has cast her out I need to learn the serpent way more than ever. But where am I to go, Gayalla, to a three-shekel seer? You know the old ways better than anyone."

Better than my mother, rang his unspoken statement of the obvious.

Gayalla ran a hand over her face and looked out the window at an empty wren box on a post. She had always fancied the drab little darlings, preferring their spunky, unmelodious chirrup to the graceful trill of a lark. She stared wistfully at the box as if it held the mysteries of the universe.

"Once there was a woman who could have helped. I don't know—she's probably gone."

"Gayalla, no!" Heganna hissed and arched her back in reproof.

Anu looked from mother to aunt. "Who is she? What's the great mystery?"

Lilla roused herself from motherly pursuits long enough to interject.

"The real mystery is why the Lukur failed to glean her knowledge while she was around to give it."

"Lilla! She spurned them, teased the councils with unprovoked taunts."

"They were dull and unwilling to learn."

"They were devout servants of Inanna!"

"Who carried out her rituals to the last drop of wine, but couldn't pull a bullock from the mire. The women were not receptive to instruction, Mother, their vanity prevented it."

"Well! I certainly never heard so strong an indictment from you at the councils. Perhaps I've raised me a daughter with backbone after all."

Anu raised his voice to be heard. "Will one of you please tell me who we're talking about?"

Gayalla waved his entreaty away. "Oh, stop straining at the yoke, Anu. Her name isn't important anymore. She was old even when your mother and I entered womanhood. Now tell me more about this remarkable Bedu couple who pulled you out of the swamp."

Anu heaved a sigh and leaned an elbow on the table, propping his head with one hand. He desperately needed information but Gayalla wanted a story.

"She sewed my leg with a sliver of boar tusk while she told jokes and made love to me with her eyes. Later, Gunzeks attacked. Her husband died in her arms, she was taken in her own tent, she crossed one lout's throat with her kitchen blade and cut me loose. I took down three of her husband's killers, but she married his brother with her husband still warm in his grave because that's Bedu honor."

Gayalla closed her eyes and bit her lip. "In one breath you cover nine years of life hunting lions with the Hani. I've probably heard more of it from my gardener."

An awkward silence ensued, in which everyone attempted to cope with the sudden change of mood. He hated the telling, as futile as sifting cold ashes for a trace of flame. The hunting life was too harsh for table chat.

Resilient even in old age, Gayalla swept aside her heavy mood and returned to his earlier question. "The woman of whom I spoke lived way up in the north country, where the Tigris stream used to wander, tending her little flock of goat herders. She knew the serpent ways and more. She was the last of the great queens, before she went crazy."

Heganna pointed an accusing finger at her sister. "Not the witch! The lunatic from Edin?"

Anu felt the blood leave his face. Edin! He stared at Gayalla and she stared back.

"Rahnee," he said simply.

Gayalla looked straight at him, her dark eyes boring deep for the slightest flinch. "Where have you heard this name?"

"I'm not sure it was a place so much as a dream. She was—she was old and wise and exquisitely beautiful all at once."

Gayalla shook her head. "Can't be the same. Rahnee was indeed this woman's name, and, oh, what a wizard she was! She could change a lizard into a prince, make the wind stop and start, cause the moon to disappear. She commanded fire and was said to have conjured a curtain of flames to smite her enemies. But the stories about her were already dying out when we were girls. She must have been old beyond counting then."

"Could she be alive? Maybe she wasn't as ancient as you thought."

"Anu, the woman is dead!" cried Heganna. "She has to be! Listen to your aunt, not your own dreams."

"Let Gayalla answer, please, Mother." He turned to Gayalla. "I'm curious why you would consider her at all if she was ready for the grave when you were both children. You seem to know a lot about the lady."

Gayalla gave her answer in a measured cadence.

"No one ever saw her die. She simply stopped showing up. I did not know Rahnee myself," she said, with a furtive glance in her sister's direction. "I saw her once from a distance—or I convinced myself it was she..."

Gayalla stopped as if the memory had jolted her back to a moment in the distant past. Anu pressed for more.

"What did you see, Auntie Gaya?"

"Oh, she's going to carry on about that again!" said Heganna.

Lilla tapped her mother's arm and frowned irritably. "Quiet, mother! I want to hear this, too."

Gayalla locked her hands together on the table and closed her eyes, turning inward to a vision from her past.

"I was fifteen, a priestess to Idumma, who was Lasori's three-times granddaughter. We were performing the last rites for Damuzi at Kilgal temple, which is now gone. It was after dark, and I stood in the torch light at Idumma's left hand, holding the holy robe of sacrifice in my arms while the Entu chanted the sacred words. For some reason, I looked down into the crowd at the base of the platform—it was a public event in those days—and there she was. Her hair was as black as kohl and it flew on the wind like a raven's wings. She put a question to me, or into my mind, for she did not move her lips. But I heard her, oh yes, I heard and I nearly dropped the robe, she startled me so."

"What did she say?" asked Anu.

"Oh, Anu, so many years. I've forgotten. Something to do with the sun, or maybe it was the moon. Always with Rahnee it was moon business!"

Without thinking, Anu repeated the words from Sikkim: "The sign of Heaven's Door is cast in stone. When the full moon shadow meets her hand..." He spread his hands in apology, "I don't know the rest."

Heganna's cup fell to the floor with a clatter and she stood up from the bench to stare at Anu in wide-eyed astonishment.

Gayalla sucked air into her lungs with a long, shrill whine, and she too stared, as if struck by some terrible, fascinating power.

He reached for his aunt to give reassurance, but she shrank from his touch.

"Tell me what it means, Gayalla!" he begged. He turned to Heganna. "Mother? What do the words say?"

Heganna lifted a hand toward Gayalla to indicate the authority of that knowledge rested in her sister. For once she was at a loss for words.

With a slow wag of her head, Auntie Gaya dropped her gaze and fixed upon a pot of pinks set in the corner, as though the answer might come from the gay little heads dancing in the sunlight. She gathered herself gradually and lifted her shoulders with an enormous sigh.

"Tell me where you heard it," she said with weary resignation.

"With Uruna, just a few days ago in Sikkim. We had just—we both heard the words."

The two older women exchanged glances. "Think she knows?" Gayalla asked her sister.

"Of course she does." Heganna had recovered both haughty manner and bold spirit. "They've chanted in her ear since she was a girl of seven. She knows what every temple elder knows, which is precious little. It's no wonder she seeks the serpent."

Anu was near the point of exasperation. "She knows what? Will one of you please tell me what it means?"

Gayalla answered: "Your mother and I don't know how it's to be taken. We have heard the phrase attributed to Rahnee's explanation of the Sleep of Serpents."

Anu shot a glance at his mother. Heganna looked quickly at Lilla, who dropped her eyes.

The Sleep of Serpents! Words from his childhood, snatched once as he listened at the door while his mother taught the codes to his sisters.

Gayalla remained oblivious to the visual exchanges going on around her and ploughed ahead, explaining that the precise meaning of the words was a matter for the chosen couple to discern and act upon. However, a few had hazarded a guess.

"The reference to Heaven's door is ascribed to a holy place," she told him. "In ancient times a door of stone guarded secret chambers behind Inanna's altar. The workings of the door and the exact nature of its construction are a puzzle lost in antiquity. Temple altars are now set flush against the wall, in an attempt to invite Inanna's presence through a more direct route. However, it's just possible that an ancient temple still exists whose stone face bears the markings of sacred glyphs. To speculate more would be presumptuous."

Anu clutched his cup and caught himself grinding his molars. It all fit. Everything Gayalla said matched the temple ruins at Edin—too well to be coincidence.

"What is said of the part about the moon?"

"A complete mystery. Might be the hour at which the gods open the seals of knowledge and grant a flash of vision. A few have hinted at a more symbolic meaning, that the shadow is the royal consort and the hand is Great Mother's outstretched palm offering the vision. No one is sure."

"But you say Rahnee knows. Where can I find her? I've got to learn how to be of use to Uruna! I must find out!"

"You must this, and you must that. Everything with you is urgent, everything must happen quickly. What is so dire that you cannot allow time to take its natural course?"

"We must prepare Sumer for the impending fate in store."

"What sort of fate? A storm? Another invasion?"

"I don't know. That's what Uruna has to find out."

"I can tell by the look of you that you're determined to carry out your quest, regardless of the consequences. If indeed she exists, Rahnee would not dwell around these parts. Start your search at Edin, if the wretched place is still standing."

"Where is it?"

Heganna's laugh was a harsh bark. "Smack in the middle of the Akkad! Surrounded by the most abominable wasteland you can imagine. When the river left her, Edin dried up like a husk of grain."

Gayalla cut the air with a swipe of her hand. "Her people vanished in a fortnight. They quit their houses and parched land and rushed away to the south. Rahnee was left with a congregation of crows and lizards. All of that happened thirty years ago."

"More like forty, Gayalla," said Heganna. "We forget how quickly time passes with advancing age."

Anu felt his heel bouncing with nervous excitement. He was close! He could feel it!

"I was there myself once. Nothing dreamy about it, but I don't know how I got there or how I left. If she's still there, how will I find her?"

Gayalla took his arm and looked into his eyes with new warmth.

"At one time there was a connection between her house and Hanza. It goes way back in time to Lasori and before..."

Her voice drifted and stopped. "Wait here," she said, and disappeared through a doorway into the main hall.

Anu turned and found Sebbu watching him with avid interest, Heganna's arm wrapped about his waist. Somewhere in the last few minutes a spark of renewed affection had touched them both. The sight gladdened his heart.

His mother spoke first. "You're a man, Anu, full-grown. And I've been thinking of you still as my little boy. Forgive me. You make me very proud."

He was still recovering from the shock of hearing his mother speak words of warmth when Gayalla returned, cradling an oilskin pouch. As she laid the pouch on the table, a choking sound escaped

Heganna's throat. Gayalla flashed a warning glare at her sister as she took a paring knife and slit the outer flap. With delicate fingers she gently pulled away the corners and removed two neatly wrapped packets. The larger was sealed with sheep tallow and stamped with an intricate design showing a priestess holding up a serpent in each hand. Its mate was enfolded in a strange fabric coated with a glossy varnish.

Anu looked over at his mother. Heganna had covered her mouth with one hand and tears were streaming down her cheeks. Never in his life had Anu seen his mother weep. Watching her now, he felt his self-assurance slip a notch as he swallowed a lump of emotion to staunch the flow of his own tears. He focused his attention on the packets as Gayalla spoke with hushed reverence.

"For your journey, here are two gifts. The smaller is for Rahnee, if by the grace of Inanna you should find her. The other is for your bride, should you obtain her. These treasures, Anu, have been kept under seal in our family for many generations. I have no daughter to give them to. Perhaps the time has come for the covers to be lifted, if indeed Uruna is the one to unleash the powers again. However, if she turns out not to be the chosen one, you must return the gift to me."

Anu felt Rahnee's pouch. The oblong shape fit neatly into the palm of his hand and felt extremely light. The smooth covering, he could see now, was made from palm fibers woven into a fine mesh and dipped in a preservative. The original dun color had reddened and darkened with age and bore creases of ancient origin.

Gayalla re-wrapped the packets in the skin and gently pushed the pouch toward Anu.

"Put these gifts in your tuck and guard them from peril. I am saddened to have to part with them, but I am only a steward."

Gayalla looked suddenly tired and fragile and he took up her once-beautiful hand, now veined with age, and kissed it.

"Now you are part of Uruna and me," he told her. "You share in what we do. I will keep your trust whole, Gayalla, as with your gifts you bless me and my quest."

Her bright eyes saddened as Gayalla squeezed his fingers.

"Anu, you may yet curse me for what I've done. Sending you on the serpent path is not a bestowal of favor. Any treasure worth having comes at a cost. You have great strength and great courage, but I hope you also possess your mother's strong will. You'll need it to endure the tests of the spirit yet to come, as well as those of the flesh."

Anu faced Gayalla squarely. "I shall never curse those who love me. Whatever befalls me is the will of the gods, but I go forth the better for your generosity, Gayalla. As for my mother," he turned with his arm around his aunt and faced Heganna. "She gave me life, to which she added her strength of spirit. Our wills often clash, but I wouldn't trade places with any man."

He addressed Heganna in the quiet voice of Tezu-Mah. "You are the reason I shall prevail and win for you another daughter."

His mother's face softened and she pressed her lips together. "Win her for yourself first, beloved. I shall take my greatest reward when you return happy."

Anu spread his arms wide. "Then I have my family's blessing!" he announced cheerfully, to break the solemn mood.

He kissed his aunt and sister, embraced his Baba with a tight hug.

Heganna moved close to receive a kiss and pressed a purse into his hand.

"Take the canal road all the way to Beshum and go north to the house of Zinat. He tends a small flock up there and will put you up for the night. Give him this money and my blessing in return for instruction on the correct path to Edin."

"How does he know where Edin lies?"

"Zinat was born to a woman fleeing Edin on the road south. His family put down at once for the baby's sake, and Zinat grew up taking stocks of goods to Rahnee every week."

"He saw her every week?"

"Ask him yourself. Now be on your way with my blessing."

Anu put himself on the road at once, pulled by the call of the Akkad and the mysterious woman whose power he needed to transform himself. His new calling might be fraught with danger and deterrents, but he took encouragement from the turn of events that put him once again on the path to wilderness. He belonged out there with the gods and animals and Mother Earth, where perilous existence made life more dear.

For the first time since the lion, he felt he was running toward his destiny.

CHAPTER THIRTY SIX
Temple Treachery

For several days after the consecration debacle, Marduk made scarce company for Uruna. He slept and dined elsewhere in Serpenthood's immense expanse—precisely where she did not know, but it was never with her. Twice more that week she sent two different girls to him with invitations to dine with her, and when he failed to appear the second time, she stopped.

She no longer cared to prolong the pretense of marriage.

Suba appeared in her window on the second night with a strange expression on his face.

"Nords are on the move. Left this morning for Kish."

"That was fast. I thought you were going with them."

"I am, just stayed to round up the last smiths."

"Who's forging weapons?"

"Done."

"Already? A thousand arrows? Copper shields? Sword and axe for every man?"

"As I said, done."

"Suba, that's imposs—"

At once the truth dawned on her. Na Purna had prepared in advance. Her Nords had needed only her approval, and likely not even that. They'd probably mobilized when the first Gunzek crossed the horizon.

Suba took note of her comprehension and simply nodded his head. "What about Anu?" she asked.

"He taught us what we needed for close combat, then took off on some quest of his own. We could have used him to lead the first assault, but something else is driving that man."

"Any idea what that might be?" she asked.

Suba peered down at her with a soft look, then leaped onto the window sill. "The same dream we're all chasing. Be safe."

He dropped from sight, but this time she did not follow his path through the garden. A surge of hope locked her in her steps.

Anu was on the hunt again.

But he was finished with the lion. He'd vowed as much under the grape arbor at Sikkim, and she believed him to be true to his word.

Then she recalled his other promise. Had he now turned his hunter's eye to the serpent?

𒀭 𒁲 𒅗 𒎙

Enguda insisted on attending every worship ceremony, and he was adamant that Uruna's husband who behaved unlike a mate should accompany her at each performance to learn the rites. Following evening service, Marduk took pains to surround himself with a handful of Lukur and several of Uruk's visiting priests sent to learn as well. Did the man fear she might expose their sham marriage?

Apparently his evasion was a ruse to get her alone, for no sooner had she emerged from the changing vestibule than Enguda thrust himself upon her from the side. Once again he resorted to intimidating brawn, this time to steer her beyond earshot of her ladies.

"I must join the others," she complained. "My husband waits by the stair."

"The sisterhood is overly demanding of a royal husband," he countered, then drove straight to the matter of concern to himself. "If you could devise a compromise over this coupling with serpents, we might get on with more pressing matters of state."

"One does not negotiate with the serpent god."

"I was in mind of appearances more than the actual experience itself."

The priest dug his strong fingers into her elbow just as he had on the Burum quay, and maneuvered her further still from the awaiting procession. "Rather, consider an alternative means to impress Council that the deed is done."

"What do you suggest I tell them?"

"The truth," answered the Bull.

"Admit that the marriage was never consummated?"

"Nonsense. You must have forgotten while you were in the trance."

"I was drugged. We didn't even enter the first Door. Your son saw fit to remove me from my senses completely and fashion his own version of the events."

"You remember incorrectly. I say again that you had your vision and you gave account of it twice—once to your husband and once to me."

"That is utterly untrue!"

"Uruna, be reasonable. A woman's memory is a fickle thing."

"Your design has nothing to do with womanhood or the nature of memory."

"It has everything to do with both. You were completely caught up in the ecstasy, as rightly you should have been. The god entered the room and—"

"Holy Enshiggu does not enter rooms!"

"—and announced the will of Inanna. 'To Ekur falls the priesthood of Shedu. A certain prophecy for the days of despair, when a man shall rise up and make peace with the gods. A priest with holy counsel.'"

Enguda made no attempt to disguise his invention. He would push and push until his ambitious desire became a reality. Any ruse would do, so long as it lent legitimacy to his cause and put a priest inside Ekur.

"You will go to any length, won't you?" she said.

"Not my will, but Inanna's be done," pronounced the Bull Priest of Eanna.

She glanced over at Marduk. He was looking the other way while her patient ladies waited at the top of the stair for Enguda to be done with her. Each woman had supper and family waiting at home. Uruna dropped the last pretense of civility and shot an accusing glance at her captor.

"I know what you're doing," she said in a low voice to the Bull. "You'd put *him* in Ekur to lead sacred worship, because a son made high priest by the queen will assure your own ascension to king. Especially if you can arrange his appointment to seem like a mandate from on high."

Enguda closed his eyes with a gentle shake of his head, the master indulging an errant apprentice.

"Again, such an idea came not from my lips but yours, Uruna. Your vision for the people, a man to lead the country to victory against its enemies."

His fabricated nonsense did not deserve a response and she realized he did not expect one. Still, he would hear her view of him anyway.

"The threat to Sumer comes from neither Kish nor the Akkadian plain," she declared. "Sumer's worst enemy lurks inside her councils like a tapeworm, eating the moist entrails of its host. I am unable to satisfy your wish, for it runs counter to everything I stand for."

"That would be unfortunate, madam," Enguda said mildly, peering into the distance where river haze blurred the horizon. "We had really counted on your support."

"My support is *for* the people, not against them!"

"Lower your voice, you'll make a scene." He turned toward her, his eyes flashing. "For once, look at the matter from another perspective. Claim the triumph that's rightly yours and retain the allegiance of the people. They'll rally to fight the foe in the north."

She dropped her voice to a hoarse whisper. "You cannot subvert the holy gift of Sight without penalty, priest. You will pay personally for your plunder, whether you believe it or not. But in your mad dash for a power you're unprepared to handle, you'll slip and drag the rest of mankind into the pit after you."

She started away, but Enguda tightened his grip to mutter a quiet rejoinder in her ear.

"Thank you so much for your weighty concern, Uruna," he said with biting sarcasm. "The people's queen, ever loyal and sacrificing—until a real threat stares us down from two days' march away. What's it going to take? When will you listen to reason?"

"When you start making sense. Will you let go of my arm, please, this is holy ground."

The hard grip stayed in place. "Uruna, what makes no sense is to keep waiting for divine favor to fall when it may not happen at all. You'll help the country more if you affirm the vision. Unite public sentiment against the common enemy. It's true, the situation is urgent, but it's not lost. My men can hold the Kurg as matters stand right now, but he won't stay in place indefinitely."

Uruna shook her head, recalling Suba's words only a few nights ago.

"A horde chief doesn't listen to priests and emissaries. He does whatever moves him at the moment. He's one step away from wild. That's how Yagga-Tor got where he is—by taking what he wanted, never mind the human cost. Right this moment, he wants the Sumerian plain. He sees year-round grasslands and a constant flow of water. To a Kurg, that's wealth beyond his dreams. His mind cannot conceive how all that grazing pasture got there in the first place. He doesn't comprehend what he can't see, that this land goes barren after two years without irrigation, forms dunes like the Akkad in five. He doesn't care that all this grass he sees was put here by man for mankind's use. He just wants more fodder for his goats and asses because that's all he knows, that's how the land operated for him where he came from—a barren plain without tree or shrub, iced over more than half the year."

"Where did you get that nonsense?"

"From your son, you arrogant sod! He whom you sent to Aramdan's icy keep for eight god-forsaken years. So, if you think an armed savage is persuaded by reason and bound by the words of men, you're a greater fool than your blithering *gubna* priests."

"I have the man's word before the governors of six cities, or whomever we led him to believe were governors. Nippur's the last to join, and we'll get that treaty as soon as Marduk takes over as head priest. Yagga-Tor is a sensible man, he'll take the easier path rather than squander men on the battlefield."

"No wonder the men haven't been ruling. You're worse dupes than any priestess in her dotage. At least a Lukur knows when she's beat before she starts. Enguda, you've got nothing but the empty word of a primitive goatherd!"

"Then your personal wisdom advises that we race up to the Akkad and engage the horde forthwith? Do the rest of us have any say in the matter?"

"After experiencing firsthand your influence with at least one Council, I'd rather put behind the folly of consensus and do as Sight reveals to me."

"You haven't got the Sight, woman. And you'll never get it on your own because a man's got to be involved. Marduk and I are just trying to make it easier for you."

"No, not your way ever. When I attain that peak it will be without either you or your son."

Careful, she thought, you don't know where you're going.

The Bull's mouth twitched with righteous disapproval. "I'm sorry, Uruna, but Council can't allow that."

"You're not in any position to argue for Council."

As soon as she said it, she realized the error of her presumption.

Enguda was the tacit master of one council already. Her hasty betrothal to the man's son was ample evidence that he commanded Ekur successfully as well. She had just sealed her doom, and the black look on Enguda's face confirmed it. As he began to move her toward the stair top, he pushed his head up close to hers and spoke in her ear, his voice a rasping whisper.

"Please reconsider what you just said, madam. It's not too late. We've no interest in shedding your blood. But if you make yourself an obstacle, you'll leave us no choice but to remove you by force. Other lives are at stake."

With a violent tug she wrenched her arm from the Bull's grasp and whisked away before he could detain her further. The man would move her to blasphemy if she listened to any more.

Marduk was still staring off into space when she overtook her retinue and stomped past without a word to any of them. She reached the street before the others could assemble a dignified procession. She didn't care how it looked or whom she offended. She could no longer countenance a man who let his father do his thinking for him.

Other lives at stake! The only lives of interest to the Bull Priest of Uruk were slaves to toil on his planned domain. The man's ambition was boundless, a guarantee of his downfall. He was too clever, too sure of himself, to realize his ill-advised schemes would set Sumer against itself and the resulting paralysis would do the Kurg's work for him. Unopposed, Yagga would loose his lethal charges upon a helpless populace and the annihilation would be total, the devastation permanent.

What added further grievance was Enguda's overriding scheme to maneuver his priests into Nippur's temple at any cost. He would accept no other course but to press hard for his goal until it was done. Any attempt to dissuade him only spurred him on and added to his conviction that women were self-centered traitors by nature. The man deserved her back and whatever pain he was doomed to suffer.

She spent the evening alone, certain that Marduk would keep to his old room at the other end of Serpenthood where he had stayed every night since Enshiggu's door closed with resounding finality.

She had released the serpents to the garden now that they were no longer fit house guests. A more complete disaster she couldn't imagine. She had relented before Niccaba and a crew of cowed advisors, she had wed a man she didn't love, she had provoked a deadly adversary. Not the stuff of wisdom, she thought, as she realized she needed Anu more than ever.

The hunter's simple courage would have withstood all the bribery and chicanery of the past week. He had asked her to wait, that he would come. Instead, she had blindly followed duty, never once listening to her heart.

She reached for the talisman at her neck: the claw was still there, its curve snug between her fingers. Was there power in its ivory crescent? Was there hope yet for a lost lioness?

Nippur's streets were shuttered and dark when the Bull's soldiers came for her that night. The Sedduan leader was hurried but considerate of her comfort. She was allowed a small box for some clothes and a cloak to ward off the chill, and he personally led her unbound from her room, down the stairs, and out through the doors of Serpenthood House. On the concourse a four-man litter waited. She turned around and paused for a last look at her home.

"Where are you taking me?" she asked over her shoulder.

A different voice answered, "If you would, madam."

She spun around and saw a man cloaked in leather from head to foot. A polished leather mask hid his face from view in a tradition that had not seen use since Lasori's edict forbidding execution.

The soldier gestured at the litter with its curtain drawn aside for her to enter. "Not a sound, please, if you would stay unbound."

His voice pleaded with a wistful reminder of Ekur's most unpleasant past, when the unforgettable edict came forth from Lasori herself, that her traitorous husband be put to death according to the code of the time. To such faceless voices Entus of the distant past had remanded the condemned, with regrettable assurance that the sentence would be carried out with irreversible efficiency. Tonight, judgment had twisted back upon Ekur's latest queen, and now she was beyond recourse.

An executioner was sworn to obey the empowered.

THE AKKAD

CHAPTER THIRTY SEVEN

Gunzek Occupation

Enguda moved quickly to put a military face on the Sumerian plain. Gunzek malice served him well, and with Uruna removed, the threat of a public clamor for prophecy was no longer a deterrent. It would take him only six days to move his army up the river to Nippur and beyond.

On Enguda's instruction, Nafti captain Borok posted four ranks of combat-ready Gunzeks inside Nippur's gates to secure the city, sixty-four men in all. He then sent eight ranks upriver, dropping off one rank to secure the garrison at Amaninda grain house Number One. Another rank would take the queen inside the huge granary and see to her execution, while he led the larger contingent on to Kish to engage the Kurg force.

Meanwhile, Enguda launched his campaign to fill temple offices with *gubna* priests. He then began a program of taxation to finance his administration. But money soon proved not to be a solution to the avalanche of woes that quickly beset his all-male order.

The men knew absolutely nothing about agriculture. The entire economic apparatus was a complete mystery to them, and without sufficient time to learn it, they were forced to stand aside and watch the ladies perform.

With the onset of winter things got even worse. Most of Enguda's priests were city-dwellers. Few had left Uruk's civic bounds except to go fishing. Where duty required them to venture afoot to the countryside and slog knee deep in field and canal muck, they foundered.

A *nigenna* clearing priestess was usually assigned to stem water flow with a precision sometimes as narrow as an hour. To do a proper job she must devote a lifetime to the fields, starting from childhood. A citified priest could only waddle into the mire, wave his *gubna* wand stupidly at a reaped field, and hope his effort appeased the gods for the spring floods.

Grain stores had to be shifted according to signs only a *nigenna* woman could discern. Left in one place too long and rot might set in. Or red rust. Or mice. Or attacks from a dozen invisible sources. A priest could only follow his female counterpart around the barn and wonder as she plunged a stick here, pulled a fistful of straw there, sniffed the air for signs only a practiced nose might detect.

A *nigenna* counter performed further tricks with stylus and tablet. Her counts were far more than hash marks for sheaves. The symbol system had evolved over generations as a body of knowledge passed down from mother to daughter, or aunt to niece. But never to a lad whose strong legs and back served better wielding hoe and plow. There were symbols for harvest grade and color and age. Symbols for barley, rye, and emmer wheat. Symbols for field of origin and planter, as well as for selling agent, buyer, shipper, and destination.

In every task the novice priests were overwhelmed. The ponderous weight of female acumen forced them again and again to step aside or risk causing a serious economic mishap by interfering.

For their part, the women were quite willing to part with their knowledge, but not at the expense of efficiency. If they had time, they would indulge a *gubna*. Otherwise, it was business—women's work—as usual.

A culmination of *gubna* shortcomings rose to the attention of *nigenna* chief Kalumma-Dalla, who had all she could handle readying distribution for the lean winter months. One of Uruna's strengths had been her infallible memory, sorely missed in her absence. So Kalumma was surprised when the Nord girl appeared one day in her counting room to report Na Purna's tiny crop yield.

After stating the counts and types of grain with incredible precision, Retha presented an accounting for products of the forge. Kalumma's stylus poked furiously in a struggle to keep up—until she looked up in astonishment.

"Six *hundred* arrow heads?"

"Yes, in addition to those already in the field, fletched and stocked."

"For what purpose? Retha, such numbers are forbidden. This is very dangerous."

"Which is why I was told to reveal the counts only to you. There are more. Four hundred spearheads, mounted and bound to hafts and field-tested. Plus thirty bronze sword blades. And more still. Shall I go on?"

"That's enough for a whole army!"

"I certainly hope so. How else are we to survive in combat?"

"Who sent you with these counts?"

"My father."

"Outrageous! He's Nord."

"Thanks be to Inanna. It's clear no Sumerian is fit—except maybe the hunter."

Kalumma suddenly felt her age and took a chair. "Where are these weapons kept now?"

"In safe hands."

"Retha! If Uruna heard such tyranny she would have your father strapped in bonds."

"I doubt it. The idea was hers to begin with. Baba only prepared a little early for the obvious."

"Did he also tell you what I'm to do with such information?"

"He hoped you might convey it as a warning to the Bull Priest, but that is up to you. I wouldn't advise it, the way things are going for his Bulltails. I told Baba you weren't one of those. You aren't a Bulltail, are you, Kalumma?"

"I'm *nigenna* through and through and that's...what is a Bulltail?"

Her work done, Retha crossed the room and stopped at the door. "Someone a Bull Priest uses to cover his arse."

CHAPTER THIRTY EIGHT
Suba Steps Forward

One man alone stood little chance of turning the tide against a whole Gunzek army. Suba knew a dozen Nords would do better, but not against the swarm now rowing silently past his position beneath patches of stars. The first winter rain was brewing, a moist breath on the wind, bringing a chill that settled on his bare shoulders. He should have brought a cape. Fat lot of good he'd do anyone if he caught the shivers.

He counted the four-man boats as they slipped past his patch of reeds. They had just left Nippur, probably after dropping off a small contingent to join the half dozen Ensi guards left from the wedding.

Something amiss there. He had sneaked into Uruna's apartment earlier tonight but found no trace of her or her things. The whole Aniginna complex was eerily silent. He suspected the Bull had driven out all the women so his priests could start running things. But Uruna too? That didn't make sense after all the trouble he'd gone to, pushing the marriage on her and then feting the ceremony afterward.

Peculiar, that too. Not a word about the Sight, not even from his best resource. The old peach seller had fled the city, along with half a dozen of Suba's other contacts. Only a casual remark by the tailor's boy had given him a hint: the lad had noticed the queen's empty litter on a side street—not terribly strange until you realized the bearers wore leather armor. Moved at a trot, too.

The Gunzek flotilla continued its march upriver. He wanted to follow the lead boats as they headed north, but the higher priority was to reach Anu and marshal the Nords, regardless of their combat readiness. Those blokes would probably revert to type in the first contest and lay bloody waste by sheer muscle power.

Enough with the counting. He had what the hunter would need.

He slipped backward from the river and used overgrown field brush for cover until he reached Nunbirdu Canal. From there he jogged east past Nergal Gate, scaled the wall at its lowest point, and entered the city.

He knew the watchman at Hanza House by sight, from having conveyed a few secrets to Heganna in her garden by night. He'd never shown himself to the staff, so this fellow didn't know him from a sneak thief. He took a chance and presented the small tablet with the Hanza seal. This might be the rare emergency its display called for.

"Don't make no difference," the fellow said. "Can't let you in."

Exasperated, Suba brought a hand to his brow, struggling for an idea. His luck turned, however, when he offered to leave a message for the hunter.

"Save your breath," the man said. "He's away hunting again."

"I heard he was finished with that."

"Not lions this time, something secret. Could be about one of the queen's snakes. Heard something like that from cook—wup, can't say more. You best begone or I'll have to use force."

The skinny watchman couldn't know how such a tiff might end, but Suba needed information, not a fight.

"One more thing, when did you see him last?"

"Couple days ago. That's all I'm saying. Shake a leg, now."

Suba thanked the man and got himself back out of the city and headed straight for Na Purna. The Hanza hunter had removed himself from the field. His reason no longer mattered. Not with the Gunzek driving hard for Kish with a hundred men.

He hoped he might find the girl with her family. She'd likely know more about Uruna, and possibly the hunter too.

If the Bull hadn't gotten to her already.

CHAPTER THIRTY NINE

Amaninda Atrocity

Uruna was still alive and counting miracles as she looked up at Amaninda Number Two and cringed in the deep shadow of the giant storehouse. Limned by tiny star points, the tall spectral shape blocked an entire quadrant of the night sky, giving the impression she was standing at the base of a mountain rising straight out of the Akkad. She clung to the hope that within its massive presence lay her salvation.

First she had been spared when no one came out to meet the boats. Her masked charge had sent his party away to find the *galla* guard, leaving her with a witless fool more afraid of the dark than his master's wrath. She had convinced the poor dolt to leave her alone beneath "the little eyes that peep."

Now, if chance continued to fall her way, she might endure on her own, but first she had to cut her bindings. The linen wad in her mouth was secured by a cloth strip torn from her hem and her wrists were bound to her back with a piece of coarse twine. The rough braid chafed whenever she twisted around at a night sound. At any moment the soldiers might come back and finish her.

She prayed silently to the grain god inside Amaninda Two and wished she had Anu at her side. Or Gar or Suba. What would the hunter advise if he were here?

Manage your own rescue.

She checked her bindings. The superstitious idiot who had tied her had been in a hurry to join his friends. She worried the twine over a mooring post until it frayed and split. The tight knot at the back of her head was a more difficult matter, and she stopped fussing with it and simply pulled it down around her neck like a scarf. She spat out the wad and shook her hair free.

The urge was strong to bolt for the water and swim to the other side. But the Bull's hirelings were loose and might be anywhere. Rather than risk swimming straight into their hands, she crept silently away from Amaninda's immense shadow and crossed the military commons. An empty watch hut gave her pause. The whole compound appeared deserted.

She moved behind the shack and slipped into a bank of rushes abutting the Kish road. Her night vision had improved, so she made a daring inspection of each roadside hut. All were empty. A long, reed-thatched *mudha* at one end of the commons proved empty as well. Had Kish purged the storehouses and fled so quickly?

Whump!

A bumping sound came from behind the command shack. Uruna stopped to listen.

Whump, whump...whump.

Someone rapping on the rear wall. But without pretense of concealment?

She listened again, but the night had grown quiet again.

The outer wall offered a pitch-black refuge where she might move to the rear unseen. She slipped along the side of the command building and turned the corner.

A shadow suddenly swooped at her from above. Uruna ducked and shrieked as a man's figure leaped out at her. He struck her a glancing blow and she went sprawling. The man jerked away and bounced against the rude siding, legs flailing in the oddest way. In the dim starlight she noticed a length of rope shivering above his head, tightening as he swung by the neck from a roof spar.

Oh gods, what was happening?

She grabbed desperately at the bobbing, lunging pair of feet. Straining to see through the murk, she stumbled to her knees twice before she finally managed to bring the swinging body to rest.

Was he from Kish or Nippur? Gunzek or *galla*? Whoever he was, he had to be cut down. She couldn't leave anyone hanging in the air.

She looked about for a box or crate to stand on, but the ground was bare. She knew what she must do, and decided quickly.

In the man's belt she found a sliver of honed obsidian. The knife fit neatly in her hand, a dining tool, but it was all she had. It would have to do.

With the blade clenched between her teeth, Uruna grabbed the man's shirt and hauled herself up his front. Dead eyes set in a dark face bulged at her in the wan starlight. A black tongue protruded through distended lips, so close to her own that she feared she might touch them.

She sawed through a few strands, the going awkward, her stomach threatening revolt. Suddenly the shirt ripped away, and down she went, landing in a heap beneath the swinging corpse. She fought to her feet, jaw aquiver with revulsion for what she was doing.

One more try and we're done, poor soul.

She climbed up the carcass again and hooked her knee over his sword hilt to hang on, telling herself it was someone's son she was helping.

As the last strand unraveled she came down hard with the body beneath her and the knife in her hand. She rolled away fast and got to her feet.

Now what to do, drag the body indoors away from view? Little difference that would make! The Bull's men were sneaking around in the silence like wolves after prey. How many others had fallen?

"Well done, lady!"

A deep baritone resonated from directly behind her as a huge arm grabbed Uruna around the waist and lifted her off her feet. "A mighty effort for such a little one," he rasped in her ear. "I commend you."

Uruna kicked and twisted in the man's powerful grasp. "Let go of me!"

"Too bad you wasted your strength on that one. Now you'll just have to join him."

"Bastard!" she cursed. "Let me go!"

The small knife had fallen on the ground somewhere.

But the needle! She felt along her hem for the sliver of bone she kept for repairs and slid into her hand.

"Give me your name before you die!" she said.

"Say your prayers, it is you who shall die, woman. We can't have you getting back to Nippur now, can we?"

"Tell me who gives your orders!"

"Nosy, aren't we? Too bad. You're full-bodied and probably a delightful bed mate. Now die like a good—"

The arm suddenly released her and Uruna swung the needle up to the man's eye, but her abductor fell away backward.

A hulking shadow stepped over the body and took Uruna by the shoulders. "Did he harm you?"

The man was huge! Uruna shivered in his hands and tilted her face high above the hairy, exposed chest. "Gar? Is that you!" she cried.

"Uruna! Gods and ghosts, what're you doing on the goddamn river? Tell me you're not hurt."

"I'm all right, but I could have used your height a few moments ago." She pointed to the fallen enemy. "You certainly laid this one out quickly. Have you found the men who took me captive?"

"Yes, I killed two outright, and eight more lie in the fields."

No wonder her captors hadn't returned. "Are you sure there aren't more lurking around?" she said. "One of them boasted of a large garrison."

"Soldier talk. This bugger's the last of Borok's garrison to roam these barracks. I got the whole lot of them. But there's more out in the hinterland."

"What if we swung east around the farms?"

"And follow the canals?" His tone said he thought it a stretch.

"We could take the narrow feeders down through the fields by night, hide in the rushes by day. Maybe hook up with Great Redeemer before they catch us."

Gar chewed on the idea. "Likely they're out there too, but there's a chance they're spread too thin to find us. You'd actually be safer up north by Kish. Pretty quiet up there as I came through. Gunzeks decamped for Nippur, it looks like. Couldn't draw Kurg blood there."

"No, we'll go home. Nippur is where I belong and he can't stop me."

She was groping without plan or reason. Her foolish determination could get Retha's father killed, but they were in it up to their necks, all of them, and things were happening too fast to consider what was best or safest.

Gar stood up and grunted from the effort. "You sure you're up to it?" he asked, offering a last-minute way out.

"What can I lose by trying?"

I've lost everything else.

"Then come with me. I've got two men standing by a boat stashed away in the reeds."

"Two? Are they *galla*?"

"Nord. We had just hooked up when these louses started tramping about. Got one of your ladies with us. Telgen says the woman was wandering beside the road not a stone's throw from a Bulltail patrol. Lucky for her we came along when we did."

"What's her name?"

"Demiah. Says she's a counter with the temple agent at Amar Town. Borok's men took it over, kicked the women out of the granary. Lucky they didn't do worse."

"We'll take her back to Nippur with us. It's too dangerous for a woman out here alone. Come on, let's have a look inside the storehouse before we make a run with the boats."

A smith called Telgen and a big farmhand named Otan greeted them in the looming shadow of Number Two. Ponderous stone counterweights were rigged to close the monstrous doors against the strongest weather. Telgen and Gar used forgesmith power to push aside one of the doors far enough to allow the others inside. Otan kicked a huge wedge of wood in place to block the door open.

The interior was completely dark until Telgen struck a flint to a bundle of straw and stuck it into the black murk ahead. The small flame illuminated a row of straw stacks flung against the front wall. Otherwise, the earthen floor was barren as far as the edge of the light.

Three years of harvest gone. The thieves had come in earnest.

"Rat food," said Gar, kicking apart several bundles strewn about the floor. "All of it unwinnowed wheat and worthless. They didn't even bother with jars."

"Higher," said Telgen, who had ventured back onto the fringe of illumination.

Uruna frowned. "What did he say?"

"Put the light above your head, man," called Gar, "and look up."

The big blond lifted his torch high overhead and flinched. Uruna heard her own shrill gasp over a chorus of groans and clamped her jaw shut to keep from retching.

From each timbered rafter down both sides of the ceiling, a body dangled at the end of a rope. So this was the fate of Amaninda's *galla* regiment! Each man hung motionless, his struggle done, chin on chest, hands bound behind the waist. Uruna swallowed bitter gall as she surveyed the gruesome sight.

"Take them down, please," she said, to no one in particular.

Another torch was lighted and Gar's two men walked the center between stacks of baled straw and clay urns, looking up at each contorted face to try to recognize features bloated purple in the final throes of agony and humiliation.

"Get a count," said Gar to the others. "Then cut them all down."

"Where will we find a pole tall enough?" asked Otan.

Gar's voice cracked with emotion. "I don't care how you do it, just get yourself up there and bring them down to ground."

"No need to bother!" bellowed a booming voice from behind them.

Uruna whirled around so see a tall man just inside the door, dressed out in leather armor and a helmet of gold. His sword, the weapon of a captain of guards, was drawn and pointed upward to show his intent to use it.

"You'll be joining those soon enough," the captain added.

Several men quickly filed in after him, wielding axes and clubs. They made a half-circle behind their leader, twelve against Gar and his two. The captain gave his instructions.

"We'll just finish the night's work with this lot and have Nippur's great attack force properly routed before sunup."

Gar glowered at the captain. "You're the ugly pig-sticker they call Borok. I saw you once in Kish, disguised as a man. What are you doing here?"

The humorless smile warped into a sneer. "Taking Nippur for money. And you're next for my purse. I'll hang your ears round my neck, Nord."

Gar barked an order to his two torch bearers. "Telgen! Otan! Give light to these butchers. Now!"

The two Nords understood instantly. Each flung his torch into a nearby straw stack and the flames leaped up the wall in a rush for the stick roofing. Gar drew his sword and slammed Uruna into the wall behind him.

"Break them, boys!" he yelled to his men.

The Kish soldiers sprang forward to the attack, axes drawn high. Three fell upon each Nord with wild, savage swings, but none landed a blow as Gar's men, despite their beefy size, neatly dodged and feinted with mace or ax. Whenever a Nord swung, Uruna heard the sickening thud of metal meeting flesh, and the opponent went down and stayed there.

Borok called for his survivors to regroup. The odds were now eight to three, and the soldiers approached with cunning feints and dodges of their own. Borok took on Gar himself and expertly separated the big man from Telgen and Otan. But the attackers wore the looks of the damned as their futile parries lost ground to the Nord advance.

Gar's broad shoulders blocked Uruna's view as he parried Borok's first swing and brought his halberd up to break the arc of the next. He slammed the Nafti predator in the face with the butt end and staggered into his foe with another swing. Borok caught Gar's blade on the hilt of his sword and both weapons cracked and fell to the floor with a clatter. The men locked arms, pitting Gar's older but meatier strength against a younger power that countered every move with steady, measured calculation.

Suddenly, Borok seemed to crumple and Gar sent his weight in the direction of yielding limbs. Too late, he realized his mistake as his opponent twisted and slammed a fist into Gar's gut.

Stunned, Gar stood a moment as the other fist smashed into his face. Gar fell back, grappling for a hold as he pulled the younger man down on top of him. Borok drew back a fist for another pounding and stopped, mouth open in agony as Gar's knee rammed home to the groin. Borok toppled aside and doubled over. Gar brought his mace down on the man's neck to finish him.

Uruna looked on in horror. There was blood everywhere, but the offal of battle stopped none of the opponents. Gar waded back into the fray like a huge bear, pairing off to equalize the odds, oblivious to the raging inferno that billowed behind.

The flames now advanced toward the door and would soon cut off escape. Uruna started for the opening, but Borok's supine body was in the way. As she stepped around him, the man raised his ruined body onto an elbow and aimed a glassy stare in her direction. His chest and throat were caked in blood and a huge flap of skin hung loose from his jaw. Uruna spun away in revulsion and shouted a warning to Gar.

"The door, Gar! Run for the door!"

Fallen bodies littered the floor, but she managed to pick up the remnant of Gar's sword on her way to the narrow opening. Behind her, roars of combat filled the fiery space as the Nords grappled with the last of their foes. Gar backed toward Uruna and the door. When he was within two paces of the opening, she lifted the sword and swung it against the chock with all her might.

The wedge didn't budge.

She looked up. Borok was on his feet and facing her. Gar took his current opponent by the hair and wrenched the man's ax away with his free hand. In a lightning move, he spun around in place and brought the ax up through the Gunzek's rib cage, nearly cleaving the man in two.

Uruna shrank inwardly from the carnage but held her place as she took another swipe at the chock. Again, no effect. Gar staggered toward her, saw what she was up to, and neatly cleared the chock with a kick of his toe. Uruna jammed the blade in behind it and stepped aside for Gar to operate the short lever.

The door rumbled as the huge counterweight began to do its work.

"Can't hold!" Gar gasped as he strained against the broken sword. "Too short."

Telgen burst through the door and plunged outside, trailing a desperate pair of assailants. Borok's soldiers made easy targets on the ground and Gar dispatched both before they could get to their feet.

Uruna glanced past Gar's straining shoulders. Number Two's arched beams and woodwork crawled with flames. The dry reed roofing and spanning joists made ample fuel. The inferno pressured the remaining Nord to swing with desperate finality. Otan swung his mace into his opponent's chest and the man fell back with a scream, landing at the feet of his commander who with monumental effort had staggered upright. Borok stepped over his own man and stumbled toward the door, raging oaths at his adversaries.

Now Otan fled past Borok and dove headlong for the narrowing gap. Borok leaped after him and caught the Nord by the foot, sending him spinning to the floor just inches short of the door. To get their own man to safety, Gar and Telgen would have to drag the enemy officer with him. Gar had no choice.

"Pull them out!" he grunted.

As he turned, the blade cracked and the door rolled to. Gar and Telgen grabbed their comrade by the arms and heaved, but with

Borok's added dead weight, the Nord only made it half through. Gar struggled for a second grip, which gave Borok the break he needed. Borok pushed himself up to a crouch and charged forward head down, feet stomping over the fallen man's legs and back. Before the Nords could react, he knocked them aside with a vicious lunge, broke clear, and took off at a run.

"After him!" Telgen shouted.

"No! The door!" screamed his fallen brother, who already felt the door squeezing in upon his hips. Uruna's hands found the chock, but Otan's body blocked the way.

"Up!" she shouted. He struggled upward on hands and knees, which brought him forward a little. The door moved another inch and he screamed.

Uruna shoved the chock beneath his chest and Gar slammed it home with a foot.

Too late.

The door crept on, an unstoppable dreadnought filling the night with a high-pitched squeal as the stone chock ground to powder beneath a weight equivalent to twenty oxen.

Uruna dropped her gaze and screamed as Otan was cleaved in half before her eyes. The shrill squealing stopped and his torso toppled forward onto the ground, eyes bulging in their sockets at unbelievable agony, mouth drawn open in a scream that never came, for Gar's mighty arm came down with swift mercy and swiped the man's throat clean through.

Uruna went down on her hands and knees and gave in to hysteria. None came to her rescue or consoled her uncontrollable sobbing. The others were too spent by their own horror and hid their faces in wretched grief. Gar stared into the darkness after the vanished Gunzek and gnashed his teeth, making silent vows and clenching his huge fists again and again.

At length the flaming massif gave up its body to the night. Uruna sat before the blazing spectacle in stunned silence, scarcely aware of a woman's form emerging from the rush brake. When Amar's counter, Demiah, failed to rouse Uruna's band from their stupor, she too sat and watched the crippling cataclysm play itself out.

Telgen got up listlessly and stood beside Gar, looking to his leader for the next step.

Uruna raised her eyes to the stars and wondered if her hunter was looking at the same night sky and thinking of her.

What would you tell me, my warrior prince? You're all I have left, and I may die tomorrow. Give me your strength. Point the way and I shall follow.

CHAPTER FORTY

Anu Seeks Edin's Queen

On his second day out of Demshalla, Anu was barely an hour beyond Zinat's outpost when he caught sight of Edin's bleached bones on the horizon. He hadn't expected much, but the destitute ruin filled him with sorrow. Edin's desiccated remains offered little to hope for.

Even Zinat's house, a hardscrabble hut at the edge of the hostile Akkad, could hardly be considered a refuge. He had dutifully conveyed his mother's blessing and bestowed her alms token to the old shepherd, in return for which the grateful Zinat had quartered his benefactor's son in the comfort of his own loft instead of with the hens in the fowl coop.

Beyond Zinat's house the land went from scrub-bare to bleak. Uninhabited silt barrens stretched as far as the eye could see, preventing the hardiest weed from clutching subsistence from the sun-ravaged clay. He tried to imagine how the north country might have looked in Rahnee's day, with shiny rows of ripening grain bracing the wide track of water running to the horizon. Old Akkad must have been truly beautiful before capricious Tigris turned her face and wandered afar. According to the hardy old shepherd, the river's present course lay a full two days' trek to the east.

Heganna had been right about one thing: for a short time, Zinat had indeed journeyed weekly to Edin with stocks for the wizard queen. But last night the old man had laughed when the hunter asked about her.

"She lives with the gods now!" he exclaimed. "The gifts I left were always taken, or maybe destroyed, I don't know which. But as for seeing her—can the eye behold the wind? Does a spirit show herself to mortals?"

Whatever confounded the simple gentry usually became cloaked in mystery and ambiguous lore.

Now he could see the ruin for himself, a low silhouette of ancient temple barely clearing the horizon. Hope welled in his chest and he trotted forward despite a lingering stiffness in his leg.

However bleak his expectations, Edin in the raw disappointed even more. Where once her gleaming ramparts had stood proud and tall, only a stubble of clay brick remained. He recognized none of it from his dream.

From a distance, the ruined memorial appeared as a low bump on an otherwise flat horizon, but as he drew closer, the crude shape of encircling wall came into sharper focus and he saw the blunted tip of its ravaged monument rising from the center. After the endless monotony of uninspiring brown lumps, Edin displayed his first view of man's imprint on the wilderness, and he stumbled on, gaining the enclosure more quickly than he had expected.

Even in her glory days Edin had been little more than a town, but the swift exodus of her people had reduced her civic center to a dry swale. Circling to his left, Anu came upon the western gate, now just a break in the wall between empty hinge sockets. He stepped cautiously between the skewed pylons to get a view of the inside.

Edin's two intact walls reached no higher than his waist, each segment weather-worn to a nub that wouldn't hold a small goat. One gate was gone entirely, probably having served out its last days as fuel for a nomad fire. Saddest of all were the houses, sickly reminders of a failed stand against the elements. The collection of fragile box shapes sagged in the heat, open to sky and weather, their rooftops crumpled or blow away, rent sides tilting crazily where they broke each other's fall. As dwellings they had enjoyed only a fleeting existence. In another decade, nothing would be left.

A short distance away, the wood-ribbed skeleton of a low fence followed a crooked path that once had separated domestic animals from the living compound. Now the fence was a catch for drifting sand, cleft at its center by a lopsided gate of brittle slats. The fragile device splintered and fell at his touch. Zinat had warned him not to expect too much.

On every hand lay signs of decay, neglect, abandonment. The temple roof was gone and the beams had fallen in. Anu stepped around small piles of dried animal dung and peered into the ruin. Drifts of sand filled the corners of the tabernacle that had become an overnight refuge for wild beasts. The compound resembled the abandoned residue of a battle. Hardly fit quarters for a renowned priestess.

He next approached the sand-filled remnant of a fountain. A great urn in the center had toppled from its mount long ago, leaving shards half-buried in the gathering sand. He pondered who might have drawn the last water from its basin. Rahnee herself? A wandering stranger?

Zinat had mentioned a deep cistern from which Rahnee reputedly drew her daily supply of water, but he saw nothing to indicate its existence. No doubt the well had fallen to decay like everything else.

He called Rahnee's name, but only a dull echo answered.

Gone, gone, gone. The venerable sage of serpent lore existed no longer. His memory of her was no more than that, a figment of delirium, the shock and stress he had since thrown off.

There was no point in staying. If he left now he could make Zinat's place by midday and possibly Great Redeemer before nightfall.

"What in Heaven's name are you doing here?"

He spun around in a crouch, his hand instinctively reaching for his knife, prepared for attack until he recognized the familiar face, the same ancient robes falling from straight shoulders. Rahnee stood a few paces away, scowling at him as if beholding an errant fool.

Anu sheathed his knife. "I was just wondering that myself," he replied.

"Gods, look at you. Restored whole in body but as mindless as before. There's nothing here for you."

"I wasn't expecting a palace."

"What then, a god-sent miracle?"

Her people were gone and her temple dissolved to dust, but the legend's gritty self-possession struck him spellbound.

Anu gathered his wits and formulated his mother's message in his mind before he spoke.

"Thy sister in Inanna, Heganna of Hanza, sends thy humble servant Anu, her son, with greetings and tribute to Rahnee, Wise Mother of Edin."

From his pouch Anu withdrew the small wrapping and stepped closer. Rahnee extended her hand to receive it. Her skin was surprisingly cool in the full heat of the day, and he kissed the ring of stone etched with the star of power, expecting her to vanish at any moment a puff of smoke. When she did not, he placed the parcel in her outstretched hand and lifted his eyes to her face.

Rahnee regarded the tribute with irritated disdain.

"We require no tribute from Hanza House," she declared. "In the name of Sacred Mother, I have lived forty years and more in this crumbling hole without benefit of company or tribute, and done quite well, thank you. But your mother is kind, and well-intended..."

Her mouth fell open with a catch of breath as she saw the talisman nestled in the folds of the opened skins. Slowly she reached for the small object and brought it to her lips.

"It comes to you from the keep of Toth," Anu explained. "My mother's sister says you will understand."

The parched lips smiled sweetly, the eyelids closed, and Rahnee turned her back to him and withdrew to an inner sanctuary. Did she visit the memory of an early lover? Did she glory in some victory over an ancient foe? Whatever the cause, when she turned to face him again, her delight was plain to see.

"Thy mother be blessed. Now let's get out of this dreadful heat."

She turned abruptly and headed toward an arch in the far wall. Now what? How could she possibly offer shelter in the sun-scorched squalor of Edin's rubble?

Play it out, he told himself. She's full of surprises and she might spring a few more before you get out of here.

Rahnee moved at a quickened pace, and he followed her into the cooler shadows of what must have been the supplication hall. She moved past the small dais stripped of decoration and approached the empty shrine at the back. For a moment he thought she intended to pray, but she moved around the altar to one side of a wide buttress centered against the rear wall. Instead of stopping, she squeezed into the wall and disappeared from sight.

Anu darted across the chamber after her. The buttress was not joined to the back wall but was separated by an opening just wide enough for a human to squeeze through sideways. Immediately inside the aperture, the floor plunged away in a steep staircase of clay brick. Rahnee was already at the bottom, having exchanged her shepherd's crook for a lighted torch from a wall sconce.

"Watch your step," she warned and disappeared through yet another hole below.

Anu grasped the remaining torch and descended after her, holding the light aloft. At the bottom, a wash of cool air wafted toward him from the subterranean interior. The stair landing made a right angle into the low doorway Rahnee had taken a moment ago. Anu stooped beneath the lintel and emerged in a world of amazing color.

Daylight angled into the chamber through slots arranged along the top of the far wall. He stood at the edge of a large room filled with magnificent artifacts of old. Tapestries in brilliant hues covered the walls with pictures of gardens where imaginary beasts and heavenly gods cavorted together. Rugs from the finest Magan looms softened a tiled floor laid out in patterns to simulate garden paths. Golden urns decked the walls, their sinuous contours etched with fine lines to depict serpents and lions. An array of vases spewed a profusion of cock feathers, some fringed in fluffy white and others bejeweled with iridescent blue ovals set in a brilliant green field. Even the home of the world's richest woman had never seen such sights.

The sound of trickling water distracted him from the ornate furnishings. Rahnee was already seated beside an underground fountain decked with gleaming colored tiles. She beckoned him to join her.

"Quench your thirst here beside me, Anu."

She took a cup from the water's edge and dipped, her legs gracefully bent to one side. Her eyes roved over his face as he drank lustily.

"Where did all this come from?" he asked between gulps.

"Edin was old even when I was born. Her ancient past lies in dozens of rooms like this one, buried beneath the mud of a hundred floods. You ask, How can an old woman keep it? And I tell you truly, everything you see here will soon pass away. But enough of this. You seek something precious, a mystery. I see it in your eyes. You have been with her, haven't you?"

There was no point guessing who she meant.

"Yes, just days ago. We met in a grape arbor—I—she is more than the sun, greater than the hunt. You were right, we each found our mate."

"Congratulations. Couldn't happen to a nicer couple. Now tell me why you aren't with your queen this very moment."

"Serpent business. She needs a man who can take her through the Sleep of Serpents to prophecy. I have no such ability."

"And you came all the way out from Nippur to acquire it."

"Yes. Or rather, to learn from you. If you're willing."

"Did she send you? Was this Uruna's idea?"

"Actually, not so much. Something my Aunt Gaya said."

"Too bad, can't be done." She sniffed and looked away. "Too late for me, too late for you. I'm sure Uruna told you how arduous it is. Now let's finish our tea so you can be on your way home."

"Rahnee! I'm serious! The gods did not bring Uruna and me together only to dally in the city as husband and wife."

"What do you believe?"

"I believe in you."

"That, my friend, is your first mistake. Serpenthood is an inner journey, long, arduous, seldom successful."

"I don't understand."

"The path you seek must begin by believing in yourself. But to take even that step you must first know yourself."

More riddles. She had grown tired of his ignorance. She would send him off to his own folly and be rid of his foolish desires.

Instead, she had one more surprise in store, for her eyes gleamed with pleasure as she bet forward and smiled into his face.

"Tell me more about this remarkable tryst with Uruna. It sounds most intriguing."

"I cannot if I'm to make it to Zinat's for lunch."

"That old fool can't make a meal to satisfy a dung beetle."

"Then what?"

"I changed my mind. You're staying."

CHAPTER FORTY ONE

Desert Sojourn

Utu's reddened eye had just lifted beneath a layer of woolly gray overcast when Uruna jerked awake at the sharp prod of an oarsman's foot. She blinked and rubbed the sleep from her eyes, then gave the man a questioning look.

Astern of their swifthull a second boat had joined up soundlessly in the night. She remembered turning over as Gar quietly explained that six Nords now defended her and they were on the way to meet more.

Telgen nodded over his shoulder at Gar, who squatted in the stern, scanning both sides of the canal.

"Something ahead, he says."

Uruna glanced at her commander's troubled face and remembered the fabled Nord ability to smell trouble before it showed on the horizon. So, they were in for more grief, as if they hadn't had enough at Amaninda Two, just as the woman who had emerged from the reeds there with grief of her own. She was called Demiah, a refugee from Kish caught in the Gunzek turmoil.

Uruna spoke to Telgen. "Are we on the channel into Nippur?"

The man shook his head between pulls. "Same narrow feeder line we found last night. Cuts into Great Redeemer somewhere up ahead." He squinted into the gloom. "We disembark at the locks, pull the boats over the embankment, then follow Redeemer south to the *Idsha-uru*."

When he sighted the locks, Gar shouted for Telgen to hold. Uruna twisted around to peer down the straight ribbon of water, black against the dike's dull grey. A slender obelisk of mortared brick stuck its head above the desert floor a half mile ahead, marking the weir that shored their narrow feeder ditch against Redeemer's more powerful channel.

Uruna's skin prickled at the sight of dark-robed figures hunkered on both embankments. Dozens more dotted the desert floor on both sides.

"*Moshti*," said Gar. "Mountain nomads."

Uruna shuddered, recalling Suba's vivid account of the dreaded tribe who had ravished the plain above Elam a century ago. Would time have healed their savage nature?

Demiah must have heard of them as well. "Are they still dangerous?" she asked.

Gar kept his eye on the distance. "Sometimes. Under great hardship, they can be fierce. Strange for them to appear so far south. They usually keep to the hills above the Zab or farther north along upper Tigris."

"They don't look hostile from here," said Uruna. "In fact, the way they're lying about they must be travel worn."

"Don't expect them to stand in armed formation. A sleeping *moshti* can turn vicious in a heartbeat. They're probably just arising from sleep themselves."

Demiah swiveled her gaze to the flat outline of canal forming the southern horizon. "Could we make a run for Redeemer and beat them to it?"

"They'd easily outrun a woman."

Uruna spoke more from hope than conviction. "Maybe they only want money for us to pass."

Demiah stiffened. "Do you mean to bargain for our freedom?"

"Yes," said Gar. "It's done all the time out in the Shem lands."

The elder woman made a rueful face. "So much for their regard for life. Look, that one's coming closer."

A lone figure broke away from the rest and emerged from the gloom at a hesitant gait.

Gar cursed and spat over the side. "He's scouting us to make sure we're takeable," he said.

As the *moshti* drew closer Uruna recognized the marks of nomad raiment—tattered cloak and broken sandals. But the adornment for his head was a different matter. A cloth of ochre swathed his crown and swept to a tuck at the nape of his neck. Four shimmering jewels studded the front, the facets doing a gaudy dance in the wan light of pre-dawn. Gar explained to the others.

"He's their chief or spokesman, or as close to that as they make anyone. The gemstones are probably stolen." To Uruna's astonishment he addressed the man first.

"*Silim-Ma-Inanna, zu moshti.*"

The chief stopped, considered the implications of his counterpart's ability with his tongue, and grinned. He kept his arms crossed inside the cloak, leaving Gar and Uruna no choice but to conclude that his hands held weapons.

"We travel to Nippur," Uruna said, and Gar translated. The chieftain showed no evidence of understanding, but fastened his eyes on the boat in which she sat.

"*Uzwah mushadi,*" he said. "*Dembuah mushadi. Gineh shub-shub. Gineh zin-zin.*"

"He says they are watchers of the sacred water. He warns us not to pass, not to upset the waters."

Uruna comprehended the veiled threat and watched the *moshti's* face for a sign of his intent. The fixed smile was a disturbing cover for whatever emotion the man harbored, but it was obvious he was playing for time while his tribesmen gained position.

She looked at Gar and saw the muscle in his jaw twitch nervously. Her Nord captain had fit himself for battle and was holding himself in check while the situation developed.

"He's a demon in a man's skin," Gar said to her. "He'd kill me where I stand if he weren't outnumbered for the moment."

Uruna kept her eye on the *moshti*. White teeth gleamed in the gray light as the chief ran an appreciative eye over the boat's polished rails. She sensed the significance of the boat's sleek lines to a people who floated in leaky goatskin tubs. Control of the situation was slipping away with each moment. The *moshti* chief was a primitive soul with the irresponsible nature of a child. What he desired, he took. Whosoever stood in his way, he destroyed.

"Gar, he only wants the boats," she said. "Let's not provoke him. Just give him what he asks and move very carefully."

"You don't understand. He wants our hearts as well, Uruna."

Gar's use of her name was a signal. He was saying farewell, or telling her to run for it, or both.

Uruna abruptly stepped from the boat. "Take the boats out of the water," she ordered the men.

"We should try negotiating coins at least," Telgen objected.

"Take them out now."

The Nords went about the business of heaving the heavy-hulled craft onto dry land. When they were finished, Uruna retrieved her small tote and threw it over one shoulder. She walked up to the *moshti* chieftain, looked him in the eye, and declared her intentions.

"*Mu-shikku*," she said, holding up her prayer cup for him to see. "I perform the morning prayer to Inanna. Demiah, come with me."

The counting woman uttered a quiet moan as she obediently followed Uruna down the embankment and onto the desert floor. The soft outline of hills was a few hundred yards distant.

"Don't look back," Uruna told her. "Just keep walking until we make that rise over there. We'll pretend to make an altar."

With each step she expected to hear a shout and the sound of running feet. If the *moshti* pursued, she didn't know what she would do. Right now it took all her resolve just to keep plodding forward and convince herself that each step gained brought them closer to freedom.

They got as far as the base of the first sloping mound before the clamor started. A fierce ululating war cry spread across the morning stillness as the *moshti* streamed forth. Above the din Uruna heard Gar's sharp bark exhort his men to form a defense.

"Don't watch, just run!" she told Demiah. "Run to the top!"

She gathered up her skirts and milled up the slope, not daring to look back until she had made the crest. Demiah lumbered up the hill after her, slow and heavy. If the devils gave chase, the poor woman would never get away.

Uruna raised her sights to the canal top just as Gar plunged a spear into the chest of the knife-brandishing *moshti* chief. The nomads saw their man fall and broke into a run, swarming the tops of both embankments and charging the Nord position. The ones on the opposite bank dove into the water and swam to the other side to join the fight.

Gar and his five defenders were hopelessly outnumbered. Uruna turned away, unable to bring herself to watch good men go down beneath the wave of dark cloaks. Out there in the Akkad she and Demiah would face dangers of a different kind but just as perilous.

No time to think about it. Just run or die.

But where to go? To the east and north stretched mile after mile of unending desert, shaped by Euphrates' earliest mud flows and untouched by Sumerian engineers, to whom the Akkad's gullies and mounts presented insurmountable obstacles. A pair of women might find refuge in its maze, provided the barbarians did not give pursuit.

They both stood in full view of the dike. As soon as the soldiers were finished, the *moshti* would seek the women. She turned around to pull Demiah up the last few steps, but the scene below brought her up short.

Bodies of the slain lay about on the ground like squashed insects. She couldn't make out who was friend or foe in the thick melee. The *moshti* had forgotten their dead in a heated squabble for possession of the boats.

Uruna choked back a sob and sent a silent prayer for Gar and the other men. Nothing would be gained by staying any longer. She could only lend value to Gar's sacrifice if they managed to get away. She grasped Demiah by the shoulders, rolled off the top of the hill and tumbled several feet down the back side.

Demiah came up spluttering and defiant as she fought to get a purchase for her hands and knees.

"What is wrong with you!" she cried.

Uruna sat on her heels and dusted off her blouse. Her hair had fallen loose and she swept a lock from her face, mindful that the comb had dropped out.

Demiah still didn't understand the situation. They were hunted prey now. In the blink of an eye, the gods had left them to earn life by their wits moment by moment. If Demiah snapped now, Uruna couldn't carry on for the two of them.

"Demiah, we can't stand in plain sight!" she explained. "The Nords are fighting to buy us time. If we head south we'll eventually touch one of Redeemer's arms, or maybe even the main stream. But the savages will expect that and easily overtake us. So we go east."

"Into the Akkad?"

"Yes. They'll take us for lost and probably lose interest. The desert offers nothing for them."

"And for us?"

"A chance, Demiah! Do you want to perish in a *moshti* camp?"

"Better that than die in the claws of wolves."

"There's nothing out here to keep wolves alive," she said, hoping it was true. The savages wouldn't kill them outright. They were more useful as slaves. Only later, when they were no longer able to work, would the rabble finish them off.

Demiah struggled to one knee and crouched before Uruna, the two of them facing each other on hands and knees.

"Give me your knife," said Demiah.

"No! We're staying together!"

"We cannot. You're younger and stronger and much more

important."

"This not a matter of rank, Demiah. Together we can survive, apart we both die."

"I think not. I think you should go east into the next valley and from there take a route north into the Akkad."

"But that's barren wilderness. There's nothing out there but abandoned pastures and rock."

"That's true, until you get to Tigris' other leg."

"Oh, Demiah, that land is all ruined! Now enough of this talk. Let's get up and leave before those cutthroats catch sight of us. Come on, get up."

Uruna struggled to her feet and stood for a moment to beat the dust from her cloak. Demiah rolled over into a sitting position and refused to budge.

"I want the knife," she insisted.

"Demiah! Give me your hand!"

"No!" Demiah's eyes flashed. "Now is not the time for noble sacrifice. Look at us. We're a full two days from Nippur under the best conditions. The gods have put you in the desert against your will for good cause. I believe I understand where they are sending you."

"You are coming with me."

"I cannot. I do not see my life going beyond tomorrow."

"Don't talk like that, Demiah. You are too precious—"

"Stop! Be a queen, Uruna! You have never shrunk from duty before. Terrible things are happening to us, tests that demand strength and sacrifice. Now do what you know you must. Give me the knife. I'm not afraid. I know what to do."

Tears blurred Uruna's vision. It wasn't supposed to happen this way! Not with horrid bloodshed showing up at every hand. She had lost everyone who meant anything to her. Why must she lose a good woman as well? What did the world stand to gain by Demiah's death?

Demiah stirred her feet in the sand. "Help me up."

Uruna hauled the priestess upright. Demiah stood and faced her with a grim smile.

If she can do it, thought Uruna, so can I.

She unsheathed the knife from its scabbard and held the handle outward. Demiah gave her a look of gratitude and pressed Uruna's hand and the knife between her palms.

"Go with Inanna and find your dream, Uruna. Great Mother has a place in Heaven for you. Even greater sacrifice than this will you be asked to give, and greater courage will you show in return."

Uruna bit her lip and sobbed. "I'm not ready to say goodbye."

"The last moment always comes upon us quickly. Thank the Goddess for this small chance. Save yourself for the vision, Uruna. Take my hope with you into the Akkad and don't look back. I am in Her care now."

"We've had such a short time together. But I treasure your friendship. This wickedness will pass, and we will both live to see that day together."

Demiah released her hands and stepped back.

"Go."

"I will see you in Nippur, Demiah," Uruna pledged.

"Go on, girl, and get yourself to the farthest side of the world. Find your dream, and find your love."

CHAPTER FORTY TWO
Lost in the Akkad

There was a way to tell direction by watching shadows: they pointed west at sunrise, and eastward after midday. But the cloud cover that saved her from the killing sun also denied Uruna the signs she needed. For most of the morning, she kept to an eastward track, reckoning a path where she had watched the red sun peek above the horizon before vanishing in thick overcast.

She maintained her spirits by telling herself that soon she would top a rise and behold the verdant farms of Tigris. But the gullies became canyons, and the walls turned into steep ramparts, forcing her deeper below the vantage of skyline.

Whenever she ascended for a look around, the landscape was the same pale brown monotony of eroded rock and clay, utterly devoid of vegetation. The skies were empty of birds. No humming insect sang in the stillness. Not even a lizard skittered among the rocks. Hers was the sole life about. Only the desperate wandered the Akkad's dead oblivion.

Eventually, the gully she was traveling opened on a wide valley bordered by towering escarpments of limestone. The bluff face was eroded with deep trenches and hollow recesses where she might find a sheltered spot to rest.

Near a crack in the west wall, a sand drift pushed against the cliff base. She was weary from strain and lack of sleep. Tomorrow could turn hot. Travel by night made more sense. She found a clean expanse of soft gray sand and lay down upon it.

North up the valley lay an opening between the walls. She would head for it after she rested. Give the sun plenty of time to pass behind the bluffs, in case the cloud cover lifted.

She relaxed, and visions of the assault at the weir flooded her mind. Gar flailing at a swarm of assailants. Black *moshti* cloaks flapping about his fallen carcass like the wings of carrion birds. Demiah's tear-stained face beseeching her for a blade to end it all.

What a waste. She must concentrate on what lay ahead. Stay alive.

She resolved not to perish. Death did not frighten her, but neither did she welcome an early end. Demiah was right. There was a purpose in everything that happened. The gods had removed her from the temple. They had brought Anu to her with his vow of love and a new door open to hope. Now she must obey instinct. Reverse the appearance of things. Find her way the same as the hunter. Somewhere over the tops of those bluffs, destiny waited. Over the tops...

A finger of cold sand swept across her cheek and Uruna spluttered awake. Her eyes fluttered open, but she saw nothing. She had never known such darkness. Not a single star shone above. The moon had shifted to the other side of the bluff and no light, not a ray of it, came through the clouds that now blotted out the sky.

The entire valley was a black void, obliterating her view of the faraway opening to freedom with an obscurity as complete as if she were sightless. Uruna crawled a few feet, stopped and shivered with cold. She had heard of night things that slithered out on the sand to lie in wait for fumbling flesh. If she got up and walked, how could she make her way blind?

She was starved and utterly disgusted by her carelessness. Being attacked and forced into the wilderness was bad enough, but now she had added folly to the bargain...

Rain. She smelled rain.

Was it possible in the Akkad? The landscape around her certainly was scoured and gouged by weather's rage. Everyone assumed it fell in winter, but everyone she knew lived in the south.

Get away from the cliff. You saw the rocks on the valley floor. The gods didn't put them there.

Clutching her cloak tight around her shoulders, she staggered to her feet. A heavy drop pelted her forehead, then another. She moved away from the wall, feeling her way down the shallow slope of dune.

Find higher ground, even if you have to wander in the dark.

Spring rains were usually warm. A little discomfort would sharpen her wits and keep her on the move. There was nothing to fear from getting wet as long as she found shelter. But she didn't have long.

Stones and pebbles littered the valley floor and her feet seemed to find every one. She caromed off several boulders, staggering through he inky darkness on a ragged course. What insanity! She might wander in circles all night this way.

A clap of thunder cracked the air as a bolt of lightning struck pinnacles high atop the bluff, momentarily lighting a clear path ahead. Either the gods or her own fears were sucking her into the open to meet her doom.

She didn't care anymore. She was moving.

Another flash, followed by a crack-boom. White glare diminished the canyon features, showing the walls to be gully size, the valley floor a washed-out stream bed.

Night closed round her again. She focused on a clearing she had glimpsed in the flash and stumbled through it, sightless but determined. She would make it if she clung to either wall.

Rivulets flowed down the rocks now, forming streams that rushed across the ground to sluice about her feet. She stopped in mud up to her ankles to get her bearings. A shower broke overhead and she raised her upturned mouth and drank from the sky.

"Beloved Inanna who cares for her children," she sang aloud to the heavens. "Blessed am I to receive thy bounty. Lead me in thy path, Great Mother. Show my feet the way. Take me to my fate."

The rain was warm and soothing and she swept open her cloak to let the flood wash the salt and grime from her body. She would be cleansed for tomorrow's journey. The water's restoring power was giving her new strength. Tomorrow she would enter the valley—

A deep rumble.

The sound rolled down the valley, reverberated through the soles of her feet, deep and steady, gathering momentum until it drowned the claps in the sky, a lion's roar above the bay of yapping dogs.

Landslide!

The entire mountain was coming down! But from which direction? If she chose wrong she would blunder right into its path.

She snatched her sodden cloak from the ground and dashed forward, heedless of rocks cutting her feet and legs. A prolonged flash of light cast the entire valley in a stark, blue light, and she glanced over her shoulder.

The sight stopped her in her tracks.

An immense section of rock wall shifted before her eyes and slid downward, falling in on itself and sending huge boulders crashing down to the floor with a resounding roar.

The light vanished and Uruna turned and fled down the gap. Lightning flashed all around, but she kept running, running, straining at each flare to see a way out.

She was near the end of the canyon when a great crash resounded from behind. A blast of air jolted her off her feet and sent her flying. She rolled onto one side and stared in disbelief.

A mud wall filled the canyon to both sides. The whole mountain was bearing down on her.

She leaped to her feet and dashed blindly through the gloom. Ahead she caught a glimpse of the canyon mouth, its flanks outlined in flickering blue light.

Her door to safety? Or her doom?

She rushed forward, praying for refuge, and at once tripped and fell headlong into the runny muck. Pain racked her feet and a sharp stone jabbed one rib. She rolled off the protrusion, sucked in her breath, and heaved to her knees.

The flood was coming on fast, filling the canyon with a rolling jumble of mud and rock. She couldn't outrun it in the few seconds remaining before it caught up with her.

She looked up, hoping for lightning to reach forth its hand and end the torture. The next flash nearly blinded her as it struck the limestone tops.

The cliff!

She dashed to the base of the rocky ruin and clambered up the first fallen rock she came to. The top was maybe six feet above the floor. The surge would sweep it away and her with it.

She reached for the next boulder, and climbed higher. The stone trembled in her hands as the flood's fury tore at the walls, close enough now to send a message of doom to her body.

She shook her wet hair out of her eyes and struggled up the face of the next huge rock in a miraculous discovery of handholds, footholds, crevices and platforms. Up and up she went, her broken nails biting the wall, fingers scrabbling with a will of their own, reaching higher and higher without stopping…

The surge of mud and rubble swept the base of the cliff. She felt the sickening groan of titans grinding boulders underfoot and peered down.

In the flickering light, an angry roiling melee sucked rubble toward the canyon mouth.

She still clung to the cliff face, shivering from exhaustion, but she would not last the night without better sanctuary.

A deep shadow above and to the right looked likely. Maybe if she made her way to that shadowy outcropping…

She climbed. Away from the raking and scouring beneath. Away from the cascade's roar. Away to the angled escarpment, every foot of ascent an agony. The rain had moved on, leaving the rock face damp and pungent. Exhaustion claimed her limbs. She dared not rest for the shortest moment.

Then she saw the hole.

Really no more than a shallow depression between two rocks, cramped and uninviting. Sharp nodules of gray-white stone protruded into a space that would barely accommodate her. She raised her head to scan the bluff top and stopped.

The rim was only a few yards higher.

Her hands and feet had learned on the climb up. Now she gave them to the cliff, and almost immediately encountered holds carved in the cleft at such perfect intervals that she could step upright as though climbing a ladder.

Her body cried out with fatigue as she gained the cliff top. She wanted to collapse right there and wait for morning, but she willed herself away from the edge and crawled across a flat of plateau. She was ready to give into exhaustion when she saw a light in the near distance.

Firelight? So soon after a torrential rain?

She looked again. A steady flickering, like a wall backlit by a fire.

Someone would be there. Someone who could feed her broth and let her sleep and see her on to the next habitation.

She staggered up on legs stiffened by exertion. The strain to put one foot ahead of the other was almost too much. The broken terrain forced her into more dips and gullies that maddeningly cut the firelight from sight. Yet at each rise she managed to find the orange glow.

Nearing the end of her strength and close enough to make out the licking flames, she fell in a heap, utterly spent.

A long, low wail escaped her lips as she despaired of ever reaching the fire site. She lay on her back, watching the stars wink in and out through gaps in the clouds.

Where are you Demiah?

Does Niccaba hear my call?

So far away from rescue. So close and yet so far.

Coarse hands lifted her head and pressed water to her lips. A deep voice spoke a subdued command, and a strong arm slid beneath her shoulder and lifted her up from the hard, rocky bed. She was being carried against a man's bony chest. Carried to the mouth of a cave and inside, where a fire danced and voices clipped the air. An imperative here, a question there.

A figure loomed above her and Uruna struggled to focus. The skin was dark and weathered and something about the face was terribly recognizable and terribly wrong.

And then she knew, and her head reeled as the weight of destiny's cruelty pulled her down to the deep well of despair.

She was not on the road to freedom. Liberation was not within her grasp. In her ordeal she had followed the inevitable circle, the twist and turn leading her in a roundabout return to the very tribe she had fled that morning.

She had wandered straight into the camp of the *moshti*.

CHAPTER FORTY THREE
Retha Safekept

Retha sat on a cold bench outside the council chamber and waited to be called inside. The Bull was back from Uruk and exerting his will upon anyone who opposed him. She had no idea who was in there with him, nor what he had in mind. The man could be nasty. Still, she'd rather be in there where it was warm. It was winter, the middle of the night, for god's sake, and she was shivering.

Two men had burst into her room, dragged her from sleep, and hauled her outside before she could grab a wrap. The younger one was nice, but the other had given her a mean look and told her to stay put on the bench.

The Bull had moved upon Nippur with sharp efficiency. His soldiers were everywhere, inside the Aniginna, roving Gipar halls, trooping up and down the concourse—bursting into *kadishtu* dormitories. One of them stood watch now, a burly fellow picking his teeth down the hall. What a boring job. He couldn't have much of a brain to put up with looking at walls the whole night through.

Her father hadn't been home for nearly a week. He knew how to handle trouble, but life was dangerous with Kurgs lurking about. She hoped the Bull had favorable news to give her.

The door opened and a tall man in a hooded cowl nodded at her.

She had almost reached the door when she recognized the face inside the hood as that of Suba.

"Quickly, follow me before the Nafti scum shows up."

"But what about the Bull's summons?"

"Your father has countermanded it."

"He's alive?"

"Yes, but no time for that. Move now."

Suba took her by the arm and propelled her through the colonnade shadows. A door on the left lay open but he pulled her instead to the right into a narrow passageway. At the far end stood three figures in hooded robes of coarse wool. She recognized the voice of one as that of the Hanza matron.

"Good work," said Heganna to Suba, then she took Retha's elbow. "Not a moment to lose, dear, before the Bull sounds the alarm."

Suba moved away quickly and jogged back the way they had come.

"Where is he going?" Retha asked no one in particular.

Sebbu bent closer and spoke in lowered tones. "To dispose of more Gunzeks. Or create a diversion while we leave for our plantation in Gishon. Your mother asked us to take you along."

"My mother? How did she do that?"

"We'll explain on the way. For now, we must hurry."

Retha peered at the third figure and received a terse reply.

"Kinar."

Sebbu produced a cloak for Retha and they set off at a fast walk across the concourse. The sentry at the Aniginna gate made a surreptitious glance around before waving them through.

Big sentry, Retha noted to herself. Nord big.

A *kadishtu* had talked of carrying food to imprisoned *galla* sentries replaced by Gunzeks. Suba had no such resources at his disposal, so the Gunzek here had probably suffered the same fate as the sentry outside the council chamber. Suba's methods were swift and permanent.

Sebbu took the lead and ushered the three women across the outer street and into an alley. They continued on a broken course through more alleys and back streets until they came to the *Idsha-Uru* central canal bisecting the city. An empty raft awaited them, and Sebbu took the pole. With Enguda's Gunzek guards all clustered inside the Aniginna compound for the night, their passage north through the city went undetected.

At Nippur's north wall, Sebbu planted his pole and pushed the raft into the canal's bricked embankment.

"Here's where it gets dicey," he told everyone. "Mama, Kinar, I hope you two are up for a climb."

Retha knew of a staircase west, closer to Nergal Gate, but Gunzeks were sure to be posted there.

It turned out two burly Nords positioned atop the wall provided hoisting power. Each woman placed one foot in a loop of rope and rode it up the wall. In the same fashion they descended the other side. The Hanza troupe plus one then cut across open ground to a footpath leading to the Nunbirdu Canal. Three swifthulls with oarsmen took them eastward under the stars to the canal's end. Sebbu cautioned complete silence, for the water carried voices afar.

After they debarked, Heganna put an arm around Retha's shoulders and drew her close.

"We'll make Sinar House by daybreak," she said. "Your mother is already there waiting for you."

"You're very kind, and I'm most grateful. But why me? Why my mother?"

"It was Uruna's plan. If anything were to happen to her, we must secure you and your mother against the Bulltails."

"I'm still not sure what Enguda had in mind for me tonight."

"We got word he intends to carry out his original plan regardless of Uruna's death. I think she balked at one of his demands, and he had her killed. So he settled for his second choice."

"Me? But I'm just a girl."

"You're also Gar's daughter. We couldn't allow him to win both contests so soon. "

"Why take me to this place of yours, this Sinar?"

"Because it's safe—for now—and the city isn't. We're all hostages there, every Lukur priestess, every landowner, every merchant—anyone in power of any kind. Enguda would have us killed in a trice. The only reason he hasn't so far is that our spies revealed his plans."

"And what of my father?"

"Gar leads the fight against all Bulltails, but especially those bearing arms."

"Where is he now?"

"Only the gods know—and possibly Suba. Retha, that man and your father are performing feats beyond imagining. Sebbu and I would be at Sinar ourselves this moment if Suba hadn't shown up to set up your escape."

"Have you any idea what became of Uruna?"

"Your father sent her over a dune to hide, but when he sought her after the battle…" Heganna drew a deep breath. "No trace. The land out there…it's brutal, fit only for the dead and dying. She is lost, Retha. We've lost our beloved serpent queen."

"And where was Anu all this time?"

Heganna bit her lip and stared ahead into the darkness for several steps without speaking. At last she broke her silence.

"Probably lost as well."

She seemed unable to explain further, and they continued on in silence, each caught up in her own thoughts.

The first light of day broke over the Hanza plantation as Retha neared the end of her strength and stumbled to a halt. Before her lay the outline of a vast house atop a low rise. Orchards spread to the horizon in all directions, row upon row of plums and olives and cherries. A cow lowed in the distance, and Retha started as a tall, angular woman in a white linen shift appeared in one of the doorways to lift an arm in salute.

"Mother!" she cried.

At once her legs found new strength, and she sprang forward and raced ahead toward Milsah's open arms.

In a matter of hours the world had turned cruel and deadly.

Though she might fear for her own life, a worse fate awaited if she didn't give Enguda what he wanted, or could not, he would vent his wrath on those dear to her.

For torture that vile she had no defense.

CHAPTER FORTY FOUR

Struggles At Edin

Rahnee leaned back from the tea table and regarded her guest from heavy-lidded eyes.

"So you are smitten with Uruna. So is every able-bodied Sumerian male. What makes her special to you?"

"She moves about without fear. She hunts the hearts of her people and wins victories by her wisdom. She can laugh at herself and yet she is completely devoted to duty. I can love no other woman."

"She arouses you more than the pretties of the temple?"

"We've never made love."

"But you are in love with her."

"Yes."

"And she with you."

"Perhaps."

"Don't demure with me, you're the heart's desire of every woman in Sumer. Why shouldn't a queen be smitten?"

"Because I'm unworthy."

"Do not dally with me, hunter. Spit it out. Why this unworthiness?"

"Because I know nothing of snakes!"

"There!" she exclaimed, regarding him with a look of triumph.

"You are so stubborn when it comes to self-examination, Anu! We must work on your introspection. You see wondrous possibility for both yourself and Uruna, yet you hold back. Where's the bold hunter? Why do you cower before your feelings?"

"I'm untrained in affairs of the heart," he said weakly, but his face broke into a mischievous grin in spite of himself. "But I learn quickly."

Rahnee did not smile. "Then prepare for a long stay. This will be like the lion. We have much work to do."

He spent the afternoon alone locked inside Edin's tomb after Rahnee, without a word of explanation, shoved him through a door in her underground maze and gave his backside a good whomp.

"Don't sleep!" she shouted as she slammed the bar from the outside. He listened to her fading footsteps and called out, but she was gone.

The darkness inside his small compartment was complete. A few moments of exploration proved it to be absolutely empty and apparently without function. Four earthen walls and the one door. He had plenty of air to breathe and he squatted on the floor to listen for the old woman's return, thinking how none of it made sense unless she was mad and had imprisoned him there for all eternity.

No, she was clever, not mad. So it must be a test of some sort, perhaps his first. He was elated by such quick success, but she had left him no instruction.

Except not to sleep.

All right, what was he supposed to do? Sit and think? Ponder his love for Uruna? Ruminate over his shortcomings with the hunting god and come up with a list? Count the hairs on his head?

Ridiculous!

He was still the hunter. For him, sitting in complete solitary darkness was no problem. The *ghana* had put him through as much and worse.

He considered taking a nap, then decided against it. Why invite a wrathful glower from the Edin mistress?

At length she came for him. Just opened the door, turned about and walked away. He followed her down the hall, blinking and realizing he was in for more strange behavior if he stuck around.

"Was that a lesson of some sort?" he asked when they reached Edin's great room. She ignored him and busied herself with an arrangement of boxes and ornaments laid out on a bench.

"I'd like to know what's going on so that I can do well. There isn't much time, Rahnee…"

"You talk to ease your discomfort."

"I'm perfectly comfortable. I've sat longer than that in mud with flies tickling my face while killers prowled as close as six feet."

"Good for you. So you can behave like a pig, go live with pigs."

"What was the closet all about?"

"More talk. The answer is not with me, it's with you. Look inside."

It was useless to ask the simplest question of her. She was a stubborn old woman with nothing better to do than amuse herself with the young man who had suddenly dropped into her life.

Rahnee quickly finished whatever she was doing and started out for the stairs.

"Where are you going?" he asked.

"Up to the roof to watch the sunset. Come along if you wish."

Rahnee clambered up the ladder ahead of him like an agile child at play. She seemed to get about quickly wherever she went, as though age might never catch up with her. Twice today she had disappeared and reappeared with none of the trappings of sorcery—just gone and back again.

The Akkad was cooling off as Anu hoisted himself between the ladder rails and walked to the parapet where his new teacher sat with her feet dangling over the side. Had she always been such a capricious soul? He warmed to a notion that Rahnee had confounded everyone with an undying zest for adventure and took chances few others dared to risk.

He faced west where the sun had dropped beneath a sullen band of crimson, painting the undersides of clouds a brilliant orange.

"Where do I start?" he asked his errant tutor.

Rahnee answered by pointing at his feet. "Right where you stand, hunter. Look inward, move outward. Stalk your new quarry. Discover who he is and find your path to him."

He knew she was using his own terms to make the task seem easier, and he admired her all the more.

When the light had faded and their rooftop stood beneath a canopy of stars, he asked the question that had dogged him ever since leaving Demshalla.

"Tell me about Uruna's trance with the cobra," he said. "I want to know what I should do."

He waited while the Edin queen gathered her thoughts for the answer.

"The Sleep of Serpents has six stages," Rahnee began. "Each stage opens a door inside the woman, letting in more light, raising her spirit higher to perceive a larger view. Uruna can get through the first four Doors at will."

He had no idea what she was talking about, but apparently the feat was astounding. "How do you know?" he asked.

"I inquired. Never mind my sources, just take my word for it, she's unique. Never heard of any woman like her. All the others only developed Sight after seeking another seer's help."

Rahnee's troubled countenance was disturbing.

"Is it wrong?" he asked. "Has she breached a trust, offended a god?"

"No, Anu, there are no rules for Serpenthood. She's just a little...imposing, is all."

"Strange, but you don't strike me as the awestruck type."

Rahnee ignored his remark and continued.

"To reach the peak, the supplicant has to have help. Six priestesses to prepare her raiment. Six serpents to test her readiness for each of the six Doors to Heaven. Six potions, each rightly mixed to remove her from the world. Six lovers, or one lover six times, to raise her senses ever higher as each door opens to her."

"An elaborate procedure," he observed.

"Too fancy, if you ask me. The Lukur turned it into a spectacle and lost the spirit of the way. But every component is essential in one form or another. The mixing of potions will be one of your duties."

"How do the potions remove her from the world? What's in them, anyway?"

"Listen to me, Anu. Each Door is different. The potion is always a mixture of cobra venom, strong ale, and herbs, but in different proportions and amounts. The venom defies her will to extend mortal life, the ale encourages the senses and loosens fear. The herbs are to hone her sensual perception of the divine.

"Serpenthood taught Uruna how to draw venom from the cobra's fangs. The same showed her how to measure out the droplets in a vial, how to measure the brew, and how to count the grains of flower seed. This most delicate of processes was usually handed down from one seer to the next. You see, an improper mixture can kill her."

"That's not very encouraging. You'll have to show me how to get it right."

"But you see, the measure is different for each of us. Let Uruna show you, but make sure she's not in the trance. Later, she won't be herself and you'll have to do it for her."

"But I might make a mistake!"

"Don't."

She was right, it was very much like hunting the lion.

"Tell me more about the ceremony," he said.

Rahnee narrowed her eyes as though measuring his capacity for shock. Every answer was a test. She knew he could face death bravely, but were there any soft spots in his resolve? Was the hunter equal to the demands of the serpent god?

"You make love to her six times in the night. First with the little serpent in attendance, the small brown master who opens the first Door to Heaven. Then he stands by with the second, and so on until it is the large animal's turn. He takes her through the last Door, and then you wait."

"Hold on, you're going too fast for me. I make love to Uruna with the serpents looking on?"

"Yes. You can do it, Anu. Believe me, it's much easier than having the Lukur council for an audience."

"So, when and *if* we get to the Sixth Door, I'm supposed to make love to Uruna with five live cobras watching."

"Yes, they're there to see you do it right."

"And if I don't?"

"Then they will strike you dead—oh, Anu, such a look! You believe everything I say!"

"Well, what will they do?"

"Mourn for her, return to their baskets, who knows? I never saw it happen. You don't think about what the lion will do if you miss. You don't wonder how your bones will look afterward, because it doesn't matter much, does it? What's really important is to do it right in the first place."

"All right, so let's say it works and she's—up there, out there, somewhere with the gods. And you said I wait for her to waken. How long does it take? I'm no good at waiting, as you'll attest."

Rahnee folded her hands and leaned forward. "Anu, you have to understand one thing with the Sleep." She rocked several times, as though thinking to herself. "It's a form of death. The venom does it. When she's all the way gone, she looks dead."

He swallowed. "So I won't know she's back until she—this cadaver—sits up and talks to me. How dead does she look?"

"Very. If you need a graphic description, I can..."

"No, thank you anyway."

A night hawk suddenly swooped through the desert night and darted away. "Look, do you see it?" he said, pointing at its phantom shape in the murk.

"You have good eyes, hunter."

"In the wilderness I can act without thinking," he told her. "I see sign, I follow spoor, I use my senses, and I go. I'm less sure what to do with Uruna. It's all so new and strange."

"Listen to you go on," said Rahnee. "Now stalk the serpent. Put your mind to it and move ahead. Look for signs of his presence and remember he's the way to all knowledge."

"Sort of like Tezu-Mah."

"Your god also answers the seeker who is pure in heart. But the serpent spirit is hard to see, for he bends his body to conform to the earth and changes his color to appear as sand. Seek him not directly, but let him come to you."

"Also like Tezu-Mah."

"Yes, from within the heart."

"I think this is going to be different."

"Unlike anything you've ever tried."

"And more difficult."

"Hardly the word for it."

"Challenging?"

"Try impossible."

CHAPTER FORTY FIVE
Hunting Serpenthood

Sand in his face.

The cold breast of broad dune pressed hard against Anu's cheek as he shivered and lifted one eyelid. Overhead, bright stars spilled across a cloudless night sky in random sprays of light. Dawn was a distant promise.

"Get up, hunter! You sleep too much!"

Rahnee's foot jabbed a rib and he spat sand from his mouth and twisted over onto one side to escape another blow. She pursued with agile purpose and landed another kick.

"Lazy! I told you to be watchful and look at you. Stretched out like a wallowing sow."

Anu struggled to one elbow and spent several moments rubbing his head before he realized he was not in a Lukur bower, but out on the Akkad with the ancient witch from Edin.

"Where's nagga?" he mumbled, fighting to get his wits together. "You told me yesterday I should stay here and learn. Have I done something wrong?"

"Not if you count it a virtue to have slept half the night. What's this 'nagga' business, anyway?"

He sat up. "Did I say that?"

The strange word meant nothing to him now.

"You were dreaming. Not vigilant at all, just the same old Anu, nodding off at the precise instant of opening."

"A door. I was supposed to open some sort of door."

"Not *a* door, hunter, *the* Door. Six Doors, I told you, six to command before you kiss your cobra queen, but at the moment there is only one Door for you, the first."

"Well, it's hard to do!"

"Of course it is. I warned you before we started. It's the most arduous work anyone can undertake. But you were so sure."

"I'll make it. Give me another chance. I'll do it right now."

He crossed his legs, took a deep breath, and pulled the sharp night air past his throat and into his lungs. The dry intake caught in his gullet and he coughed.

"Get up."

"I can do it."

"Get up! We're going back."

"Not until I get it right."

"You'll get nothing right if you catch your death out here. Look at yourself, no cloak, no robe, not even a shawl for your head. It's winter, or close enough to it. The Akkad is the lion, Anu. Desert night kills just as swiftly as the beast. Now get your feet under you and we'll go home for a warm breakfast."

"I'm fasting."

"Not anymore, you're not. Come-come-come! Up!"

He got to his feet and shook his limbs to get the circulation going. She was right, of course. He was miserably cold and he could hardly stand, as weak as he was from hunger. Once many years ago, starting out on his own, he had almost perished the same way. On that occasion a passing Bedu had pulled him from the brink.

"But why are you taking me away so soon?" he objected. "I just got here."

Rahnee held up four fingers. "Fourth day. You wanted to do it in ten days, and what did I say?"

"You didn't say anything. You just laughed."

"Yes, and then I told you that if you have excellent concentration, and if the god is in a particularly good mood, then maybe—just *maybe*—three months."

"I can do it in ten days."

"You!"

She stormed off the ridge and stomped down the sloping tail of dune, following the imprint of his tracks from half a day ago. He trailed after her, resigned to bear her chastisement all the way back to Edin.

"The strength of a god carries you past peril," she continued, "you're a marksman without equal, your love for the supplicant is pure. That gets you no credit with the gods, but you'd do it anyway, and so I send you out to the ideal spot, with the clearest air and the purest, most unadulterated sand available. No distractions except your own inner voice. I give you Akkad. I take you through it all. So what do you do with your time? You sleep!"

"I was in a garden with an angel. She kissed me and whispered—"

"That was mere dreaming! A mind trick! You sat and watched the sand and you got bored, and so your mind thought up a dream. 'Oh, Rahnee, I had a vision from on high. She was this, and she was that.' You couldn't explain a bit of it to me if you'd really gone through the Door. Words simply fail."

"I didn't claim to go through the Door, but I shall."

Rahnee stopped in mid-stride and cast her arms to the heavens.

"Inanna, I plead for recourse. Please find another soul foolish enough to counsel this densest of men!"

She wheeled around and confronted him, her face caught momentarily in the flat reflection of white-sand-sea and the star-appointed canopy. Fold and crease melded and he saw her as she might have appeared in early middle age, a woman of compelling beauty and awesome intelligence. She ignored his stare and pointed a finger straight at him.

"First you have to *see* the Door, Anu. All you're seeing right now is your own creation. You're listening to the eternal dialog with yourself, convinced it must be a conversation with angels. You must shut it off, cut out the mind-play completely, and you cannot do it by falling asleep."

Rahnee turned around and struck off down the slope again, and Anu trudged after her, thinking his own thoughts.

What she had not done was send him home. If she were truly finished with him, she would say so, and if the ten-day goal were absolutely impossible, she wouldn't have bothered with him in the first place. Instead, she exhorted him, applying insult and outrage to goad him along. He jogged ahead and fell in step with her, intending to pledge his intent to try harder, but Rahnee spoke first.

"Don't try to talk right now. Use this moment like all other moments henceforth. Tell me what you're doing."

"I'm walking."

"You're thinking about what to say next. The body is walking while you're out there somewhere with your mind. Now be the walking."

"Be the walker, you mean?"

"No. Find the business of walking. You've been doing it all your life, it's become such a habit that you don't watch any more. Now watch the walk. Feel the foot touch earth, the leg extend, the chest muscles stretch. Find as many parts of the walk as you can and watch them. Move yourself into the walk. Like the hunt."

"I can—"

"Don't talk. Do it. Forget me, forget you, forget serpents, just do one thing. Walk."

The eastern sky was gray when the walls of Edin finally fell behind and Anu slumped to the ground in a heap. Rahnee ignored his fallen form and continued on across the courtyard and into the darkened temple, where she disappeared beneath the arched doorway. He dragged himself after her and climbed down the stairs with exaggerated care, unsure his legs would support him and wondering if he wasn't a little crazy from lack of food and sleep.

Had he squandered his time with Rahnee? There were moments

when he doubted her existence as much as he questioned his own sanity for coming to Edin. It was one thing to place one's hope in the ghost of a lost legend, but quite another to pursue that ghost endlessly into the chaos that forsook everything he knew to be real about himself, his gods, the world.

For a week he had toiled in the caverns beneath Edin's temple, returning each night to his mat exhausted, not from physical exertion but from an endeavor more arduous than any he could have imagined.

He had to stop thinking.

And to stop thinking, he had to start doing strange things that made no sense whatsoever.

Like stare at a blank wall until he disappeared into it, a seemingly benign little exercise in contorted thought which taught no lesson but the absolute conviction that if he had to look at the same pock pattern another minute he would go stark, raving mad.

Or the task of pounding Edin's old bricks into dust, one after another, just hammering clods with a fist-sized rock until Rahnee called or the sun went down, whichever came first. He had quit before either could occur and earned a mute glare from his teacher.

As the days rolled on, he lost track of time. He would sit alone for long stretches inside his chamber watching shadow play on the wall patterns. Often he would rise from sleep to find Rahnee gone without a trace. Even his expert tracker's eye was useless to him. He never knew which way she had gone or how she might have traveled, but eventually she would return, suddenly reappearing in a portal like a wraith. At times he suspected he had fallen in league with a clever spirit who had left mortality long ago and took pleasure from tormenting him.

At dusk on those days when she chose to be seen, they would climb together to the roof of Edin's Goddess Shrine and sit cross-legged, facing each other on the empty pedestal while the western sky changed colors. On one such occasion, as he caught the play of lemon light in her black-and-silver tresses, Anu put a question to her about the Sleep of Serpents.

"What is it, exactly? I mean, what happens?"

"In the old tongue it was called 'Holy Stone of Sacred Lust,'" she told him. "But its true significance has been lost over time."

As practiced at Nippur's Ekur temple, she went on, the rite was a departure from the sacred tradition of old. Long ago, the coupling of queen and consort had degraded to ritual copulation. The original practice, preserved in rite but lost in spirit, had involved a much more spiritual union in which copulation was only the beginning step. Thereafter, the couple transcended level upon level into higher realms of ecstasy. Occasionally, every thousand years or so, a pair might conjoin who were so spiritually advanced and so perfectly mated that they attained absolute unity. These sacred beings became gods and ascended directly to the throne of Inanna.

Gradually, the secret of ascension became forgotten, or so intermingled with fable that its power diminished to insignificance, and another path had to be found.

"The Sleep of Serpents was developed by an ancient order of elderwomen in the mountainous country of Anshan, far to the east. To these women Inanna entrusted the knowledge of alchemy and of beasts. Combining the serpent's venom with a mild drug, they induced the trance by altering the blood of a priestess queen.

"For ages afterward the practice was infallible. Each queen so indoctrinated was able to attain the Sight."

"Did Rahnee of Edin so attain?"

"What do you think, Anu?"

"I think that Rahnee has gone beyond the first sight of Sacred Lust. I think she sees at will."

"Touch my hand," she commanded suddenly.

Anu obeyed and immediately entered a trance. His soul sought and fused with the soul of the woman of Edin, and in a heartbeat he became Rahnee. He was in her body and he watched the world through her eyes, felt the pulse of her heart and the strong grip of the young man seated before her. And with that awareness of contact, he went back into himself, and Rahnee suddenly appeared as a young woman of compelling beauty and appeal. He felt the urge to bed her at once and recoiled. Instantly he became the young woman, pleased by her ability to arouse the young man, aware that she desired him and wanted to take him between her loins. And in the heat of her desire he became Anu once again, Anu reaching for her hand in the darkness, reaching across years of time for the hand of the exotic maiden who bade him join her bower, whose secrets were yet to be revealed...

...who watched him as a sharp-eyed old woman breathing contentedly the evening vapors atop a desert shrine.

Anu flushed bright crimson as the stately queen regarded him with open candor.

"You are forgiven for assuming responsibility," Rahnee told him. "There is no will involved; it simply flows, most *un*willingly at times. As with most gifts, the Sight is both blessing and curse."

"What did you just do?"

"You mean what did we do? We were together, were we not? And when? Time is not a road across the desert, Anu, nor are the souls in Inanna's keep scattered asunder. All exists in eternal unity."

"I shall never understand such mysteries."

"Have patience. Understanding is already within you, just forgotten is all. You have only to rediscover it."

On another evening, Rahnee surprised him inside the shrine hall. He had been sitting across from her for several minutes as was his custom after a day of work. As he watched the light fade and felt the peace of Edin's raw simplicity, Rahnee abruptly addressed him.

"Thou art ready."

Before he could utter an objection, Rahnee pressed her hand to his forehead and immediately the space inside the room opened, and he found himself standing at the foot of a broad staircase with the open air all around. His eye followed the steps up to a throne at the top, where sat a woman of extraordinary fairness. Eyes the color of sapphires gazed down at him from a glowing oval face rimmed by soft, golden curls. The woman smiled a welcome and her smile was Rahnee's, but then it was another's. He felt himself drawn into the smile and he went inside it and became the smile itself. And then he became the woman, gazing at the man whose face radiated golden light.

A bond of love instantly filled the space between them, a visible, tangible ribbon of light shining and shimmering and filling with sound until it grew into a melody he recognized as belonging to the him-and-her one he had joined. An enthralling peace coursed through him, rising from a spot just behind his navel and vibrating outward along his arms and legs to his fingertips and toes. A question brushed his mind, light and soft like the touch of myrtle leaf against his window sill, and abruptly he was the man again, looking out at the world from male eyes.

But the woman had vanished, and in place of the alabaster throne stood a small nub of stone. He stared at the stunted throne for some time before he realized it was not a royal seat at all, but a simple birthing stool. In the distance an infant bawled its first cry.

He came to his senses alone on Edin's rooftop, without an inkling how he'd gotten there, the calm serenity still with him.

He sat the night through beneath the stars and never once asked Rahnee what it had meant. For the first time in his life he'd had an intimate experience that was solely his to recall and to cherish. The beauty of its uniqueness filled him with abiding peace and unshakable clarity on at least one point.

He was changing.

CHAPTER FORTY SIX

Brief Rescue

The aroma of barley cooking over a campfire brought Uruna awake with a ravenous appetite. She sat up and winced, muscle-sore and light-headed from her race with the floodwaters. Outside the cave, the gray light of a clear dawn promised heat. She squinted to make out the figures roaming about on morning chores.

Her shifting beneath the robes caught the attention of an old woman and Uruna quickly found herself staring into two of the darkest eyes she had ever beheld.

"Let me look at you," croaked the peasant voice as a wrinkled hand stretched forth to examine eye, cheek, nose, tongue. "M-m-yah, you'll make it. Strong, like Kurdeshi, but pretty. Too pretty. Bad boys out there like to take you for a lover, but I keep them away. Here, eat."

A spoon clacked against her teeth and Uruna opened wide and swallowed whatever it was. The thick gruel tasted rich and creamy and she reached a hand through the blanket folds for more.

The old woman looked down at Uruna's bare legs poking from beneath the bedding and gave her a grim frown. "Cover yourself, girl!" she spat, "unless you want to attract those vermin."

Uruna made a perfunctory attempt to rearrange the covers and grabbed for the bowl, but the old woman pulled it away. Uruna glared like a neglected child and gnashed her teeth viciously.

"I've been attacked and beaten and chased into the wilderness. I want food!"

The old woman regarded her with a sly look and slowly passed the bowl back. Uruna snatched the vessel and brought it to her lips without another word.

"Finish quickly," said the old woman. "We're breaking camp soon."

"Why? It's early yet."

"Kurdeshi always move at daybreak. No use wasting any light."

Uruna gulped on her porridge. "You're not *moshti*?" she asked.

The old woman looked away toward the cave opening before answering. "He was, the man who brought you in last night. But he's dead."

Uruna brought the bowl down and watched her hostess for a trick. "What do you mean, dead? He looked well enough in the firelight."

"He died in the night. The watch found him an hour ago, dead on the ground. He showed up yesterday. What do you make of it?"

"Of what, a *moshti* in a Kurdeshi camp?" Uruna shrugged. "I'm not surprised. They're all over the place. Killed my soldiers over on Redeemer."

"Which redeemer do you speak of?"

"Great Redeemer is a channel that brings the river east to water our fields. Where are you from?"

"North. We were chased from our mountains by the disease. The *moshti* may have caught it—another reason we hasten to be on our way."

"Would you take me with you?"

"It is not for me to say. Ask him."

The old woman nodded at a grizzled man of advanced age whose silhouette momentarily blocked half the circle of sky. Uruna pushed the covers away and stood, nearly bumping her head on the low ceiling.

The man glanced at her once and squatted before a bundle of

wrapped skins which lay on the floor. He untied the bundle and withdrew several sharp-looking instruments which he held to the light for examination.

"He's in the earth," he mumbled over his shoulder to the women. Apparently the men had buried the dead *moshti*.

"I want to go with you," Uruna declared.

The man stood erect and looked her up and down, as though gauging her fitness for travel and labor. "Can you cook?" he asked.

"I'm a quee—No, I do not cook. Not well, that is. I c-can make a broth but nothing more."

The man continued to stare at her several long moments. By her remark, Uruna had just consigned herself to menial burden-bearer, and they both knew it.

"You will last a day, maybe two, in the Akkad."

"I've already spent two days afoot and one without food or water. I can get you safely into Nippur."

"We have no interest in Nippur. We go east beyond the mountains. We forsake the land which forsakes Kurdeshi. There is no place for Kurdeshi here."

"Please, I—I'll do anything required."

"Careful what you say, girl," warned the old woman.

The man looked long and hard at Uruna, then suddenly smiled. "I'm too old for you. No, you'll help Nash-Tyna tend fires and cook. Maybe learn to cook what you eat. That is Kurdeshi way. Everyone cooks."

When he was gone, the old woman spat on the ground where he had stood.

"He lies," she said simply, as she picked up her bundle and started for the opening.

"About the cooking?" Uruna asked.

"About everything."

The old woman picked up a blanket bundle near the mouth of the cave and started toward the fire with it. Uruna called after her: "May I have that for myself?"

The old woman stared at her steadily until Uruna caught on. They were the *moshti's* wraps. If she wanted coverings of her own she would have to appropriate a dead man's things and risk contracting his ailment.

Uruna watched the infected garment smolder and catch fire.

Like your hopes, little fool, like your hopes and your chances.

The Kurdeshi were eleven in number and Uruna made a fifth woman among six men and a frail girl of indeterminate age, whom she guessed to be ten or so. The child had lost her family to the pestilence and begged her way into the band's company the same as Uruna. Nash-Tyna quietly confided to Uruna her misgivings for the girl's future.

"She was weak and ailing when we found her. Now she is worse and we can do nothing for her."

The men were all tradesmen and thus inept hunters and worse cooks. Each fared for himself and took no interest in the welfare of the women. What little food the group managed to acquire came from fields or cupboards left behind by those fleeing from the curse. Uruna could expect neither sympathy nor assistance if she fell behind. The Kurdeshi had no charity to give.

"What about my bowl of broth this morning?"

"The *moshti's* ration." Nash-Tyna shrugged at Uruna's reaction. "Akkad is harsh and demands much suffering. The dead make way for the living."

Into that brutal existence Uruna plunged for her welfare. Because too much exertion had depleted her the day before, she soon sought the child's company, which turned out to be little more than shared misery. After a little prying, a name, but no more. Gudma, as the girl called herself, closed up to conserve her energy for the trek, and Uruna soon perceived the waif's wisdom as her own attempts at social chatter quickly depleted her breath.

The land dropped away from the high, broken terrain of bluffs on which the Kurdeshi had camped and fanned out upon the flat plain below in a maze of winding gullies and washes. The wrinkled surface had been cleaved and gouged by the slicing vehemence of the storm, and showed not a trace of moisture from the night before. Had she not experienced the wild, demented torrent herself, Uruna wouldn't have believed rain had fallen there for a hundred years.

By midmorning she and Gudma were far enough behind the others to be in trouble, and by noon the ten figures she had watched dance above the shimmering reflection of sky ahead were only a dark spot on the horizon. Soon the Kurdeshi would pass beyond view, a moot point since they had already passed out of her life.

Out of *their* lives.

Uruna looked down at Gudma and winced. The girl's hood shaded her pale brown face, wizened from too many days without food, and hid the rest of her emaciation from the sun's abuse, but she desperately needed water and Uruna had none to give.

"Stop here," Uruna said, casting about in her mind to make some effect on their plight. The girl had no will to disobey and simply dropped to her knees in the dust. Uruna knelt beside her and put an arm around the narrow shoulders. "We'll rest a moment, Gudma."

The girl said nothing, only stared ahead past heavy eyelids that waved their desire to close for good.

Uruna took the child into her arms and held her close, choking off a sob of despair as she came in contact with the tiny bundle of bony limbs and sharp angles, the coarse, loose flesh of the dying. Gudma's fragile frame pressed into her lap with scarcely more weight than a newborn babe's, as Uruna wrestled with grief. A hundred unanswered prayers for a child of her own came to mind and she despaired that Gudma's slim hold on life might snap in her hands before another word of care passed between them.

She must be the strength for both of them. Hadn't she survived the previous day? She could do it again, if she tried hard enough. If only that treacherous sun would hide behind the clouds the way it had yesterday.

And what clouds might that be? She looked up at the bright, unbroken sky and felt the killing, merciless heat upon her shoulders.

On your feet, and take the girl with you.

"Up, Gudma," she said quietly. "Let's try another few steps."

She struggled onto her feet with the girl's limp frame dangling from her arms like a rag. "Gudma, use your feet, dear," she said.

The child did not stir.

A terrible shriek tore from Uruna's throat as the ominous shadow of fear darkened her hopes.

Please, not so quickly, Inanna! Don't take her so soon, take me instead!

She turned the child over in the cruel sunlight and knew in her heart what she would find before her finger traced the scrawny neck, pressed the skeletal wrist, lifted the eyelid.

Another life had passed before her eyes.

The child had lost everything. Had she ever known love, comfort, a warm bed in a safe hut? Or had her life been one long ordeal of hardship and sorrow? Could a queen in flight for her life have stopped long enough to tell little Gudma that she was dear, that her name would be remembered in someone's heart?

She looked down at her own hands. She was on her knees, digging.

Her fingers clawed the ground, raking clods and prying up rocks and piling them over Gudma's inert form. She moved in a dream, the gully walls a hazy backdrop to her grisly task.

She must cover the dead. Cover it all, erase the terrible evidence of her failure so that the calamity she brought with her everywhere was hidden from the world.

Great Goddess, what am I to do? Take me now, this day, out here in the Akkad. Take me before I bring another wretched soul to a miserable grave!

The body was covered, a piteously small shape beneath a pitifully small amount of earth. She had draped the tattered cape over the mound as an emblem of her grief, and now the gesture looked foolish. Nash-Tyna would call it a waste of goods.

The dead make way for the living.

She put on the cloak.

Forgive me, Gudma. I shall wear it for you. By your garment let me live to remember you in prayer.

Now came the most terrible hours of the day, when the desert heat rose from the earth like a lion to full height, leaped upon the weak, and beat down its prey with overwhelming might. She wandered through the maze of dry, packed mud, following the downhill course of phantom streams through ever shallower cuts until she reached the hard pan of the ancient lake bed.

The land stretched north, east and south without a break. Somewhere out there lay death or salvation, and she hadn't enough strength to meet the latter. She pulled the hood tighter about her neck, and watched the horizon slip sideways and up.

A blue band of sky tilted away from her at a strange angle. Had she stopped walking? She couldn't tell, but her feet weren't being very obedient. And she was drifting, drifting in the warm sun beneath bright, puffy clouds...

Not clouds, but a long, flowing gown of purest white, streaming from the waist of a lovely woman who came to her out of the sun.

Inanna! her heart sang. *You heard me! Come for me and lift me up from mortal strife. Take back your failed daughter and press her to your bosom, and tell her she is forgiven.*

Take me, Mother. Just take me away...

CHAPTER FORTY SEVEN

Left To His Own

The going was slow. No matter how much Anu pleaded, Rahnee would tell him nothing about serpents.

"Drop the hunter," she told him. "You need to lose your hunter's mind. It loves the chase, the thrill of being caught in the lion's sight. All this business of pursuit is a waste. It works for lions, but you cannot hunt down a god, nor can you finesse him into hunting you. This you know from your experience as Tezu-Mah."

"I was never Tezu-Mah. He came to me and worked through me. Now he's gone."

"As you wish. Enshiggu is no different. Enshiggu decides whose heart is open. You can only empty your vessel so that he may fill it, should you please him."

"Must I take up snakes in my hand?"

"Most likely. Does the prospect frighten you?"

"No, I just don't know how to do it properly without getting bitten."

"And if he should bite you with his fangs and you perish, is that frightening?"

"Only if it prevents me from serving my queen."

Rahnee paused and gazed into the fading glow illuminating the horizon. He waited for her to continue.

"Wild serpents such as are brought to temple from the desert are utterly worthless. You can't train them. The temple women will only take such snakes for a very special rite, and use them with extreme caution. The serpent of choice for the Sleep is the cobra."

"The 'ring of death.'"

"Well, no, the one with the white ring on its hood is Naja, hostile and difficult to work with, although some things can be done with the more intelligent members of his kind. The best you can expect of Naja is to lull him into compliance by making a sound in your throat."

"The suitor from Uruk can do it. Uruna didn't think much of his accomplishments."

"Rightly so. These entertainers may impress bazaar crowds but a true adept goes to Meluhha for the king cobra. Uruna rejects Naja because he is fearful and unsound of spirit and therefore very dangerous. Only the king is attuned to the voices of gods and offers entrance to Heaven's secrets."

"And where do you keep such a beast at Edin?"

Rahnee turned her face slowly from the light. "I do not. If you wish to learn cobra magic, you must go to Egypt or to Ajram east of Elam. Or you could try the woman in Nippur."

Anu sighed. Rahnee's playful attitude was getting on his nerves. If Uruna could have helped him, she would have done so. Still, he nodded his head agreeably.

"I see. No other snake but Uruna's will do. I should have just marched into her room and asked *her* for the wisdom! Why did I come all the way out here?"

"Well, yes, why did you?"

"Because Uruna explained that I'm not adept, or at least not as adept as the snake charmer the Lukur found for her."

"What would you learn from me that you could not learn from your queen?"

"How to assist her during the ceremony, whatever that is."

"The Sleep of Serpents, yes. Well, there is a way, but it is most arduous and exacts a terrible toll from the supplicant."

"A penalty for serving the god?"

"More like wages for living the lie. You have to give it up."

"Give up my life?"

"Not quite. You have to relinquish the lies in which you believe, give up all you hold dear, everything you believe about yourself, all your fears and convictions, your pride, your treasured memories. Throw it all out and become as a gnat on the ear of a bull ox—empty, no-man."

"I will give up anything for Uruna."

"Don't be so hasty to answer," she cautioned. "You've no idea how much of your lifetime you have wasted. You must undo all of it. And to completely rid yourself of your wasted self can take a lifetime and more. In your case I don't think there's enough time because the path means years of toil and hardship, and always the prospect of failure."

"You're trying to discourage me."

"Yes, I'm telling you how impossible is your quest."

"Then you would advise me to quit without trying."

"I have no advice for a hunter of lions who wishes to reunite with his spirit. The choice is not mine but yours to make."

"And if I start this moment..."

"Then I shall do all in my power to work a miracle in you."

"Can it be done in ten days?"

Rahnee chuckled without warmth. "Good heavens, Anu, that would require an act of divine intervention!"

"And what miracle does not?"

"The miracle that I continue to put up with you!"

Rahnee continued to reproach him scornfully, grudgingly consented to try the impossible, and thus he spent four nights falling asleep to the drone of his own mind, looking inward without victory while the self, the sole enemy of his serpently aspirations, rattled on with its incessant litany of delusion.

He slept most of the fifth day and awoke to find himself alone in

Edin's underground warrens. Before seeking Rahnee's whereabouts, he took the tiny incense burner from his tote bag and offered *mushakku* to Shumu-gan, keeper of the wild, and asked for a pure heart to lead him. For several more minutes he sat and watched the faint light from the stairwell, trying to detect each nuance of fading illumination. Once, a shadow shifted at the left corner of his vision, but he kept his eyes straight ahead, knowing he was unprepared and dared not face the god. He tested his response, probing for evidence of something new or different, then shook his head. The god would not let itself be found if he sought too earnestly.

Up on top, he found Rahnee watching the setting sun from her usual aerie on the shrine's dilapidated roof. He told her his intention to return to the Akkad for the night.

"Is it stubbornness that drives you," she asked, "or have you really found a reason?"

He weighed what was happening with him at the moment and shrugged. "I go again, that's all."

She looked across at him and turned her face in the orange glow. "Take a wrap. I'm too old for any more jaunts like last night's."

"Meaning, if I sleep again and freeze, you'll send Zinat to my mother with condolences."

She considered his jibe as the red orb sank below the empty Akkad. "Meaning you'd better find Kukhmet any way you can. My way isn't working. It takes more time than you're prepared to give."

He watched the colors change on the horizon, astounded by his own calm as the terrifying implication of her words amplified an unspoken threat: she had consigned him to Fate. She was done with him.

"I'll go hunting tonight. That is my way and I can't change it."

They continued their watch together until the light dwindled to a faint rosy streak. Anu got to his feet and bent over the wise woman and planted a kiss on top of her head. Without waiting for her to respond, he climbed down off the parapet and walked out into the night.

CHAPTER FORTY EIGHT

Akkad Night Vigil

Anu let his feet follow a path of their own, taking him on a straight course across the pan-hard desert floor.

Eventually, as the land started to lift, he found himself in an altogether different realm of winding rills and folds. The ancient river path had pushed the mud around like rolls of dough on a bread board, making shallow troughs and gullies that were knee-deep, then waist level, then deep enough to block the horizon from view.

The mind told him to climb to where he could see, and he closed off that channel of thought and let the twisting path take him deeper into the confusing maze.

The mind called up terrible portents. He would become lost. Predators would attack his lower position from the crests. He would flounder in a sink hole.

The terrors went on until he shut down all avenues of thinking altogether.

No more hunter.

Be the walking.

At length his body told him he needed rest and he stopped in a hollow between two hillocks. Just above the lower crest hung a slender crescent of moon, already well down its descent into blackness. He looked at the stars overhead and thought of Uruna. Was she too watching the spangled canopy? Or did she bend to duty inside the candlelit confines of some Aniginna chamber?

See the night with me, Uruna, he said to her. Know that I'm on the path to you. Feel my love which burns hot and keeps me warm as I approach your beloved Kukhmet for admittance.

He squatted and crossed his legs beneath him. The contour of the terrain was irregular and uninteresting, the detail of horizon lost in a fuzzy surround of shapeless undulation.

Watch the breath, he told himself, and he began the introspective tug and pull of attention as the mind fought for entertaining memories, spooky speculations about night crawlers and wind spirits, games of star counts and kill counts and minute-by-minute time counts. He threw all of it away, and every morsel obstinately returned to plague him again.

For a thousand upon a thousand lives, Rahnee had told him, you have let the mind do everything. You cannot break such a cycle in an afternoon of trying.

Nor in a night, obviously, nor in five nights—or was it six now? Ah-ah! Counting again.

He grew irritable with the tiresome business and worked himself through that phase and into the next—rage. They were all against him, the gods wanted him to fail. The Lukur had already picked their man. Heganna wanted him to spy on Uruk, and Sebbu—well, what could a father do about anything? Rahnee was old and cranky and out of tune with the times, sending him out here to freeze in a stupor. And even Uruna... No, that was unreasonable, and now he proceeded to hate himself for being so stupidly simple.

Then from rage he moved into self-pity, to self-contempt, and on, remembering with each occurring emotion to see it, watch what happened but suspend judgment. Just remain detached.

Ah, yes, here came the doubt, the limitations; can't be done, never could be, fooling yourself, wasting time out here in the Akkad. Now the arrogance; I was chosen, it is mine by right, I have earned the key to the Door by my life of sacrifice and pain. Ayah, ayah, ayah.

Look to the left. Is the horizon gray yet?

No, of course not. You're not even sure that's east over there. And what if it was light? That would only mean you'd spent another night in failure. Look for the night! Look for stars—yes, up there, try counting *those* points and quickly get a feeling for how uselessness are mind counts!

He fidgeted. He shifted on his buttocks and relaxed his shoulders. He watched the breath come in, go out. In and out. Ye gods, what a worthless pastime!

Get over it.

Back to Uruna. Why did she always come to mind when it only meant he couldn't have her? Why continue the torment?

Back to the god. What would it be like, seeing the image of Enshiggu? He might show himself as a serpent, or in human form, or a many-horned beast. One look at Anu and he might slam the Door in his face. Maybe Enshiggu would invite him in only to attack him and eat his mind, and send him back to Earth as a mewling idiot.

He began to drift in a vision with a woman. She was the same woman he had seen before, golden hair to her shoulders, eyes of palest blue, and lips the color of a rose. She took him to her bosom, and he smelled the essence of her, buried his face in the folds of her garment as stars swept over the sky beyond, a great wheel...

A nudge in the ribs. He was sprawled on the ground again and coming awake to the awful realization that he had not kept his vigil.

He waited for Rahnee's other toe to land and the tone of disgust to rain castigation upon him again. But something was different. The foot pressure was softer and it was still pressed against his rib.

He knew without moving.

Could feel the slender shape coiled against his torso.

Smelled the musty, scaly odor of serpent flesh, an oddly pleasant scent, as he sensed the displacement of space beside him, the aura of "other" sharing the ground with him.

A tiny tendril of fear crept into his heart and tried to establish a toe hold. He banished the fool's reaction and reasoned an explanation to himself.

The snake, having grown cold in the night, had crawled on its belly in search of heat after the last of the day's warmth had escaped from the ground. But what was this? A great warm body, lying as he lay and coiled upon itself as he coiled. Large and protective, a body to which he might cleave, a refuge until the sun's rays returned.

Anu lifted an eyelid and tucked his head to get a better view. The animal was curled against his thigh and abdomen, its body dirt gray to match the soil, telltale triangular head tucked into a curve just beneath his chin. Stretched full length it would measure no more than four feet. He examined his new companion with interest, suddenly struck by the significance of the event.

The serpent had come to him! The god was signing to him by sending its smallest messenger: *thou art worthy of further test.*

What could he learn from the small but potentially deadly beast nestled against him? Was its wisdom enough to show him the way? Did the lesser serpent possess power of its own, or was it simply a nod of assurance from the god?

He emptied himself of desire, or tried at least to remove his own designs for what should happen next. The answer to the next step lay beside him on the floor of the Akkad, beneath ten thousand stars. Perhaps its message was simply to wait out the night until the sun roused them both to wakefulness with its empowering heat. He was the hunter; he must keep a vigilant watch for sign, a stirring of the flesh beneath his breast or a lifting of wind, anything that signified change.

The light in the east had just kissed the low hummock behind him when he caught himself nodding off. His head snapped upward with a reflexive jerk that roused the serpent, who peered out from its adopted lair and began to sniff the air with its black tongue. Oblivious to his presence, or else totally adapted to it, his scaly companion settled back against him with all the comfort of a child in the protective embrace of his parent.

What do you do upon rising, little master? Do you hunt or bask for warmth?

Probably both. His own first thought was for food, which might be a reasonable expectation for the serpent as well, and so he stirred first one foot and then the other as he brought a hand slowly, gently under the slender neck and lifted.

The serpent came up with him, and he placed it about the warmth of his shoulders, pleased by the contact of smooth animal flesh. Then he got to his feet and began to walk.

𒍡 𒁹 𒃵 𒑱

The sun was poking its head above a flat line stretched out beneath a thousand thousand stars when Anu stumbled past Edin's naked ribs. His rider stiffened and took note of the stark shapes pointing into the luminous sky. Their journey from the dunes was fading to a pleasant memory not unlike others Anu could recall after covering great distance without effort or thought.

The little master coiled about his left arm in search of support, weaving its head in a searching motion as it probed the space ahead.

Curious are we? he thought. *This place will be kind to you. The woman who lives here will make you at home.*

The torch was gone from the staircase behind the altar, and he picked his way carefully down each step through the pitch dark, his free hand pressed against the wall for balance. After several moments of fumbling, his fingers found the sconce and he struck the torch with a piece of flint. The serpent shrank from the sudden burst of light and bared its fangs.

Here's light and warmth for you, he told it. *Put your trust in me. I'll bring you no harm.*

The snake relaxed slightly, still alert and sensing every crevice.

Where was Rahnee? He thought he heard voices up ahead. Had someone discovered Edin and broken in?

He crept cautiously toward the far end of the corridor where a faint light slanted across the deep shadow of Rahnee's crowded cupboard. The old woman was probably engaged with a spirit or, worse, had transformed herself into a dreadful underworld creature to harangue him upon his return.

As he neared the lighted doorway, he heard another voice in a higher pitch like that of a child. He turned the corner and entered the room.

Rahnee sat on her bench, gazing up at the standing figure of a girl, or what better qualified for a beggar. The small frame was wrapped in a filthy cloak of coarse brown wool, patched and re-stitched in numerous futile attempts to thwart the wind's probing fingers. From a large hood intended to protect the wearer's head peered the dusky, grubby face of an urchin.

Rahnee looked up, an unusually vibrant welling of jolly pleasure stretching the corners of her mouth into a most becoming smile. She saw the serpent on his arm and her eyes lighted up.

"Who have you brought to us?" she asked, stretching forth a hand.

He reached with his own and the serpent wriggled across the bridge of locked limbs as though eager be reunited with a long-lost mistress.

"He seeks his home, I think," said Anu.

Rahnee waited for the serpent to find its comfort and settle upon her arm.

"A wee one to push open such an immense portal," came her enigmatic reply, as she looked the snake over, like a weaver appraising a fine cloth at market. She shifted her gaze back to the urchin with a look of fond adulation, then looked at Anu with a twinkle. What was she up to?

"You two know each other, of course," she said pleasantly.

Anu squinted at the face inside the hood. Something about the angles and proportions was familiar. Yes, he had seen the child before, but where?

The girl stared at him with a look of rapt awe.

"What are *you* doing here?" she exclaimed.

Anu looked to Rahnee for an explanation, but the old woman only smirked as though she harbored yet another secret he had failed to detect. Was he supposed to remember a dirt-smeared waif from the Akkad who had wandered errantly into Edin in the dead of night?

A movement brought his attention back to the girl, and as he turned, the hood fell away and a length of lustrous dark hair swung free and tumbled about her face.

The face of a woman.

Anu stared in shock as he whispered her name.

"Uruna."

CHAPTER FORTY NINE

Union

"If I intrude, only ask and I shall leave."

Rahnee's remark went unheeded. Hunter and queen had eyes only for each other, the two of them suddenly transported to that special realm where lovers leave the world behind to bask in timeless rapture. For several moments they stood without moving, eyes locked, spirits entwined, senses oblivious to her presence or the passage of time.

"I did not send for her," Rahnee offered as a defense.

Anu's expression flicked with a brief expression of annoyance, as if at a bothersome fly, and he was again with Uruna.

To the queen from Nippur: "He also came unbidden. Do not blame me for his sudden intrusion."

Uruna dismissed her subject absently with a twist of wrist.

Rahnee lighted a new taper and set it on a small table in one corner. Love needed no shepherd to work its magic. She chuckled to herself and quietly withdrew.

Uruna gazed into eyes brimming with worship and knew inexpressible joy. She entered upon a profound peace, suffused with the warm glow from a deep, unshakable soul. In an outpouring of devotion, Anu's powerful arms reached for her and gently gathered her to him until she was completely enfolded and supported. A rapturous sensation of belonging washed over her like a warm, cleansing tide, pulling her ever closer to him with wave after wave of purest adoration, and locking their two hearts together in an inextricable bond. With a single ecstatic pulse, all the lonely nights of empty solitude and hopeless longing ceased to exist, and she knew she was forever free—liberated from her self-imposed prison of doubt. Now she would be whole, worthy to love and be loved without equivocation, and she was ready for it. She wanted the moment to last for eternity.

Anu pulled the drawstring of her cloak and lifted it away. He bent his lips to the curve of her bared shoulder and kissed the soft hollow of her throat. She felt the swell of his body press here, and there, and there again, and she thought she would swoon as she surrendered her will with abandon.

Yes, she said with her eyes, and he lifted her in his arms and took her upward into Heaven's bliss.

CHAPTER FIFTY

Basket Surprise

A spirit of morning celebration graced Edin's cavernous enclave, where Rahnee entertained her guests as royally as means allowed. From an urn she produced dried plums and apricots, and the oven yielded freshly baked pastries. Anu hauled a piece of meat from the coals and Uruna wondered where the lamb hock had come from. The secret might be worth prying from the old sister.

The two women dined in nibbles while Anu ploughed through his porridge. Rahnee jerked her head in his direction and spoke out the side of her mouth to Uruna.

"My cupboard was never intended to keep this man fed. He eats for twenty women. His escapades in the marshes have developed an appetite disproportionate to his worth, if you ask me. Goodness, my dear, you are quite ravenous yourself!"

Uruna had just removed her hand from the pastry jar for the third time and bit delicately into a honeyed soft roll. Her other hand was enclosed in Anu's great mitt and she could feel the strange crease of flesh where his thigh touched hers. He craved constant contact and his adoring glance followed her everywhere. She was giddy with happiness.

A thought struck her.

"I shall do Morning Call," she announced, and promptly rose to her feet, dragging Anu's hand upward as his other stubbornly clung to a lamb bone. She realized an explanation for her sudden declaration was due her hostess. "My heart is full of joy and we haven't thanked Great Mother yet."

Rahnee smiled. "Edin has gone too long without a voice of authority. I shall assist you, daughter of Ekur."

"Let me go too," Anu pleaded like a little boy.

Rahnee looked at him with mock annoyance. "It isn't a masculine ceremony, you know. However, we do require a blood sacrifice and your finger will do nicely."

"My finger."

Uruna joined in the jest. "We offer Inanna the juice of life as we greet the day. Usually a lamb or a chicken will do—as long as it's male. Quite generous of you to oblige, as I'm sure there are no livestock about this place."

Anu proffered the lamb bone. "I say this poorly-cooked offering will stand Great Mother's test and I willingly sacrifice its remains without further repast."

"He is noble," said Uruna.

"Very well, noble son," agreed Rahnee. "Bring your offering to start the day, although Utu is nearly half through his journey, thanks to your extended slumber."

The day was already hot when the three stepped cautiously from behind the altar stone and crept across the square to the doorless shrine. Anu watched Uruna set out flour and dried leaves in two bowls and place a small candle in an alcove. She then draped her shoulders with the coarse woolen shepherd's shawl she treasured as much as himself, and took her place at the far end of the courtyard.

"This is my first *napishtu*, you know," he informed her. She smiled up at him brightly and blew him a kiss.

"Watch closely," she said. "Someday I'd like you to welcome the day for us."

"But a man can't perform worship," he replied.

"True enough, an ordinary man may not," she admitted. Then she flashed an enigmatic smile. "But a priestly man…"

He was pondering the implication when Rahnee bumped him from behind.

"Out of the way, hunter, can't you see we're about pious business?"

"I was hoping that with your poor eyesight you'd mistake me for a statue and drape me with royal garlands."

"I'll dress you in garlic cloves if you don't show more respect. Now off, off!"

She pushed him aside and deftly flared a diaphanous cloth over the altar and guided it into place on a cushion of air, a task she had performed probably a thousand times, but her effortless flourish had a dancer's grace.

Next she laid out sticks on the floor in a curious five-pointed pattern. "Remember," she cautioned. "We must remove all evidence of the ceremony afterward. I'm not interested in attracting the next curious brigand who wanders through."

Uruna communed with her Goddess, marched across the broken tiles, did a neat pivot with her eyes closed, and stood with the two sticks crossed over her breasts. Anu glanced at Rahnee, whose quizzical expression told him this was not the usual order of things. At length, Uruna snapped her eyes open and beamed at him with a shy smile.

"I was thanking Her for you," she told him.

Anu swallowed and sank to a squat with his smoking copper incense burner in hand and placed the tiny tube on a tile. Then he closed his eyes and said his small prayer.

Inanna is great.
She gives me the lion's heart.
I see Her heart in my dream lady.
She comes to me.
She fills my cup.
She is pure.

She is Inanna's face on the river.
She is water in a dry land.
I give my heart to her.
And my heart returns to Inanna.

He pinched the glowing red tip to let the pain remind him of his humanity, and he touched the knife edge to his thumb and drew blood across his chest to honor the lives taken by his hand. He returned the copper tube to his waist pouch, listened for the god to speak to him, then opened his eyes.

Uruna went to him and pulled him close, her eyes full of tears. "I have found the right man," she declared, placing a finger tentatively on his lips. "I see his beauty with my eyes and feel in my soul the goodness of his heart. But now his lips sing a most beautiful song, and I love him more."

Rahnee gathered up the sticks and bowls and started past them, her eyes crinkled with mischief.

"That was some *napishtu*," she said. "I can hear all the little gods wailing laments from here to Dilmun. 'Where is the grandeur?' they cry. 'Where's the aplomb, the dignity that sanctifies worship call?' And to them I say, 'Look where a hunter makes a place in the desert with sticks and sand, and know who warms Inanna's heart.'"

The happy couple spent the morning naked on Edin's roof, taking the sun and doing what lovers do. Toward midday, as Uruna sat cross-legged facing Anu, he glanced over her shoulder and squinted.

"What's that out there?"

She turned and looked over the wall behind her. A nomad was coming in from the south, leading a donkey straight for Edin's post.

"You know," Anu said, "I think it's old Zinat, my mother's herdsman. He put me up the night before I came out here."

"What do you suppose he's looking for?"

"Probably checking in to see if I'm all right. I've been up here for weeks without a word. He's a good man."

"What's the donkey carrying?"

"No idea. We'll have to go down and see."

"You go down. I'm not presentable."

Anu raked his eyes over her and flashed the grin that started things between them. "You're plenty presentable to me."

"Stop," she chided half-heartedly, feeling randy and bold and only partly concerned that a servant might witness desire on a rooftop.

She slipped below to the cool darkness, where she donned a light smock that had magically appeared in the night. Then she poured water into a gourd and climbed back upstairs, her curiosity rising with each leap.

Anu was stroking the donkey and talking to his friend. He made introductions and then Zinat gulped gratefully from the gourd.

"Took me longer than I thought," he said with a smack of lips. "I'm getting old and my last trip out here was long ago."

Two casks were yoked to the donkey's back and a wool tarpaulin covered the wicker. Anu lifted a corner and gestured at the cargo.

"What did you bring us?"

Zinat gave him a peculiar look. "I thought you'd know."

"Well, I don't. How did you get him?"

"It was very strange, let me tell you. I awake late at night and I am disturbed to find myself walking. Never before have I walked in my sleep. Never.

"So there I am, on the road to Nippur just above the Lulub canal where it crosses east to hook up with Tigris. I say this to give you an idea how far I had traveled. Must have been on the road four, maybe five hours. And here comes this ass up the road toward me! I see his dark shape in the light from the stars."

Zinat suddenly noticed the donkey happily munching Anu's skirt hem and batted the animal's flank. The animal flattened its ears and stamped a foot to show proper disrespect, but Zinat ignored the animal and continued.

"What should I do?" he said. "I'm stunned. My mistress sends her son to inquire about Rahnee. After thirty years of silence from the witch. He wanders off in the desert and a couple weeks later this ass shows up. Well, I figure it's provisions for Anu, maybe the doings of the Edin queen. She works in ways I do not question. So here I am."

Anu's curiosity was getting the better of his caution. "Let's pull the straps off and see what sort of mystery found its way from Nippur."

The old herder squinted and looked to Uruna for relief. Clearly Zinat wanted nothing to do with whatever was inside those casks.

"Here's my knife, dear," she said to Anu. "Open it yourself."

Anu examined the small utensil she held out and kissed the air in her direction. "I'll try untying it first. Zinat will need the ropes in one piece for the return trip."

"Oh, no!" the old man protested, backing away. "He's yours! I'm leaving right now, got to be back before dark. Flocks, you know."

"But we have nothing to feed him!"

"Look, what you do is unpack his load, you give him a sharp slap on the rump, and he'll find his way back to my place. Or wherever."

As the old flock-keeper turned to go, Uruna stepped up close and kissed his cheek. "Inanna with you, Zinat."

A gap-toothed grin was her reward. Zinat touched his cheek where her kiss had landed and left with a flustered nod of appreciation.

"He'll be walking in his sleep the rest of his life for that," the hunter remarked. "My mother's flocks are doomed."

"Shush, you, and open the casks. Maybe it's date meats from Ekur's bakery."

"Well, you take one side and I'll get the other. This is a partner sort of thing, you know."

She grinned at him over the donkey's back and expertly undid the knots on the animal's left side. The tarp came away with a flourish of Anu's hand and Uruna's heart skipped as she beheld the familiar designs on the cask tops, patterns in wicker she knew like the back of her hand.

"Oh, great!" said Anu, obviously disappointed. "More baskets!" He reached for a lid and Uruna shouted.

"Don't touch it!"

He jerked his hand back and frowned. "What's the matter? Are you playing games with me again?"

"Anu!" she said excitedly, "these baskets are mine!"

His look was even more puzzled. "Are you sure? How could anyone in Nippur possibly know you're out here?"

"Doesn't matter! He's here, right in this basket in front of me! Anu, it means—she did it!"

"Who did what? Will you please tell me what's in the basket?"

"It's Kukhmet!"

His eyes went wide as the full significance struck home.

"The god!" he exclaimed. "We couldn't—without him you wouldn't be able—he had to come all the way out here to Edin. But Uruna, only if he had a purpose. Uruna, we aren't ready!"

She leaned across the donkey's back and lifted an eyebrow at her big, handsome, lion-slaying lover.

"What do you mean, 'we,' hunter?"

CHAPTER FIFTY ONE
Rite in Edin

Edin's drab altar chamber awaited the exalted ceremony. Inside, the hunter had prepared a courting bower for his mate. Smoke curled from a low fire banked in one corner. The kindling's soft red glow throbbed with the slow blink of a contented cat. On the offering table, a trident of tarnished silver held three lighted oil wicks. A pathway of thread-bare rugs bordered with baskets pointed the way to the table.

Uruna reckoned he had found the silver, rugs, and baskets among Rahnee's keepsakes, but where in the barren Akkad had he found the wood and the oil? Part of Serpenthood's magic was to marvel at its wonders, and Anu's delightful gifts showed he had captured the spirit.

Anu stood to one side to usher his bride across the threshold. She stepped quietly to the center and stopped, feet together, head tilted back, and breathed a sigh of satisfaction. This was the house of her heart. Edin's ruined face was magnificent, a most fitting sanctuary for seeking prophecy's gift and grander than the grandest temple hall.

At the far end of the room sat Kukhmet's large basket. The king held his head erect, watching his human charges with avid interest, his round black pupils gleaming with anticipation. He understood his role. To this he had been born, and he was ready.

Anu followed her inside and heaved one of the fallen planks into place. A crack in the wall showed the moon round and full, beginning its climb above the edge of the plain. Her heart started at the sight, and she called Anu to her side and pointed.

"When the full moon shadow meets her hand..." he gulped. "I wasn't watching."

She turned her gaze back to the room. "The sign of Heaven's door! Anu, it's got to be here, somewhere inside these poor old walls."

"But it's just bare plaster on brick. Maybe the stone in the saying got moved away from the altar."

"No, it's here." She felt the light touch of a wise and timeless presence. "We just aren't being careful enough."

"Well, we can't figure out in a single moment what the temple hasn't found in centuries of looking."

"Then give it to the god to show us. We'll know at the right time."

Anu set himself to the task of pushing more planks across the entrance while Uruna knelt on the floor before the altar. Firelight amplified shapes on the wall behind, making the tall-necked vase a scepter beside Kukhmet's tree-sized curl.

She belonged here. She fit Edin's hallowed enclave, and her mood felt right. The serpent sustained her, the hunter protected. She felt his love as a palpable presence, and she responded with yearning of her own, sent her electrifying desire across the room to him even as she gazed through the broken arch at a patch of starry sky. The room was charged with their hunger, but each held passion in check to give serpent energy its chance. Anu would follow her lead, but she had no idea what to do first. She wanted to feel all the pleasure he could summon, to experience the abundant satisfaction he was capable of giving her. But how much was too much? At what point on the arc of ecstasy should she stop her own soaring ascent and listen?

The surface of ancient stone beneath her hands was cool and growing colder. She knew only a handful of the carved runes, barely enough to figure out where to place herself for the various stages of the ceremony. The proper positioning was essential, for the power in the stone was part of the magic. Anu could work with the serpents only if he remembered her position for each of the six steps.

He went down on all fours beside her, so that they were like two oxen yoked up to plow a serpently furrow.

"Is there a right way to start?" he asked.

She faced the altar and realized she had forgotten the words to the chant. "I'm sure there is, but I don't know it."

"What did the serpent god tell you?"

"To attend my own desire and wait for the serpent heat to arise. He had no advice for this step."

"We're on our own."

"Completely."

"Good."

He unfurled the thick robe and rolled it out in front of her. "I think the floor's too cold. There, is that about the center?"

She crawled onto the robe and stretched out on her side, watching the nightscape through the arch, her body naked except for the loincloth. Anu's hand traced a line from the soft hollow of her spine down the swell of hip, over the smooth sheen of buttocks, and down to the spot where the loincloth curved in between her thighs. He had coupled with her on a mat in Edin's underground lair, he had tasted her on Edin's lone roof, but tonight, in the ceremonial performance of his life, he must make love to her before Enshiggu on the royal dais.

She reached up to him and gently covered his mouth with her own, pressing her firm breasts against his chest and leaning into him. Anu closed his eyes and drew a breath of her, then bent his face close. The scent of his skin was intoxicating, her senses quickened to the latent power behind his gentle caress.

The ceremony was supposed to start with anointing of the two supplicants. Robed priestesses were to accompany them to the grand altar amid a chorus of voices raised in flaming celebration. Pomp and tradition would attempt to grab the attention of celestial witnesses. All Uruna knew was that she wanted her hunter. She nearly burst with desire, but she couldn't have him yet, and the tension of wanting and denying was a thrill almost as exquisite as the getting.

She rose to a sitting position and took a jar of oil and drew a daub down each of Anu's cheeks, then one between his eyes.

"To anoint my lover's face," she told him.

He took the oil from her and gently rubbed her breasts with it. Then he made an oil design over her belly and drew it down to the cloth between her legs and stopped.

"To anoint my queen's loins," he told her.

She took back the oil and shook out a great glob of it and smeared it over his abdomen, and then she set her eye on his scrotum and drew the oil slowly toward his member

"To anoint my—" she broke up laughing.

"Enough with the oil," he said, lunging for the jar, but she playfully pulled it away and dribbled the contents down Anu's chest and over his legs, smearing as she went.

He grabbed for the jar and knocked the oil into her lap, and she started laughing again as he pulled her down on him, and their oiled bodies slid over each other, and soon they were writhing in a delicious lather of sweat and oil and juices while their hands sought limbs and torsos and orifices and appendages.

He rolled on top and pinned her wrists to the floor as he gently touched her between the legs and pulled away.

"Mm-mm," she crooned. "Slow torture. Are you going to devour me, lord rogue?"

He pushed more assertively, and she gave a little involuntary gasp, and he drew back again. "First, I'm going to hunt you down," he said. "Every bit of you."

She arched up to meet him. "Can you hold your lance high?"

"Save me if I fall."

She had known him the night before, when they had used wild, hungry love to punish the world for denying them each other. Tonight's love should be a performance for the gods. They should embrace wisdom while wrapped tight in each other's arms, glimpse eternity while drenched in each other's gaze. Tonight they should meet somewhere between chastity and abandon, suspended in bliss yet alert for the opening of the gap, that narrow crack of light through which she might slip into the eternal. The hunter would not know. She would have to tell him. She must be in command of them both while she straddled the razor edge between physical indulgence and the approaching spirit world.

"Fetch Kukhmet," she said, to get things started with some semblance of propriety.

"He's for last," Anu objected.

"I know, but I want to show you how to draw his power."

When the cobra was in place, she picked up the timepiece from the offering table and held it aloft for Anu to see. Two gourds the size of a man's fist were hinged, one above the other, to a pair of poles mounted in a frame. One gourd was painted reddish brown, the other gray. Each was truncated at the top so that its hollow insides could receive a measure of sand. A small hole in the bottom was fitted with a wooden stopper.

"Where did you get such a curious piece?" Anu asked.

"It came with Kukhmet," she told him, tracing a finger over the strange glyphs on one gourd. She did not know their meaning, but she demonstrated how the sequence of the gourds could be inverted simply by flipping the frame end over end. The stopper in the lower gourd allowed it to capture and hold the contents of the upper. She poured fine white sand from a vase into the stoppered gourd and flipped the ends. The sand dribbled in a slender trickle into the captor gourd. She made Anu repeat the process several times until he got the operation right.

"I shall be in trance for two falls of the sand," she explained. "If I haven't roused myself by then you are to do the following."

She then gave Anu instruction in how to restore her respiration.

"And if you don't respond?" he asked when she was done.

"Don't worry, I'll come back to you, my love."

"Maybe you'll want to stay with Inanna and Enshiggu."

"Not while you're here."

Next, they weighed and measured the sacred vial, a slender translucent tube of thinnest calcite upon which were etched thread-thin lines of calibration. Anu held the trident flame behind the vial to aid Uruna's mixing of wine and herbs. She spoke the sacred words to Kukhmet and then it was Anu's turn to hold the stoppered vial as Uruna gently bent Kukhmet forward. The cobra tested her with a hiss of objection, but she spoke to him the words of the supplication.

"In the name of Inanna, Mother of the World, the Great Goddess who summons her servant Uruna for counsel, we ask thee, Kukhmet, to share the power of thy milk."

The venom flowed.

When they were finished taking the cobra's blessing, they knelt together in the light of the trident and Uruna began the alchemy. Too little venom, and she would awaken far short of the goal; too much, and she would not only fall short, she would die, never to return to Anu and the world.

They were beyond words now, their deep concentration forbidding speech. She held his gaze for a moment and then, still on her knees, took the cup.

The brew was bitter. She winced at the foul taste, but sipped as instruction dictated.

Nothing. Anu's eyes flickered in the light and he waited.

She let go of the world and quit willing and caring, so that the magic could happen.

Still nothing. Wait a little more, let it come, and...there.

Serpently, to be sure, but so different from before! Something new, a lifting of weight, then mild confusion as the sweet essence settled down like a nesting wren and surrounded itself with Uruna-ness. The presence expanded with a suffusion of warmth that started at her center and moved outward along her limbs and up her spine. Tingling and teasing, the flush of euphoria raced around inside her like a giddy child testing the bounds of delight and discovery, and finally burst into a sustained chorus of sensual arousal.

Her connection to the world suddenly broke and she was floating, light-headed and slightly disengaged.

"I think I should be on the floor," she said in a quiet voice, and abruptly grabbed for Anu, who was a good deal less relaxed than before. He kept her from swaying off balance while he watched her face with intense concentration.

"It's all right," she assured him, trying to give herself encouragement.

"Do you feel it now?" he asked. "Are you still waiting?"

"Whenever he's ready."

She suddenly tilted off-center, and Anu caught her and laid her gently on the robe in the center of the room.

"Hunt me now, Anu," she commanded. "Take me—"

His mouth smothered her, leaving no question of his desire. She was feeling deliciously sensuous everywhere. Ripening goodness pushed outward through every pore. Her breasts felt full and enormous and her nipples were hard under his mouth, and when he ran his hands down her ribs she thought she would scream with pleasure. Instead she whimpered, and his hands kept moving down across her belly and she bent her knees and lifted her pelvis, and he brought her up with the strength of his powerful legs, lifted her, carried her as she opened for him and loosened. She was his instrument, a pleasure realm made for Anu's love.

Now the serpent sound came in, a vibrant warp in the fabric separating her flesh from his flesh, full of warm golden song that annealed her female to his male, releasing the tension while attracting, drawing, sucking their bodies tight together, flesh filling flesh, every crevice and orifice bonding to the swelling new ripening that came from them both. Growing out of her was life abundant, pouring out a new and wholly astounding possibility, something bright and miraculous and unexpected, and springing not from herself, but from the fundament of being, from the All.

They raced together, chasing self-restraint and bringing it down with reckless abandon. She knew her heat was rising too fast. She would peak too soon and miss the serpent's call while she blindly rode the steed of her own passion through the mist of their wild orgy.

Go back! warned the voice of common sense. You must follow each step, observe every detail, summon back your will.

She really must command Anu to stop. Really must. A corner of her mind signaled trouble, but his hands were doing amazing things and she didn't know how to set aside the wonderful, glowing sensation rolling up inside, filling her with warm, vibrant goodness. She was ripe fruit pushing up moist earth. She was a sea net gravid with flashing promise. She was raving female sensation not to be denied and she wanted to make Anu want her. She could make him lose it with a push here, a prod there, a murmur or a soft sigh, a fluid, welcoming caress. Every inch of her, every ounce, was made for his pleasure and she wanted to hold back nothing and give it all to him. But she mustn't. They were both crazy-mad in love, brawling on the floor, using each other's passion in wonderful new ways. But she had to be the one to hoist them back from the brink. It was all up to her.

Hold back your desire, she told herself. Save it, save it for the serpent. You must push Anu away...

Instead, she reached for him, sang him every song in her body, and when he answered, she knew they were lost, lost in sensual oblivion where the Sight could not reach and the gods could not hear. And she didn't care.

It was Anu who pulled them back from the brink.

What are you doing? she started to ask, but he spoke to her first.

"It's here," he said.

"What's here? What are you talking about?" She started to lift her head.

"Lie still," he said. "It's the moon. Let the god bring you the moon, Uruna."

"But it's outside."

"Look at your right hand—don't move it. Keep it exactly in place."

She rolled her head to the right, saw the small circle of light inching across the floor toward her hand. It was very close now, almost touching. She looked up at the ceiling, saw the round hole, and knew in a flash what it meant. She brought her gaze back to Anu's smiling face.

"When the shadow touches..." she began, but the god locked her jaw shut and she bucked, and at once lost sight of the room. She struggled to remain calm, remembering she was supine on the floor, and then impossibly she toppled over backward and went tumbling, tumbling into empty space.

A voice cried out from far away: *Uruna...love...Uruna.* The sound of the name grew stranger until it became just a lovely melody wafting through her mind, simplicity playing a fading refrain. A great peace settled over her like a cloud of comfort, and she drifted, drifted...

Abruptly she came to herself. She was walking an earthen path in brilliant sunlight. The course meandered over grassy green hills dotted with flowers and thick copses of trees. The lie of the countryside was familiar. She had been to this place. She had traveled the road before, many times.

Many, many times over.

CHAPTER FIFTY TWO

Living End

Anu watched sand dribble through the cups. Six falls had passed, and still Uruna lay supine on the floor in the center of the room, her arms folded over her naked belly, her feet pressed together, her eyelids shut as in slumber.

The circle of moonlight had fulfilled its purpose and moved past her hand and up the wall to form a slender oval of light. Soon it would flatten and disappear altogether. He wished he knew the rest of the saying, whether the moon dot carried any more significance.

He looked down at Uruna. *The sign of Heaven's door is cast in stone.* They had been looking for a carved glyph but now the meaning was clear: Uruna was Heaven's sign.

She was cast in stone too, the way she lay with her chest immobile like a cadaver awaiting the tomb. A soft gray light between her heavy eyelids was his only hope for her return. He prayed it was not the Hani mark of death called "the seeing that sees not." Uruna was simply elsewhere, her loving attention withdrawn from her hunter as she feasted on Eternal essence.

Did the cobra know more? Did Uruna remember the man she had left behind? Did she care anymore for him? Or was she sprawled on a distant shore with a divine being of fantastic beauty, her hunter forgotten? He might have lost her already, but he wouldn't know for sure until he fought for her.

He was making himself wretched with all this thinking. The tedium of watching grains of fine sand eke from an antique talisman was wearing him down.

Hurry, sand.

Uruna didn't look right to him. Her skin was glossy and pallid, her lips parched. She remained beautiful to the eye, but he had no use for a lovely piece of frozen statuary. He yearned to feel again the thrill of her touch, to see vibrant desire in her eyes, to experience her direct engagement that said: *You are mine and I am yours and we belong together.*

The sand was nearly gone from the last turning. The time for Uruna's return was close.

His mind repeated the saying she had given him, stumbling a bit at the end. Then he resumed his vigil, keeping a close eye on Uruna's unchanged form as he scrutinized her features for the first sign of return.

The sand stopped.

Uruna remained motionless on the floor, her face unchanged

He grasped her wrist in his hand and cringed. Not a trace of pulse. Her arm was rigid, her flesh cold to the touch. She had not made it back—if she had tried at all.

No, he must keep his faith. He was her only anchor in the world. She might be reaching for him right now, but what else could he do for her? Somehow he had let her down in the final hour, omitted a detail so vital—

The chant! How could he have forgotten the song of Serpenthood? Its lilting collection of disjointed, meaningless phrases had connected him to a power that was somehow connected to Uruna too. They were not finished! He must call her back with serpent strength.

In a loud voice he began to say the words, letting the strange utterance come not from the shallow soil of memory but from the innermost fount of his being.

Uruna...
Kirith azzeh manna.
Sigah, selah, selashum.

Kukhmet raised his head from the basket, yellow-banded chest scales extended like protective wings. The serpent lord plunged to the floor and raced over to Uruna as if propelled on feline haunches. The blunt snout began a restless weaving motion just inches above Uruna's upturned face, keeping time to the cadence of the hunter's chant.

Anu repeated the arcane verse over and over, earnestly praying that it would magically summon her return. And when at last Uruna turned her head aside, lips parted and an eyebrow wriggling upward on the stony mask, a jubilant shout burst from his chest.

Sigah!
Selah!
Selashum!

He felt the power of each syllable, yet Uruna's eyes remained closed, the death mask relaxed only slightly.

He grasped her hands and lifted her arms away from her sides and back, but the rigid spine resisted, the joints refused to flex.

The salts! He shook loose the bag of camphor spirits and wafted the salts under Uruna's nose. Her brows came together, her nose twitched, her mouth twisted.

Now she was responding!

And now her instruction came to him like a familiar lyric. Dip a rag in a bowl of water. Daub her forehead in three places. Bathe her neck and arms three times with lemon oil. Now fetch another sack and sprinkle the powder lightly over Uruna's upper lip.

Uruna shook her head slowly and moaned, and he bent close.

"Uruna, I'm here with you."

Gods, he sounded as somber as a burial priest. Don't be the voice of doom, you idiot, give her a reason to come back!

"It's Anu!" he tried again. "I'm still here, right with you. And look, here's Kukhmet! Uruna, listen to me if you can. You've got to wake up!"

She grunted, as if trying to revive the breathing process by pumping her lungs with air, but all she got for her effort was a rapid rise and fall of chest as her lungs fluttered with an invalid's shallow wheeze. In a feeble gesture, she raised a finger to her lips and tried to brush away the salts. Anu gently restrained her.

"Uruna, love," he said to her, "be the lioness. Tell them to let go. Tell them you're going back to the cobra, back home to your hunter."

Uruna managed a low whine and strained against invisible forces, twisting her face in a tight grimace of frustration. Her pulse was slow and delicately tenuous. He forced open one of her eyelids and brought the taper close. The tiniest speck of pupil showed. The gods were pulling her back. He was losing her.

Rahnee would know what to do. Why didn't she make one of her magical appearances now, in Uruna's most desperate hour?

No time to rail at what ought to be. He was out of chants and potions, and his store of hope was just as bare. What was left?

Get her up and get her moving. Give Uruna back her body. Get her to feel the physical sensation of balance and pressure.

He stretched out her limbs and flexed each arm at elbow and wrist. Then he moved to the knees and ankles. She only seemed to go deeper into slumber, except that now her muscles felt less stiff than before. Her pulse was erratic, her breathing rapid and shallow. Uruna had started to move back into her body, but now she was dying in it.

Quickly, he ran over the rituals in his mind. He must have overlooked something! The prayer had fetched her from the demon realm, the salts had started to revive her. What was missing?

He looked up, hoping to see Rahnee standing at the window. Details of the altar sharpened in the gray light of early dawn, and as he watched, the sun's first ray pierced a crack in Edin's shell and struck a bright golden vein across the ceiling. He looked down at Uruna, desperate for a miracle. She remained motionless.

They had lost. Uruna had placed all hope in her hunter, but he was untried in serpent lore. The two of them had reached too far too fast, and now she was gone.

Beneath the arch, fading stars matched his dying hope for a sign of resurrecting his love. Inanna had turned away. Instead of winking assurance from on high, the spangles blurred before him.

He was weeping.

CHAPTER FIFTY THREE
Throes of the Damned

Uruna had become Andira. Rather, she *was* Andira, soul and body, squatting inside a tent on the edge of the British campaign in Assyria, clamping her hand over a compress to stanch an officer's wound. She could not fasten the binding, since he would not lie still. The men inside with him attended his every word, for he was of great importance to them, a man possessed of answers, who knew how to respond to great danger. They feared his loss would precipitate their doom.

She sensed all these fears without understanding how she knew. The unceasing din all around rattled her thoughts. She had wakened to a thunder clap only to realize it was not a storm but the sound of big guns from a descending battle. And her rockbound home was in the thick of it.

The man she tended at last stopped fighting her efforts and fell back on his pallet. The others had a name for him she could not pronounce, and a title that signified he must be obeyed above all others, even their own need to live. She sensed his dread of dying, but a deeper fear made him restless, drove him beyond his own pain, a fear that their side was losing the contest and more would fall.

Without warning, the tent flaps flew open. Two men in helmets rushed in and fired short bursts. One soldier leapt before the officer and took the shot meant for his superior. The officer pulled a handgun from his own belt and fired at the intruders. Both fell dead.

One of the British, not much more than a boy, lay on top of her, his eyes glassy, blood seeping from a corner of his mouth as life left him. She turned toward the wounded officer, saw his weapon swing around at her.

"It's better this way," he said before firing.

The impact was like the blow years ago when a grain sack had fallen on her. Oddly, there was no pain this time, just a rapid flutter of breath, a closing of light to a small circle, the officer's words fading.

"The Turks have no mercy…"

𒅗 𒌨 𒆠 𒌋𒌋

She floated away from Andira, gliding among feathers falling softly from above, swinging to and fro as gentle breezes soughed through endless space. No destiny, no desire, no urgent call demanding action. Just adrift in an effortless meander…

𒅗 𒌨 𒆠 𒌋𒌋

MAN THE BOATS! All hands on station!

The shrill bleat of a pea whistle.

Over the side, soldier! Make it quick!

Thirty-six GIs crammed in a Higgins boat, guys up front and to either side, packed like sardines. Diesel throb grinding your gut.

There's the whack-whack of waves slapping the prow. Welcome to the English Channel, McBride, Omaha Beach dead ahead. We're not in Kansas anymore, Toto. Or Nebraska either.

Keep yer fucken head down! You'll see the beach soon enough!

Fella up front just keeled over. Kee-rist, didn't even get outa the boat.

Mortar screaming in on both sides, but we're still moving. Gunny getting ready to drop ramp. Wait for his order, wait…

Where's Gunny?

Down on the deck between two other guys. His head's gone.

Mary, Mother of God!

And me a Presbyterian.

Move your ass, man, outside now! Hit the beach!

Into the briny. Water's cold, man.

There's the sand, bodies all over, damn Gerries got us pinned down. Move up, move up.

Uh, oh, the guy up front just bought it. I gotta keep moving, keep…unh.

…so this is it…

That girl at the lunch counter. Looked like someone I knew. Shoulda asked her out.

𒀭 𒐊 𒅅 𒌋𒌋

Oil. Hot, steaming oil. Vats and buckets of it. They were pouring boiling oil between the palisades atop the parapet and onto the first assault wave. All across the wall. Liquid flame drenching jerkins and peeling flesh from skull and bone. The screams filled the night, and she winced as a second ladder went down.

Harald was somewhere off to the right with his lancers. Where was the charge? Why hadn't he attacked?

An arrow drove into her left thigh and the horse went down beneath her. She leapt away at the last second and staggered over the barren field, her sword unsheathed, gritting her teeth against throbbing agony that dragged at her like a witch's claws.

Nay, there were no such things. Witches, demons, all imagined horrors of a superstitious rabble. You won or lost by your own wit and grit.

Had not her father told her so a hundred times? Even on his death bed, his last words. Not "I love thee, Winifred," but "Go forth and do unto my enemies as they have done to me. Avenge thy father!"

The last arrow split the air and struck her square in the chest. She reeled and fell backward, saw the night sky alight with flame, heard the rumble of a catapult nearby.

I knew him not once. Nor e'er shall I gain sight of his beloved face. 'Tis too much I ask of Heaven.

Blessed Mother of God, pray save thy wicked daughter…

𒀭 𒈨 𒆠 𒐖

Anu ripped the planks from Edin's entry and heaved them outside onto the courtyard floor. Then he sat Uruna in the doorway to face the broad plain stretching away to the east. Beyond Edin's crumbling wall the land fell away in purple shadow and stretched toward the flat line of lemon horizon.

"Look into Utu's face, Uruna," he said aloud as he tasted salty tears.

Her head lolled forward onto her chest and he grasped her chin and gently held her face upright to confront the dawn. "See Utu light the sky once more before you leave, my love," he whispered into her ear. "Open your eyes and behold his glory."

Uruna took a deep breath and grunted. She was trying! Now he cupped her chin in his left hand and used the fingers of his right to draw back her eyelids.

"See the sun, Uruna. Old Utu beckons. He knows you well from your thousand morning calls. Reach to him, Uruna, let his heat warm your heart and loosen your limbs."

A low moan escaped Uruna's lips, an exhalation of despair. Could her eyes see at all? Did she even know where she was?

The horizon broke with the bright tip of the sun's orb and suffused the balcony outside in golden light. A warm breeze ruffled Uruna's hair and lifted a corner of the drape on which she sat, but Nippur's queen did not stir. They were both dying in this god-forsaken tomb, she by venom's thrall, he of a broken heart, and in a short while no one would know how close they had come.

He heard a rustling from somewhere behind, and a sigh, and he craned his head around as Rahnee moved away from the corner shadows. She might have been watching their plight for hours. The light fell across her face to reveal an expression of horror, and for the first time since the lion Anu felt gnawing fear.

"What's wrong with her?" he asked. "What's going to happen?"

Rahnee moved closer to the center of the room and stopped. She stretched both hands forth from her sleeves and Anu heard a loud clap, and a blinding white flash filled the room. He blinked hard and saw spots in front of his eyes, and beyond them the most wonderful sight.

Uruna's eyes snapped open and she bolted upright, drawing herself erect in one long, extended gasp of air.

Anu started to put his arms around her. "Uruna! Thank god you're back…"

"YA-A-AH!"

Uruna's voice exploded in a long, raging scream.

Her jaw dropped open and her face reddened. Distended neck tendons stood taut as her bellow piled into him like hard stone. Revulsion twisted her lovely mouth. Monstrous pain contorted her body. Something hideous and all-consuming gripped her will and refused to let go. She could not stop, and the scream went on and on.

Anu fell back as if physically struck. The sound was deafening. Uruna wasn't looking at him. She wasn't looking at Rahnee or Kukhmet or anything else in the room. Whatever she saw was somewhere back in Enshiggu's serpent space.

She rolled forward onto her hands and knees, tears streaming down her cheeks and a stricken look marring the miraculous return of color to her skin. Anu reached for her and she lunged away.

"Stop it! Stop it!" she screamed, and her voice broke again and dropped in an agonized groan.

"Uruna! Tell me what's wrong!" he shouted.

Her shoulders quaked and she shook her head over and over. "They won't stop!" she cried. "Oh, Mother, make them stop! I can't—I can't make them stop it!"

She pounded the floor with her fists as her voice trailed off in a whimpering wail. Then she lifted her head and the grey eyes looked up and stared blankly at him for several long moments.

She didn't know him. She had lost her mind. The Sight was too much for anyone, and the gods had chewed her up and spat her out.

Then, as she looked into his face, a brief flicker of recognition lighted her eyes, and her face crumpled as she reached for him, her hands clawing the flesh of his arms as though grappling for life.

"Uruna, I'm here!" he shouted, trying to get through the haze to her clouded mind. "I'm with you now, you're back home safe in Edin."

The corners of her mouth pulled down and she bared her teeth like a wild animal.

"No! I'm not safe! I can't make it stop, they won't stop! Won't stop! Won't…" Her voice trailed off in a wail.

Anu looked over at Rahnee in helpless appeal, saw her luminous eyes wide with awe, and he knew they were doomed.

He turned back to Uruna. "Who won't stop?" he asked in a soothing voice. "Tell me, precious. Tell me what happened."

"I saw it," she said simply. She wouldn't face him and she looked wretched with her long black hair hanging loose about her face, the love-look from hours before lost in red rimmed agony.

"You saw too much," he told her. "Sometimes the gods—"

"I saw the times ahead, and oh, Anu, it's an abomination! It's not what we thought, not at all!"

Uruna pressed the heels of her hands tight against her temples, as if to squeeze out the images torturing her mind.

"It doesn't matter what you saw, Uruna, it's all a dream. It must be Sight's way…"

"No!" she yelled. "Oh, how can I make you understand? How can

I… Anu, what happened to me…it isn't the Sight!"

He stared at her dumbly, reeling from the enormity of what she was saying.

"If not Sight, then what is it?" he asked. "What else did we come for? We followed the steps, you went into the trance. We did everything Enshiggu asked, we did everything right. What happened, Uruna?"

She stared at him, the heart gone out of her, and he feared she might never love him again.

"I went there," she croaked, her voice deeper than he remembered. "I went into it and *I was there*. I wish to Inanna it was a dream, but *I was in it! I lived in it and I died in it! Over and over!*"

He looked over at Rahnee, thinking surely she possessed the answer, having been to this place before, but he hardly recognized the once-proud face, now haggard and scored by time's ravages. Her gaunt frame seemed more stooped and frail than before, and her haunted eyes told him something was horribly, dreadfully wrong. The unexpected had happened to Uruna.

"It was always possible that it might go this way," she offered. "I had hoped not…"

Her voice dried up and she looked away.

"Go which way?" he asked. "What do you mean?"

"She saw the place. We all saw it, every one before her. We saw and despaired and drew away before the terror consumed us, and we never went back. We stayed within Sight's narrow comfort."

Rahnee shuddered and drew a sharp breath. "But she went in. Uruna went all the way inside, and by miracle or curse, I don't know which, she has come back."

"What are you talking about? What sort of place is this?"

"It's the abyss, Anu. The world of our children's children for countless generations. It belongs to the damned and tortured souls who follow us through endless tribulation. How they can endure their existence is beyond comprehension. How Uruna survived is more than I can answer. She is…"

The wizened face grew soft and reverent as her eye again fell upon Uruna, seated on the floor and looking more like the Uruna he remembered.

Rahnee brushed a tear from Uruna's cheek and let her hand linger as if savoring the contact.

"I have touched—" she began, her hand trembling as if suddenly taken with the infirmity of ages. Then she whirled away and sped for the door.

"Rahnee, wait, please!" Anu sprang after her. "What about Uruna? Tell me what to do now that she's back."

The keeper of Edin kept walking, and Anu raised his voice.

"For Inanna's sake, for Uruna's sake, Rahnee, help me!"

Rahnee stopped at the door and looked outside where the new sun was painting the land a dusky gold.

"She's not *back*, Anu. She's still in it and will be for the rest of her time in this body. There's nothing I can do for her because she's beyond my reach, far beyond any of us."

"But this place you're talking about—where is it? How can she be sitting beside me and be some other place at the same time?"

"Anu, what did I tell you when you first asked who I was?"

"You said 'we are one and we are many.' I didn't understand then and I still don't."

"That's because you think of yourself as separate from others, which we all do until we move from that narrow view to a larger world where all are connected as one. Most of us never take that step, or if we do, we draw back from the void where I am not threatens our very existence. The woman you love stepped into that breach. She's out there on her own where no seer dares venture, and one day you will leap out there with her. The two of you are tied together by an inscrutable power beyond my experience. I had expected her to pull back like the rest of us, but she went ahead to a place of unbearable pain, where life is cheap and death is king. I only hope she lasts. Make your courage a medicine to her."

"What are you saying? Didn't Uruna get the Sight? Please help me understand what to do."

"You'll have to ask your lioness, Anu. Ask Uruna what happened, because I didn't go. I was like every other seer, I couldn't stand the agony. Your little serpent queen is stronger than all the rest of us put together. Sixth Door, pah! She burst all asunder and broke the seals in a trice, every one. And now neither she nor the world will ever be the same."

Anu glanced back at Uruna, who appeared now to have achieved some measure of self-control as she blinked and struggled to get her legs under her. What had Rahnee done by releasing her? In what way was the world forever changed? Would they ever know?

Right now he didn't care. All that mattered was that Uruna was back alive and his to love again. He turned to thank the Edin seer, but the desert outside was as empty as the deepest Akkad.

Rahnee was gone.

CHAPTER FIFTY FOUR
Tamed By Jealous Gods

Uruna's first hours as herself were spent in a push-pull nightmare of living and dying as everyone *but* herself. Yet, each time she came out of another's experience, Anu was there. Each time she returned horrified and abandoned, Anu held her, caressed her, crooned assurances that she had not lost her mind and the ordeal would diminish.

And it did abate somewhat. At least by mid-afternoon she had learned a few ways to temper the plunge so that she didn't always land in the jaws of death or flesh-rending combat. Gradually, she developed a willful resistance to "going down" at all. The enticing ecstasy eroded to become a suggestion of discomfort resembling human hunger. Her mental exertions paid off in a return of her familiar self and a semblance of control.

And the walks. Anu had come up with the idea to keep her walking the whole time, following his conviction that forcing her body to move had brought her back from the dead. Now those walks seemed crucial to each subsequent return. The hunter's reliance on action had become her bridge to salvation.

But as daylight waned, the sere Akkad imposed a new imperative. Without Rahnee and her magic, Edin's accommodation had made an erratic switch from romantic bliss to harsh rejection. A handful of beans and two water gourds greeted their search of the ancient warrens. Barely enough for an hour or two on the road.

At first, Anu was baffled by the absence of stores where he had seen whole barrels of grain, a huge cistern half-filled with water, a shelf stocked with wine jars.

"She kept me fed for weeks," he argued. "Now I can't find cook pot or ladle. It's as if she took the lot with her."

"She couldn't have," Uruna replied. "She wasn't here long enough. Anyway, it's clear there isn't enough here even to feed the serpents. Speaking of which, have you seen them?"

"I thought they stayed in the altar hall."

"We'd better have a look."

Anu followed her up the stairs to ground level. She squeezed through the slot behind the dais and was turning to pull his larger bulk through when she gasped aloud.

The hall lay empty.

All evidence of their precious ceremony had vanished. A thick layer of unbroken dust covered floor and altar stone, even the very steps she had trod hours ago as Anu brought her back. Drifts of sand filled the corners of the ancient room with the accumulated neglect of years. The undisturbed dais surface showed no sign of recent serpent activity.

Anu took one look and leaned against the wall, stunned.

"This is exactly how it looked the day I arrived. One of my first tasks was to sweep it clean."

"Anu, we performed the rite on that stone. Just last night! And look. Do you see it?"

"I don't see anything."

"That's just the point. Kukhmet was right there beside his basket. His head was directly above my face. I remember looking into his eyes. I know it happened and I know he was there."

"Rahnee tricked us." Anu spat to one side. "That witch and her magic!"

"If so, then which was false? Edin restored? Or the Sleep of Serpents?"

"Well, you're still half in and half out of the abyss, that much is real. So it must be Edin that was the mirage."

Uruna shook her head. "No sign of the donkey, either, or your sleepwalking shepherd friend. I guess it doesn't matter anymore."

Anu took her hand and led her back to the altar stairs. "We'll have to leave before sundown. Let's make sure the serpents aren't hidden below somewhere. We can't leave them to perish here without water."

A quick search of the premises revealed no trace of Kukhmet or the others, nor even their baskets. It was as if Rahnee had swept up all four in her robes and vanished with them.

Uruna concluded the obvious truth of the situation.

"There's no purpose for us here."

"Let's grab what we can find and start for Zinat. I hope he's got tuck we can use for the road."

"Because we're not stopping there, is that it?"

"Uruna, everything's changed. We found each other, blessing enough, but we also found the Sight, or whatever it's called. Now Fate has something further in store for us. And the task won't wait for us to get comfortable."

Moments later under a cover of clouds, they set out for Zinat. Uruna sensed massive changes ahead where the road led to new purpose and new challenges. She fell into her old habit of summing up the situation.

She had left her temple friends in the hands of Uruk's despotic abuser of women. A task unfinished begged her return.

If by some miracle Gar and his Nord enclave had survived Moshti savagery, they probably struggled now to vie with an army of superior numbers.

Anu's mother and her family stood directly in the Bull's path. Hanza House would feel the brunt of Borok's fury and suffer Enguda's grab for riches.

And Retha, dear Retha. What would become of her dreams for prophecy?

She clung to her hunter's arm with tight resolve.

𒅎 𒁹 𒆜 𒎙

Retha walked the ditch along the western edge of the Gishon orchards. Eastward, rows of almond trees stretched nearly to the river. To the west, desert hard pan shimmered under a cloudless sky.

Daily reports from Heganna's spies indicated the Bull's interest in Hanza affairs had given way to a preoccupation with taxes and brutal displays of power. The man had enough on his hands to manage city and temple life, as well as tend to the logistics of an occupying army. After receiving a third such report, Milsah relented to her daughter's constant pleas to ply the plantation's open spaces.

But Retha's solitary forays soon proved dull. Gishon was a lovely place, but she had memorized every quadrant boundary and even knew the tree counts. Her elders consigned her to kitchen chores because she was female and knew the drill from temple days. She hardly expected Nord forces to retake Nippur anytime soon. All the more reason to check the horizon these days, hoping for a sign of someone appearing out there...

What was that?

Two figures, dark shapes bouncing in the distant haze. Coming her way, and not from the west but from farther north. Why was anyone running around in the Akkad?

As they emerged from the bright reflection, each figure began to take shape. One was tall, with big arms, a man. The other seemed to glide smoothly over the ground. A woman's graceful step with a little side-to-side sway. She had known a woman who walked that way...

Retha rubbed her eyes. It couldn't be.

She looked closer at the man's broad shoulders. The hunter. Anu was coming home to Gishon.

And he had Nippur's queen at his side.

"Uruna!" she yelled, and leaped the ditch. "Uruna! I see you Uruna!"

She lifted her knees and ran straight out into the flats, flying over the ground like a deer, her heart bursting with joy and a great uplifting of relief.

Uruna was back! Uruna was alive and walking the land again. Uruna the indomitable, Uruna the supreme, Uruna the conqueror.

Retha called out her name again as she raced triumphantly to embrace her queen.

CHAPTER FIFTY FIVE
Family Talk

Summer's heat mellowed to golden days and longer nights, as Uruna and Anu settled in at Sinar House. Heganna's ebullient welcome on their surprise appearance shifted quickly to quiet, almost offhand, acceptance. She had acquired another daughter, the consummate fulfillment of a life spent waiting and hoping. To Heganna's mind, her son's destiny with his intended was complete.

Likewise, the entire Hanza fold enjoined Uruna in an intimate embrace unlike any in her experience. At once she became theirs and they hers, and they rallied round her in her darkest moments with assurances she could scarcely believe at first.

"In many ways, you've always belonged with us," Sebbu pointed out when she expressed her wonder. "That was the reason for our earliest hope in the first place."

"Which hope was that?" she asked.

"That you would love Anu as we do and share your life with him. What you have brought us is so much more."

One day Uruna came upon Heganna on her knees, brushing carrots from the garden. She grabbed a bunch to work on herself and spoke her confusion about Sebbu's remark. Heganna's reply astounded her.

"I loved you from the first moment I saw you in the Gipar scullery. You were scrubbing pots, up to your elbows in soapy water, your hair a tangle, your face red with the heat, and I thought you were magnificent. 'Get that girl out of scrubs!' I told Kikki, and she did so, the very next day."

"That was you? No wonder everything went so fast."

"Wasn't fast enough for me, but here you are—look there, you got some dirt on your cheek. No, let me get it."

Uruna remembered mornings at Serpenthood as the busiest time of day, crowded with affairs of all kinds, bustling with industry. She would be up before sunrise and off to Morning Honors, then back for a round of discussions over a hasty breakfast, then a civil case or two at court, then more meetings, and so on without letup until noon.

Not so in the Hanza household, especially with winter coming on. Morning was a time for soft comforts and quiet introspection. The family members trickled into the longroom in stages, with no agenda except to stay warm and let one's body manage the climb out of lethargy at a pace of its own.

Sebbu was already seated at the hearth, cloaked in a brown woolen blanket, when Uruna came in from the cookery carrying two hot bowls. His face lighted at the sight of her and he winked mute appreciation for the tea. They had needed no time at all to establish an easygoing camaraderie.

He looked the question at her: Did you sleep better?

Uruna answered with a light shrug. To her, the object wasn't to rest as much as it was to harvest whatever energy remained after her "excursions abroad," as she referred to them. For some reason, each foray into the spirit world regenerated enough body heat that she was able to sit out most gatherings in a simple woolen shift with wide sleeves. Today, the bowl's warm touch was adequate, and she immediately took interest in a faded crown imperial in the garden outside, struggling to hold its pale yellow face to the wan light.

Presently, Heganna shuffled into the room, all blanket-clad

bunches with mussed hair and a surly regard for the world. She set a scone on the hearth to warm and proceeded to stare sleepily into the low fire while her normally restive spirit arrived at its leisure. Her disposition at this early hour always put the rest of the household on notice that their crotchety mistress would tolerate no boisterous disruption until she gave the order. For that reason, prudent Lilla kept her newborn boy to herself in the south wing until the rest of the house was buzzing well enough to accommodate a hungry baby's bawling demands.

Last to arrive were Anu and his Uncle Obi, suitably blanketed against the cold. Anu propped himself against the door frame and blinked around at the other occupants until he found his wife. Her presence duly noted on his mental roster, he shambled over to her side and sat heavily on the couch, pulling the cushion down so hard that she toppled happily against him.

He seemed disconnected after any protracted absence of physical contact with her. Knowing her hunter as she did, Uruna totted off his frequent touches as a lover's reassurances, a sure sign of his abiding attachment and not any dependence of spirit.

On the window ledge across the room, Obi proudly flounced his favorite blanket, the gray one with the indigo stripe.

"Uruna, your cheeks are red as ripe plums today. Are you sure the chill isn't too much for you, dear? Come sit with me, I've an extra length of blanket for you."

"Watch him," warned Sebbu. "He's got lecherous intentions."

"Impossible," retorted his brother. "I just awoke."

"Your lechery begins upon rising and quits only when you start snoring."

"I was just being solicitous of Uruna's comfort. Obviously my virtues are not appreciated by my own family. Uruna knows me better, don't you, dear?"

"Mm-hmm," she murmured without getting up. "I think I'm fine with Anu."

Mild chuckles all around. Obi was not one to give up easily, however.

"An unfortunate choice," he sniffed. "Sleeps on the ground, you know. Rats and ticks for bedfellows. He'll wander back to them soon enough, and then you'll be thankful to have your old Uncle Obi's companionship."

Anu stirred against her and regarded his uncle from heavy-lidded eyes.

"Remember who you're talking to, Obi. This woman's bedfellows wear fangs and curl happily against you the night through. I find them rather pleasant myself, as long as I'm careful not to roll over too fast."

Obi glowered at his nephew. "Must you win every argument, Anu?"

"Of course," piped up Heganna with her first remark of the morning. "He's Hanza, in the best sense of family tradition."

"Well, he's also Hadrach, which I realize accounts for little around here or anywhere else, but he carries the courage of his fathers."

"For which we are all eternally grateful, dear Obi," she responded. "Rest assured, your legacy lives on. I only wish the temple showed more appreciation."

"For which, his courage or his bride's?"

"Both."

"Well, they seem to have little regard for either. I'm convinced the best of the Lukur have left temple service and fled to more sensible occupations."

"They were chased," Heganna said, reminding everyone in the room of what was only too painfully apparent. "The Uruk queen saw quickly their interference with her husband's plans and removed them."

"She's cool and efficient, you have to admit."

"More like cold and calculating."

Anu interjected a comment before the going got too thick.

"Don't put all the blame on Udea. Council had the chance to hear Uruna. They just chose to ignore her story."

"It doesn't fit their idea of a solution. Ekur wants one warrior race to annihilate the other while they stand by to pick up the leavings."

"Nicely put, Mother. I think that's the most accurate assessment I've heard yet. But it doesn't get us any closer to putting Uruna's vision to use in Nippur's defense."

Uruna stirred against her husband's thigh. "I'm not entirely convinced my version of Sight is right for this world."

Silence.

Gods, she'd stepped into the breach with that one.

She discovered her attention had fastened on Heganna. Couldn't keep her gaze off the woman. Those snapping black eyes were fully alert now and boring in on her like the horns of an angry bull ox. She waited for the rebuke sure to follow.

"Right now, this is the only world we've got," said the owner of one tenth of all arable land. "This is the time we live in, not some age past or yet to come. I know one truth beyond question, which is that we belong to the world Inanna created, and not some fancy of our own creation."

Anu cocked his head and shifted a foot. "Mother, Uruna does not create the images she sees."

"I realize that is your perception and hers. And I won't refute it. I simply don't know. But I do know what makes the world run, and it isn't dreams or wishes. It's the work of our hands and the sweat of our bodies, the same as made this land when we came out of the hills and put up towns and dammed the rivers. Now we have cities and canals and the rite and rote to keep it going. Great masses of people depend on us to hold it together. And this plundering jackass with an insufferable hatred for women comes knocking at our door with nothing else in mind but to tear it all down. It has to end, Anu. We draw the line here. If we don't, there'll be no rebuilding. We won't have a Hanza House or a Hadrach legacy of service. We won't have a devout sisterhood to gather the scattered tribes again. Sumer will fall asunder because we didn't get our backs up and fight."

Anu looked long and hard at his mother as the tendons in his jaw flexed and clenched. Uruna sensed he was compelled by her unflinching diatribe to rush to the fray, yet he held himself in check. She wished sometimes he would tell her what it was, but she wasn't sure Anu had the clearest grasp of it either.

At length he found his words. "The Bull's potential for devastation is nothing compared to the abyss Uruna foresees," he said. "We must tell that story, so that someday our children can pull the world out of it."

Heganna shook her head. "But no one listens, Anu."

"That's unfortunate for Enguda and his pretentious young wizards. But you listen, Baba listens. Others will hear and believe, and that's all we need."

"No," Uruna heard herself say. She placed a soothing hand on his arm. "I'm sorry, my love, but no, it's not the world's way to believe in something beyond our own lifetime. Inanna brings the river, the river brings life, so we worship Goddess and her helper, Buranun, the river god. What can they see for themselves in a world that lies generations ahead, beyond counting? Nothing, and so they turn their heads and close their eyes, and try to face today's tyranny with brave resolve, forgetting tomorrow's."

"You know what this means. You realize what you're saying."

"Yes, I knew it as soon as I awoke at Edin."

"And you didn't tell me."

"I was like you. I wanted to try."

He looked away at the window. "We're both giving up too soon."

"People are asking you to provide a defense."

"I told you before, I'm finished with fighting and killing. That's for others now. Tezu-Mah left me months ago and Enshiggu took his place."

"Will you watch good men die at the end of their own pikes for lack of training?"

Her husband's black eyes burned, mirroring his mother's intensity. Whatever was on his mind went unsaid. For the moment, she could ask no more from her hunter, and she settled back against the cushions.

So much grief, so many forces vying for Sumer's future. And for some reason queen and hunter were appointed to resolve it all.

A new voice from the abyss called out in her head. She blinked hard and shifted her attention back to the family around her.

Family! At last she belonged to a family! Where she could love and be loved. Converse as an equal, partake in arguments, cajole and bicker, as well as joke and laugh and share small confidences. Where she could join in the give and take of moments such as this.

Yes, this life was hers!

The voice in her head fell away and she forced her mind to dwell on the present.

She had no idea what this day or the next might bring. Not knowing gave her comfort. She knew only that she and Anu were together for the path ahead. Her lifelong wish for a clan of her own had been answered in full.

But having just completed one excruciating journey, she was about to embark on the next without rest. Now she must go at it again, lose and win once more, endure the pain and cherish the love. But this time with new assurance from on high, for the terrors of the abyss had not consumed her. She sensed a new venture already in motion, this time with her mate at her side. Felt the certainty of it with crystal clarity.

They had run with the divine, vied with cosmic powers and survived. Now the gods were pushing them back into the world of man.

NOTES ON THE TIMES

Uruna's Sumer was Iraq 5,000 years ago. To this day the rivers wash the desert with silt each year, transforming the topography over time. Modern-day Basra once lay deep under the Persian Gulf.

These *Sumerian Chronicles* begin and end around the Great Marsh which has defined the Tigris-Euphrates river delta for thousands of years. Marsh people lived there without change until Saddam Hussein closed it off and burned it in 1994 to destroy his enemies who fled there, as countless persecuted refugees before them. (The marsh has been recovered.) I dubbed it the *ghana*.

Sumerians were industrious, assertive people of round skull, beaked nose, black hair. They were assimilated as a race by Semitic Akkadians c. 1800 BC. Sumerian firsts include the wheel, writing, a code of law, schools, and the first love song (by a woman, of course, Enheduanna (2334-2279 BC).

Sumerian cuneiform writing didn't coalesce as a unified body of texts until 3,000 BC. Their invention of the wheel coincided. Earliest cuneiform tablets recorded kings and their victories in war.

The Sumerian pantheon contained more than 400 gods and goddesses, for all types of human situations. Thus, the story's characters speak of gods the way we might say "I think" or "what a coincidence" or "how did that happen?" They spoke of anthropomorphized deities they believed lived and died and ate and drank and magically flew and all sorts of things. I tried not to go all Fantasy with this notion because I want the story grounded in realism.

Ziggurats! The most famous is of course the semi-restored monster at Ur, which American soldiers brought home in still image and video. It didn't exist in 3200 BC. Those temples barely rose above 10 feet in height. The platforms weren't finished. Sumerians built one on top of the other. Leonard Woolley in 1921 dug at Ur 40 feet below surface to find streets and houses under 5,000 layers of silt. I stretched fact a little with Ekur (at Nippur) and Eanna (at Uruk).

ACKNOWLEDGMENTS

To do justice to my resources is difficult because so many of them are no longer living. Truly, Sumerian scholars are few in number and largely unheralded outside academia. Add to that the destructive effects of two recent wars in the region, and it's a wonder anything is left to ponder. So in that regard, I owe a huge debt to the writers, scholars, and adventurers from times long past. Much credit goes to my fellow writers and friends who encouraged me to proceed, to women who dare and the men who support them, and to those of you who take an interest in human history, wherever it may lie, and yearn to understand ancient humanity, passion, and sacrifice.

This book could not have come together without my beta readers, Brandee Guard and Catherine Skinner, both of whose canny plot flow analyses and sharp-eyed proofreading saved this project from the abyss.

My heart-felt gratitude to my wife, Sue, for her patience, wit, support, and sharp intelligence. I worried this story out of a deep belief in the value of countless women whose achievements often get subordinated in the mad rush toward human greatness. For they already stand at the finish line and wait while the slower remnant jogs across to claim the win as usual. To their honor and abiding love I am indebted.

GLOSSARY

Since we can count on the fingers of one hand the number of humans literate in Sumerian, a glossary might help your understanding of this book's who, what, and where. If your e-reader permits, feel free to bookmark this page and bop back and forth as you read Uruna's story.

Places

Nippur	(nee-POOR) sacred city of Inanna; capital of northern Sumer
Ekur	(eh-KOOR) Nippur's temple
Aniginna	(ah-nuh-GHIN-uh) Nippur's enclosed administrative center
Euphrates	(yoo-FRAY-teez) one of two main rivers through Sumer (Iraq); Sumerian *buranun*, Akkadian *ipurattu*
Tigris	(TIE-griss or TIGG-riss) Sumer's other main river; Sumerian *idiglat*
ghana	(GAH-nuh) the Great Marsh, swamp, river delta where Tigris and Euphrates rivers meet the Persian Gulf; refugee hold; wilderness
Uruk	(OO-ruck) Sumer's largest metropolis, civic center, Enguda's headquarters
Eanna	(eh-AH-nuh) Uruk's temple
Senarib	(SEN-uh-rib) open meeting square inside Eanna complex; seat of Enguda's personal power
Aramdan	(uh-RAM-dan) snow-bound town in Turkey's Anatolian mountains
Kish	small city upriver from Nippur, Kurg quartering nearby
Kudu Mahti	(koo-doo MAH-tee) backwater marsh settlement

Burum (BOO-rum) port town on Euphrates delta
Meluhha (meh-LUH-huh) trade center at the mouth of the Indus River in what is today Pakistan

Gods

Inanna (ee-NAH-nuh) supreme goddess, mother protector; Great Mother
Enshiggu (en-SHIG-oo) god of Serpenthood prophecy
Enbilulu (en-bee-LOO-loo) god of agriculture
Shumu-gan (shoo-moo-GAHN) god of hunters; keeper of the wild
Guda Abzu (GOO-duh AHB-zoo) bull god; the Bull Priest's chosen deity
Utu sun deity
Nanna moon deity

Terms

disikku (di-SICK-oo) midday worship ceremony
Emesh Sumerian god of summer and personification of summer; brother of Enten, god of winter. Depicted as a farmer.
Enten Sumerian god of winter who watched over the birth and health of animals during the cold, rainy season.
gipar (ghi-PAR) women's temple dormitory
kadishtu (kun-DISH-too) acolyte priestess
meh a power or ability conferred by a deity; god-endowed strength, talent, right, custody, possession
mudhif (moo-DEEF) large communal house of the marsh people; guest accommodation, gathering place for weddings, funerals, etc.; constructed with bundled and woven reeds.

mushakku	(moo-SHOCK-oo) incense offering to a god
naditu	(nah-DEE-too) caste of businesswomen; temple order who conducted commerce with traders from abroad
napishtu	(nah-PISH-too) a sacred rite; a woman of sacred bloodlines
nigenna	(ni-GHEN-uh) temple-owned farm lands
swifthull	slender water craft with upswept prow; Sumer's speediest transport; paddled like a canoe or with a long pole
uzba	(OOZ-bah) group of forty elected landowners who lobby with temple authorities over entitlement, seed allotments, and price-setting

READING LIST

_____ (ed.) *Splendors of the Past,* National Geographic Society, Washington, D. C., 1981

_____ (ed.) *TimeFrame 3000-1500 BC, The Age of God-Kings,* Time-Life Books, Alexandria, Virginia, 1987

Baring, Anne, Cashfor, Jules, *The Myth of the Goddess: Evolution of an Image,* Viking, 1992

Bibby, Geoffrey, *Looking For Dilmun,* Penguin Books, 1970

Black, Jeremy and Green, Anthony, *Gods, Demons and Symbols of Ancient Mesopotamia,* Univerity of Texas Press, 1992

Campbell, J., Muses C., *In All Her Names,* New York, Harper San Francisco, 1991

Childe, V. G., *New Light on the Most Ancient East,* New York, W. W. Norton, 1969

Cles-Reden, Sibylle von, *Realm of the Great Goddess,* New Jersey, Prentice-Hall, 1962

Cottrell, Leonard, *The Quest For Sumer,* New York, Putnam, 1965

Dalley, Stephanie, *Myths From Mesopotamia,* Oxford Press, 1992

Eisler, Riane, *The Chalice & The Blade,* HarperCollins, 1988

Friedrich, Johannes, *Extinct Languages,* Philosophical Library, 1957

Frymer-Kensky, Tikva, *In the Wake of the Goddesses,* Free Press, 1992

Gimbutas, Marija, *The Civilization of the Goddess,* HarperSanFrancisco, 1991

Gimbutas, Marija, *The Gods and Goddesses of Old Europe: 7000-3500 B.C.,* University of California Press, 1982

Gimbutas, Marija, *The Language of the Goddess,* HarperSanFrancisco, 2001

Hawkes, Jacquetta, *The First Great Civilizations,* Knopf, 1973

Heyerdahl, Thor, *The Tigris Expedition,* Doubleday, 1981

Hooke, S. H., *Middle Eastern Mythology,* Baltimore, Penguin Books, 1963

Kramer, S. N., *From the Tablets of Sumer*, The Falcon's Wing Press, 1956

Kramer, S. N., *History Begins at Sumer*, Doubleday, 1958

Kramer, Samuel Noah, *Cradle of Civilization*, Time-Life Books, 1967

Kramer, Samuel Noah, *The Sumerians*, University of Chicago Press, 1963

Mara, W. P., *Venomous Snakes of the World*, T.F.H. Publications, 1993

Postgate, J. N., *Early Mesopotamia*, London, Routledge, 1994

Pritchard, J. B., *The Ancient Near East*, Princeton University Press, 1958

Reade, Julian, *Mesopotamia*, Harvard University Press, 1991

Roaf, Michael, *Cultural Atlas of Mesopotamia and the Ancient Near East*, Equinox Ltd., 1990

Saggs, H. W. F. *Everyday Life in Babylonia & Assyria*, New York, Dorset Press, 1965

Scarre, Chris, *Smithsonian Timelines of the Ancient World*, Dorling Kindersley, 1993

Steinman, Marion, "Chicken scratches written in clay yield their secrets", Smithsonian, Dec 1988, p.130

Stone, Merlin, *When God Was A Woman*, New York, Dorset Press, 1976

Thesiger, Wilfred, *The Marsh Arabs*, New York, E. P. Dutton & Co., 1964

Weidensaul, Scott, *Snakes of the World*, Chartwell Books, Secaucus, New Jersey, 1991

Woolley, L., *Excavations At Ur*, New York, Thos. Y. Crowell, 1955

Woolley, L., *The Sumerians*, W. W. Norton, 1965

AUTHOR NOTE

Thank you for taking the time to read *Eden's Bride*. If you enjoyed it, please tell your friends or post a short review. Word of mouth is an author's best friend and much appreciated.

Visit my website at www.danielphalen.com to learn about current and future projects. You'll find some interesting facts about Uruna's world and where it stands in the annals of human history.

Dan Phalen